WOLF

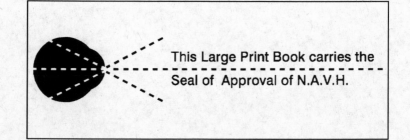

This Large Print Book carries the
Seal of Approval of N.A.V.H.

WOLF

MO HAYDER

THORNDIKE PRESS

A part of Gale, Cengage Learning

GALE
CENGAGE Learning·

Farmington Hills, Mich • San Francisco • New York • Waterville, Maine
Meriden, Conn • Mason, Ohio • Chicago

GALE
CENGAGE Learning®

Copyright © 2014 by Mo Hayder.
Thorndike Press, a part of Gale, Cengage Learning.

ALL RIGHTS RESERVED
Thorndike Press® Large Print Peer Picks.
The text of this Large Print edition is unabridged.
Other aspects of the book may vary from the original edition.
Set in 16 pt. Plantin.

LIBRARY OF CONGRESS CATALOGING-IN-PUBLICATION DATA

Hayder, Mo.
    Wolf / by Mo Hayder. — Large print edition.
        pages ; cm. — (Thorndike Press large print peer picks)
    ISBN 978-1-4104-7104-8 (hardcover) — ISBN 1-4104-7104-7 (hardcover)
    1. Caffery, Jack (Fictitious character)—Fiction. 2. Large type books. I. Title.
PR6058.A9776W65 2014
823'.914—dc23   2014012594

Published in 2014 by arrangement with Grove/Atlantic, Inc.

Printed in Mexico
1 2 3 4 5 6 7 18 17 16 15 14

WOLF

PART ONE

PICKING ELDERFLOWERS IN THE EVENING, NEAR LITTON, SOMERSET

Amy is five years old and in all of those five years she's never seen Mummy acting like this before. Mummy's in front of her on the grass, standing in a weird way, as if she's been frozen by one of those ice guns what the man in *The Incredibles* have got in his hand most of the time. She's on one leg, with one arm out, like she's been running and got told to stop and stay still as a statue. Her mouth is open too and her face is white. It would be really funny if her eyes weren't all opened up and weird, the way her face goes when she's looking at something scary on the television. Behind her is a line of fluffy white clouds in the sky — like on *The Simpsons* — except the sky's a bit darker, because it's nearly night-time.

'*Amy?*' After a while Mum puts her foot down. Stops balancing on it. She does this funny little sideways dance like a puppet what's about to fall over, and when she gets her balance again her face changes. 'AMY?'

She starts running and as she runs she's screaming, 'Brian!?! Brian, I've found her. *Brian?* Come NOW. I've found her. Over here in the trees.'

Before Amy can say anything Mum has grabbed her up. She's still screaming out to Dad, 'Brian Brian *Brian,*' and she's hugging Amy the way she hugged her that day she was about to go into the road and almost got squished by a bus, which Mum says is the most scary thing what ever happened to her, but Amy didn't think was even *half* as scary as the Puzzler man off of *Numberjacks* on CBeebies.

'Where've you *been?*' Mum puts her back down on the ground with a bump. She squats and runs her hands up and down her arms and legs, straightening her blue dress and pushing her hair out of her face. Staring at her, all worried. 'Amy? *Amy,* are you all right? Are you all right, darling?'

'I'm all right, Mummy. Why?'

'Why?' Mum shakes her head, like the times when Dad says something really stupid. '*Why?* Oh baby, baby, baby. My baby.' She closes her eyes, drops her head against Amy's chest and squeezes her. It's a really hard hug and Amy can feel her insides squishing up, but she doesn't want to squiggle away coz it might upset Mum.

'Amy!' Dad comes running along the path. The field is very big and very green and sloping and all the people from the cars that were parked here before have got out and they're all standing staring at her. 'AMY?' Dad's not carrying the container they were putting their flowers into any longer, instead he's got his phone in his hand. He's taken off his nice jumper and his shirt's all wet and yucky under the armpits. Mum says that's where he leaks when he runs too fast so he must of been running for a long time. His face is just like Mum's, all white and scared, and Amy wants to laugh a bit, coz they do look funny both of them, all white like Halloween masks, except it's hard to tell if Dad's really cross or really sad.

'Where were you? Where have you *been*?' His voice is really shouty. 'How many times have I told you not to go out of our sight?' He turns and yells at the people over at the cars. 'We've found her. We've found her.' Then he turns back to Amy. He's cross, definitely cross — you can tell by how squinty his eyes have gone. 'You've been ages, you've made your mother *cry* now. This is the last time we pick elderflowers. The *last* time.'

'Brian, be quiet. She's all right, that's the main thing.'

'Is she?' He puts a hand on Mum's shoulder and moves her out of the way so he can bend and look into Amy's face. His eyes go up and down and side to side, taking in every inch. 'Are you all right? Amy? Where've you been?

11

Have you spoken to anyone?'

She bites her lip. Her head feels all nasty and hot and there are some tears in her eyes that fall out of under her eyelids and go running down her cheeks.

'Amy?' Dad shakes her arm. 'Did you speak to anyone?'

'Only the man. That's all.'

Dad goes all funny when she says this. Suddenly his hands aren't nice any more but are like bird's claws, digging into Amy's arms. 'The *man*?'

'Yes.'

Mum's mouth starts quivering. The black make-up stuff on her eyes has gone runny and it's all trickling down her face. 'I told you we shouldn't be out here at this time of day, Brian, this is when they all come out — all of them. And we're not far from the Donkey Pitch. Remember? The Donkey Pitch?'

'What *man*?' Dad says. 'Amy, tell me in the most grown-up way you can, because this is serious. What man?'

She turns towards the woods, lifting her hand to point. But as she does she sees that he's gone — the man who likes dogs. He's gone away. And he must of taken the puppy, coz that's gone too.

'He was really cute.'

'Cute?' Mum says. *'Cute?'*

'The puppy was called Bear.'

12

'The puppy?'

'Oh, for God's sake!' Dad rubs hard at his forehead. 'There's always a puppy. Always a shagging puppy.'

'Brian, *please.*'

'It's the oldest trick in the book: *I've got a poorly puppy — come into the woods and I'll show you.* We're taking her to the police. She needs an examination.'

Amy frowns. The man in the woods didn't say that the puppy was poorly, and he didn't ask her to come into the woods to look at it. She was the one what found the puppy, before she met the man.

'I don't want no exam, Mum — I don't want one of them.'

'See, Brian, you've scared her. Now, Amy . . .' Mum sits down on the grass. She pats her leg. 'Come here, sweetie. Sit down.'

Amy sits on Mum's lap. She wipes her nose with her hand. Sniffs up the rest of the snot, which is yucky. She wishes Dad wasn't cross — she doesn't understand why he's cross, coz the man wasn't horrid. He looked a bit funny, with a big hairy beard like a goblin, or like a Santa Claus in reverse, because his beard was black, but he spoke to her very *very* nice and made her a promise, a proper pinkie-promise which everyone in the world knows is the most proper. And another thing is that he called her Crocus, which was the bit she liked the best — when he said she was as pretty as a crocus. Because crocuses are really pretty and they're sometimes purple and sometimes yellow and sometimes both. Miss Redhill at school says they're the second flower of spring after the snowdrops have died and gone back into the ground.

'Amy,' Mum asks. 'This man . . . was he nice to you?'

'Yes. And he was nice to the puppy.'

'Was it his puppy?'

'No.'

'Then whose puppy was it?'

'I don't know.' She puts her finger in her nose and picks it thoughtfully. She thinks that maybe the puppy wasn't a puppy for real but a grown-up dog — sometimes a big dog can be little if it's a puppy and sometimes an old dog can be smaller than a puppy, even though it's really lots older. It's all about something called 'breeds' what can be small or big. 'He came after I found the puppy. I just said that, didn't I?'

Dad straightens up. 'Come on. Show me where you found this puppy.'

Mum lets Amy jump off her lap. She holds her hand as they walk into the trees. It's a bit more spooky in the wood coz it's dark in here now. But she can see Dad's white shirt, and Mum does that thing as they go, with her hand, where she squeezes Amy's thumb to let her know everything's OK. Amy squeezes her hand in return.

Amy takes Mum and Dad to the place she met the puppy. It's getting really night-time now and the trees are all silent and dark. No puppy. The man made a promise to take the puppy somewhere safe.

'I was here,' she says. 'And I was putting the flowers in the . . . There it is!' She sees the Tupperware container. She goes and picks it up and turns round to show Mum and Dad all the flowers inside. Which are the best flowers without none of them worms like the ones Dad found earlier.

'I was only getting the flowers off of here and I was getting the flowers and this puppy comes up and he's got a poorly paw.'

'A poorly paw?' Dad looks at Mum with his eyebrows all arched.

'Yes, with blood and stuff. And the person of it wasn't there and the man didn't know who the grown-up of the puppy was neither, so I was going oh puppy puppy and I was going to bring it back to you, Daddy, because if it didn't have a nowner, it needed to be —'

'*An owner,*' Mum says.

'An owner,' Amy repeats. 'And if it didn't have *an owner* then it needed one and I thought that it could of lived at our house, under the cooker — coz there's that place that gets really warm, and I don't mind giving it my pocket money, Mum, to buy it some milk.'

Mum wipes her eyes and laughs a little.

Which is nice. She hasn't laughed at all since all of this happened.

'Amy . . .' She gives her a hug. More gentle this one. 'He didn't touch you, Amy, did he? Did he ask you to do anything you didn't like?'

Amy sucks her fingers for a while. They taste of grass and the stems off of the flowers. She wishes she could of kept the puppy.

'*Amy?* Did he ask you to do anything you didn't like?'

'No. *He didn't do nothing.* He was nice to me and he's going to help the puppy. Honest, Mum. Honest.'

Dad lets out his breath in a long sound like a balloon what's had a pin put in it. He shakes his head. He tucks the phone back in his pocket and stands up and walks around a bit with his back to Amy and Mum, shouting into the woods.

'Hello? Hello — do you want to come and have a chat with me? Any puppies you want to talk about, you fucker?'

There's a long long silence. Then he comes back and it's amazing coz Mum doesn't say anything about the rude word he just said.

'Come on, let's go — you should have been in bed hours ago.'

Mum takes Amy's hand and they follow Dad back to the van — Dad's white van he drives for work. Amy uses her thumbnail to try to get rid of the green stains what's got

16

themselves all over the inside bits of her hands. The flowers here are supposed to be very puffy, which is why they've come here today, and you can make really really nice drinks out of them if you put in enough sugar, but that takes a grown-up because of the heat and how hot it gets. Hot enough to make your finger fall off if you put it into the saucepan. With blood and everything.

Amy's teddy, Buttons, is on the front seat. She clambers in after Mum and snatches Buttons up, holding him to her face to get his fluffiness on her. When Dad turns the engine on with the keys, Amy moves the seat belt around so she can kneel up, put her nose to the window and look back at the woods. Mum doesn't stop her.

Dad drives the van off of the grass and on to the road. It's bumpy going along and Amy bounces around, but she doesn't stop watching the trees. She wonders if the reverse Santa Claus man will find the puppy's owners.

When the van gets further up the road and she can't see the trees any more and can only see the road and the other cars and buildings whizzing past, she sits down and gets the seat belt more comfortable. She puts Buttons in her lap. He looks up at her with his nose what needs mending and his bad paw, just like the puppy.

'Mummy,' she says when they get to the place that's at the end of their road, the place where someone has sprayed a picture of a Moshling on to the road sign. 'Mummy, what word does it make if you put that "huh" letter Miss Redhill makes when she puffs on her hand —'

'Aitch you mean?' says Mum.

'Yeah — what happens if you put aitch next to eggy "e" and lollipop "el" and the "puh" sound. You know, that letter you make when you blow out candles on your birthday cake? "Puh"?'

'Aitch, ee, ell and peee?' Mum says. 'That spells "help". Why?'

'Help?'

'Yes.'

'And what about umbrella "uh", and snakey "sssss"?'

'You and esss? That spells "Us". Help us.' Mum looks down at Amy, a puzzled smile on her face. 'Help us? Why? Why are you asking that?'

Amy bites her lip. Something was attached to the puppy-dog's collar. A teeny-weeny piece of paper what had been writed on in blue pen. It was all torn and the letters were all smudged and spread into big blue pools so you couldn't read them properly. Except for those letters.

Help us.

'Amy? Why're you asking?'

Amy looks at the side of Dad's head. If she mentions puppy-dog again, Dad's going to

18

start shouting. So she shakes her head.

'Nothing,' she says as they pull up outside the house. She wishes she had a little puppy-dog. And different parents. Parents what would not get cross when she told them things what are true. 'Nuffink.'

EARLIER THAT DAY:
THE PIG MAN

The pig man. That's how Oliver Anchor-Ferrers views himself. Like something lifted whole from the pages of a Victorian bestiary. Nine weeks ago the doctors in the Mayo Clinic in London gave him drugs to thin the blood. They opened his pericardium with stainless-steel rib retractors, connected multiple cannulas to his body and rerouted his blood to mechanical membrane oxygenators which carried out the job his heart should have been doing, delivering oxygen to his tissues and organs. His own heart the medics stopped by injecting a cardioplegic solution to induce paralysis. For almost an hour on the operating table Oliver was dead. Once they'd cut out the valves he'd had from birth and replaced them with valves from a specially bred pig, the surgeons closed the aorta and secured the sternum with steel wire. In spite of his appearance — that of a perfectly normal man in his sixties — the truth is that Oliver Anchor-Ferrers is being kept alive by a piece of foreign flesh flickering inside his heart. He's half man, half swine.

Valve replacement is a common enough procedure, an operation that's been in use for years — there must be several thousand pig men walking the planet, by his reckoning — but Oliver can't rest easy about it. Since the moment he woke in the ward he has been listening to his pulse, wondering how it is linked to his brain and whether the mechanical, ancient survival parts of his cerebellum have yet recognized the foreignness. Since the op he lies in bed at night listening to it thrum-thrumming in his chest. He wonders what control he has over it. He wonders who is choosing to live — him or the pig.

Keep beating, he sometimes whispers under his breath, *pig-heart, keep beating . . .*

Oliver is sixty-four and he is worth several million pounds. England is his native country — he owns two properties here. His chief home, a Regency end-of-terrace, is in Knightsbridge. But it is in the second, where he is now, a rambling Victorian house set high on a hill in the Somerset Mendips, that he feels most at home. His favourite chair, scruffy and old and moulded to his skeleton, is in its usual place, next to the inglenook. He's been looking forward to this chair for what seems like ages. It's taken almost two months for the London doctors to give him the all-clear to come down here.

He stretches out his legs and settles back, gazing around in contentment. The fire isn't made, not now that it's summer, and there is a basket of dried flowers in the hearth to fill the space. But all the familiar hallmarks of a family visit are here. They left London at the crack of dawn and arrived late morning and it's a typical first day, passed in amiable chaos. Everywhere are dotted the groceries and bits and pieces that Matilda brings down from London: endless Waitrose bags and papery deli bundles and boxes of cereals and fruit juices. The only unwelcome addition is his pale pink medication tray on the window-sill.

Matilda comes hurrying in from the boot-room, all colour and fragrance. She is dressed in her blue-and-pink gardening apron — the one Kiran gave her years ago. She's tying a spotty-print tool pouch to her waist and Oliver notes that, as is her custom, she has wiped her face of London make-up. Instead of postbox-red lipstick and foundation her skin is bare and peach coloured. Her lips are their natural soft pink, like the inside of a fig. Matilda is sixty, and grey now, but her skin is as clear as a cloudless sky, and when Oliver looks at her the light still does the same strange dance around her that it has always done, from the moment they first met all those years ago.

'Sweetheart.' She stops and smiles at Oliver. It's a smile that conveys everything: love and pity and a shared desperation that it's come to this — to heart surgery and medication in numbered boxes. 'Sweetheart, do you mind if I . . . ?'

She wants to go into the garden. It's less than half an hour since they've arrived and already she wants to be outside. In the twenty-eight years they've owned this house she has poured her heart into the flowers, shrubs and borders. He smiles. 'You must, darling. In fact, I think I can hear the plants calling you.'

'Are you sure you're all right?'

'Of course, of course, I am perfectly fine.'

Matilda finishes tying the belt and leans over him. She slides her hand into his shirt, presses the palm coolly across the scar on his chest.

'How's it feeling?'

'It's behaving.'

'Not grunting? Not squeaking or squealing? Doctor says I've got to listen out, especially for the squealing.'

He presses his fingers over hers and holds her hand tighter to his chest so she can feel the thud thud thud down there.

'Good.' She takes a moment to button up his shirt, smoothing it until she's satisfied. She kisses his head. 'Nurse Matilda's a bit of a dragon, so get ready for the regime. Drink your tea, pills in three hours. And that cake'll be ready in twenty minutes, so I'll be back.'

She leaves the room, rummaging in the tool belt for secateurs. He watches her straight back, her refined profile. No one would know how tender she is inside. Just like no one would look at him and think there were pig parts keeping him alive.

'You all right?'

He looks up. Lucia is sitting in the window seat, the kitchen table pulled up close, drawings and magazines and poems spread out everywhere. The sun is spilling in behind her, catching all the highlights in her spiky black hair. Her skin is white, and her eyes are outlined so many times with make-up they make deep smudged holes in her skull. She's studying him in her challenging way. Steady and dark. He and Matilda call it 'the Lucia look'. Lucia might be nearly thirty, but she still behaves like a sullen teenager.

'Yes. Why?'

'Just . . .' She puffs out a bored breath. Shrugs. 'You know, just think I've got to ask. Be polite.'

She goes back to her work and Oliver watches her scribble and scratch her head, poring over her books, every few moments reaching automatically for one of the black grapes that sit in the bowl in front of her. Bear, their Border terrier, is asleep under the table, half draped across Lucia's feet. Bear doesn't look like a bear at all, more a small teddy with unevenly set ears that have to be cut differently to make them sit parallel. She is little but she runs like the wind and has to be tied up the first day they arrive here. She's got a habit of making a bolt for it, heading for the forests, so she's wearing her collar. The lead is under the leg of Lucia's chair, Bear's head is resting on Lucia's boots — Doc Martens with pastel trolls' faces covering them. Ridiculous children's cartoons, all over her feet.

Oliver picks up his cup of tea and sips slowly. The familiar musty tartan blanket he loves so much is over his legs, there's the smell of Matilda's cake in the oven and he's holding tea in the chipped mug she sometimes uses when she's gardening. It's got a cheesy photo of Kiran and Lucia on it, their arms around the old golden retriever they used to have when they were children. A year ago he wouldn't have drunk from this mug, he'd have been embarrassed by its sentimentality.

'Oliver.'

Matilda has reappeared in the doorway, secateurs still in her hand. Her expression is no longer calm — it is wary and alarmed. Immediately the pig valve flutters.

'Yes?' he says guardedly.

At the table Lucia lifts her chin and stares curiously at her mother. 'Mum?'

'Oliver,' Matilda says, levelly, ignoring her

25

daughter. 'Have you got a moment? A chat?'

'What sort of chat?' Lucia says.

Matilda won't meet her daughter's eye. Instead she tips her head meaningfully at Oliver, suggesting they need to speak in private. With an effort he gets to his feet, ignoring the now familiar swoop of nausea that sudden movement brings. He clutches up the walking stick and crosses the room as fast as he can, feeling Lucia's eyes on him all the way. When he draws level with the pantry Matilda puts a finger to her mouth and touches his wrist, pulling him out of the kitchen.

'I'm so sorry,' she whispers. 'Sorry to do this to you. But you've got to see it. Or else I'll think I'm going mad. I'm so sorry.'

Silently beckoning him to follow, she steps out of the back door. He moves after her, conscious of the air wheezing in and out of his lungs. *Keep beating. Pig heart.*

Outside, the sun has almost reached its midday summit and is glaring down on the hilltop. Matilda puts a hand under his elbow to help him walk away from the house. They go slowly. In spite of its location, high up on the hill, surrounded on all four sides by sky, the garden feels more like a series of rooms than an open space. A path leads from walled garden to a walnut orchard, through a hedge into a formal knot garden, then through a gate to three descending parterres with crumbling, ornamented balustrade steps. One can wander through the areas in any imaginable sequence, from a paddock of grass that sways knee-high, studded in the summer months by meadow flowers, to the moss-covered stone walls of the kitchen garden where giant rhubarbs spring from the ground like fountains. It's a maze, a maze and a monument to Matilda's love. Her energy.

Every now and then the eye catches on a black spot. Like dots of fungus. Or a scatter of pathogens on a Petri dish. These are the places Lucia has sabotaged Matilda's colour scheme on the many occasions she comes back to live with them. She sneaks into the garden and secretly plants black tulips and blood-purple hellebores; her way of staking a claim on the property, making sure her mark is made. It drives Matilda mad and the moment Lucia leaves home again, the moment she appears, even temporarily, to have got her life back on track, Matilda takes the opportunity to weed out the offenders.

At the bottom of the flights of steps the land drops away, leading to a series of small, half-sunken coppices; from afar they resemble a puckered string in the landscape. At the first coppice Matilda lets go of his arm and hurries on ahead. He follows at a short distance, using his stick for support. She stops about twenty yards away in a small clearing where a rake leans against one of the

27

trees. Next to it is a trug, cast aside, as if Matilda has been interrupted in the middle of picking up leaves.

'There.' She turns to him. Her grey hair is pulled back from her face, her lips aren't pink any more but white. The bottoms of her teeth where they meet the gums are visible. 'There. See what I mean? Or am I going mad?'

His eyes track back to the silver birches beyond her. He sees what is there and for a moment has to lean against a tree for support. Every muscle begins to shake.

It can't be. It just *cannot* be.

THE HAUNTING

Matilda Anchor-Ferrers believes the house is haunted. Not haunted in the conventional sense, by the spirit of the long dead, but haunted by the shared memory of an event that occurred fifteen years ago, when Kiran was sixteen and Lucia was just fifteen. It was, in Matilda's eyes, a watershed in their lives. A happening that changed everything beyond repair. It happened on a summer's day, not unlike today. And in woods identical to these.

Lucia in particular hasn't recovered. She was the most affected and to this day carries the dark energy of those events, which is why Matilda didn't ask her to come out here now. She is the one who must be protected from the unbelievability of what is in the trees.

'Was it like this when you found it?' Oliver stands in the clearing, one hand wedged on the trunk of an elder to support himself. The sudden walk and the shock are etched in his face. 'Was it?'

'Yes. I was gathering up the leaves and I . . .'

She trails off. She doesn't know what to say. 'I couldn't believe what I was seeing.'

'It's pure coincidence. Chance.'

'Coincidence?' she echoes. 'What sort of *coincidence,* Ollie?'

'Something's been brought down by an animal — it's just fluke the way it's . . .' He waves his hands vaguely at the bushes. He's trying to sound gruff, confident, but he looks as if he might be sick at any moment. 'The way it's ended up like that.'

'What sort of animal would be big enough, tall enough to do something like —'

'Mum?'

Matilda breaks off. Behind Ollie, standing timidly at the entrance to the copse — all black T-shirt and white skin — is Lucia. It's hot out here but she's wearing Ollie's old Barbour as if she is cold. It swamps her, hanging to her knees.

'Dad?'

Oliver sways away from the tree and turns awkwardly. 'Lucia.' He begins to walk painfully up the path towards her. Pointing to her with his walking stick. 'Didn't see you there. Let's go back to the house.'

'What's going on?'

'Nothing.' Oliver puts out a hand to try to shield her view. To move her away. 'It's nothing. Go back to what you were doing.'

'So fake.' She tries to sidestep him, craning her neck to see down into the clearing. 'I know you, Dad. You're lying.'

Matilda comes forward, trying to block her view. 'Lucia, darling, why don't you go inside and get the cake out of the oven. It's going to burn.'

But Lucia has seen it. 'Oh,' she says, her hand coming up to her mouth. 'Oh, no.'

Matilda takes her daughter by the shoulders. Turns her bodily in the direction of the house. 'Listen to me. Do as I told you. Go into the house and get the cake out of the oven. Your dad and I will deal with everything out here. It's not what it looks like. All right? *Lucia?* Is that all right?'

The skin around Lucia's mouth is blue. After a long time she nods numbly. She takes a stiff step towards the house, then another. Her head is down, her legs awkward and uncoordinated. Watching her go, Matilda feels that familiar pang of guilt . . . as if she's somehow let her daughter down. Maybe every mother is like this and has one child destined to be a worry. For Matilda it's not Kiran, it's Lucia; she just can't seem to settle in life. She's started and ended careers more times than can be counted — one minute she's performing with a punk band, the next she's designing clothes for a goth store — and as for boyfriends, well, the rapidity with which they change leaves Matilda dizzy. Every time a job or relationship goes sour Lucia comes limping back home to lick her wounds. She's been back with them for the last two months. Fate, of course, would put her here now, of all times.

Matilda raises her eyes to the house, with its dark walls built of the local blue lias. It's a four-storey building, including the vast towers put in place by the second owner in the 1890s, hence its name: The Turrets. Dark as a crow. God, she thinks, they should have sold this place back when it all happened. But fifteen years ago there wasn't a property in the area that would have sold — you couldn't have given them away. People were superstitious and scared and nothing could induce them to come and live out here, especially in a location as remote as The Turrets. *How long would it take the emergency services to get here?* they asked. Look at that driveway — it must be more than half a mile long. And the nearest police station is in Compton Martin.

The sound of Lucia opening and slamming the back door punctuates the silence. Neither Matilda nor Oliver speaks. Somewhere a bird sings, the breeze shifts the branches.

Eventually, certain that Lucia won't come back, Matilda turns and stares at the mess, the way it's been mingled and studded with plant matter and earth. It's been here a while, more than a few hours she guesses from the shiny patina. Drying out in the heat. Bluebottles landing on it, some lingering. Laying eggs, she supposes.

Oliver rubs his nose. 'I think we're making too much of this.'

'Are we?'

'We know he can't be back.'

'We know, Oliver? Are you so sure of that?'

'Of course I'm sure.'

'Do we know he hasn't been let out? I mean, I haven't checked on him recently. Have you?'

Oliver huffs something about having other things on his mind. Not having time to check up on prisoners. 'I'm sure he can't be free. We'd have been told. Everyone would be talking about it.'

'Well, that's fine then.' She grabs the rake from where it leans against the tree, and turns for the house. 'That's fine, and of course I believe you. But I'm still going to call the police.'

THE REFLECTION GROVE

Fifteen miles to the east of the Anchor-Ferrers' house the weather is more troubled. Small clouds bump restlessly across the sky. The sun flashes on and off and sudden localized rain-bursts punctuate the day. The West Wiltshire countryside is alive with birdsong and the new, acid greens of May. In a small grove on an otherwise deserted hillside, almost a hundred people have congregated. A middle-aged woman in towering stilettos, mini-dress and black veiled hat, holds centre stage on a beribboned platform. She appears to be holding back tears as she delivers a speech to the waiting journalists.

'Lots of people are going to come here just to think about their lives and stuff.' She opens her arms to indicate the grove they stand in, its bunting and flags and hospitality tables. 'It's a place for them to have a really good think about what's happening in their personal journey, so what the clinic and me have decided we're going to call it, is . . . the

"Reflection Grove".'

Oooooh, murmurs the crowd appreciatively. Clickety-click go the cameras.

'Yeah,' she says. 'The Reflection Grove. And I want to say thank you for this, from the bottom of my heart, thank you to everyone who made it happen. It would have meant everything to my beautiful daughter to know other people are going to get something out of her tragedy. It's so beautiful to be able to give something back.'

This is Jacqui Kitson. Two years ago her twenty-two-year-old daughter, then a minor celebrity, wandered away from a rehabilitation clinic located a mile away from this hilltop. She'd taken a lethal mix of drugs and alcohol and, disorientated, she eventually collapsed and died at a spot right under the feet of the gathered journalists. Her body lay for several months before it was discovered among the leaves.

Jacqui Kitson has lived through the trauma and come out the other end. In its wake she's raised £15,000 through charitable donations to buy this glade on behalf of the clinic. A memorial for her daughter, a place for the residents of the clinic to come with their solitude and their thoughts. A willow-weave pagoda has been erected in the centre of the glade. On its lower floor are cut-away arches, with benches on the interior so that people can sit and gaze out at the view of the Wiltshire plains.

Ten current patients have attended the celebration. They wear an assortment of clothing, tracksuits, denim, trucker hats, and they stand in shuffling formation around the platform. The directors of the clinic are here too: three women in suits, each of them itchy with the desire to speak to the waiting journalists. Only one man doesn't want to be part of it. One man who stands alone, keeping his distance, set a little apart from the melee in a place shielded by the lofty birches. A place he can watch, not participate.

DI Jack Caffery is a CID officer in his mid-forties. He is here out of duty, to show a police presence, but he will do anything to keep removed from this spectacle. He stands quite still, hands in his pockets, watching as people crowd around Jacqui Kitson. She smiles and nods and shakes hands. Poses for a photograph with one of the clinic directors. They hold up glasses to clink for the cameraman. Green tea, not champagne — this is, after all, a place to escape from the reach of intoxicants. Someone asks her to sit in the pagoda for photographs. She does this without blinking an eye, her hands resting demurely on her knees, her chin lifted in the direction of the sun.

Caffery is a seasoned detective; he has worked a lot of the country's most notorious and difficult cases. He has seen things, a lot of things, and been in many situations that have made him uncomfortable. But he's never wanted to get away from something quite as much as he wants to get away from this.

BEAR

The Anchor-Ferrers are all back in the house.
They've locked the doors and windows in a
mood of subdued panic. Lucia watches Dad
in the hallway, his head bent. He is using a
butter knife to prise open the cordless phone
and check the batteries, frowning because
Mum's tried to call the police and inexplica-
bly can't get a line. Sunlight is coming
through the great stained-glass window, falling on his face. Jewel-bright greens and reds,
harlequining his expression into something
monstrous. As if the day wasn't surreal
enough to start with.

Here in the kitchen, Mum is busy tidying
things. The bags are all unpacked, the cake
has come out of the oven and is sitting on
the wire cooling rack, and every now and
then Mum stops to smooth her clothes down,
almost as if she's expecting guests.

Except it's not guests she is expecting, Lucia thinks. At least not the kind that come to
eat cake.

'Lucia,' Mum says. 'Look after Bear. She wants some attention.'

Lucia stares numbly at her mother. She wants to respond, but nothing comes out of her mouth. It's like being shot through with anaesthetic; her face, all her muscles are immobile. What is in the garden is just like it was before. Exactly the same and there is no escaping it. She knows what the scene is *meant* to look like — and she can guess who has done it — but now it's upon her it all feels so unexpected and wrong.

'Lucia? Did you hear me?'

With an effort Lucia blinks. She tries to focus on Mum's face but her eyes can't help wandering past her, out to the coppices and the woods beyond. The funny thing is the trees themselves are the greatest shock. The normality of them. The fact they haven't changed or reacted when everything else is all so wrong.

'Deal with Bear.' Mum is getting exasperated. 'Lucia. *Please.* Stop her barking, I can't hear myself think.'

Under the table Bear has been made nervous by all the activity. She is giving small, querulous yaps and tugging on the lead, making the chair scrape across the flagging. Lucia comes back to herself with a jolt. It's happening. It's really happening.

She crosses the room on legs that feel like rubber. Sweat is soaking into her T-shirt. Bear

39

turns agitated circles, getting herself tangled in the lead. They should have got round to chipping her, then she wouldn't have to be tied up here. She's been known to head for miles — once as far as Farrington golf course. It's as if she's always known there is something bad about this place, despite the fact she wasn't even born when the murders happened on the Donkey Pitch.

'It's OK, Bear.' Lucia unhooks the lead and bundles her up. She sits in the window seat and holds Bear's wiry body against her chest, hushing her, whispering. 'It's going to be OK, I promise, it's all going to be OK.'

It breaks Lucia's heart that Bear is scared like this. She loves this little animal more than anything in the world, and most of the time she thinks Bear's the only living creature that really cares about her. Lucia might be silent and dark a lot of the time, but she's not stupid and not much gets past her. She knows perfectly well that she's not Mum and Dad's favourite; she's lived with that knowledge all her life. And as for what happened fifteen years ago . . . well, she will never, ever recover from those wounds.

Hugo . . . Hugo.

She will never, ever forget Hugo. Since his death the only thing she has felt safe to love is this little dog.

LIGHT

There is a homage to the Anchor-Ferrers family in the huge stained-glass window that Oliver installed twenty years ago above the minstrel's gallery. It shows the four of them: Matilda, Oliver, Lucia and Kiran, standing on a shrunken globe, surrounded by radiating sunrays, tangerine and yellow.

Oliver loves light. Loves it possibly, Matilda feels, more than he loves his own family. He worships it and considers it in every waking hour. Her friends tell her that at least light is free, whereas golf or flying a single-engined Cessna or fly fishing in Peru — well, those things certainly *aren't* free and Matilda should consider herself lucky. Nevertheless she's always felt a little envious of light. Even the children are named after light — there's Kiran, meaning beam of light, and Lucia, which to many people's ears sounds too close to Lucifer for comfort. Matilda has never been totally happy about it.

The window depicts the family as subjugated to light and to the heavens. The sky is like something William Blake might have painted, ablaze in glory. The house behind them is meant to be The Turrets, though it's a poor and clumsy representation, in Matilda's opinion. There is no dog there either — which is wrong, because there's always been a dog in the family's life. And no garden. Nothing to capture who they are. No flowers being picked or cakes being cooked.

A stupid thing to worry about, she thinks now, because actually nothing could matter less. Ollie stands under the window, busily fiddling with the phone. Alarmingly, it has chosen this moment to lose its power. Lucia is huddled in the window seat with Bear scrunched up against her chest, and Matilda doesn't know where to put herself. She's done nothing more constructive than walk agitatedly to and fro, moving things around, trying to put the place in order. Double-checking doors are locked and windows closed.

'Check the back door again,' she tells Lucia. 'Do the top bolt too.'

Lucia goes down the small corridor and can be heard rattling bolts. Matilda can't recall if the front door in the hallway has been bolted, but as she turns to go to it something brings her to a halt. She stares down at the floor, her heart beating low and slow. Four or five drops of something brownish red are there, each a long teardrop shape.

She drops to her knees and uses a thumb-nail to scratch at the biggest. It comes away in flakes on her thumb. She raises her head and scans the room. The kitchen is huge — it straddles the side of the house and incorporates a small dining area, as well as a living area with a vast inglenook. It's all familiar and old as the hills to her, except something is not quite right. It's more than just what is looped in the bushes down in the coppice; something *inside* the house is out of place too. A smell? A vague unfamiliar scent. And this? She rubs the flake between her thumb and forefinger. It disintegrates and softens down into the grains of her fingerpads. Blood? Is it blood? No, good God, no. Of course it can't be. She goes to the sink to rinse her fingers. There's no connection between these drops of red — which could be *anything, let's face it, anything at all* — and what she has just seen in the trees. Oliver is right. Those belong to an animal which has been brought down by a predator. An entirely normal occurrence and to assign any other significance to it is sheer hysteria.

She wipes her hands furiously. Dips at the waist and leans forward so she can peer back down the corridor into the huge hall where Oliver is still picking away at the telephone. What's keeping him? It should take him two minutes to replace the batteries.

43

He stops fiddling with the phone and rolls his head to the side, fixing her with a look. His face is very puffy from the medication and there's a single blue vein in his forehead that Matilda has never noticed before. As if the surgeons have given him an extra blood vessel during the surgery.

He holds up the phone. 'It's not working,' he mouths. His expression says: *What do I do? Is this really happening?*

Matilda doesn't react. Lucia has come back into the room and she mustn't be panicked. But inside Matilda is screaming. The house phone is their only lifeline. When the doctors finally told Ollie he was free to leave London they asked whether he had quick access to a hospital, The Turrets being so isolated, and Matilda said she'd drive him into Wells or call an ambulance. There's no mobile signal up at The Turrets, but there's a perfectly good landline. There's never been a problem with it. Not until now.

Matilda has a runaround car they keep locked in the garage, but the keys are in Oliver's study at the other side of the house. The Land Rover, their London car, they park down the drive. That'll be quicker. She goes into the mudroom and puts her hands into the pockets of her oilskin that's hanging there. Ferrets around for the Land Rover keys and mobile phone. There is a weak phone signal at the bottom of the driveway. She'll

44

have to drive down there and call the police. But the keys aren't in the oilskin. Maybe they're in her handbag, hanging on the chair in the hallway.

She goes back into the kitchen and stops short. At her seat in the window Lucia has her face up, her mouth hanging slightly open, and is staring in amazement at two men who have appeared in the kitchen doorway with Oliver, who stands next to them, regarding them in bewilderment, the broken phone forgotten in his hand. Beyond them, in the hall, the front door is ajar.

The men are dressed in dark grey suits and both wear serious expressions. One is short and long-armed, with freckles and ginger hair cut close like a soldier's. He wears black-framed glasses and stands a little awkwardly, his eyes roving the kitchen nervously. The other is calmer. He is tall and straight-backed, with a large nose and very pale green eyes, fringed with fair lashes. His fair hair is curly, but it has receded back so far that the top of his head is as naked and shiny as a monk's, giving him the look of a young Art Garfunkel. He is holding a police warrant card.

'Mrs Anchor-Ferrers?' he says. 'Detective Inspector Honey. This is Detective Sergeant Molina. Sorry to barge in — we buzzed the intercom by the gates at the bottom of the driveway, but no one answered so we had to

45

walk up.'

'No,' Matilda says distantly. 'We've been outside in the garden.'

Sergeant Molina exchanges an uncomfortable glance with Inspector Honey, who clears his throat. Puts his card back in his pocket. He doesn't smile.

'I wonder,' he says, 'could we have a word with you?'

THE SICKNESS

DI Caffery is a good-looking man. Medium height, clean shaven with close-cropped dark hair. He's a senior officer in his unit too, so he is often sought out by journalists. Their affection for him isn't reciprocated; he avoids them whenever he can. He still has not learned how to give them what they want to hear, and despises the fakery and game-playing. Today, however, the journalist has got to him before he can escape, and now he is obliged to answer her question, 'What does today mean to you and the rest of the force?' He does so quickly and efficiently, bending slightly to speak into the small microphone she holds. He's careful not to meet her eyes so she doesn't see the lies in them.

'Mixed feelings. Of course we were devastated by the family's loss and that we couldn't bring the search to a happier conclusion, but now, seeing the way Jacqui is rebuilding her life so positively . . .' He gestures to the clearing where the crowd is gathered. 'Then I can say we — the force — are delighted that the family are moving on with their lives.'

'Do you think Jacqui has closure? I mean, her daughter's body may have been found, but it's still not known exactly what happened to her.'

Caffery stares at her. He hates the expression 'closure'. It sounds like something connected to solicitors and house purchases. She sees him hesitate, and prompts: 'Closure? Has she got it?'

'I don't know. I'm not even sure what the word means. Thank you.'

He nods and, ignoring the next question, moves away, heading for the cover of the trees where he can monitor events without having to speak. Startled by his rudeness, the journalist is momentarily lost for words. He manoeuvres himself further back into the trees, so she isn't encouraged to follow him.

He remains there in the shadows, leaning back against a tree, because today he is struggling to keep upright. Caffery is ill. For two weeks now he has been blighted by the sort of headache that won't be dulled by painkillers. He can't sleep, and on the rare occasions he does sleep he dreams of being tied down. Of sinking in mud or quicksand. He hasn't been to the doctor — doesn't even know who his GP is — and anyway, he knows there will be no diagnosis. There is no physical root to the pain, he's sure of that. It's coming from something deeper, something intangible he can't quite pinpoint. But he does know that listening to Jacqui Kitson talk about her daughter will make the pressure in his head worse.

The journalist, apparently having given up on her pursuit of Caffery, has found her way to Jacqui, who by contrast is eager to talk. She rolls out the same old lines, about how awful it was for the months when her daughter was missing, the agony of not knowing what had happened. Caffery's hands twitch in his pockets with every sentence she speaks. It's true that he knows more about the disappearance of Jacqui's daughter than anyone else — he's the investigating cop and there are things about the case no one will ever know, fabrications around what really happened that will never be revealed. But that's not what's troubling him today. It's something more profound than that. Something about Jacqui's demeanour and words scrape like sandpaper in his head. Every time she opens her mouth, the tension increases.

He pushes himself away from the tree and shuffles a few feet further into the woods, just to keep himself moving, get some life into his body. But it doesn't work. He is tired. So very tired.

Oliver is a scientist, but a physicist, not a biologist, and he isn't too sure if he understands exactly what is going on in his body. He has noticed that since the operation his thoughts come more slowly. Sometimes it's like being in a dream — as if people are speaking to him from a different room. When the front door handle first turned, opened, and the bigger of the two put his head round the door, peering at Oliver in the hall, he struggled to work out how they'd got here. Who called them? He was sure it wasn't him because the phone wasn't working.

The men say they are here to investigate a murder.

'Have you been here in the house all morning?'

DI Honey, the tall man with the monk's pate and tight curls, is grilling Matilda, who is answering automatically, her voice distant, as if she's reciting a long-forgotten poem that has suddenly come back to her.

'No. We didn't get here until after eleven. This is our holiday home — we drove down from London this morning.'

'You didn't hear the sirens?'

'No. But we don't hear stuff up here, we're very isolated.'

'The victim lives just down here in the valley.' He lifts his hand to indicate the west. 'Down there, not far from the bottom of your driveway. In the house where the lane turns out on to the main road.'

'The yellow house, you mean? The one with the stone tiles and the yellow walls?'

'That's the one.'

'My God. Oliver? It's the one that has the satellite dish. You know?'

He nods numbly, still struggling to catch up to the reality of all this. It's a single woman who lives in the yellow house. He doesn't know her by name but he's seen her around. Brunette, mid-forties, quite attractive. Mostly he remembers she wears red jeans and leather jackets, like a city person, and insists on driving her four-by-four down the centre of the road — as if everyone else should pull to the side to let her pass.

'The offender came in through the . . . the downstairs window. It was open.'

DS Molina — the red-haired one, who reminds Oliver of someone, a politician, or a singer, he can't quite place it — puts his hands on the back of a chair. He looks as if he's about to deliver a well-rehearsed speech. 'We're going to have to take you through a few protocols, have community liaison come over and talk you through some basic home security measures. If this is a holiday home it'll come in handy anyway — to know about window locks and the like.'

'First you need to tell us what has happened,' Matilda insists. 'And if you've arrested anyone.'

'Until we've got a positive identification and we've informed the relatives, we can't give out details.'

Oliver finds his voice. 'I'd expect more people for a murder investigation — especially if your offender's still out there. A helicopter maybe.'

'There was a helicopter — didn't you hear it?'

'Like Mum said, we don't hear anything up here,' says Lucia. She manages to make it sound like an attack on her parents. 'Not a *thing*.'

'We're asking people if they've had any break-ins — anything going missing. Have you got a garden shed?'

'A garden shed? Yes. There's a garage too.'

'Do they lock? And have you checked they're locked today? We're wondering if anything's been taken. Any tools. Like a Stanley knife . . .'

Stanley knife. A long cold silence comes

down on the family. This is the final confirmation. Now they know it's not their imagination. This is happening.

Keep beating, Oliver tells the pig valves. *Beat the next beat. And the next . . .*

'You really should apologize!' Matilda is suddenly pink with rage and bewilderment. 'Is that what this is? A belated apology?'

Honey doesn't answer for a moment. He seems confused. He glances at his sergeant for support, then at Lucia and Oliver. 'I'm sorry,' he says. 'I don't . . .'

'What happened to the notification from the CPS? The CPS are supposed to let us know if there've been any changes or reviews to that man's sentence. We're supposed to be informed if he's out.'

'I'm sorry. "That man"? I don't —'

'Because my daughter was deemed vulnerable. She was only fifteen when it happened — *fifteen.* My husband and I were given the same rights as a family spokesperson. We were entitled to be informed if he came out again, and nobody's said a word.'

'Mrs —'

'Look at my daughter.' She gestures at Lucia, sitting on the sofa with Bear, who has picked up on the tension and is growling menacingly. 'Look at her and tell me that she didn't deserve to have some warning. And my husband's just had serious surgery, so we're not exactly equipped to deal with any

53

of this. Meanwhile he, HE — he's light years ahead of us, as usual. He's already cut the phone line, or at least done something to stop it working. So you're a bit late. We were supposed to have been given notice a long time ago. A bare minimum would be ten days — but no. Not a word. And now *this . . .*'

DI Honey holds up a defensive hand. 'Look, I'm sorry, Mrs Anchor-Ferrers. I can hear you're angry, and I want to respond to that, but until I know what you're angry about there's nothing I can do.'

This makes Matilda subside a little. Though her eyes don't leave his face, she does at least move back from him, giving him a bit of space.

'Kable,' she mutters, bad-temperedly.

'Kable?'

'Well, of course! I mean, please tell me you *know* Minnet Kable is responsible. He's out again, isn't he? And nobody's told us.'

There's a long, breathless silence. Oliver notices that Lucia has closed her eyes and he knows why. It's the first time in the last frenetic forty minutes any of them has actually said the name aloud, though it's what they've all been thinking. It feels like speaking the name of the devil.

Minnet Kable. Minnet. With the emphasis on the first syllable. Usually the name is never spoken aloud in this household.

Minnet is white, British, and the Anchor-

54

Ferrers have no idea how he came to be given such a name. There is nothing in any of the legal transcripts to suggest his heritage. Ollie, not having grown up in today's multicultural England, is embarrassed to admit even to himself that the name has a guttural sound to it. Like a curse spoken in Aramaic. Something a demon in a film would say. And Kable is a demon. Fifteen years ago Minnet Kable murdered two people. One of them was Lucia's ex-boyfriend, Hugo Frink.

DI Honey's eyes roll slowly to meet his colleague's, as if none of this had occurred to him. As if expecting an answer. Then he puts his hands in his pockets and stares at the floor for a while. 'Yes,' he says eventually. 'I admit I hadn't thought about . . .' He glances at DS Molina. 'Don't suppose you remember Minnet Kable. It was before you joined the force.'

Molina's eyes are wide, as if his pulse is forcing them open. 'I do remember him. I mean, Jesus!' He runs his finger nervously around the inside of his collar. 'Doesn't everybody?'

Oliver shakes his head in resignation. And they call this modern policing. He's seen more efficient police forces in the Third World. 'You seriously didn't think of Minnet Kable before?'

'No. We didn't. Though I agree it seems obvious.'

'We need to take you outside.' Oliver speaks

in the most measured tone he can summon. 'There's something you're going to have to see.'

THE DEER

All five of them — the family and the two
police officers — leave the house. Matilda
locks the side door carefully and puts the key
in her tool pouch before they set off down
the path together. Lucia is with them. It's
against Matilda's wishes, but she refused to
be left alone in the house. She has brought
Bear with her, clasped in her arms so tightly
the dog can only move her head.

It is hotter now, the sky is so clear it's
almost white, just a few faint vapour trails
drifting slowly high overhead. The land
stretches away, not another house or building
to be seen, only the distant pylons and a flank
of a hill patchworked with fields. It had been
this uninterrupted view that Matilda had
loved about The Turrets, so different from
the view out of their London windows. Now
it's what she hates the most.

They go tentatively, Oliver leading the way.
He supports himself on the stick he's been
told by the doctors to use. From behind he

doesn't look to Matilda like her husband. He looks like an old man in baggy corduroy trousers. Infirm and bent. Past his prime.

They stop in the clearing and gather around. The flies react sluggishly, lifting half-heartedly from their meal as if to acknowledge the presence of the humans before drifting back down to gorge.

Earlier, when Matilda first happened on this scene, her initial impression was it was some sort of decoration — a paper chain, or a string of deflated children's balloons, draped almost delicately in the bushes. It had taken a moment or two to recognize them for what they actually are: intestines.

'We were hoping they were from an animal.'

'They could be,' Oliver asks the police, a note of hope in his voice, 'a deer, perhaps?'

'A deer?' DI Honey says softly. 'A deer? I doubt it.'

'I'd say there'd be some domestic dogs around here big enough to do this to a deer.'

'And hang them up in the trees?'

No one speaks. They can all smell the decay. In the short time the family's been up at the house, the intestines have begun to smell. The white fascia stretches around the bulbous pink sac, the last meal of whatever creature these came from visible as dark shapes behind the semi-transparent wall.

'Insane,' DI Honey says, clearly embarrassed. 'Completely insane.' He fumbles a handkerchief out of his pocket and wipes his face. 'It's very hot today, isn't it? Unseasonably hot.'

He folds up the handkerchief, taking his time to make it neat or, Matilda thinks, buying time to collect himself. 'This could be —' He pulls back his shoulders. Scans the horizon. 'I'd be lying if I said this might not be relevant. This is . . . consistent with the case we're investigating. The injuries to the victim.' He pushes the handkerchief into his pocket. Pulls back his jacket to reveal a radio nestled in his breast pocket. He runs his fingers over it and appears about to summon backup, then thinks better of it because instead he again pulls out his handkerchief and mops his face.

'Mr Anchor-Ferrers,' he says in a strained voice. 'I wonder — could we go inside? It's hot. We had to leave the car at the bottom of the drive and it was a long walk up. I wonder if we could trouble you for a glass of water?'

THE CHAUFFEUR

A shower works its way restlessly across the Wiltshire fields. It travels up the hillside and brings the opening ceremony to an end. The group breaks up, people hurry for cover, holding cardigans and handbags over their heads. Only DI Caffery lingers. When the glade is deserted he stands for a while, surveying the place. The bunting is streaked with rain, the smell of earth and grass hangs in the air. The sun comes out again, but the sight of the rain dripping from the pagoda roof drags on him, lowers his mood further.

Eventually he turns to go. His shirt is hot and scratchy. He has never been comfortable in a suit, though he lives in one day after day, and as he walks he tugs at his collar, undoing the tie. At the bottom of the path, at the entrance to the car park, two women are waiting for him. One is Jacqui Kitson, a light mac draped over her shoulders, the other, also dressed in sky-high heels and a tight dress, is a sergeant from his unit: DS Paluzzi. She is holding a dripping umbrella and has one hand jammed into her hip. She doesn't look impressed.

He shoves the tie in his pocket. His head is still throbbing. He is sure the smallest conversation could crack his head in half. Split open the thing that's been building inside him these last few days. 'You OK?'

She nods. 'Uh huh.'

'What can I do for you?'

'Just spoke to the superintendent. He's suggesting you could drive Jacqui back to her hotel.'

There's a brief pause. He can feel Paluzzi monitoring his reaction. She knows how welcome this news is going to be.

'The unit is quiet,' she presses. 'Nothing's happening, he can spare you. It's a courtesy for Jacqui, and also nice for the press to see how we treat people.'

'Don't worry.' Jacqui Kitson smiles, her bracelets jangle. She's got a line of lipstick across her top teeth. 'I won't eat you.'

Caffery's hand in his pocket finds the smooth metal casing of his V-Cig under the tie. He's trying to quit them, but times like this he knows that isn't going to happen.

'You'll have to take my car as you find it.'

'I'm happy with that. It'll be like old times.'

As senior officer on the case of Jacqui's missing daughter, he's spent a lot of time in her company. He's never been one hundred

61

per cent comfortable around her. As he leads
Jacqui to his car he senses Paluzzi's eyes on
him. Usually she's one of the detectives he
likes, always on his side, but lately she's been
sarcastic. Keeps making comments about the
fact he's mid-forties and not married. She's
recently divorced and there's a suggestion
doing the rounds that she's lonely and wanting company.

As Caffery unlocks the car and holds the
door for Jacqui to get in, he feels Paluzzi's
eyes on his back. Right, he thinks. And I am
the last place you should look.

THE DONKEY PITCH

A wood pigeon chortles softly somewhere in the trees on the other side of The Turrets. It's the only sound. The Anchor-Ferrers and the cops go back to the house swiftly. No one acknowledges the sudden sense of dread the surrounding woods seem to have taken on. As if something is watching from among the trees.

As they go, DS Molina mutters into his radio, which gives off bursts of static but no voices, no intelligible reply. When they reach the house he stays outside at the side door, waiting for a response, while the others go inside. DI Honey and Oliver check all the doors and the windows on the ground floor. Matilda isn't quite sure why, but to busy herself she instinctively begins making tea for everyone. She warms the pot and tips the cake off the cooling rack on to a plate. No time to ice it — they'll have to eat it as it is. She cuts it into slices and puts it on the table. It sits there untouched until she feels foolish to have imagined food was appropriate in these circumstances.

When Oliver and DI Honey come back they sit at the table together. DI Honey makes notes. Oliver is helping him recall the details of the case.

'It's been, what? Fifteen years.'

Oliver nods. 'That's why I can't understand why he was let out so soon.'

'We don't know that he *is* out. The system isn't perfect.'

'You can say that again.' Oliver's back to his old self. He seems as angry and anxious as Matilda feels. He glances up at Lucia then turns his back to her, putting his elbow on the table and speaking to the detective in a whisper that Matilda can only just hear. 'You do understand, don't you, that my daughter knew the victims. The boy had been . . . well Hugo Frink was her boyfriend . . . before. They hadn't been long separated when it happened.'

Matilda comes to the table and sits, her hands jammed between her knees, staring at the plate of cake while Oliver continues in a low, monotonous voice. As he speaks, Hugo's death all comes back to her: the first phone calls, the rumours that something had happened on the Donkey Pitch, then the confirmation, the visits from the police. The slow, ugly unfurling of details turning from whispered hints among the neighbours into cold hard facts.

Hugo Frink was just seventeen. Tall, broad shouldered and green-eyed, with a love of rowing and music. He was living for a while in his grandparents' house on the other side of the valley while his parents were abroad. Hugo met Lucia at a Guy Fawkes party in the local village and they dated for six months. But in late spring Hugo met another local girl and broke off the relationship with Lucia. If that wasn't enough to destroy her, his murder, just weeks later, was the final nail in the coffin. She has never recovered.

Kable was insane, convicted over and over for a string of offences — arson, sexual assault, car theft. No one knows what made him cross the line and turn to killing that summer night, or why he targeted Hugo Frink and his new girlfriend, Sophie Hurst-Lloyd. It happened about a mile away from The Turrets, in a section of wood at the far end of the valley. Now it is used by youngsters to ride BMX bicycles. Back then it was just a piece of unchartered woodland called 'the Donkey Pitch' because someone had once, years ago, kept donkeys there. The land was adjacent to Hugo's grandparents' property, but too far for anyone to hear the teenagers screaming. Kable's final signature was to remove the intestines of both teenagers. He twisted them together and used them to decorate the trees above the corpses in the shape of a heart. Which is exactly what has been replicated today, in the woods next to The Turrets.

'Kable,' says Oliver, 'is a psychopath. He is completely unstoppable. He shows no remorse and no fear.'

DI Honey massages his temples, as if the outrageous unreality he's wandered into has only just hit him. 'We're sorry. We're going to find out why we weren't told he's out. Just give us time.' He glances to the side door, still unlocked. Molina stands in the doorway with his back to them, speaking urgently into his radio. 'When did you find it?' DI Honey asks. 'You know — what you showed us in the wood?'

'Just before you arrived. It's the first thing Matilda does — go outside to garden. She loves the garden.'

'You have to pass the yellow house to get here. Do you know what time you drove past?'

'I have no idea. Elevenish?'

'And you didn't notice anything odd? No cars you didn't recognize parked there? Anything that wasn't quite as you'd expect it?'

'No.'

A few beats of silence. Oliver waits for DI Honey to ask another question, but instead the detective blurts suddenly, 'I don't understand why you didn't move. Don't you find it . . .' He searches for the word. 'I don't mean to be rude, but there's an atmosphere here. Can't you feel it?'

'There is.' From her place in the window seat, Lucia raises her head. 'A terrible atmosphere.'

Matilda studies Lucia. She's always said she hates this place, even before the killings. She is more sensitive than anyone in the family, always has been. Kiran, on the other hand — well, Kiran is completely the opposite. Though Oliver is firmly in the nurture versus nature camp — that every child can be moulded by society to be a productive and happy citizen — Matilda couldn't disagree more. Having brought up two children, she believes that children are born. Like planets they fall into their natural orbit no matter what you fire at them. You might hope to nudge them slightly off their route, but you'll never turn them around. Kiran was born with a clear, straight, solid core. From the word go he's known what he wants from the world. Lucia is the polar opposite. She gets pulled and reversed and cannot keep in line. Hugo's death exacerbated the problem.

'Boss?' Everyone twists round. Molina has come into the kitchen and closed the door behind him. Sweat is beading on his forehead. 'Problem.'

WHAT ANGELS WANT

'My little girl would want me to be happy. She was an angel, my daughter, a complete angel. And I suppose she's an angel still. She's up there and watching me.'

In the front seat Jacqui Kitson has her legs crossed, her right arm up over the back seat so she is turned in Caffery's direction. She's relaxed in his car. He keeps his eyes on the road, conscious of her proximity and the red lipstick blur as her mouth moves.

'I know she wants this for me, Jack. She wants me to have happiness. What do you think? Do you think she'd want me to be happy?'

'I don't know.'

Jacqui sighs. 'I think she would.' She uncrosses her leg, pulls down the visor and uses the mirror to check her reflection. She finds the lipstick on her teeth and rubs it away with a noise of irritation. Then she snaps the mirror back to its place and says, 'I don't know why, but a drink in the afternoon always cheers me up. Are you the same?'

Caffery would like a drink, but not with her. He judges by the smell that she's already managed one or two this morning, in spite of the green tea for the cameras.

'Aren't there any pubs around here?' she asks. 'Somewhere intimate? One of those thatched-roof thingies?'

'Realistically, it wouldn't be appropriate for me to drink while I'm on duty.'

Jacqui gives a long hiccupping laugh. 'Oh my GOD! *Realistically, that wouldn't be appropriate?* You've got your professional face on then?'

'It's my job.'

'Maybe, but when you say it like that I can't help wondering what is "appropriate". A little drink with me? Wouldn't kill you to be friendly, would it?'

Caffery makes no comment. Jacqui has always flirted with him. Usually she's drunk and he can slide out of her way without too much argument. He calculates it's another hour's drive to her hotel in Bristol. A long time to hold her at bay.

'Come on, Jack. We're old friends. Just a quick stop. Look at all these places we're passing. One of them must do a nice Pinot.'

'I said no, and that's what I mean. Let's drop the subject.'

That deflates Jacqui. She sinks back in her seat, arms folded, her mouth twisting as if trying to come up with a witty retort. For a while there is silence. The roads are quiet so he can put on some speed, the fields and hedgerows zipping past the car. Clouds play rapid cat and mouse overhead, occasionally opening up to reveal huge, cathedral-like blue stretches of sky.

Caffery pities Jacqui, but he'll never go in the direction she wants. He has a lifelong dilemma with women and maybe that's contributing to the sick way he feels. The blinding flashes of red, the headaches and the dreams of quicksand. He's never been able to get it right. Never married or had kids. The only girlfriends he's had have been screwed up in some way. There's only one woman he has ever imagined he could get it right with. She's a police sergeant. Not DS Paluzzi, but the head of a specialist search unit over at Almondsbury, and he's been through a lot with her, both professionally and personally. Somehow, when he pictures the end of the story, he always imagines her in it. He's never told her this or acted on it. He's not sure why.

And he's not sure if that is the cause or the effect of this atom bomb sitting in his head.

Jacqui begins to fidget. She opens her bag, takes out a packet of cigarettes. She pulls out a gold lighter, appears to think better of lighting up and puts everything back. She closes her bag and sits with it clutched on her lap, her manicured fingers tapping lightly. Eventually she can't resist speaking.

'I don't get it. There's no ring on your finger, you're not spoken for, so what is it? The age gap? You're what? Forty? I'm only late forties. It's not like I'm some *cougar.* And even if I was, would it be a sin? Or is it that you don't think I'm allowed to be happy now? Is that what it is? Hmm?'

Caffery says nothing.

'Yeah!' Jacqui says. '*That's* what it is. You think instead of enjoying myself I ought to be wearing black and crying all the time. Believe me, I've done my share of that. And you — people like you, you'll *never* know what it feels like, so don't judge.'

'Is that right, Jacqui?'

'Of course it's right. You do all this sympathy stuff, but you don't know. Not really. Nobody does. They might have had people die on them — in a hospital bed or at home. A body to bury, a funeral service, time to grieve, etc etc. But no one really knows what it's like to have someone you love go missing. Not knowing. Day after day after day — it's hell on earth. You never sleep. Did you know that?'

Caffery's pulse beats slow and hard. He grips the steering wheel until his hands are white. 'Jacqui, I'd like you to stop now. I do know what it's like, so please don't tell me I don't.'

'*But you don't.* You have absolutely *no* idea what it's like. Nobody knows. Every day you try to sleep, you close your eyes, but it's not real sleep. You dream about them all the time. You get all these images — horrible things happening. You think there must be one stone that hasn't been turned, one person that hasn't been questioned. You wonder, Is she alive? Is she hurt? Is she dead? That just goes round and round your head all the time, till you wonder whether you're mad and —'

A sudden sensation in the side of Caffery's neck. An almost audible pop, as if a blood vessel has burst. He slams on the brakes and swerves the car to a halt in a lay-by. He unclips his belt and leans across her to open the passenger door.

'What?' She looks down at the kerb, then back at Caffery, then around the car. Baffled by the reason they've come to such an abrupt halt. They are on a suburban street in Keynsham. There's nothing. No bus stop, no buildings. Just a row of houses and a newsagents. 'What? What the fuck're we doing here?'

KNIVES

DS Molina locks the side door, goes straight to the kitchen sink, turns on the tap and bends, his mouth to the opening, letting the water gush directly into his mouth. No one speaks while he does this. They stand and stare at him. Oliver plucks at the sleeves of his shirt to get some air in there, to stop the sweat pricking his underarms.

'Well?' DI Honey comes and stands next to his colleague, one hand on the work surface, half bent to scrutinize his face. 'What happened?'

'Nothing.'

'Did you see him?'

'I saw something.'

'Something? What does that mean?'

'I don't want to talk about it. If you don't mind.'

'I do mind.'

Molina pauses and looks up, his eyes magnified behind his glasses. Water streams off him. Oliver thinks something dark crosses his face, but Molina quickly contains it. He straightens, finds a tea-towel and dries himself off.

'What did you see?' Honey insists. 'What?'

Lucia suddenly puts her hands over her ears. 'Oh, please don't. I don't want to hear it.'

'I do.' Honey is adamant. 'I want to hear it.'

'You're upsetting her. Can't you see that?' Molina takes the radio out of his pocket and throws it on the table. 'Useless. I can't get anyone to answer me.'

Everyone stares at the radio. Oliver in particular finds this impossible to believe. He knows a lot about communications and this just shouldn't be happening. 'I beg your pardon? You've got a whole new radio system. How can you *not* get an answer? There isn't supposed to be a place in the British Isles you can't get a signal.'

'I know — go figure. But then all of this is —' Molina gives a helpless gesture in the direction of the coppice. 'It's gone beyond a joke. This is like a bloody movie.' He licks his lips and looks at Oliver. 'Where's your phone?'

'Over there on the worktop. But it's not working.'

'I beg your pardon?'

'My wife did tell you. Earlier. She mentioned it to you because it was odd. The

74

house phone not working. No wi-fi. And there's never been a mobile signal here.'

Honey pulls his mobile from his pocket and studies it, frowning. 'What network are you?'

'Orange. But no company has a signal up here. It hasn't worried us before.'

'Shit.' Honey puts the phone back in his pocket. 'Haven't you got an alarm fitted?'

'The phone line is down and usually that would provoke a call-out. I can only assume the alarm's been tampered with — otherwise we'd have been visited a long time ago.'

Honey appears lost for words. Oliver can't help but give a satisfied smile at the way the inspector is slowly waking up to the seriousness of the situation.

'There isn't an SOS signal either. The only place is at the bottom of the drive. Even there it's weak.'

Honey pushes the radio back across the table at his sergeant. 'That's where the car is, at the end of the drive. Go down there. You can radio from the car.'

Molina doesn't respond. He blinks rapidly behind his thick glasses.

'Mate?' Honey tips his head on one side, puzzled. 'You're still here.'

Molina's jaw moves slightly, as if he's chewing. As if he's trying to find the right words. 'I'm sorry. I'm not sure I want to.'

'It's come to this, has it?' DI Honey pushes the chair back and stands. All eyes are on him. Oliver can't decide if this tall man with the shiny head is someone he can place his confidence in or not. The inspector claws back the radio, puts it in his top pocket, then reaches inside his jacket. A gun, Oliver thinks, but tells himself, No, of course not. This is the UK. Detectives in the UK aren't armed. Sure enough Honey pulls out handcuffs and a small canister of something that looks like mace. Oliver's spirit sinks. If Kable is out there in the grounds of The Turrets, mace and handcuffs aren't going to stop him. He is a psychopath. He will stop at nothing.

'Where's your car?' Honey asks Oliver.

'We leave it on the next level down — too many trees around the house. Why?'

'I'm going to drive down to the gates.' Inspector Honey goes to the window and stands for a moment, measuring the distance between the door and the next level of the driveway where the family's Land Rover is parked.

'There's another car in the garage — my wife's runaround.'

'The garage is . . . ?'

Oliver indicates the sunny courtyard. Beyond it is the garage. 'Not so far.'

Honey puts his hands on the windowsill, leans forward and presses his face to the window. He peers out to the right and to the left. Then his attention is caught by the knife block sitting on the windowsill, the black handles facing up. He crosses to them.

'One serrated, one smooth.'

Honey glances at Oliver. 'I beg your pardon? What did you say?'

'I said take a smooth knife for the initial target, and a serrated knife for when he's down.' Oliver nods very slowly. 'The smooth knife goes in faster and will set him back, but it might just go straight into muscle, which won't finish him. A serrated knife gives you the best return for your money if you're thinking blood loss. If you're clever, the best damage can be done with a serrated blade.'

'How do you know all this?'

Oliver doesn't answer. No one looks at him and believes even for a moment that he can look after himself, because after all he has a frail body and a middle-class accent, neither of which fits with being capable. He's lived with the middle-class thing for years, that's a given, but the frailness, the creeping atrophy of his muscle, skeleton and fibre, is something new. He wonders what he looks like to this healthy man, who may have a receding hairline and a shiny forehead, but is muscular and not bowed or running to fat. He wonders if he, Oliver, gives away any of the secrets of his life. Old and sick though he appears, he has seen more horror, more reality in one hour at work than this boy Honey has seen in his entire life.

'You'll have to trust me. Take two types of

77

knife. You won't regret it.'

Honey pauses. He looks at the knives then back at Oliver then at the knives again. He chooses two. A serrated and a smooth, just as Oliver suggested. He puts one into the right-hand pocket of his trousers and the other in the left. The correct place, Oliver thinks approvingly. It's the best option, given all the constraints. The least likely place for him to be injured by the blades if he falls, and the easiest place to retrieve them in a hurry.

The keys to the garage and the runaround are kept where all the other keys are — in the study at the end of the corridor under the western turret. Oliver gets up and heads out of the kitchen. He feels stronger, as if the anger and the fear have given breadth to his shoulders, energy to his pig-heart. He's in the hallway when Molina catches up with him.

'I'll come with you.'

Oliver looks down at Molina's hand, which is extended, ready to steady his elbow. 'I'm OK. I can get there on my own.'

'I'm sure you can. But I want to know how much of the woods you can see from the windows back there. We don't know which side of the house he might be.'

THE WOMAN IN THE
YELLOW HOUSE

Ollie goes with Molina to get the garage key and Matilda is even less able to keep still than she was earlier. She busies herself clearing the cups, pretending to be calm. A few moments later DS Molina comes back — he's left Oliver hunting for the key — and stands with his inspector in a huddle at the side window. They seem to be discussing how far it is to the garage and who is going to be the one to get the car, muttering to each other under their breath. Molina keeps tapping on the pane, to draw attention to something outside — just out of view.

DI Honey nods. He turns and, bending slightly at the waist, cranes his neck to see out of the front window where the driveway makes two serpentine loops just below the parking area at the front, then drops out of sight to travel down the hill to the road. He glances at the ceiling, then asks Matilda, 'There are turrets on the top of the house?'

'Yes.'

x

79

'Can you see the driveway from them?'

'Yes. You can see all the way to the gates.'

'Can you take me up there?' DS Molina says. 'I need to see.'

'I'll take you.' Lucia lets Bear down and stands, pulling the sleeves of her cardigan around her hands as if that's going to protect her somehow. 'Come on. This way.'

They go, leaving Matilda and Honey alone together. She watches him for a while, hoping he'll say something reassuring. But his eyes are dancing from side to side, monitoring everything out of the window. She dries and puts the cups away, folds up the dishtowel.

'Inspector Honey, I didn't want to say it with my daughter in the room, but here are some spots of something on the floor — over there. I'm sure they're nothing, but perhaps you should have a look.'

'I'm sorry?'

'On the floor — there. Just please don't mention it when Lucia comes back.'

He follows her eyes. Crosses the room. Crouches and dabs his fingers on the drops, looks at them.

'I don't know. It could be anything.'

'Are you sure it's not blood?'

'I'm fairly sure.'

'Fairly?'

He raises his eyes to her, solemn. 'Everything's going to be OK, Mrs Anchor-Ferrers.

80

You can calm down. I promise you there's nothing to worry about.'

'Isn't there?'

'Absolutely nothing.'

But she doesn't relax her scrutiny of him. She pulls off her gardening apron and throws it on the table with a clatter. It's more to do with the adrenalin than an act of irritation but it startles him. He gets up and begins to pace around the kitchen, trying to prove how relaxed he is by pretending to show an interest in objects. He runs a hand admiringly across the back of a tapestry-covered chair. He inspects an oil portrait of the children which is propped on the mantelpiece and nods approvingly at the collection of Sèvres porcelain on the Welsh dresser.

Then, as if to impress her with his nonchalance, he goes to the table and inches a piece of the cake on to a plate. He sits and begins to eat, swallowing each mouthful with evident difficulty.

'Very good,' he says eventually, putting the empty plate down. 'Molasses. I'm a keen cook myself.'

'Do you think he's somehow been in the house?'

'Did you get that here? Or in London? Tastes like a London cake to me.'

'You think he's been in the house, Mr Honey, don't you? Right here in this kitchen. Which means he's probably somewhere near the house now. Very near. So what are you going to do if you don't get to the car? I mean — he's obviously disabled the phone and the alarm. And God only knows why your radios aren't working. Maybe that's down to him too.'

DI Honey goes to the sink and runs the tap. Without asking her permission he takes a glass from the draining board and begins to fill it.

'I've been a cop for a long time,' he says while the glass fills. 'Since I was twenty. I can't even guess any more what it's like to be civvy. I've seen a few things, believe me.'

Matilda sighs. She reaches down and picks up Bear. She sinks into a chair, burying her face in the dog's fur, just the way Lucia has been doing. A comfort. 'I'm sorry, but I'm not much interested in what you've seen in the past.'

'I've seen a few things,' Honey continues, still with his back to her. 'But I've never seen anything like what I saw down in that yellow house. What he did to that woman . . . It doesn't even begin to make sense.' DI Honey drinks the water in one. He sets the glass down in the sink. He turns and smiles apologetically. 'Not that I'd want to upset you, of course, Mrs Anchor-Ferrers, but I've never seen anything quite so ferocious. He'd cut her here.' He places a finger on his stomach. 'Pulled everything out. Makes me wonder

82

what he was thinking — as if he wanted to empty her out.'

'Please,' she begins, but is interrupted by a loud noise overhead. She jumps, turns her eyes upwards.

'It's all right. It's only my man and your daughter.'

Matilda stares in silence at the ceiling. Footsteps can be heard on the stairs — hurried footsteps. A moment later the door opens and Molina comes in. He's taken off his jacket and rolled up his sleeves to reveal his long, almost ape-like arms, sprinkled in auburn hair.

'Everything OK?' asks Honey.

'Driveway's clear. And round the back of the house too.'

'Good. That's worth knowing.' Honey's voice is slower. He smiles. 'I was just telling Mrs Anchor-Ferrers about what Kable did. To the woman.'

'The woman?'

'You know, the one in the house. I was telling her how he cut her. So it looked like he was trying to empty her out.'

Molina hesitates. He glances at Matilda, then back at his DI, as if he doesn't know how to respond to this.

'You know, the way he took the knife to her. Opened up her stomach and emptied it. Almost like he wanted to get inside it.' •

'Yes,' Molina replies eventually. 'Yes. That

was bad.'

Honey shakes his head regretfully. 'Bad. Really bad. If you ask me, he was thinking about cutting off her breasts too.' Honey's eyes rove briefly to Matilda's chest. 'He didn't actually do it, but you could tell from the cuts he made it's what he was thinking.'

Matilda looks from one man to the other. Her heart is thumping. Something has shifted, but it's happened so rapidly, so smoothly that she can't quite work out what. She says, 'Where's Lucia?'

Honey blinks. 'I beg your pardon?'

'Where's Lucia? My daughter. Did she stay upstairs?'

'Yes. Sorry — you confused me then. Your daughter. I mean, she must be someone's daughter of course. I knew she must have been born from someone, on some level I knew it. It's just she's sort of . . .'

'Sort of?'

'She never strike you as a bit common, Mrs Anchor-Ferrers? Have you never looked at your daughter and thought, Whoa, now that's not a pretty trait in a lady. That level of sluttiness?'

Matilda's face goes slack. 'Where is she?'

DI Honey turns to DS Molina, his eyebrows raised questioningly. Molina seems to be thinking about this, but in the end opens his hands, a pained expression on his face — as if to say *You've caught me out! What do I say now?*

Honey laughs. 'Well, Molina old boy, are you sure she didn't say something about helping Daddy find the car keys?'

EWAN CAFFERY

When Jack Caffery was eight years old — an average boy growing up in the deprived and overrun southern boroughs of London — his older brother, Ewan, aged nine, vanished. One Saturday afternoon he walked out of the family's back garden and simply disappeared into thin air. He hasn't been seen since. A hundred and fifty yards from the family home, on the other side of a railway cutting that ran along the back gardens, was the house of Ivan Penderecki, an ageing paedophile. There was no doubt Penderecki played a part in Ewan's disappearance, but he was never convicted. There was simply no evidence. Absolutely nothing to prove what happened. Least of all a body.

When Jacqui says Caffery has no idea what she's suffered, she is wrong. So wrong. He's been in her position most of his life. Except that whereas her daughter's remains have been returned to her, Ewan's haven't been found. Not to this day.

Eleven years ago the paedophile Ivan Penderecki hanged himself. Not because he was ashamed of the countless children's lives he'd destroyed with his habits, but because he'd been diagnosed with cancer and was too much of a coward to face the treatment. At first it seemed the trail to finding Ewan had died with Penderecki, but then Caffery discovered the old guy's stash of child pornography. It had been well hidden, and well disguised, but once Caffery had cracked the code it turned out to be a lever into the paedophile ring Penderecki had belonged to.

Somehow Jack always knew there had been something cleverer at play in disappearing Ewan so easily. A level of sophistication that surpassed the knowledge of a sixty-year-old laundry worker. Penderecki had to have had help and Caffery was sure the answer lay somewhere within that ring. However by the time he found out about them many of the members were already dead or locked up. There remained only one person he could trace: Tracey Lamb — a satellite member of the ring. He homed in on her, certain she knew Ewan's final resting place.

It took weeks to decide she was jerking his chain, messing him around and wasn't ever going to give up what she knew. His revenge on her was swift and merciless. He delivered her to Scotland Yard's paedophile unit — she spent the rest of her life locked in Holloway

Prison in North London.

Now Caffery sees where his headaches and dreams are coming from. It's taken Jacqui's haranguing to make it clear.

'Get out,' he says. 'Get out of my car.'

'What?'

'You heard me. I don't want to have to repeat it.'

'What the hell is the matter with you?'

'Just get out.'

Fingers trembling, Jacqui undoes her belt. She grabs her coat from the back seat and climbs out. 'How'm I supposed to get to my hotel? Your superintendent isn't going to be happy about this.' She fumbles her phone from her bag and holds it up to Caffery's face. 'I'm going to call him. I fucking am. And then I'm calling the papers. It's a fucking disgrace, what you've done, a fucking —'

He slams the door on her and, without indicating, floors the accelerator. The car shoots into the road. Horns blast, tyres scream. In his mirror he can see Jacqui Kitson yelling after him. He ignores her. He knows where life is taking him now and it's nowhere she can follow.

A PARTY

There's a moment when it could have gone differently — a moment when fate might have been tricked into letting Matilda grab the fire poker from the hearth to defend herself. Or letting her run to the back door and out into the garden, where maybe she could have raced into the woods and down eventually into the village to raise the alarm. But that moment passes so smoothly it's like silk slipping through a ring, and before she knows what is happening she is handcuffed, on the floor with her arms around the table leg. She hasn't even resisted. In fact she's so numb and confused that when DI Honey said, 'Hold out your hands,' she did. She let him fasten the cuffs and obligingly sat on the floor while the two men lifted the heavy oak table and dropped the leg down inside her arms.

DI Honey is wearing really nice shoes. Expensive shoes. It's a stupid thing but she fixates on those shoes, thinking that a policeman who wears nice shoes like that can't mean them any harm. There must be a mistake, an explanation.

The men leave the room. Matilda immediately tries to wedge her back under the table and lift it, so she can pull her hands out, but there's a wooden cross-member linking this leg to the other, effectively holding her hands at ground level. Her arms just aren't long enough to get the right position.

In the corner, Bear barks for all she's worth. She's alarmed and protective, but she's not quite sure of herself. She looks as if she'll turn tail at any moment and disappear. Matilda twists round as far as she can so she can see the doorway to the hallway. Whenever Bear stops to take a breath she can hear whispering and shuffling out there. Lucia? What did they *mean,* she was helping Oliver find keys?

The door opens then, and Oliver is pushed in ahead of Molina. He has his hands tied behind his back and he comes silently, giving the kitchen a quick, hopeful scan. He sees Matilda, and, immediately deflated to see her cuffed to the table, lowers his gaze to the floor. Shakes his head.

'Ollie? *Ollie?* What's happening?'

Molina pushes Oliver against the cooker and forces his hands roughly around the handle. He uses another pair of cuffs to fasten Oliver there. While he's doing it, DI Honey heads back to the door. 'Wait,' Molina says.

His glasses are slightly askew and there are sweat stains on his shirt. 'Don't go without me.'

He finishes with Oliver, then hurriedly follows his colleague back into the hallway. The door closes.

'Ollie?' Matilda hisses. 'For heaven's sake, what's happening?'

He doesn't answer. His head is hanging low, sunk in despair.

'Speak to me,' she hisses. *'Speak to me.'*

He turns his head slowly and peers at her over his shoulder, revealing a saggy and bloodshot eye.

'What's going on? What are they *doing*?'

'I don't know.' He shakes his head and turns away.

'Oliver — they can't be the police. Why would the police do something like this?'

'They're not police.'

'Then *who*?'

'I don't know.'

'Did you see Lucia?'

'No.'

'But she's OK? Isn't she? OK?'

'I just said — I don't know.'

Matilda stares at him. All their lives Oliver has been the one with the answers. Whatever the question, he always has an answer. Except now.

She looks around herself, completely bewildered. The kitchen — the place she feels most at home — is a different landscape. Yes, she hung those candy-stripe curtains. She chose the pink range kettle to match. She stocked the painted shelves. There's a jar at the back no one would ever notice, its lid open to release the smell of cinnamon. All of this is familiar. Yet somehow they've crossed into a different reality.

A door bangs overhead and there's the noise of scuffling on the staircase. Again Matilda strains to lift the table with her back. It goes a tiny way but the effort is too much. She squats, panting. '*Oliver?* What do we do?'

He glances at the door. The men are in the hallway now. Talking in low voices. 'Just do what they tell you,' he murmurs. He folds his arms under his ribcage, as if the place he was cut by the surgeons is hurting. 'That's all.'

'*Oliver?*' Her voice becomes a whisper because she doesn't want to know the answer. '*Are you feeling all right?*'

There's a pause, then he nods.

'*The scar?*'

'Fine.'

'You sure?'

'Yes.'

'You're not light-headed, are you?'

'No.'

'They haven't hurt you, have they?'

'*No.* Do what they say and this will be over quickly.'

'I will.' And then, after a deep breath, 'I

92

love you, Oliver.'

The two men come into the room. In front of them they are pushing Lucia. The gauge of hope in Matilda's head moves down another notch.

Lucia too wears handcuffs and her left eye is half closed, her cheek red and swollen. One of her boots has come off to reveal a black and purple sock. She has a downtrodden, lopsided lurch. She's talking to the man, but it's a confused and rambling string of words. Matilda realizes that the sound overhead was the noise of DS Molina, hitting Lucia.

Oliver suddenly comes to life — outraged to see his daughter like this. He tugs at his cuffs. 'Don't even think about hurting her. Who are you? What the hell do you think you're doing?'

'No,' laughs Honey. 'That's not the question. The question is what the hell do *you* think we're doing?'

'You're not the police.' Strengthened by Oliver arguing, Matilda starts to talk. 'You lied to us. You won't get away with this. Do you know who my husband is?'

Honey laughs again. 'God, I just *love* it when people say that.'

Molina pulls Lucia across the kitchen and handcuffs her to the handle of the fridge. The moment he lets go of her, she flings herself away from it, wrenching the door wide open. Bottles fly out and smash on the tiles, the fridge lurches forward drunkenly as if it's going to topple. But it's a solid, American thing and no matter how violently Lucia fights, it just rocks back on to its heavy base, dribbling out food and drink and salad dressing.

Bear yaps at the top of her voice, and Honey grabs her. Half bent, he pulls the little dog across the floor by the collar.

'No!' Lucia yells. 'No.'

Bear snaps and whips her body back and forth, trying to sink her teeth into the man's wrist, but she's no match for Honey. He pulls her to the sink then, using a leash Molina passes, tethers her — the lead looped over the tap so that the tension almost lifts her off the floor by her neck.

'No!!' Lucia begs. 'No. Don't hurt her.' She redoubles her efforts — twisting and slamming at the fridge door. She succeeds only in throwing more of the food out. A carton of milk explodes in a white star on the floor. 'Don't hurt her, you fuckers!'

'Lucia,' Oliver says. 'Don't fight.'

Lucia stops struggling and faces him, her hair plastered to her face, her chest heaving. She seems about to say something, but Honey crosses to her and looks her in the eye. The words die in her mouth.

'Put your head forward.' DI Honey has taken off his jacket and undone the top couple of buttons on his shirt. Matilda can see he is muscled under that shirt. It isn't the body of a detective with a desk job. She didn't notice all this before, she can't imagine why. 'Just put it forward. Like this.'

He pushes Lucia's head down and parts her hair at the back. For a moment Matilda thinks he might slide his hands around her neck, or into her bra, but he's unfastening her necklace. He untangles it from her hair, turns and drops it on the table. Then he unsnaps her watch and adds that to the necklace.

Molina goes to Oliver and rummages in his pockets, pulling out his phone, the garage keys and his wallet. He removes his watch and glasses and drops everything on the table.

Then DI Honey comes to Matilda. 'Put your head down,' he says, and pushes it down. He unfastens her necklace. While his fingers are busy at the back of her neck she stares at the buttons of her blouse, the soft flesh spilling against it. A frozen part of her brain is chugging into life. This is a robbery. Bizarre and cruelly elaborate, but a robbery nonetheless. It will be over soon.

Honey finishes undoing her necklace. The cold slip of the chain touching the side of her neck, then it's gone. He crouches and starts removing her rings, his hands warm and damp on hers. He doesn't wrench the jewellery off, but eases her wedding ring slowly over her knuckle, giving the skin time to fold itself under the metal so it doesn't hurt. She

95

stares mutely at what he's doing — her hands seem to belong to someone else. Beyond them there's the weave of his suit trousers, and once again it flashes into her head that with a suit so well made this man can't possibly be a real criminal.

He straightens and drops her rings into the growing pile on the table. Molina is thumbing through Oliver's wallet, unhurriedly, counting the banknotes.

Eventually, when all the family's phones and jewellery and money have been thrown into a pile in the centre of the table, Honey hooks his jacket from the back of the chair and pulls from it a crumpled carrier bag. He begins loading the belongings into the bag.

'Right.' He holds up his hand in a friendly fashion. Turns and smiles at each member of the family, as if he's thanking them in turn for a particularly good party. 'That'll be us then. Thank you for your time, you were rewarding. In a freaky sort of way we almost enjoyed ourselves. Didn't we, Mr Molina?'

'Yes,' says Molina. 'We certainly enjoyed ourselves in a strange way, Mr Honey.'

Molina goes to the door and opens it. Honey pauses and, hand lightly on his stomach — with the poise of an Edwardian man who keeps a precious timepiece in his waistcoat — gives a mock bow, circling the air with his hand. He straightens and follows Molina out.

The door closes.

There is a long, long silence. Bear is twisting and whimpering and opening her jaw convulsively as if to get more air in, but none of the family members speaks. No one knows what to say.

Then Lucia lets out all her breath. 'Oh my God,' she mutters. 'Oh my God, my God, my God.'

'Are you both OK?' Oliver's voice is shaky. 'Lucia? Tillie?'

'I'm fine, Dad.'

'Tillie?'

But Matilda is not fine. She doesn't want the men to leave. She's staring at the back door. 'They can't go!'

'It's OK, they have — they've gone.'

'But they can't!' She whips her head round. 'They can't leave us here. They've left the door unlocked — he could come in and do anything. They can't leave us here, he'll see them go and then he'll . . .'

Her voice subsides. Oliver is looking at her sadly. She closes her mouth with a wooden snap.

'Minnet Kable?' she says querulously. Oliver sighs. He averts his gaze. She stares at him, absolutely incredulous. *What?*

'I don't think Minnet Kable is out there at all, darling. I think they did it all to scare us.'

'You mean they . . . ?' Her eyes dart from the door to the window that overlooks the courtyard, then to the window that overlooks the copse. Her brain leaps over images. The intestines in the tree. The woman who was murdered. Minnet Kable out of jail, roaming the woods. 'All those . . . those *things*? They made them up?'

'I think so. I think they really were from a deer.'

She lets out a long breath. 'Why? Why would anyone do that?'

'I don't know. Some people are just sick by nature.'

'But that's awful. All the things they did. That . . . *stuff*.' She thinks about the jewellery — the rings. Sophie Hurst-Lloyd had been given a ring by Hugo and it had disappeared — it was taken by Minnet Kable and it never turned up again. 'Then they must know Minnet — they must have been in jail with him.'

Lucia says, 'It's OK, Mum. We're lucky they're gone and that all they did was rob us.'

'But they're insane — they're as bad as he was, they're copying him. We've got to tell someone! They're going to do it again, to someone else, and it's —'

'Stop now, Mum, please. We got away lightly.'

But Matilda can't stop the shock and the anger. And the relief that Minnet Kable isn't out there, stalking around the house. 'My wedding ring — they've taken the ring you gave me, Oliver.'

'We can replace it.'

'Why did they have to do all of that? If they just wanted to rob us, why go to so much trouble? They're worse than Kable even — *worse.*'

'I know, but they're gone now. They're gone.' He coughs and repositions himself. 'Really, darling, they've got what they wanted and they're gone.'

Eventually she subsides. Ollie and Lucia are right, of course. The family is lucky to have got away with just being robbed. Being handcuffed to the table is nothing compared to having to face Minnet Kable in the woods — or being cut to pieces with a Stanley knife. Having her stomach opened and her breasts cut off.

Except then she realizes something even worse. She snaps her eyes over to Oliver.

'What?' he says. 'What is it?'

She shakes her head quickly. She's noticed what the other two haven't. They are all tied, all manacled, they have no phone, no signal. No means of escape. They could be here for hours and hours. Overnight even. Oliver needs his medication. And he needs it soon.

THE LAST STONE

When Caffery leaves Jacqui Kitson, swearing and shouting on the roadside, he drives for a long time. He goes in no particular direction, sees nothing of his surroundings, and ends up lost. It doesn't matter. All he needs is to be moving. He needs the time to work through what's happening.

His headache has vanished and at last he sees where the sickness was coming from. He can't believe he hasn't identified it earlier; perhaps subconsciously he's avoided thinking about it. What Jacqui said about turning every stone has knocked something loose in his head. And it's got a name on it.

The name is Tracey Lamb.

Tracey Lamb. *She* was Caffery's last stone. The one that wasn't turned in the search for Ewan. She died two weeks ago, in Holloway. When he heard the news he told himself it didn't matter, that he'd closed that chapter of his life, but now he sees of course it matters. Very much. Her death was the end of his hope of finding Ewan, and the beginning of his sickness. He might have tried to convince himself he wasn't affected by it, his body has been telling him something different.

He pulls the car into a lay-by. Sits for a while breathing slowly. He reaches up and angles the driving mirror so he can see his surly reflection. Eyes himself suspiciously. If Ewan had lived he would now be mid-forties. Maybe he'd look the way Jack does now, maybe not. Somehow Jack thinks Ewan would be heavier — stockier and taller. He tries to imagine Ewan doing this in a similar mirror in a similar car somewhere and finds he can't.

You think there must be one stone that hasn't been turned.

It's all broken open again. Come back to haunt him. He can't leave it, won't ever leave it.

He taps his fingers on the dashboard, his head working fast. Where does he start? He's already done everything a human being could do. He's torn the world apart looking for Ewan's body. But he's got to be tenacious. What do skilled cops do when the trail runs cold? They go back to the beginning and they *revise* . . .

He pulls out his phone and dials a number in London. Johnny Patel is an old friend. He retired after his thirty in the Met and is now a probate detective in Catford, South London. Every day for hour after hour Patel sits in front of a computer screen searching the birth, marriage and death records — the hatch, match and dispatch records, he calls them — in an effort to track down the rightful heirs to unclaimed estates. Back in the days when Caffery was Patel's inspector in Sydenham he used to turn a blind eye when Johnny would slip away early, knowing, as everyone else knew, that Patel was using the job as a cover for the affair he was having. Patel's affair went wrong, his marriage was wrecked, but at least he kept his job.

He owes Caffery.

'Jack!' he says. 'You've been on my mind.'

'How so?'

'I was trying to work out when I last saw you face to face. It was ten years ago — at that retirement thing? The one where the two girls had a fight?'

'I don't remember it.'

'On the floor — proper catfight? No mud, of course, but one of them was wearing a mini-skirt.'

'Amazing, your powers of recall.'

'I know it. Why do you think the Met valued me so highly? Cop's memory. Mind you,' he adds ruefully, 'that fight — it was a difficult thing to watch. It's all stored — every second — just can't wipe the memory. Very traumatic.'

Caffery shakes his head. Some things never

change. 'I feel your pain, mate, feel it like a knife. Johnny, do you remember Tracey Lamb? Died in prison recently?'

'Tracey Lamb, the fat slag. Overdosed on pork pies. They banned that cartoon, didn't they — "The Fat Slags". All the fat slags in the North of England got together and said it violated their rights to heiferdom. They should have formed a political party, if you want my opinion.'

'Is there any way of knowing if she left a will?'

'Every way. That's my job.'

'How long will it take?'

'Twenty minutes. Leave it with me.'

Caffery finishes the call. He puts the phone on his knee and stares out of the window at the row of shops he's come to a halt near. Their hoardings, their posters and adverts. He sees none of it. His brain is cantering forward.

On his knee the phone jerks to life. He turns it, sees it's DS Paluzzi.

'Jack, Jack,' she says, 'you are in so much shit. Why can't you be nice?'

'I take it Jacqui called.'

'Yes, and this is a gentle heads-up — the superintendent is going to be calling you any second now and he is going to eat you alive.'

'Thank you. Can you give him a message?'

She sighs. 'As long as there are no rude words in it. Only words I could use in conver-

103

sation with my mother, OK?'

'Of course.' He digs into his pocket, feeling for the V-Cig. 'Tell him I'm having a break. I'll let him know when I'll be back at work.'

There's a small intake of breath at the other end of the phone. 'You can't expect me to deliver something like that! You know the rocket that comment will launch.'

'Yup.' He braces the cartridge between his knees and clicks it into the holder. 'Well, that'll be the only communication he'll get from me. I won't be answering his calls. And if he's that worried about me not being in the unit, ask him why he's used me as a fucking chauffeur today.'

'You promised, no bad words.'

'I apologize.'

'Yes, but not sincerely.' She pauses. There's a shuffling noise, then she comes back on, hissing, 'Too late, he's here now, he wants to speak to you.'

Caffery hears the superintendent's voice, the muffled sounds of him talking to Paluzzi. He doesn't wait to hear what he has to say. Before the superintendent can speak, Caffery kills the call and turns the phone to silent. Then he sits back in the seat and takes a long drag on the V-Cig.

It's the first time since Tracey Lamb died that he feels calm.

THE HOUSE ON THE HILL

Matilda is exhausted, trembling uncontrollably. She's tried over and over again to move the table and she just can't get the leverage. The only angle she can get her back up to the underside of the table is where an iron brace is mounted, and the metal digs into her shoulder. She's already bleeding where her thin skin has torn from the friction.

She rubs the sweat from her face on to the other sleeve and breathes, trying to calm herself. She glances up at Oliver.

'How do you feel?'

He shakes his head, tries to smile. 'I'm OK. I promise I'm OK.'

'No, he's not,' says Lucia. 'Look at him.'

'Honestly, I'm fine. I'm fine. Let's not panic. Panic is the worst thing we can do.'

Matilda closes her eyes. Three feet away Bear is still twisting and whining, trying to free herself from the leash that strains down over the edge of the sink. Maybe if she struggles enough she'll slip the leash, thinks

Matilda. And then what? If the doors were open she'd be off — she'd run and run, the way she always does. Then someone would find her. She's got no chip — but surely someone would think she seemed lost. People in the area don't know Bear, not like they do in London, but a lost dog? Someone would investigate, surely?

Except, the doors are closed. Bear can't get out. No point in even thinking it. So what else?

The family has a cleaner — Ginny Van Der Bolt — who comes in the day before they arrive to ensure the hot water is on; to stock the fridge with a supply of essentials, such as milk, butter, bread; make up the beds; and in general get the house aired and ready. Usually she makes sure there are some flowers in the windows, on the table. Not this time, Matilda notices now.

Ginny lives locally and often on their second or third day at The Turrets she will make a point of coming all the way up the hill just to say hello and pass the time of day, in the way that people out here have the leisure to do. She brings with her eggs and squares of honeycomb from the hives in the valley, or runner beans piled high in a basket, or great swathes of hollyhocks cut from her garden. Ginny wears a sunny blonde milk-maid's smile and Matilda cannot think of her without imagining Ginny dressed in an apron and mobcap, dropping little curtseys wherever she goes.

It's usually the second or third day, Matilda thinks. But sometimes it's the fourth. Even the fifth.

'Hey,' says Lucia. 'Listen.'

Matilda's eyes fly open, every nerve on alert. At first she can hear nothing, just the distant cawing of rooks. Then there's a crunch of gravel outside. A footstep. *Ginny?*

'In here,' she yells. 'In here — we're in here.'

'We're here.'

Another crunch of gravel — to the side this time, and the family swing their eyes to the door.

'In here. Here.'

The side door opens. Molina and Honey stand in the doorway. Honey is grinning from ear to ear.

'You didn't really think that was it, did you?'

REVISION

The place Caffery calls home is a sodden, cramped thatched cottage tucked away on its own in the Mendip Hills of Somerset. The curtains are all drawn — he was in a hurry when he left this morning. He goes around opening them and checking cupboards in a hunt for alcohol. He finds a bottle of scotch and fills a glass. It's two in the afternoon and the craziest time to be starting to drink but that doesn't matter. He's not going anywhere. It's going to be a long day in this tiny cottage. Just him and his renewed commitment rattling around together.

His phone shows four message icons hovering over the voicemail inbox — the superintendent giving vent to his rage. Caffery doesn't want to know. This sudden urge, this clarity, this obsession — it's the closest thing to freedom he can imagine, and nothing will block him now. He deletes the messages, drinks half the scotch in one hit, then carries the glass to the landing and stands looking up at the ceiling where the hatch to the attic is.

Attics. The place all the memories go. Years ago, back in London, he worked on a case where the perpetrator — a particularly disturbed paedophile — had invaded a family's home by crawling into their attic from the roofspace of the neighbouring house. Ever since then he's had problems with the damn places. And this cottage — which has never welcomed him — has got something living in the loft. A squirrel, he's fairly sure, but it keeps him awake at night and he's been promising to do something about it.

There's a rubber-tipped pole on top of his wardrobe. He fetches it and uses it to unlatch the hatch and hook down the loft ladder. It comes with a clatter, bringing with it a few tufts of peachy-coloured insulation material. He gives the ladder a couple of rattles to check it's secure, then climbs up.

This is an old, old house with low ceilings. Parts of it were built before this area of Somerset was drained, when you had to arrive here by boat, but it's been added to over the years and this section is a modern extension. There's an electric light up here — just a bare forty-watt lightbulb, but it's enough to illuminate the timbers and the joists. At the far end there is temporary boarding where he stashed the piles of cardboard boxes brought with him from London. Everything smells of hay and mould and the chemicals he used to get rid of a wasps' nest a while back.

He crosses the attic carefully, head lowered, stepping from joist to joist. The afternoon outside is so silent he can hear the rain dripping from the trees and the distant roar of a plane. A hundred tonnes of jet fuel hurtling through the crystal-blue sky thousands of feet above the clouds.

He finds the box he wants quickly. The cardboard has been chewed by the squirrel and the notes he made back when he was investigating Tracey Lamb have spilled out. He can't carry the box so he begins tossing the paperwork towards the hatch. When all the contents of the box have been removed he picks his way back across the rafters and starts pushing it all through the hole on to the landing below. It floats down like giant flakes of ash, some pages slithering down the stairs. He descends the ladder and uses his feet to herd the whole lot downstairs. In the hallway he stoops and carries great armfuls of the paper to the kitchen table.

He takes another slug of whisky and commences sorting the pages into piles. There are reams of scribbled notes and intelligence reports. Penderecki's paedophile ring was formed before the days of the Internet and was never the huge and internationally coordinated network many people imagine when they think of paedophile rings. It was a loose collection of small-time criminals and persistent offenders who spent their time in jail sharing fantasies and making plans for their release. Most of them knew they would end up back inside. It only made them more determined to make the most of their time on the outside. They didn't care who or what they hurt. They gave up their obligations to society the day they realized society didn't want them any more.

Caffery has watched every one of the analogue videos on which the scenes of their abuse are stored. Patel jokes about the images he can't erase from his mind; there is no trace of humour in the images Caffery cannot erase. He sent the tapes to the CPS ten years ago, but he's never been able to scrub the memories. And here, amongst these books, in case he ever felt the need to revisit the information, are the notes he made before he surrendered the tapes to the authorities.

His phone pings in his pocket. He takes it out. It's an email from Johnny Patel.

Ever heard of Derek Yates? He is the sole beneficiary of Tracey Lamb's will — which looks as if it amounts to about five shillings and sixpence (that's old money, mate). That's all I can find for now.

Derek Yates. Caffery stares at the screen. Derek Yates.

The name clips at something in his memory. He can't say what.

He is still for a very long time. Then he drops the phone and searches frantically through the papers. He stops at a sheet with a list of names he's transcribed from the video tapes. Members of Penderecki's paedophile ring Caffery's never traced. Around some of them are question marks he made years ago, but now his attention is sucked straight down to the name at the bottom of the list.

Yatesy.

Yatesy?????

He snatches up the email from Patel — speed-reads it.

Ever heard of Derek Yates?

'Derek Yates,' he murmurs to the phone. 'Derek Yates. Why did Tracey Lamb make you her beneficiary?'

DEAD CHICKENS

Apparently chickens, when they have their heads cut off, will keep running around the farmyard until their heart stops pumping. As if the force of their survival instinct is blind enough to keep going even when there is no longer any control. It's like the ghost who doesn't realize he is dead and insists on getting up every day and cleaning his teeth, combing his hair, going about his business. Still mingling with the living.

Oliver has no idea if the story about the dead chickens is an old wives' tale, he's never seen a chicken with its head cut off, he's not a country boy, but what he has seen is people with their heads cut off. He's seen people injured in unimaginable ways — limbs missing, faces peeled away — and what has always struck him is how humans can mimic that chicken-like inability to stop their momentum. A failure to recognize when things are serious. Car-crash victims fight with the emergency crew, insisting they don't need to go to hospital, that they're late for a meeting. Don't put me in the ambulance, they cry, my arm's not broken, my eye's not injured, my skull is not cracked. I'll be fine, they shout, it's nothing, just let me keep going. I've got to be at that meeting!

The two men, the one called Molina and the one called Honey, are wandering around the kitchen, casually picking up things to inspect, shooting the family the occasional smile, putting their noses into cupboards as if they've just arrived at a holiday home and are checking out the arrangements. Honey, the gangly one with the shiny monk's head, picks up the piece of pottery Matilda's mother gave them the day Lucia was born and checks under it, as if to decide whether it's worth anything — in money, or in taste. Then he makes a great performance of taking a stack of ironed napkins out of the drawer and carrying them to the window to study them in a better light. And yet, like the chicken, like the accident victims, in spite of what his eyes and ears are telling him, part of Oliver's brain won't adjust.

Earlier, when the whole thing changed, when Molina turned to him in the corridor, his orang-utan head pushed forward, glasses misted, the knife held to Oliver's throat, his thoughts went into slow motion. Like Matilda, he had accepted the reality of these two men being cops and it took a jump to adjust

114

to the realization that they weren't police at all and that Kable wasn't really stalking the woods outside. Likewise his stubborn refusal now to give up that hard-won interpretation and see that the tables have turned again and that these men aren't merely opportunistic thieves. They are back and there is even more to this story than meets the eye.

Oliver wants to resist, it's in his nature to, but he can feel the subtle pulling in his chest where the doctors have opened him up. He can imagine that scar unzippering. He's made a decision not to struggle. He knows enough about hostage situations to know that the victim's best window of opportunity is in the first few moments. The family's chance to fight back has already come and gone.

Bear scratches frantically at the place her collar is hoisting her off the floor. Honey stops and gives her a long look. Then he walks to the centre of the room. Every movement is theatrical in its nature — as if this is one huge play. There is something beyond that performance of his — a nervy self-consciousness maybe — which makes Oliver even more scared. As if something in Honey could lose control at any moment.

Lucia has turned her back to the room and sullenly lowered her face, her shoulders hunched up, her attention focused on her hands, manacled to the fridge door. It's the same attitude she used to adopt as a teenager in her room whenever Matilda or Oliver reprimanded her for anything. She'd shut out the world by studying whatever homework or subject she could find to block out the attention. He hopes she can block this out the same way.

He tries to study the handcuffs. They're chainlink, not the speciality Hiatt ones the UK police use, but something American. Very strong, very efficient. He tries to think which company made them — Bianchi or Chicago or Winchester — hoping it will give him a clue as to who these men are. Anything to avoid looking at Matilda. She's in the periphery of his vision, though. Just the bottom half of her. Her right leg on the tiled floor. She's wearing slacks and comfortable gardening shoes. He's glad she isn't wearing a skirt.

Honey stops at the table and holds the carrier bag in the air. Then with a small smile he upends it. Everything tumbles out on to the table. He begins to sort through it calmly, collecting up the folded cash that's come from Oliver's wallet. He holds it in front of him and inspects it, as if it was a huge curiosity. It isn't a lot of money, thinks Oliver. Only a hundred pounds at most, but he's making a big thing of it.

'That,' he says with a frown. 'Is an irritation to me.'

'An irritation?' Molina's voice is so automatic it could be a puppet's. 'How so?'

'An irritation that these people could mistake us for the sort of scum that would do a house raid.'

'A house raid? We're not here for a house raid.'

'Of course we're not. Of course we're not. People assume things too easily.' Honey uses his fingers to fan out the money. 'Look at this. People have a fatal attraction to this. And it never occurs to them how easily it can disappear.'

He produces a cigarette lighter from his pocket and holds it under the wad of notes. It takes a moment to catch light, and when it does he drops it into the sink, standing back to watch it burn.

'What is this all about?' Oliver asks. 'Are you friends of Kable? Do you know him?'

Honey turns and regards him coolly, a smile tugging at the corners of his mouth. 'Kable? I know of him — of course I know of him. But as far as I'm aware, he's still in that high-secure unit they locked him in. Best place for him, considering what he did to those kids. You don't do the things he did with their insides, decorating trees with them and such, and expect to get away with it. Do you, Mr Molina?'

'No. You don't.'

'Then why did you do all of this?' asks Oliver. 'What's your agenda? What do you want?'

Honey smiles patiently. 'You're a sick man, Mr Anchor-Ferrers. Please, don't waste your breath.'

'If we don't know what you want, how can we help you?'

Honey thinks about this, his mouth pursed. At length he nods reasonably, as if it's dawning on him Oliver has a point. 'Fair enough — since you're being generous enough to offer to help me, I'll do that. I'll tell you what we want.'

Oliver can sense Matilda and Lucia both holding their breath. 'Please do.' He has to fight to keep his voice steady. Polite. 'Please do explain.'

'We want you to be scared.'

There's a moment's silence. Then Oliver speaks. 'OK. Well, you've achieved that. Congratulations.'

'Thank you. But actually, when I say scared, I mean *really* scared. Let's say your current rating on the scared gauge is — oh, I dunno, I'm plucking at numbers here, but let's say it's at four now. What me and my partner are aiming for is a ten rating.'

'You want us to be scared? Is that all?'

Honey laughs. 'Well, only having you scared would be pointless, wouldn't it? That wouldn't achieve much. So of course it's more than that. Of course we want something.'

'Tell me.'

'No — the first stage is to scare you. Like I said: let's aim for that ten. And when you've reached a ten, when you're so scared that you'd do anything, anything at all, *then* we'll tell you what we want. Call it a way of ensuring you do what we ask.'

'Desperation,' Molina says, pushing his glasses up his nose. 'True desperation.'

'That's right, Mr Molina. Desperation is a kind of holy state, if you ask me.' Honey wafts the smoke from the burning notes in the sink. Peers at them with interest. 'Did you ever see that film *Hunger Games*?'

'No.' Molina shakes his head. 'Can't say I did.'

'Well, don't worry — you didn't miss much. Dumb-ass film, where all these stupid Hollywood cute kids go around killing each other just to save their own skins. Desperation, like you say.'

'Sounds interesting,' says Molina.

'Not very.' Honey turns on the tap to douse the smouldering money, watching the fizz and steam. He pushes the ashes down the drain, sloshes water around and wipes the sink clean. Then he dries his hands on a tea-towel. He turns and seems surprised to see the family all staring at him silently.

'Hey, stop looking at me like that. What's going to happen here is not going to be anything like that stupid movie. It's a ridiculous premise — so just you put that idea *right* out of your minds. You understand me? Just put it right out of your minds now.'

Dog Food

Matilda's been fighting tears so long, but now there's no holding back. She can't wipe them away, so she has to content herself with turning her face and burying it in the sleeve of her blouse. Her eyes leak soundlessly into the material.

A noise. She looks up. Honey stands at the other side of the table, licking his fingers as if he's trying to cool them down. Then, with his hands folded around his middle, he bends over to peer down at the pile of jewellery.

'These must have cost a lot. I can see a lot of good things in here.' He shakes his head, as if what people spend, and what they spend it on, will never cease to amaze him. 'A lot of good things.'

'Molina', who is smoking a very thin cigar which he keeps moving between his teeth as if he thinks he's in a Clint Eastwood movie, cups his hands for DI Honey to drop a handful of the jewellery into. Matilda can see her wedding ring and her necklace tangled in his thick fingers. Molina stands for a moment, looking round the kitchen, as if trying to find the most inappropriate place to dump the jewellery. It's probably going to be the waste disposal. The waste disposal fits with the way these men are acting.

But Molina does neither of these things. Instead he goes to Bear's bowl and drops the gold into the food, then he crouches next to it and makes sure the dog food coats it thoroughly.

Honey has crossed to the sink where Bear is still scratching at her neck and hopping from foot to foot.

'Don't touch her!' Lucia says.

Honey raises his eyes to her and smiles. It's a vague, idiot smile as if he can't quite work out where the sound came from. Then he unsnaps Bear's lead from the collar and, before the dog can scuttle away, grabs her up in one hand. Bear twists and struggles but he carries her to the table, puts her down and leans over, both elbows placed on either side of the tiny dog's ribcage to hold her steady. Honey raises his eyes expectantly to Molina, who is juggling the dog food and jewellery from one hand to the other as if he's working a ball of dough.

'What are you looking at?' Honey says calmly, not raising his eyes to Oliver, who is watching the men closely, his eyes flitting to and fro, the way he does when he's concentrating. 'What do you think you're staring at?'

'You.'

Honey pauses, as if he's wondering whether to take offence. But eventually he merely smiles and applies pressure to Bear's neck.

'Don't hurt the dog,' Oliver says calmly. 'There's no need to hurt the dog.'

Honey doesn't look at him. 'Shut up. At least learn that — when to shut up.'

He leans his chest down and presses his weight on to Bear's backbone, reaching up his forearms to Bear's face. With his thumb and forefingers he prises her jaw open. Bear throws her head from side to side, but Honey holds steady and looks meaningfully at Molina.

'Do it. Don't wait. Do it now.'

Molina breaks away a chunk of the mess of gold and dog food and begins to palm it into the dog's mouth. The dog convulses, her back legs twitching, her head thrashing, but the men are intent on their objective. When Molina seems to hesitate, Honey grabs the food from him and pushes it into the dog's mouth — ramming his hand deep past the animal's teeth, not reacting when Bear twists like a snared fox.

'No! You shouldn't be doing that,' Lucia yells from the fridge. 'That's not necessary. Not at all.'

Honey ignores her. He holds the dog's

mouth closed, his face a mask of concentration, his gaze not on the dog but on the ceiling, waiting patiently for the animal to swallow the mouthful.

'There.' He releases Bear and steps back from the table, his hands open. 'There — good girl. Good girl.'

The dog, suddenly free, doesn't run but lies down flat on the table, coughing and groping at her jaw with her paws. Lucia lets out a long breath. She turns away and rests her forehead against the fridge door.

'What is it, Lucia?' Honey calmly drops the rest of the dog food into the bin. He washes his hands at the sink. 'What? Did the jewellery mean that much to you?'

She doesn't look at him. She keeps her forehead to the fridge.

'OK.' He claps his hands. 'OK, OK. The show's over, folks! Let's move this party out of here to somewhere safer.'

NORMAL AND HEALTHY

What no one in this room has noticed is that Lucia isn't as switched off as she's making out. In reality she's on red alert. She's got her head down, she's made her eyes quite opaque-looking, but actually she's monitoring everything. She's listened to Bear being tortured, she's listening to her squirming, and although it's killing her, she finds the strength to turn away. She could easily crack over this part of it, but she won't. She will contain it. Because Lucia Anchor-Ferrers is going to win this game.

She keeps her face to the fridge. A line keeps coming to her, something her counsellors made her repeat when she was in therapy after Hugo and Sophie were killed:

I am not stupid, I am not ugly or unattractive. I am a completely normal, healthy girl.

She repeats it over and over, reminding herself of what the therapists all said; that people can look at her, they can hear her speak, and they can make judgements. They can think she's lawless and wrong because of her spiked hair and pale complexion. They can think that just because she wears black and studs in her ears she's some sort of hooligan. But the important thing is that the only person who can know for sure what Lucia is, is Lucia. And at this moment Lucia is in complete control.

She concentrates on the record the two men are leaving. The record is the crucial thing. The good thing about having a father like Oliver is that he knows every modern gadget and has access to the newest security systems. Yes, the men may have tampered with the alarm to stop it working, but what they don't know is the house is networked with invisible lenses. Although Dad's the one who's put them there, he hasn't mentioned them today — not once — and Mum, if she has any sense, any sense at all, won't mention it either. The men haven't worked out the camera thing, whereas over the years she has had plenty of time to think about the system and the angles it covers. Even today, she's still finding new places, new pockets it's missed. While Bear is crying on the table, she scans the angles, finding parts of the kitchen that provided the best perspectives for the lenses, where the men's faces will be best captured.

If people think they can control Lucia Anchor-Ferrers they can think again. She is perfectly capable of taking charge of this situation. It's only a matter of time . . .

She tilts her chin slightly and opens an eye to look across the kitchen. The two men are talking to Dad.

The man who calls himself DI Honey unnerves her. He is so odd-looking, with tight curls and a shiny bald crown. He's not a cop, of course, any idiot could deduce that. And Honey isn't his real name, though it's the only one she has for him. She has to admit the choice is clever — the way it connects with sweetness and purity and things that are trustworthy.

Now he is holding out a small pale pink container to Dad. She recognizes it as his heart pills. Since the operation he's had a gazillion pills to swallow every day, something for every system in his body, it seems.

'What do you need?' Honey opens the lid and surveys the different pills. 'Which ones?'

Dad is slow to respond. He's not sure if this is another trick.

'Come on.' Honey shakes the box impatiently. 'It's your last chance.'

'The section in the top right. All of those.'

'Open your mouth.'

Honey tips the pills into his hand and places them on Dad's tongue. Then he stands and fetches a glass of water from the sink and holds it to his lips. Dad swallows painfully. The water dribbles down his chin. Satis-

127

fied the pills are gone, Honey closes the case and tips the remaining water into the sink. Lucia casts a quick look at her mother, wondering whether she's worked out that this means the men are serious, that they mean to scare the family. That they want them all alive in the process. And that it's going to take time.

Honey's shirt is laundry white and starched, his suit sober, just like a real cop. He bends and uses his shoulder to push up the table. Mum instantly pulls her hands back, but before she can get away he slams his foot down into the space between her arms. She ends up with her body canted towards him, embracing his leg.

'Get up.' He lifts his foot to release her, grabs the back of her blouse. Before she can react, he pulls her to her feet. She stands unsteadily, her cuffed hands half raised in front of her face, ready to fend off any blows, should they come. He pauses and glances at Bear, who is still choking and shaking her head as if to free something.

'It's going to puke everywhere,' he tells Molina. 'And if there's one thing I don't do, it's dog puke. Something needs to happen to it — deal with it.'

Lucia can't contain herself. She jerks at the handcuffs. 'Let me have my dog. Please don't touch her. Leave her alone.'

A shadow crosses Honey's face at this. He

is motionless for a while then very slowly he turns to her. He looks her up and down, letting his eyes travel over her legs. He smiles.

'Nice to see you. Welcome to the party, pretty girl.'

'I just want my dog. I don't want her hurt.'

'I want, I want,' he mimics. ' "I want" doesn't get — didn't Mummy tell you that? Or has Mummy been slack in her parenting skills?' He gives Matilda a shake, making her head flip violently forward and backwards on her neck. 'Slack slack. Slack slack. Have you been slack?'

'Please,' Lucia says. 'Just let me have my dog. Please.'

'I give the orders, not you. What you want doesn't come into it any more, haven't you worked that one out — with all your brain cogs turning over there?' He jerks his chin at Molina. 'Take her upstairs, then deal with the dog. I don't care what you do with it, just make sure it doesn't stay with her.'

Honey puts a knee in the back of Mum's leg and nudges her forward. She walks clumsily to the door, not looking at anyone as she goes. Dad makes a small sound in his throat as they leave the room — a tiny whimper — then he drops his head. He must be crying. Lucia averts her eyes, sickened.

Molina takes the leash from the back of the door and secures Bear to the handle of one of the cupboards. Then he comes over to Lu-

129

cia. She raises her eyes to his, expecting some communication, but gets none. His eyes are shuttered, turned in on themselves. He uses a key to unclip the cuffs — she's amazed by how slickly he does this, as if it's habitual, like cleaning his teeth — then recuffs them behind her back.

'Please can I have my dog with me. Please.'

'You heard what he said.'

He pushes her towards the door. She resists a fraction, just to give her father one last look, then allows Molina to push her out of the door.

He takes her to the box room on the first floor. It is the one that the family call the 'rose room' because everything has roses on it. The walls, the bedspread, the drapes. Even the curtain rail is printed with roses. The room rarely gets used in spite of all the money spent on it.

Molina tells her to sit next to the radiator and begins fiddling with the shackles then eases on the cuffs. He is considerate, trying not to tug at her. She is facing the door and can see out on to the landing. As Molina works, the door to the bedroom opposite, Kiran's bedroom, opens and Honey comes out. He glances once in her direction then closes the door behind him and walks calmly down the stairs. It must mean Mum has been put in there. Lucia studies his face in profile, trying to get the measure of him. There's something in his expression she can't quite identify. She can't decide if he's very dangerous or just faking.

Molina finishes what he's doing. He stands back and gives her a questioning look. 'Are you OK? Are you comfortable?'

She is silent for a moment. Then she says, 'All that made-up stuff about Minnet Kable? Was that necessary?'

Molina narrows his eyes at her. He seems to be thinking about a retort, but it passes. 'I asked, are you comfortable? Can you move?'

'Yes.'

'Sure?'

'Yes.

'And you didn't have to hit me so hard. Did you?'

He ignores this.

'Can I have Bear? I want my dog.'

'I'll do my best.'

'Thank you.'

She makes a point of holding his eye. She is conscious of the CCTV lens gleaming in the ceiling above him. It's her secret weapon. It's recording everything and Molina doesn't even realize. He goes around the room rattling the window catches. As he's doing it, Honey comes up the stairs pushing Oliver in front of him. Dad's face is loose, his mouth hanging open, the front of his shirt stained with water. He reaches the landing and spots her watching him. His eyes go to the hand-

131

cuffs. An awful resigned, clouded expression crosses his face.

Honey pushes him onwards, stumbling into the second bedroom. It's Lucia's own bedroom — the one that she's painted purple and brown and black — and as Honey kicks open the door she gets a glimpse of all her familiar things, her crucifix and her poster of Marilyn Manson. Her mothy All Saints dress on a black clothes hanger on the wardrobe door. No camera in there — she insisted when Dad put the system in that there had to be a place she could call her own.

The door closes. Lucia sits quite still. Her face doesn't change.

You are a normal, healthy, clever girl. Very clever. No one can say who Lucia is, except Lucia herself.

Yes, she thinks now, looking at that closed door. No one can say who Lucia is except Lucia herself.

THE PEPPERMINT ROOM

Matilda was the first to be moved upstairs. She is in Kiran's bedroom, directly above the disused scullery, and is fastened to the radiator by her left hand. She sits with her back to the window, her feet stretched out so they touch the red tiles of the hearth. The men are moving around the house. Doors open and close. Then suddenly Honey is standing in the open doorway, smiling at her. Under his arm is Bear. He stoops and sets the dog down, then, without a word, turns and leaves, locking the door behind him.

Bear runs to Matilda. She scoops the dog up with her free hand and holds her on her lap, pressing her face against her furry head. Either Bear has vomited downstairs or she's somehow swallowed down whatever piece of jewellery was stuck in her throat because she's stopped that awful convulsive movement. She licks Matilda's face and chin, a habit she has when she's nervous and needs reassurance. Usually she gets a telling off for it. Not now.

Matilda's head is spinning — this cannot be happening. She must be dreaming.

Desperation is a kind of holy state . . . a film where they all had to kill each other to save their own skins . . . don't think about it — put it out of your mind . . .

She hugs Bear tighter. Tries not to cry, to get her thoughts straight. She is fairly sure that Lucia has been put in the rose room, and that Oliver has been put in Lucia's bedroom — what they call the amethyst room, with all Lucia's ghastly posters. It's made Matilda's imagination boil, trying to guess what these men want, how much they've invented and how much is real. The intestines looped nightmarishly in that bush for her to find. Elaborate games, leaving her bewildered — not sure any more if the sky itself is real.

When you're so scared that you'd do anything, anything at all, then we'll tell you what we want . . .

But why? Why?

Bear stops licking, and Matilda lets her on to the floor. She paces the floor, sniffing at things. Matilda watches her. She is sure that if Bear barks or makes a fuss the men won't hesitate to kill her. That feels like a certainty — not speculation or fear, but a concrete fact.

Matilda looks around the room. It's so

familiar, but she tries to study it now with fresh eyes, to really take in every detail. It is painted in Kiran's favourite minty green, with fresh, stripey curtains. There are still Airfix Spitfires and Harrier jets, suspended by nylon wires to the ceiling, gathering dust. Kiran's daughter loves those airplanes. He still uses this room when he brings his own family here from Hong Kong for the summer — there is a double bed with a fluffy quilt and a single bed installed in the corner for her grand-daughter. Even a cot hung with a dangly carousel ready for the new baby which is due in six weeks.

How can they get a message to Kiran? Will he try to call? Sometimes he does phone when he knows they're coming down here — just to check they've arrived safely. But not always.

The windows are locked, but there's a tiny draught coming from the place in the fire-place where the two flue walls have decayed, forming a breach between the two which has been hastily stuffed with newspaper. Some-thing she's been meaning to get to for months, because the baby won't be able to sleep in a draughty room. Something glints under the skirting board about three feet away. She tries to tilt into a position to see it better; it looks like an old piece of wiring, but she can't get to it from here and, even if she could, what use would a piece of wire be?

Her eyes are drawn to another section of the skirting board. This part is closer to where she sits and she knows what it is because there's an extra section of wood which has been nailed over the board.

When the children were little, maybe six and nine, Matilda caught them smuggling notes to each other after lights out, tiptoeing on to the landing and slipping messages under each other's doors, so she relegated anything like pencils, paper, scissors, paint to a room downstairs. They could keep nothing in their rooms beyond books and toys. The children found a way past that. They found devious hiding places in their rooms. One by one the hiding places were discovered, and each time the children emerged with more sophisticated hiding places. One weekend they managed to prise away part of the skirting board and hide their belongings in there — Matilda sent Ollie up here with a hammer to secure the skirting board. He was so angry he nailed it closed, complete with the glue-pots, the envelopes, the clogged paintbrushes, in spite of the children's tears.

She kneels and lowers herself on to her stomach. By stretching full-length she can reach the section of board. The nails have been blobbed with paint over the years; she chips the paint off and sees the silver heads underneath, as fresh as the day Oliver closed it up. She tries to grip the edges of the board, but she can't, her fingers are too big to slip into the crevice. She jams at the underside of the board, but that is also too narrow a gap to slot her fingers into.

She rolls back painfully and sits up, breathing hard, rubbing her wrist where the cuff has chafed. Even if she could get into that hidey-hole the chances she'd find anything in there of any help are next to nothing. Say there was a pair of the children's craft scissors, old and blunt, what would she do? Hack her way out of the handcuffs? Hardly. Unlock one of the windows? If she was a locksmith. And anyway, then what? There are no passing pedestrians to wave at, no cars, nothing. Just the trees and the birds.

She gazes at the window, imagines herself opening it and climbing out. Beneath it is an ornate lead hopper faded to white by age. It leads to a drainpipe that goes down to the gabled roof of the rundown room that was once a scullery. It's now derelict, just a handy place to keep a lot of their gardening equipment. The drainpipe is twined with clematis; she pictures herself trying to clamber down it.

A noise comes from the hallway and Bear stiffens, gives a low, threatening growl. The key turns in the lock and the door opens. It's the smaller, redheaded one with the glasses, the one who calls himself Molina. He is holding a tray. On it are cartons of juice, a jug of water and a few wrapped sandwiches, the type you get in service stations.

Bear snarls. Molina ignores her. He comes in, kicks the door closed behind him and sets the tray on the floor in front of Matilda.

'Dinner,' he says. 'Eat it.'

Matilda looks at the food, speechless. She doesn't know what to make of it. It should be a nice thing — something generous — to be bringing food into a room on a tray. It should have happy associations: hotels in foreign lands, honeymoons, Mothering Sundays. But she decides she's never in her life seen anything as sinister as that tray of food.

'There you go.' He holds up the sandwiches and looks at the dates. 'Any preference? This one's tuna.'

'My husband. My daughter — where are they? Is Lucia in the rose room?'

'I can't believe you asked me that. I just can't believe you had the nerve.' He doesn't sound annoyed when he says it, just amused. 'Did you really expect an answer to that?'

She turns her eyes to his. 'Who are you and what do you want?'

'Questions, questions.'

'Were you in prison with Kable — is that it? Or have you just read about him? Is that what it is?'

Molina reaches behind her and unsnaps the handcuff. Then he stands and holds out a hand.

'There is blood on the kitchen floor. Did you put that there?'

'Please. Get up.'

She hesitates. Eyes the hand suspiciously. 'Why?'

'I'm taking you to the toilet. It might be your last chance until this evening. You don't want to wet yourself, do you?'

Matilda considers making a run for it, but he is stocky with an anvil-shaped head and wide shoulders, long arms. She knows she won't get far, so she struggles to her feet. He takes her hand and leads her out of the room on to the galleried landing. This feature of the house was the chief reason she wanted to buy The Turrets. It stretches around the central atrium, ending in a grand stone staircase that sweeps down to the entrance hall. On the occasions they spent Christmas here, the children used to hang tinsel from the gallery. Once Matilda arranged for a local group of handbell ringers to perform at a party. The ringers were arrayed around the gallery, each behind a lighted candle.

Now the gallery is drab, the big tapestry curtains drawn across the stained-glass window so no light comes through. The central candelabra is on, but the illumination is dim. As Molina pushes her towards the bathroom she has time to note two other doors are closed: the rose room and Lucia's room. So she is right about where Oliver and

Lucia are.

Molina pushes her into the bathroom.

'Four minutes — I'm timing you.'

She closes the door behind her and reaches for the key to lock it but of course there's nothing there. She stands in the sudden brightness, scanning the room quickly. The window is shut and locked, the key nowhere to be seen. She immediately opens the medicine cabinet to find Ollie's razor, or her tweezers, but it's empty — completely cleaned out. Her eyes dart around, hypervigilant — there has to be something. Something.

'There isn't anything,' says Molina from the other side of the door, as if he can see what she's doing. 'Don't waste your time trying to find anything — there's nothing.'

She sits on the toilet and urinates, all the time looking for something. The mirror. She stares at it. Can she somehow crack it? A shard of that could be a lethal weapon. She flushes and with the noise of the water covering her, she slams a hand into the mirror. Nothing happens except for a knock at the door.

'Don't even think about it,' says Molina. 'We're not that stupid. Do you want me to come in there with you?'

'No.' She subsides, breathing hard. 'No.'

Defeated, she begins to wash her hands, still looking at the mirror. He'd hear it if it crashed; she wouldn't stand a chance. They've thought of everything because — and the thought scares her now she's let it coalesce — they are professionals, not fly-by-nights.

She uses her foot to click open the bathroom cabinet. It swings open. It's virtually empty save for the cardboard tube of a spent toilet roll. She finishes washing her hands. There's nothing else in the room — nothing. Just a bar of soap, a small handtowel, and the mirror.

'Time, Mrs A. F. Time.'

She studies her face in the mirror: the lines and the folds and the wiry grey hair curling at the temples. She is old. But she is cunning.

'I'm coming,' she calls. 'I'm right there.'

She turns off the tap, dries her hands and at the last minute bends and scoops the toilet-roll tube out of the cupboard. She pushes it into the inside of her bra. Then she straightens her clothing, switches off the light and leaves the room.

Half a Century

The West Country is the only place in the drenched little island of Great Britain where summer is supposed to reign. Somerset is rumoured to be named after a tribe called the summer people, who always slept in the open air and danced in the sun. The truth is that although the west is warmer than the rest of England, it's also wetter. Warmed by the Gulf Stream, it's the closest to a jungle the UK can offer. In the coastal regions, palm trees look like postcards from the Caribbean. Rhododendron, with its vaguely erotic blooms, is considered a pest.

Caffery's been here for three years now, learning the ways of the land. He's learned to expect not lines of traffic and diesel fuel, commuters in rain-streaked buses, but sheep being driven home along the lanes and cows straying on dangerous corners. The suffocating smell of rapeseed in the spring and fertilizer in the autumn. He's learned that just when you think summer should be on its way, in the west it always rains.

It's bucketing down this afternoon, drops leaping from the ground and leaving gritty scars on the window. He sits in the kitchen, uplit by the screen of the iPad. He has one elbow on the table and is sucking on his V-Cig, his eyes fixed vaguely on the oily rain-streaks. He is pondering where he's come to and what it means.

The afternoon has been spent making phone calls. He's pulled strings and used the right vocabulary, been careful to whom he speaks and how. He's also used the web, flicking through everything he can find on Derek Yates to back up what he's being told from his sources.

So far this is what he knows: Derek Yates, d.o.b. 1948 (which would put him now at sixty-six) was part of Penderecki's circle. In 1989 he committed a horrific assault on an eleven-year-old girl, for which he did time in Belmarsh — which is where, Caffery guesses, he was introduced to some members of the paedophile ring, namely Penderecki and Carl Lamb, Tracey's brother. After an attack by a fellow prisoner left him with internal injuries, Yates was moved from Belmarsh and placed in the secure unit at Long Lartin — a Category A facility which has the largest 'supermax' segregation unit in Europe.

Long Lartin is in the West Country, not far from where Caffery lives now. It sends a chill through him, thinking of this guy so close all this time. The court records indicate Yates was placed there because he had family ties in the area. He was eventually released in 2005, for just one year. By 2006 he had already reoffended and was returned to the high-secure unit at Long Lartin, which is where he remains.

Does he know something about what happened to Ewan? It's an outside chance, but it's all Caffery's got.

Actually Derek Yates has proved to be not too difficult a quarry, there are huge amounts about him on the web. Even an article about him in the *Guardian.* The journalist was granted an interview as part of an article on the prison population at Long Lartin who were waiting for placement in psychiatric units. Yates comes across as a little manic — stuff about the government, the screws and the system and wanting to move out of the high-security Perrie Wing — but Caffery reads the whole thing, wondering all the while what he's going to extract from it.

Yates is in 'Rule 45' segregation as he is considered a vulnerable inmate because of his crimes . . . Has few friends . . . he refuses most requests for interviews, though has one regular visitor — not a family member, but an ex-prisoner from a different section of the prison. 'When he was on the inside he wouldn't have been allowed near me — me being what I was, him being what he was.' Otherwise his is a lonely existence . . . Inmates considered mentally ill are called 'Fraggles' by the other inmates . . . Is Yates mentally ill? . . . 'I hear things,' he says. 'Sometimes it's impossible to keep myself still. The doctors said I'm probably meant to be in a hospital. Not here.'

Where Caffery has failed is getting a visit with Yates. He's called Long Lartin, posing as a friend, and has been moved, relentlessly, around the system. The dedicated booking line for visitors asks him for a VO reference number. When he can't provide one, the woman at the other end says, bluntly, 'How do you know Mr Yates is here?'

'He is, isn't he?'

'I'll pass your information into the system, and if he is with us I will contact you with his answer of whether he wants to speak. But I can tell you now: that will never happen.'

'Why?'

'If you really are a friend of his, you'll know the answer to that.'

Caffery calls someone on the professionals' line and fails again to talk his way in. He explains he's with the major crime unit and that he's looking into a case Yates was loosely connected to and that he needs immediate access to the prisoner. But the woman at the other end is firm. He'll have to go through the normal protocol: get the unit to raise a production order and see if Mr Yates will respond to the request. If he says no, Caffery's got no choice but to send an outline of what he wants to the governor. She promises she will put through a request to Derek Yates, but explains he's very controlled about who he sees. *You will have to be very special for him to break his rules. There is only one person who visits him.*

'Who?'

'If you're a warranted police officer, you'll know that I'm not allowed to answer that question.'

So his application is in the pipeline. It could be days. What he is left with is shreds — nothing to base anything on. The headache squeezes at his temples, threatening to come back. He closes his eyes and presses his fingers to his head.

Keep revising, he tells himself. Just keep going back over it all. There's an answer here somewhere . . .

THE PEPPERMINT ROOM

In the striped green room above the disused scullery Matilda is staring at her hand. The skin is so papery thin that every vein and tendon is visible, as if age has come along and sucked out all the flesh. She's started a bleed by scrabbling vigorously at the piece of skirting board. After two hours she admitted defeat, accepted that she was never going to prise it off with her bare fingers and even if she could there probably wouldn't be anything of use in the hidey-hole. In desperation she's used some of the blood to smear around her ankle where Molina cuffed her to the radiator on her return from the lavatory. She had some vain hope the blood would lubricate the skin enough for her to slide her foot out. None of it has worked. Her hand is a mess, her right knee is aching from maintaining the same position, and her shoulder is sore from pushing up on the kitchen table earlier.

She saw a film once — an awful film that

Kiran and his wife, Emma, were watching when they were staying last year. It was about a man who'd fallen down a crevasse and had to hack off his own arm to escape. She can't stop thinking about that film now; the images won't stop flooding into her head, convincing her that the only way to get out of here is to break herself somehow. To break the bones in her foot, or cut herself. On her ankle the blood has coagulated and coated the metal and is now drying in tight flakes. Oliver is on blood thinners after the operation. If he bled like this, he would die. His life would just seep right out of him.

The house has calmed as the day has worn on. No noises from the other bedrooms, but the men downstairs are murmuring to each other, clattering around in the kitchen as if they're making tea or something.

Once upon a time Matilda considered herself tough. She did things the other girls wouldn't dare. She was the first in her village to get a driving licence, and she toured America and the Far East on her own back in the days when it wasn't the thing that every student did as a rite of passage during their gap year. Back in the days when it took hard work and courage and the only people you met on the way were the tough Australians and Israelis who had turned travelling into an art form. But somewhere along the way, perhaps because of the children, she's lost the art of being courageous. It's been leeched away from her, until taking a chance on anything is unthinkable and every move has to be choreographed and planned.

She drops her head back against the wall and gazes at the window, still open a crack. At the sun on the tops of the trees. Last week she saw an item on the news about a man who'd had an industrial accident. His overalls had been snagged by a piece of moving machinery in the factory and he'd been dragged, inexorably, through a solid-iron gap of less than nine inches. His entire body had passed through before the managers could stop the machine. He suffered a broken back, pelvis and ribcage and a ruptured bowel. But he'd lived.

That's fine, she thinks, for a skinny eighteen-year-old apprentice. But for her?

She turns and looks at the desk where Kiran used to do his homework. It's only a few yards away from her; on top of it are some old children's books that Matilda has put out in the hope the grandchildren will one day be interested. The cricketing mug Kiran won when he played in a prep school tournament. When she came into the room after the visit to the bathroom, she casually nudged the table. A few things rolled off, which she replaced. Molina came forward to help, but not before she'd managed to kick a pen out of sight under the curtain.

149

She stretches her foot over, and using her toe she nudges the pen out. Then she pulls the folded cardboard tube from inside her bra, tears it in half and begins to write, slowly and deliberately. When she has finished she pulls the elastic band from her hair and turns to Bear.

'Bear,' she whispers. 'Bear?'

The little dog lifts her head. She wags her tail and the trust in her face makes Matilda want to cry.

'Good girl. Come here.'

Bear gets to her feet, stretches and yawns, then trots over to her and sits down with a loud huff of breath. Matilda strokes her, soothingly, scratches her behind her ears. 'You're a good girl, aren't you?'

Her collar has her name stamped into the leather, but there's no tag. It broke off in London and they haven't got round to replacing it. Matilda carefully undoes the collar, winds the scrap of card around it and secures it with the band. 'Good girl.' She refits the collar then takes the dog's face in her hands and presses her own forehead to Bear's head. 'Good girl,' she murmurs. 'Good luck. We love you.'

She shuffles herself across the room until the leg attached to the radiator is stretched out and her bottom is on the hearth. Ungainly and wincing from the pain, she lies on her back so her head is in the fireplace and she's looking up into the flue. The newspaper blocking the breach is brown and wet; one push and it disappears into the neighbouring flue and falls away, down into the fireplace in the scullery downstairs.

Matilda grits her teeth. She tilts her head low and speaks to the dog. 'Come on, Bear.' She feels sick. Sicker than she ever has in her life. 'Come over here now.'

HONIG AND MOLINA

In the kitchen 'DI Honey', whose name appears on his birth certificate as Theo Honig, age thirty-seven, a British national with German parents, breaks off from cleaning the table where the dog food has spilled and calmly tips his head back to look at the ceiling. The noise overhead is a whispery, scratchy sound. Snaky and secretive. He's not at all surprised to hear the prey struggling. You expect these acts of rebellion. Idly he wonders what she's planning.

'DS Molina', whose real surname is unpronounceable, but who usually goes by the Christian name 'Ian' (or as he's known in the company, 'Ian the Geek'), is cleaning the kitchen floor where the Anchor-Ferrers' daughter, Lucia, has tipped an entire fridge-load of food.

They both stand there for about a minute, heads tilted back, not speaking. Then Ian the Geek casts his eyes questioningly at Honig, who shrugs. Shakes his head. He's not worried. They can deal with it.

When there is no other sound they resume their work, mopping and disinfecting. The two men are quite different in the roles they fulfil for their company: Honig is the superior with years of experience in the field, while Ian the Geek is the technical whizz. They've never been paired together before and Honig isn't sure how it's going to work.

He rinses the cloth under the tap and cleanses his hands with an antibacterial spray he takes everywhere with him. He can't stand dirt and smells, especially the smell of dog food. This house, he thinks, is particularly unhygienic. The moment he came in he could smell the accumulation of months and years of badly wiped surfaces and the accretion of food particles in the cracks of the floorboards. He thinks, though he isn't sure, that he can smell Ian the Geek too, as if there might be a few missed showers in his history. Honig dries his hands and inspects them, turning them over and over and checking each nail individually for any remnants of dog food.

Another sound comes from overhead and again the men stop what they are doing and turn their eyes to the ceiling. This time the scratching increases to a panicked scrabbling. There is a pause then the noise hurtles down the inside of the chimney breast, as if Satan himself is running his claws down the flue. A small thud comes distinctly from the other side of the kitchen fireplace. Then there is silence.

Honig gives a long weary sigh. He puts down the towel he is using and nods at Ian the Geek, who props the mop against the fridge. They both go quickly and quietly to the back door, unlocking it. Outside it is an oppressively humid afternoon, as if thunder is on its way. Ian the Geek knows the house better. He came a day in advance to recce and set the scene and set everything up, so now he leads the way — around the side. Here a small stone scullery — its walls crumbling and beyond repair — is tacked to the kitchen wall.

The door lolls on rusty hinges — Honig can tell it's been like that for years and Ian the Geek doesn't need to push it open wider to step into the room. Both men go in, ignoring the cobwebs that brush their faces. There's a tiny amount of light coming from the window, just enough to see the fireplace and the huge pile of soot and pigeon droppings that has been dislodged. Honig uses a toe to move around the crunchy pigeon droppings. There is blood there. He puts his hand on the chimneybreast and bends to peer up into the flue.

'It's the mother's room up there, isn't it? Where we put the dog?'

'It is.'

Honig straightens and dusts off his hands.

He scans the scullery — no dog. The stretch of floor between here and the door has been disturbed. It's obvious what's happened. The dog has taken a hit falling, but it's got up and gone. He nods at the door. Ian the Geek doesn't need to be told. He heads off, moving purposefully into the garden.

Honig is left on his own. He bends down and puts his head into the fireplace again. 'Hey, Mrs Robinson,' he whispers up the chimney. 'You're not as stupid as you look. And proper impressive in the tit department, incidentally. Proper impressive.'

Silence from upstairs. No more, no less than he'd expect. He straightens and picks his way back across the room. Goes into the garden, across the lawn and down the steps that link the parterres. He can hear Ian the Geek crashing around hundreds of yards ahead in the undergrowth. Whistling softly to the dog.

Honig goes down the steps and into the coppice — stopping at the place the intestines are. He half hoped some animal would have come by now and eaten them, but they haven't been touched. They'll have to be moved. They are from a deer Ian the Geek killed yesterday, but they've had the desired effect on the family. Fifteen years ago Kable left the intestines for the police to find. He took all that time to arrange them in the trees, in spite of the fact that someone could

155

easily have walked into the woods and caught him. Incredible.

Honig returns to the kitchen and hunts around a bit until he finds a bucket and some rubber gloves. As he goes back outside, Ian the Geek is walking towards him across the lawn from the trees. His face is red and he's breathing hard.

'Well?' Honig says, though he already knows the answer. He can see it in Ian's face. 'What happened?'

'Chased it into the trees — it's gone.'

'Is it going to die? It was bleeding.'

'Probably. If we're lucky.' He holds his hand out to Honig. In it is a ripped scrap of cardboard from the inside of a toilet roll. 'It was on the lawn.'

Honig bends and places the bucket and the gloves on the ground. He straightens and takes the scrap, turns it to the light. It has been torn across the top but the remainder reads: *We are at The Turrets, Litton. Please call the police, please take this seriously.*

'Ahhh,' he says softly. He yawns and crunches up the note, puts it in his pocket. 'Bless.'

'Dog's got no ID,' Ian the Geek points out. 'And it's not microchipped — I checked.'

Honig knows this already. The dog's not a big threat, running around out there in the woods. Nevertheless, he'd like it back. Just to keep things tidy.

'It's sloppy,' he says. 'Very sloppy. Come on.'

He picks up the bucket and continues in the direction of the coppice. Ian the Geek follows.

They stand for a moment or two, surveying the loops of innards. 'Fucking awful mess, isn't it?'

'Fucking awful,' Ian the Geek agrees.

Honig hands him the gloves and the bucket. 'Put it all in here — we'll take it up to the house. Use it as bait — see if we can't get the dog back.'

Ian the Geek pulls on the gloves and begins unlooping the intestines from the bushes — pausing once or twice when they snag on a thorn and tear, allowing the semi-fluid contents to leak out. Honig watches for a while. Then he gives a long languorous stretch and glances around — at the trees, at the gardens and terraces and the stone summerhouse. Some people just don't deserve what they have, they really don't. They don't work for it, and when it comes to paying their taxes — well, everyone knows that people like the Anchor-Ferrers are the first to wheedle their way out of their obligations, the last to put their hands in their pockets and help their fellow man. The house rises majestically above the trees, its turrets and mullioned windows all lush in the late sunshine. As if it's haughty and contemptuous of its surroundings.

One of the windows is open a crack on its latch. He's pretty sure that's the room where Mrs Anchor-Ferrers is. He looks at it for a while, thoughtfully.

When Ian the Geek has got all the remains into the bucket the two men go up to the house. They hunt around in the outbuildings until Ian the Geek comes out from a little shack, covered in cobwebs and holding up a rusting metal animal trap. Probably intended for rabbits, it's the perfect size for the family dog. Honey gets a handful of Pedigree Chum treats from the utility room and the two men go back to the scullery where they get to work arranging the trap, using the intestines and the biscuits as bait.

'Of course,' Honey says, as he primes the trap. 'One good thing has come out of this. At least we don't have to draw straws any more for who gets the first turn.'

'No?'

'No, dickhead.' He turns and smiles at Ian the Geek. 'Mrs Robinson has just volunteered herself. Nice lady.'

THE ROSE ROOM

There have been noises in the house that Lucia doesn't recognize. A strange scuffling — a scratching as if from inside the walls. She watches the door expectantly, trying to decode what's happening. The noise is coming from Kiran's room where Mum is. The place Kiran's daughter christened 'the peppermint room'.

It's the ugliest room in the house. But it could also prove to be the most important. There is a camera in there — mounted in the number twelve in the clock face. It surveys most of the room. It will see everything that happens between those walls. Dad couldn't have chosen to put it in a better place.

Even Mum doesn't know the camera is there — Dad has been so secretive about protecting the house. Ever since Hugo and Sophie's murders, he's changed. He changed at work, and he changed at home. It didn't matter that Minnet Kable was locked up in a secure unit — Dad was doubly vigilant after

159

the killings.

She hears a door slam, then the house falls into silence. Absently she rubs the side of her breast where it aches. It's uncomfortable, sitting here in this position, and her bra is painful and lumpy. She wants to unhook it, get comfortable, but she won't — not with 'DI Honey' in the house. Just thinking about her bra brings on a sudden overwhelming memory of Hugo. Hugo undressing her on the tennis court at his grandparents' house. Hugo, his body tanned from days on the cricket pitch, days swimming in the rivers. He was at Radley, where they all played so much sport, and it showed in his physique. He had a place lined up at Durham University. Even now, all these years later, the pain of it is like being eaten from the inside out.

Another noise: one of the men in the garden whistling loudly, as if calling a dog. She sits up, blinking at the window, things slotting into place. Then she hears the men's voices — they are in the old disused scullery. The scullery is under the peppermint room. There's a chimney there which has been open for years — she's often worried about Bear crawling into it. Suddenly everything falls into place. She's promised herself to stay silent, but this is all so wrong, all so wrong.

She sits up on her knees. 'Hey!' She hammers her fists on the floor, yells through the floorboards. 'Hey, you — what have you done with my dog? I want my dog! I want my dog!'

There's a pause. The men downstairs have stopped talking. She pictures them staring up at the ceiling.

'I want my dog,' she yells. 'Let me see my dog.'

The kitchen door opens and she hears footsteps on the stairs. A moment later the bedroom door is unlocked. The two men stand in the doorway. She stares at them wildly. A savage.

'Lucia, Lucia?' Honey says, all mock horror. 'What's all the noise about?'

'My dog. Bear. What's happened to my dog?'

'The dog,' Honey says lightly. 'Oh that. I'm so sorry — the way that worked out.'

'What's happened? What's happened to her?'

'Your mother put the dog down the chimney.'

She stares at Honey. She doesn't like him, she doesn't like him one bit. In a wooden voice she says, 'I told you you should have left him with me. You fuckers.'

A small, barely contained squeak erupts from Honey. He rubs his hands nervously. Shoots a tiny gleeful look at Molina, as if he's a schoolchild who can't bear how exciting this has all become.

'You fuckers!' he says in an excited voice. 'She said "You fuckers"! She made me feel

161

ever so small. Did she make you feel small?'

Molina is glaring at the floor. He mumbles something that neither of them hears.

Honey's smile fades abruptly. He gives a long, heartfelt sigh. 'Yeah. She helped the dog escape. What that means to me is that your mother regards the family dog very highly. Is that right?'

Lucia eyes him carefully. She doesn't trust him. There's something unstable about him. Unpredictable.

'I said, is that right?'

'I don't have to answer that. I want to know what happened to my dog. Nothing should happen to my dog — she has done nothing. I want to speak to my mother. In private. I want to hear what happened to Bear.'

'Yeah, like we're going to let you do that.'

'I want to speak to my mother.'

'She doesn't want to hear it.'

'Yes, she does.'

'No, Lucia. She doesn't. I mean, ponder this. Ponder the fact that maybe your mother regards the dog higher than she regards her own daughter.'

Lucia says nothing.

'I don't know,' Honey ruminates. 'You do hear it said, don't you, Mr Molina, especially with the ones further up the social scale, you do hear it said they prize their animals very highly. It's a class thing, I think. I mean, me being from the dregs of society, I don't get all this. Never saw how a horse or a dog could take the place of a human.' He makes a thoughtful clicking noise in the back of his throat. 'How about you, Lucia? Do you think your mother holds you in greater esteem than she does the dog?'

'Of course she does.'

'Because you are higher than a dog, aren't you, Lucia?'

She closes her mouth. Stares at him defiantly.

'Did you hear me, Lucia? Are you higher than a dog? Because I'm not a big fan of dogs — I don't like the way they eat. It's messy. Unappealing. Isn't it, Mr Molina?'

'Disgusting.'

'You look like a lady with poise, Lucia. I bet you can be a lot tidier than a dog when you eat, can't you? More discreet in your bodily functions?'

Lucia holds his eyes. 'What did you say?'

'There are other ugly, unappealing things dogs will insist on doing. Do you know the other unappetizing thing a dog will do, given half a chance? It'll roll in the defecations of other members of its own species. Did you know this Lucia?'

'You won't win this.'

'I don't know about that.' He makes the clicking sound in the back of his throat again. 'Sometimes dogs'll go even further. They'll even eat it. That's putrid behaviour, in my book, the sort of thing only the lowest forms of life would do. Don't you agree? I mean, when your mother places you lower than a dog, it's kind of a serious thing to level at another human being — it's implying that they're capable of eating human faeces.' He gives a long, weighty pause. 'You're not capable of doing something that disgusting. Are you, Lucia?'

She lowers her chin, keeping her eyes on him.

'Are you?' he repeats. 'Capable of that?'

There is a breathless silence. In her head she keeps shouting at him: Fuck you fuck you fuck you . . . But Lucia is very good at knowing when to lose the battle in order to win the war. Now is not the time to fight.

She shakes her head. Lowers her eyes.

'Good,' says Honey. 'Now we won't be hearing another word out of you. I'm going to close this door and you're going to be quiet now. Like a good girl. Get it?'

'I get it.'

When the two men have gone she sits in silence. Her head is inside the house and outside too, all at once, plotting and plotting. She is tracking the two men from their sounds as they move around. She's also tracking Bear in her imagination. Through the forests and the brook. Through the hedges. Lucia knows where she'll head — up to the common where they sometimes walk. To the

place where all the children go picking elderflowers on a Sunday. She's got no chip, no
collar. If someone finds her they won't be
able to track her back to the house. But at
least she'll be safe from all this.

Lucia wonders who will find her.

PART TWO

THE WALKING MAN

The moon climbs, a clear unblinking disc. A hole in the sky. In the Chew Valley, at the foot of the Mendips, Amy sleeps, dreaming about the doggy called Bear with the bad paw. She dreams about the man with the sooty beard, carrying the dog to a nice safe house with a roaring fire. The man puts the puppy next to the fire, pats her, then turns and walks away into the woods.

Meanwhile, six miles away — up over the reservoirs and forests of the Mendips — DI Jack Caffery wakes with a jolt.

He blinks at the clock. Ten thirty. The alcohol has burned through him, leaving just a vague taste of cloves in the back of his mouth. Outside the rain has stopped. He sits for a while staring at the ceiling, trying to work out what woke him. His scalp is tight — his brain feels as if it's sticking to his skull. But the sick feeling isn't back.

He picks up his phone from the bedstand. There's a text from the superintendent: *Call me ASAP.* He deletes it and opens his browser, finds Derek Yates's interview again. Yates said something odd about the only person who visits him . . .

When he was on the inside he wouldn't have been allowed near me — me being what I was, him being what he was . . .

Hurriedly Caffery fumbles for the notepad where he's listed all Yates's crimes. He stares at the dates. He looks back at the phone. He can't understand why he didn't make this connection before.

Him being what he was . . .

He knows exactly who that ex-prisoner is. Exactly.

He gets dressed quickly, finding a fleece in the back of one of the cupboards and a pair of Thinsulate gloves. He's had too much to drink; if he gets stopped and breathalysed it'll mean automatic dismissal from the job. But really, does he care any more? Does he honestly care? He snatches up his car keys.

His car smells familiar; it even has the lingering scent of tobacco from back when he still smoked roll-ups and not the designer steel things he uses now. The rain has stopped but the clouds hang silently in the west, shot through with veins of black — almost living and bleeding. He drives out from the house and goes north-east until he gets to the network of lanes that criss-cross the Chew Valley. As the stars come out he slows the car and begins to crawl along the lanes, keeping his eyes on the fields on either side. He is looking for a fire — the first of the flames that will be used to make supper for the man he is hunting.

The Walking Man is a nomad. As his name implies, his sole activity is to walk. By day he walks constantly. He stops walking at dusk and makes camp where he stands. At dawn he wakes and makes a fire over which he cooks a breakfast that will fuel him for another day's walking. He moves day by day in a predetermined pattern; over the months, Caffery has logged the pattern and is fairly certain the vagrant is covering a giant circle — one which lies mostly in Somerset, but straddles the borders with South Gloucestershire and Wiltshire. A lemming urge: he moves from the centre to the outer edge of the circle, then around the perimeter of the circle a quarter of a degree, then back to the centre. Caffery isn't sure how the Walking Man has decided on the size of the circle, but he does know he is marking the perimeter with a line of crocuses which he plants in some of the places he stops. The centre of the circle is at Shepton Mallet, the place the Walking Man's eight-year-old daughter was abducted decades ago.

This is what links the two men. The Walking Man has lost someone to a paedophile the way Jack Caffery has. He too has no body to bury. Like is drawn to like. Jacqui Kitson thinks she's been through all the grief a person can, but she hasn't.

The search for his daughter's body is what drives the Walking Man to comb the countryside day after day after day. When he finds an immovable object in his way — a road, a house, a city — he assesses it. If it was there before his daughter went missing, he skirts it. If it was built afterwards he does what he can to tear it away and check it hasn't been built over a grave. He doesn't care how often he breaks the law to achieve this. He's spent enough time inside not to worry about that.

One of the Walking Man's other characteristics is that he is almost impossible to find. It's as if he chooses when he wants to be discovered. Caffery has hunted for him for months, but in the Walking Man's mystic, sly way, he's dissolved himself off the face of the planet. Whatever grove or ditch or barn he's bedded down in, he's made sure not to be visible from the road. He is clever. Cleverer than the foxes he beds down amongst, and certainly cleverer than any cop. Tonight, when after long hours of hunting Caffery turns a corner and glimpses to his left a campfire, he knows it isn't that *he* has found the Walking Man. He knows that the Walking Man has allowed himself to be found.

He must want something from Caffery.

THE AMETHYST ROOM

It would have been better, Oliver decides, if the men had just assassinated him and the family the moment they first walked through the door. This drawn-out process is unbearable. Ten years ago, or even one year ago, Oliver might have been able to do something about it. He might have used brute force to prise apart the ageing bed he's manacled to. He might have used one of the bed struts to smash his way out of the window — on this side of the building the drop is only two floors, and he might easily survive that. But the soft pulling on his sternum reminds him of the truth: he would die in the attempt.

And if he were dead, how desperate would that make the two men? What might they do to the rest of the family? To Matilda, and Lucia. Earlier he heard shouting and scuffling. For a while Lucia was screaming — yelling at the top of her voice. He couldn't make out the words, but he heard the men come running. He has no idea what happened next.

Oliver already has an embryonic theory about these two men and what they represent. It's an accretion of subtleties — the way Honey and Molina played their invented ranks of inspector and sergeant so naturally, one instinctively subservient to the other. The way they carry their arms — ever so slightly wider than their bodies — as if the muscles there are stopping them relaxing totally, or as if they've spent long years on parade in that stance. The methods they used for marching the women up the stairs also gave something away. Molina crunched down Lucia's hand when she struggled and easily controlled her.

It is called the gooseneck manoeuvre, and it gives Oliver a hundred clues.

He isn't sure if this means the family is more likely to survive. Or less.

Whatever does happen to them it will all be recorded by his security cameras, which feed directly to a hard-drive he has had discreetly located under a set of stairs in one of the turrets. He kept their installation a closely guarded secret, hid his trail by changing contractors several times. Even Matilda doesn't know where the cameras are mounted — she's given up asking. His only regret is that he gave in to Lucia's insistence that none were placed here, in her room. Nothing that happens to Oliver in here will be recorded.

He rarely comes in here — she has kept the walls either black or purple for the last fifteen years — ever since Kable killed Hugo and Sophie. The curtains are a grey voile decorated with floating red skulls. Ordinarily he tries to avoid looking at the things his daughter decorates her walls with.

There is a clock in the shape of an electric guitar, and next to it a stark picture of a dark-haired woman in a petrol-blue ballgown, reclining so that her white breasts are almost exposed. The man supporting her at the waist — Oliver assumes it is a man — wears a high batwing collar and cravat. His black hair is long and swept to the side, his face is utterly white with the exception of his black-lined eyes and his lipsticked mouth. Oliver has no idea who this couple might be, though he knows they mean something to his daughter. Another poster is more familiar to him: it shows Patty Hearst in her olive combats and beret. Standing legs apart, her M1 Carbine aimed aggressively at an unseen foe; behind her the orange-and-black seven-headed cobra — the Symbionese Liberation Army symbol.

The door opens and Oliver turns jerkily to it. The one called Molina is standing in the doorway holding a tray. On the tray is a plate of food and a glass of water. He comes into the room and sets it carefully down on the floor, in a place Oliver can reach it. He stares at the tray, his pig-heart thumping loudly. His medication is on the tray next to the water.

'You're here because of me. Aren't you?'

Molina turns cold eyes to him, but doesn't answer.

Oliver says slowly, 'I've met you before, at one of the companies I work with. Which one?'

'Well, see, Mr Anchor-Ferrers, at this point that really is none of your fucking business.'

'I won't have you hurting my wife and my daughter, whatever the circumstances — that IS my business. I heard my daughter shouting — and that definitely IS my business. So you just tell me what you want and we'll arrange it, like gentlemen.'

Molina sighs. He shakes his head as if Oliver is a monumental disappointment to him, turns without another word and goes out, locking the door, leaving Oliver to contemplate the contents of the tray.

FIRE

The camp is next to a haulage yard where juggernauts stand like sleeping giants, the moon glinting off their windscreens. It's a blustery night and the fire is sputtering and flitting, the smoke chasing in wreaths across the yard, banking into ornate curls at the wall of the empty portakabins.

Caffery parks on the road and makes his way by foot down the track along the perimeter. The yard's night-light comes through the grilled security fencing and makes criss-cross hatching on his face. When he arrives next to the camp the Walking Man doesn't look up. He's busying himself with the fire. Preparing dinner is his ritual.

He's picked up a friend since the last time. Sitting with its back to the security fence, its face towards the fire, is a dog. A mongrel of some sort, wiry, its hair dark at the muzzle as if it has, like the Walking Man, been dipped in tar. It doesn't move when Caffery arrives, but keeps its eyes on him as he stands at the

177

edge of the clearing.

The dog may have acknowledged his presence, but the Walking Man will do no such thing. This is what Caffery expects — he knows the game now. Knows not to push. Knows that when the time is right the Walking Man will speak. And so he stands and watches the Walking Man pottering around, emptying tins into the makeshift pots he seems to be able to conjure from nowhere, sprinkling them with the herbs he's gathered from the hedgerow or from private gardens he's happened on.

He's a white guy, the Walking Man, but you'd have to peer to be sure of that, covered as he is from head to toe in a kind of primordial grease. It coats his beard and his hair, it forms a carapace on his clothes. It borders and defines him. And yet, paradoxically, the Walking Man is clean in the ways it's important. He takes enormous care of himself — especially his feet. You don't walk twenty-five miles a day, every single day, without taking care of your feet.

He finishes heating the food and dishes it out on to plates. Two are standing ready, as if to confirm that Caffery was expected. This subtle prognostication is the Walking Man's sign that he knows everything before it happens. Sees everything. Misses nothing.

'Well?' The Walking Man finally glances up at him. 'Why are you here?'

Caffery massages his temples. 'Can I sit?'

In reply the Walking Man unrolls a foam mattress. He has hidey-holes around the countryside where he keeps his belongings and somehow he always manages to have supplies on hand. Caffery sits and accepts the plate the Walking Man offers. There's a mug of scrumpy too. He eats a little of the food and sips the cider, conscious of the dog's eyes still on him.

'You let me find you. I must be in favour.'

'You read it how you will, Policeman.'

'You've got a friend?' He nods at the dog. 'He wasn't here last time.'

'We'll talk about that when you explain why you're here.'

'Derek Yates,' he says slowly. 'You visit him in Long Lartin.'

The Walking Man shows no reaction. 'Do I?'

'Yes. You visit him and he's spoken about it to a journalist.'

'Tsk tsk. What they allow in prisons these days.'

Caffery puts down his plate. He finds one of his black-and-silver V-Cigs and clicks the cartridge in. That clicking sound has become as reassuring as the sound of his Zippo lighter used to be. 'You are not known to be on the side of the nonces. In fact, you're rather infamous for the lack of sympathy you show child molesters. And yet you have befriended a convicted paedophile.'

The Walking Man tortured his daughter's murderer, Craig Evans, to within an inch of his life. Evans lives on — if living is the word to describe his existence — like a Skoptsy or like St Paul of Tarsus: castrated. Evans's genitals have made a long journey from the moment they were separated from his body by the Walking Man. They have lived at various times in a biscuit tin on the windowsill in the Walking Man's former house, in a storage locker at the mortuary in Flax Bourton, and ultimately, after undergoing a barrage of tests and having had several small amounts of tissue removed to be stored at a secure location in case of appeals at a later date, they have been incinerated in a furnace only a five-minute drive from the care home where Evans now lives.

He would have been able to sit at his window in the dayroom and watch the smoke from the incinerator burning his own genitals — had the Walking Man not also relieved him of his eyes.

The Walking Man was incarcerated in Long Lartin at the same time as Derek Yates. Caffery is convinced he is the one Yates is referring to: *me being what I was, him being what he was.*

Caffery says, 'Yates is confused by you, by why you've chosen to visit him. But I'm not. I know you — I know that everything you do is for a reason. And I know it isn't a co-incidence you befriended him.'

'Such confidence. Such intelligence.' The Walking Man pulls off the black beanie he covers his hair with and dips his head. 'I know when I am in the presence of greatness.'

'You're doing it to give yourself a weapon. It's connected to me.'

'You're a mind reader too. The fecundity of your talent is unimaginable. Just a moment. Let me pour myself another drink — I've been waiting for this and I'd like to be comfortable to hear it all.' He pours another cider and settles down, his hand resting lightly on the dog's head. He's got the gnarled look of a decaying forest god, twined with creepers. 'So tell me — what's my reason?'

'It gives you something over me, because you know — you must know — that he used to have a connection to Tracey Lamb.'

'Tracey Lamb?'

'You know who I mean. You don't fool me. You know she was one link in a long chain of paedophiles. And that the ring was operated by her brother and by Ivan Penderecki.'

The Walking Man's face changes. He leans towards Caffery. 'Ivan Penderecki? The one who killed your brother, you mean?'

Something inside Caffery goes cold. It takes him a moment before he speaks again, and when he does his voice is lower and more intense. 'Once you said these words to me — you said, "What would some old vagrant in the West Country know about a boy's disappearance thirty years ago in London?" '

'You have perfect recall too.'

'I've thought about that statement. Thought about it and thought about it. And now I understand. Because you are precise, you fucking old pedant, you care about the value of each word, nothing goes to waste. You are interested in the interpretation of words — and the interpretation of that sentence to most people is *I don't know anything about your brother.* But actually that wasn't what you said, was it? What you said was a question, not a statement. "What would an old vagrant know?" A question demands an answer — and this is the answer I give you. I think an old vagrant could, and *does,* know a lot.'

'I see.'

'I want you to make Derek Yates speak to me.'

'That won't happen. I can promise you that much — he won't see you.'

'I can make him. I've got in a request for a professional visit. He doesn't have to give consent for that.'

'But he won't tell you anything.'

'Then you speak to him. You can make him tell you,' Caffery mutters. 'Unless you already know. That wouldn't surprise me, if you already knew.'

'Because you can read my mind?'

Caffery scowls at him and the Walking Man smiles.

THE SCIENTIST

In the purple jewel that is Lucia's bedroom Oliver stares out of the window. It's a blustery but bright night; a full moon. As a child, Oliver imagined that the moon had its own light. It was only when he was at senior school that he discovered, to his embarrassment, that the glow was sunlight bouncing off the inert mass of cold rock. He was disappointed, he felt let down rather by the moon. He decided to ignore it and focus on things that emitted genuine light. The sun. Lasers.

First and foremost Oliver is a scientist. But in many circles, circles that count, he is more, much more than that.

His obsession with light came from his early physics lessons as an eleven-year-old boy — learning the basic principles. He particularly loved lasers, believed them to be science's closest equivalent to alchemy, and could spend hours watching their play, their properties and their powers. He earned an MSc at university and went to NASA, where he

tinkered for years with space-junk projects —
specifically a 'laser-broom project', the no-
tion that all the deceased satellites and cor-
roded space-station debris could be made
safe by a laser that would atomize the fragments. He left NASA and spent a short time
in the British army — the education branch
of the Royal Corps of Signals, where for a
while he was a second lieutenant, adding to
his database of communications and target
identification knowledge, which led to a suc-
cession of posts in research and development
with various private companies. 'Free space
optics' — the use of lasers in communication
— was his specialist area, but for years he
trod water, never quite finding the magic, the
practical application that suited his vision of
lasers.

Then Minnet Kable murdered two teenagers less than a mile from The Turrets. And
everything in Oliver's life changed. Outwardly
he became a success. Inwardly he became
something he still doesn't like or recognize.

It's an uneasy journey to make, but now he
travels back to the days following Hugo and
Sophie's murders. A police helicopter circled
for two days afterwards and Oliver had a
security officer from his company sent down
from London. The officer stayed for a week,
until the day Kable walked calmly into a
police station in Wells, his hands out, ready
to be cuffed.

Oliver was haunted by thoughts of what happened at the Donkey Pitch. He didn't admit it to Matilda, but privately he spent long hours feverishly trying to make sense of it all. When the family were staying in The Turrets he'd find excuses to walk alone, and invariably he'd find himself at the Donkey Pitch. He stood at the place the bodies were discovered, he studied the trees where the intestines were wound. He walked the perimeter, kicked among the leaf litter. He found a cave, a hovel strewn with beer cans and bat droppings, and hunted around in it, wondering whether Minnet knew about the cave — whether he'd slept there. Waited there, perhaps.

One of the members of the local golf club worked for the coroner's office, and for months Oliver sought him out, found excuses to be at the bar when he was, bought him drinks. Once the case had been through the courts, the coroner loosened up and slowly Oliver was able to glean some of the details that hadn't been made public. The thing that stuck in his head the most was the way Kable attacked the couple. The brutality of it, the efficiency, tormented him.

Hugo and Sophie were making love when it happened (Oliver still isn't sure if Lucia knows this detail, he doesn't want to ask). It was a warm evening and the couple were lying on a blanket at the foot of a large oak —

Hugo on top of Sophie — when Kable approached. He was holding a Stanley knife, which later he'd use to remove their insides. And an ice pick.

In one single movement the ice pick pierced Hugo's buttock. It missed his spine by millimetres, travelled through his bowel, and emerged from the front of his abdomen, where it continued its journey and pierced Sophie's stomach.

Oliver couldn't get rid of this image. Two injuries, one blow. It followed him every way he turned. Dogged him and taunted him.

Then slowly, imperceptibly, and maybe out of self preservation, the thoughts metastasized from something that hounded him into something he could use. He'll never admit it to Matilda but the only way he could deal with the images was to use them as an inspiration in his work. It took him to an arena he is still ashamed of.

And he is fairly sure that this is why the two men are in the house. The whole thing is *his* fault.

FISHING

An owl moves low over the darkened forests and fields and tracks. Weshimulo, Cailleach, Oidhche — in ancient folklore she has clairvoyance. Without her aid, Athena can only see half the truth, not the whole truth. Cailleach can uncover lies like no other. Now she skims the treetops, gliding on an air current, not moving her wings. As she rounds the edge of a coppice she comes unexpectedly on a clearing where a small campfire burns. The flames send orange light to the underside of her wings and quickly, almost as if the light is scorching, she banks left, diverting her course, away from the fire — heading to the west. As she goes she lets out a screech. A warning there is something unnatural or predatory down there.

In the clearing Caffery sits forward, elbows on his knees, his eyes locked on the Walking Man's face. He is waiting for him to speak, but the Walking Man takes his time, finishing his drink, then carefully wiping his mouth and his beard clean.

'I know when I am defeated,' he says. 'And this is one of those times.'

'You'll speak to Derek Yates?'

'I might be persuaded.'

Caffery narrows his eyes suspiciously. The Walking Man is never straightforward. 'Might be? Then what's the price? There's always a price with you — always. I know you're going to make me work for it.'

'Give a man a fish and he will eat for a day, give a man a fishing pole and he will eat for life.'

'So you're going to teach me to fish? Go on then, get started.'

The Walking Man is silent for a while. He sits back and rubs his beard a few times, thinking about this. Then he speaks. 'Come, little dog. Come here.'

He's made no movement, has hardly changed his tone of voice, but the dog instantly obeys. It trots around the edge of the fire, passing Jack without so much as a sideways glance, as if he's no more than a ghost, and makes its way to the Walking Man. Without any further instruction it sits a pace away from him, looking at him, licking its lips.

The Walking Man gives it a scrap of food. He lifts first one paw then the other, inspecting the pads, spitting on them and holding them to the firelight to get a better view.

'You're going to mend, little dog. You're go-ing to mend.' He strokes the dog thought-fully. Then he reaches inside his filthy jacket and pulls out a crackling paper bag. Jack recognizes it. The crocus bulbs he bought for the Walking Man almost two years ago. 'What are these for, Jack Caffery? Detective?'

'They mark your circle. You believe your daughter is inside the circle — and when you've searched it, you mark it — to remind you.'

'And crocuses because . . . ?'

Caffery shakes his head. 'I don't recall. Something about a story — a child who goes missing — a little girl called Crocus.'

'And the girl, on a predetermined day each year, sweetly lowers her face through the clouds to speak to her parents.'

'Does your daughter do that?'

The Walking Man stares at Caffery, his eyes reflecting the flames. He and Caffery have the same eyes. It's like looking in a mirror.

'Well?' Caffery prompts. 'Is that what you're saying — that your daughter visits you? Because my brother doesn't. I haven't seen him, or his ghost. Not once since the day he left.'

The Walking Man's voice is dry. 'Maybe she is finding ways to communicate with me.'

'What *ways*?'

'A child came to me. A little child, so big.' He holds his hand out in the air, to indicate a small child. 'Blonde, like my daughter. With grazed knees and green eyes. She came from a van — a white van.'

'The same as your van, the one Evans used to abduct your daughter.'

'She wore a dress the colour of a blue crocus, but she wasn't a ghost, she wasn't a spirit, she wasn't an illusion. She was real, she had a real voice and real eyes. She came as a signal — a signal never to give up. And I made that real child a promise.' He lifts the dog and sets it so it's facing Jack. It puts its head on one side and opens its mouth, its tongue lolling out. 'I promised her to help.'

'To help what? The dog? Is it her dog?'

'No. Crocus found this dog — it is a refugee, an orphan, a runaway. But it is also an emissary. I don't know from where and I don't know how it came here, and I don't know why. But . . .' He pauses and gives an ironic grin. 'I know a man who can find out.'

'You want me to find out where the dog came from?'

'And I want you to find out why it had this on its collar.'

He gets to his feet and comes to stand near Jack. Holds his hand out in a downturned fist, as if it's a drugs deal they're doing. But when, after a moment or two, Caffery opens his hand to receive what's there, it turns out to be a crumpled piece of grey card. He takes it, unfolds it and squints down at it. It's been

191

torn, the writing smudged by water, and most of it is missing. But two words are legible.

Help us . . .

He frowns. Turns the note over. 'What's this?'

'I don't know. It was attached to her collar.'

'A joke?' He shakes his head, not sure. 'Kids maybe — a prank.'

'A prank? Interesting. Would you care to prove it?'

'Has the dog got an address? Phone number?'

'No, just a name: Bear. Though a less likely-looking bear I've yet to meet.' The Walking Man peers at the dog, as if he's gently chastising her for her lack of bulk and height. 'Pets these days have pieces of electronic equipment inserted under their skin — tracking systems — the sort the government would like us all to wear.' He takes the note from between Caffery's fingers and goes slowly back to his place. Sits down and picks up the dog. 'Will you find out who this dog belongs to?'

'If I do, you'll speak to Derek Yates for me?'

'I will.'

The wind changes and with it the smoke turns tail like a wraith and blows into Caffery's face, making his eyes smart. But he doesn't close them. He stares at the Walking Man, hardly breathing. His heart bounces crazily around in his chest. He is suddenly closer than he has ever been to finding out what happened to Ewan.

'Shit,' Caffery says irritably, a prick of sweat starting on his back because of course he'll find who the dog belongs to. He'd go to the ends of the world if he was guaranteed a clue about Ewan. 'Damn you to eternity. Give me the dog.'

TEA

Morning. Mist clings to the ground and to the walls of the house. But the roof is so tall, so high above sea level, that the turrets stretch up into the clear air, proud, their windows and tiles lit pink by the rising sun. In the kitchen the lights are on and the kettle is coming to the boil. Two suits dangle on hangers from the curtain rail and there are two camp beds made up in the corner. In one Ian the Geek sleeps. The other, Honig's, has the sheets and covers thrown back.

He is already awake and dressed in a black T-shirt and black undershorts. He is at the cellar door, on his knees. A bowl of soapy water is next to him. He is using a scrubbing brush to clean the floor and he is not happy. Not happy at all. When Ian the Geek at last yawns and opens his eyes, Honig scowls at him.

'The place stinks. And what's this on the floor? Looks like blood.'

'I think it is.' Ian the Geek props himself

up on his elbows. 'I had to park round the other side of the house and bring everything through this way. That's how it got there.'

Honig narrows his eyes. Ian the Geek sleeps in an insane deerstalker hat. It must be a techno thing, Honig thinks, a geek thing.

'You brought everything through the house? Why did you do that?'

'If I'd left the car at the front I could have been seen. It was quicker to go through the house.'

Honig is unimpressed. Ian was sent out here a day in advance to set the whole thing up and so far he's made a number of errors. Matilda Anchor-Ferrers spotted the blood yesterday — the family could have been tipped off before the whole thing was set in motion. They can't afford carelessness. And worse, in Honig's book, to allow this level of hygiene to pass is unforgivable. A deer's entrails being dragged through a kitchen? Ian the Geek is obviously on a different plane to him.

'The rest of the animal though? You did something sensible with that?'

'In a canal.'

'A canal?'

'Miles from here. Miles and miles. Don't worry.'

Ian yawns again. He throws back the covers and pads over to the kettle. He unsnaps the fresh box of teabags that the Anchor-Ferrers brought down from London, then begins to make tea using some of the Sèvres porcelain that looks to Honig to be worth several hundred pounds.

Honig finishes scrubbing. He carries the bowl into the utility room and empties it into the sink. He washes it, then his hands, and goes back into the kitchen, coating his hands with little puffs from his antibacterial spray.

'You're making tea?'

Ian looks over his shoulder at him. 'Shouldn't I be?'

'How about coming next door to see if there's a dog in the trap?'

Ian the Geek shrugs. 'OK.' He squeezes the teabags and hooks them out of the pot with a spoon. He sets a digestive biscuit on each saucer, as if they're having tea at the Ritz or something. The two men pull on fleeces and boots, they don't bother with trousers — they aren't going to be seen — and they each carry a delicate cup and saucer out into the misty morning.

The trees are barely visible, and everywhere tall grasses loom out of the haze. It's an amazing place this — awesome — especially now with the lawn covered in dew and the crystal drops of water on the spider webs. Honig breathes deeply, enjoying the way the cool air brings him to life.

They get to the scullery and push open the door. It's still dark in here so Honig rests the cup and saucer on the window-ledge and uses the torch app on his phone to illuminate the place. It is silent, the cobwebs casting ghostly shadows. The slop trailing out of the bucket is beginning to smell, but as they get nearer they see it hasn't been touched. There is no dog clamped in the jaws of the trap.

Honig hunts around the scullery, kicking at things, to make sure the dog hasn't come in and hidden, while Ian the Geek stands in the doorway and finishes his tea, his back straight, his head up. He is balancing the cup and saucer as if he's the most delicate and well-mannered person ever born. As if he's standing in the posh drawing room of a hunting lodge, and not in a broken-down scullery, wearing just a sweater with his hairy legs all naked and goosebumpy. The deerstalker hat flaps round his ears.

Honig takes a step over to the bucket and frowns down at it. 'Kable must have been wack,' he says. 'I mean, it's one thing disembowelling a dead animal, another thing entirely pulling the innards out of a human while they're still alive.'

'Yes. I suppose it took real *guts.*'

Honig looks blankly at Ian the Geek. The comment was meant to be a joke. But it's not remotely funny. He doesn't laugh or even acknowledge he's heard. He turns his attention back to the intestines. 'You'd think something would have eaten it, wouldn't you?

All the way out here in the country — there must be hundreds of foxes wandering around. And badgers — they'd eat this, wouldn't they?'

'Maybe they don't like deer.'

'Well, if something doesn't eat it soon we're going to have to . . .' He breaks off. He's just spotted something in the mess. Something small and silver. 'What's that?'

Ian the Geek puts his cup down. He comes and squats next to the intestines. He isn't as hygiene conscious as Honig is and he thinks nothing of putting his bare hands into the mess. He digs around with his fingers and pulls out the object. 'Shot,' he says, going to the doorway and chucking it into the bushes.

'Shot?'

'Yes.' He squats and wipes his hands clean in the dewy grass. 'Yes — shot.'

'You told me you trapped the fucking thing.'

'Yeah, well, I . . .' Ian the Geek pauses, thinking about it. 'Well, it might have been shot by someone first — I dunno. That's probably how come it was easier to trap.'

'So you lied.'

'Not really.'

'OK — you were economical with the truth.'

'Does it matter? I had a lot to set up. I thought I got it quite good.'

'It only matters because if someone shot the fucking thing before you got to it, they might still be wondering where it is.'

'No. It happens a lot round these places. A deer gets shot, but it gets right up and carries on. Half the deer around here are walking around with bits of lead in them. You see it all the time.'

Honig shakes his head. 'OK, OK — but tell me you weren't lying about what you did with the rest of the body?'

'I swear.' He puts a hand on his chest, leaving a wet handprint on the fleece. 'I swear — in a canal. Miles and miles away.'

'Because people find a deer that's been disembowelled and they're likely to go around screaming about devil worship. And while you might feel free to be careless, I do not. I am not going to screw this job up because of *you.* Get it?'

Ian the Geek frowns. He seems to be trying to find a retort, but in the end thinks better of it. 'Yes,' he says obediently. 'I get it.'

'Good. And what about the housekeeper? What's her name again?'

'Virginia Van Der Bolt. She's happy.'

'Happy? Because what? Because you paid her a visit?'

'Yes.'

'And you told her you were . . . ?'

'Working for Oliver. I said the family didn't need her for two weeks. She seemed to believe me.'

'Seemed to believe you? Is that believed you

or seemed to?'

'Believed me,' he says definitively. 'She especially believed me when I paid her for the time off.'

Honig shakes his head and makes a tutting noise. He turns and picks up his cup and saucer. 'Dear, oh dear. What some people will do for money.'

THE PEPPERMINT ROOM

There's a small bar of yellow light showing under the door. All night Matilda has been expecting one of the men to come in. But they haven't.

Bear has gone. Yesterday afternoon the men were down in the scullery searching for her — one of them even whispered something unintelligible up the chimney — but she is quite sure that Bear has fled with the note attached to her collar. From time to time Matilda pictures her injured and feels briefly panicked, but then she reminds herself of the time the dog fell off the sea front in Lyme Regis and landed unhurt. The drop down the chimney wasn't as far as that fall, so she tells herself over and over again Bear will be OK. And she will have run; knowing Bear, she'll have run as far away as she can from The Turrets. It will only be a matter of time before someone finds her and gets the message.

The men are moving around downstairs. They've been in the scullery again, and she's heard them talking in the garden, now they're back in the kitchen running taps and opening cupboards. Having breakfast probably. The sun has crept up over the side of the hill and is burning shapes on the dusty ceiling and walls.

Since sunrise she's been thinking about Ginny Van Der Bolt. Ginny has a key but she always knocks. Matilda wonders what she will do when the door isn't answered. She'll have seen the Anchor-Ferrers' car parked on the driveway below the house, as it usually is, but if no one comes to the door will she have time and the sense to realize something is wrong? Or will the men be too quick for her?

A door opens downstairs and footsteps sound on the stairs. Matilda's eyes begin to water. She has to cough and shake her head to stop her neck seizing up. She moves around a bit, shifting awkwardly, trying to get her legs tucked under her so she feels less vulnerable. It's Honey coming, not Molina. She can already tell the differences in their footfalls. Honey moves faster and more heavily than Molina, who moves with slow deliberation. As if he's got all the time in the world. She doesn't know which one she's more scared of.

The door opens and Honey comes in. He's dressed in black waterproof trousers and a black blouson jacket. The outfit has vague, unsettling echoes of a Nazi uniform. He goes to the middle of the room, the foot of the bed, and stands, arms folded, scanning the room. He bends and looks behind the cot, under the bed. He even makes a show of lifting up the duvet. He goes to the window and peers out. Down on to the patch of land next to the scullery.

'Mrs Robinson? Something you want to tell me?'

'My name's Anchor-Ferrers.'

'Yes, Mrs Robinson, is there something you want to tell me?' He turns and smiles pleasantly at her. 'Have you got something to tell me? Something happened to your little lapdog?'

She doesn't answer. She locks her attention on a space in mid-air, just in front of his face.

'Come on. You'll feel better when you apologize.'

'You were going to hurt her.'

Honey's smile fades. 'Hurt her? Of course we weren't.'

'You were going to kill her.'

'No.' He has the slightly surprised, slightly incredulous look of a man who's been accused of a crime he hasn't committed. 'That wasn't going to happen at all. Now let's not make a fuss. I'm only asking for an apology.'

She stares at him, unsure. Then, in a small, cracked voice, she says, 'I apologize.'

'I beg your pardon. Didn't hear you.'

'I apologize. I'm sorry.'

Honey scratches his neck. 'I'm not sure —
you don't sound that sincere.'

'I am. I'm sorry.'

'That's OK.' He gives her a smile. 'I forgive
you.'

He comes over to her. Her hands reach up
instinctively to defend herself, but he
crouches and unlocks the cuff. He's got a
faint smell to him — not of cigarettes like
Molina, but of some sort of chemical, like an
antibacterial spray. And under that scent
something more wholesome. Baking and
fabric softener. She sees then that under the
jacket he's wearing Oliver's sweater, the blue
knitted one she'd bought him in Skye, and
realizes it's this she can smell — the comfort-
ing, warm smell of her husband.

'Where's Oliver? Is he OK?'

Honey pretends not to have heard. He
unlocks her cuff and she massages her leg,
getting the blood flowing again.

'Where is my husband?' she repeats, still
rubbing her leg. 'Is he OK? It's hard for him
— he's not well, not well at all.'

Honey still doesn't answer; he just keeps
smiling. She thinks she's never seen anything
as scary as that smile in her life. He lets his
eyes rove down over her chest the way he did
yesterday when he was posing as a detective,
describing the woman with the breasts cut
off. She doesn't break his gaze, but subtly
hunches her shoulders down. He's a young

man and she's a much older woman. But things like that only matter in places where the rules still count.

Something bad is going to happen. She can feel it.

'Please tell me who you are. What are you going to do?'

He smiles. Puts out a hand and strokes her hair gently. She flinches but she can't twist away from him, so she just shrinks her head into her shoulders.

'You're going to kill me. You're going to kill us all.' A tear rolls down her face. 'I don't know why you've chosen us, but I do know you're going to kill us all. You'd have started with Bear.'

Honey pulls his hand back, surprised. 'Oh oh oh oh oh!' He puts his head down and shakes it, laughing to himself. 'No no no no no. That's not it at all.'

'It is. You said you're going to scare us, but that's not where it's going to end. You're going to kill us, and you know it.'

He stops laughing at that. There's a long pause, then he raises his chin. His smile has gone completely. 'Actually,' he says. 'I'm sorry. You're right. That is what's going to happen. We're going to kill you.'

There is a long, shocked silence.

'What did you say?'

'Oh, don't worry,' he says soothingly. 'It won't happen quickly. It's going to take a long long time. Days probably. Maybe even weeks.'

THE VET

Not for the first time in his career Jack Caffery has become a reluctant dog sitter. He likes dogs, but wouldn't ever keep one. The sense of responsibility for another living creature would sit like a spider in his head. But Bear is more than just a dog, she's the key to getting the Walking Man to speak to Derek Yates in prison. First thing in the morning he takes Bear to the vet for a chip scan and a check-up. He leaves her with a nurse and goes for a coffee at a greasy spoon, infuriating himself by worrying about what the dog is thinking. Whether she thinks she's been abandoned.

'She's got injuries.' When he comes back after half an hour the vet is waiting in the doorway of the consulting room, holding the dog by a lead. She wags her tail when she sees Caffery and pulls at the lead, her feet scratching excitedly on the floor. He avoids her eyes. 'Superficial injury to the feet, but from an accident — not abuse. In fact, she's

207

been rather well looked after.'

'A chip?'

The vet shakes his head. 'Nothing. Ran the scanner over every inch — there's nothing there. She's been spayed and she's had money spent on her teeth. This definitely isn't a neglected dog.'

'The accident — what sort of accident was it?'

'Hard to tell. At first I thought she'd been dragged by a car, but she hasn't got any other symptoms I'd associate with that. If you want my guess, I'd say she's fallen from a height. Landed badly.'

Caffery frowns. He looks down at the dog, who looks back up at him. Falling? Falling from what? And no chip.

'Jesus,' he mutters. 'It was never going to be easy, was it?' He sighs and feels in his pocket for his wallet. Pulls out his credit card. The vet looks at it.

'Don't you want to know about the jewellery?'

Caffery lowers his chin and purses his mouth. 'The jewellery? What jewellery?'

'You'll have to come and look at the X-ray. This dog is about to pop with all the stuff she's got crammed in her stomach.'

THE WOLF

Oliver Anchor-Ferrers has spent the night in some discomfort. He's been able to move his body round so that he was facing the door, ready to wake if anyone came to the room, but that necessitated crossing his arms over his chest at an awkward angle, causing more pain. He slept for a few hours and now he lies, half asleep, half awake, blinking vaguely at his surroundings. The men are moving around the house. He can hear faint shuffling sounds, whispers in the hallway.

He sits up groggily, moving his tongue around the furred inside of his mouth. The red-skull curtains are open. Beyond the turret the trees seem to float above the mist. A thin morning light comes through the panes and falls on the blunt features of Patty Hearst.

Patty Hearst. He wonders if Lucia will end as a similar figure. Targeted for the profile of her father.

He isn't proud of it, but for a long time Oliver was one of the world's foremost scientists in the international arms industry. It's the place his fascination with Minnet Kable led him.

Kable. A man with the face of a predator. A wolf. You can see it in the police photographs at the time of his arrest. Something yellow about his eyes. He disturbed Oliver, but inspired him too. In the wake of the killings, Oliver converted his love for the science of light into a deadly weapon.

The ice pick travelling on from one body into another. It was this image that stuck. Oliver developed an application which has made him rich. A smart torpedo, capable of waiting silently beneath the waves, only springing to life when its specific target passes overhead. Its sensitivity is extraordinary: the data algorhythm is loaded remotely using free space optics — Oliver's area of expertise. This innocent MP3 file carries a unique sound signature, a way of recognizing the subtle variations and anomalies of an engine so it can identify not simply a type of sea vessel, but an individual boat. The system is so sophisticated it can carry the signature of more than one vessel. Crucially it can be programmed to pass through one hull, crippling it, then keep going for a second, even a third target.

It is known in certain circles as *The Wolf.*

It has made Oliver rich and irreplaceable. For years he had his pick of companies —

often being head-hunted in an R and D capacity. And yet, there was no pretty way of stating it, of dressing it up to be anything other than what it was: he had become an arms dealer. And when you walk in the weapons industry there is danger every step of the way.

When, thirteen months ago, he had the heart attack which would eventually lead to the operation, Oliver made the immediate decision to leave the business. He stepped away, suddenly sickened and regretful of the role he'd played. Secretly he pictured the heart attack as Minnet Kable, the Wolf, somehow reaching his unwholesome claw into Oliver's chest and squeezing the life out of him. Punishment. And the situation with the men downstairs? Punishment too. They are here because Oliver has unwittingly upset someone in the course of his work. He is sure of that — he just doesn't know what or who.

In this last year of waiting for the heart valve op he wrote his autobiography: *Luciente: A Life in the Light.* The book is currently with an agent in London. His first thought was that the men were working for someone who is worried about appearing in the autobiography. What secrets Oliver might give away. But he's dubious — he and the agent have gone to the greatest lengths to keep the contents secret until they have found a publisher. Oliver hasn't even told Matilda. There's no way the book could have leaked.

Nevertheless *something* has gone wrong with *someone* connected to the Wolf system. No doubt. But until Oliver can work out who is behind it and why, he can't even begin to bargain with these people.

THE WAIT

The vet doesn't want to let the dog go — he thinks she needs to be kept under observation until she passes whatever is in her stomach. Caffery, however, makes a decision and eventually the vet relents, warning him to call if she exhibits any signs of pain. Any swelling of the abdomen, vomiting or bleeding from either end. But the dog shows none of those symptoms — in fact the only symptoms she shows are of making herself at home in Caffery's cottage, even pattering into the bedroom when he goes upstairs, and sitting expectantly on the floor until he relents and lets her get on the bed.

'Disgusting habit,' he says, scratching the dog's right ear. She leans into his hand, her back leg twitching and half lifting in her desire to join in the scratching. 'Disgusting animal — I'll have fleas for ever. This is the last time it happens.'

He takes a shower and when he comes back Bear is still there, contentedly yawning and blinking at him, licking her chops. Caffery's known guys to give dogs all manner of names: Psycho and Chaos and Ripper. Gonner for rescue dogs, and Cluedo for dogs with a mystery father, because 'no one knew whodunnit'. But Bear? Why Bear?

He feels Bear all over, palpating her stomach, but she feels pretty regular-dog-shaped. The X-ray was impressive, he has to admit. He knows what dogs are like, that they'll eat all manner of things, things that'll kill them stone-dead. But jewellery? That's a step outside the normal. Could it be that the Walking Man has set all this up? If there's one thing he likes it's putting out hoops for Caffery to jump through. Or could it be this dog is part of something bigger. Maybe she's been used to smuggle this jewellery into the country.

He gives her a plate of cold sausages from under foil in the fridge and watches her eat. Then he nods at the garden. 'Time for some doggy action, old girl? Time to do what you all do best?'

But when Bear goes into the garden and squats, all she produces is urine. She trots back inside, yawning to herself, and sits at Caffery's feet, looking up at him as if to say, *OK, what next?*

'What next? What next? Well, next we go for a drive around the place you turned up. We go and knock on doors and you get to do your best profile. Smile. *Smile?*'

He uses his forefingers to push up the corners of his mouth. Bear watches him steadily, her head on one side.

'Yeah, well,' he mutters. 'I'm sure you'll be fine on the night — someone's bound to recognize you. And in the meantime, if you could see your way to, you know, having a crap, I'd be heartily grateful.'

JOHN BANCROFT

Oliver is a rational man and instead of fighting the reality in which he finds himself, he progresses beyond it. He conjures an image; a police officer who, in some vague, conjectural future, will come into The Turrets and find their bodies after the men have tortured and killed them. His body, in this room. Then Matilda's. And then Lucia's.

Rather than dwelling on what will come next, he focuses hard on what evidence will be left when it's all over. He decides the cop will be male, though his pedantic mind takes the time to question this and wonder if that's just his stick-in-the-mud patriarchal attitude assigning the role to a man. Rationally it might be a woman, that is how the world runs now; nevertheless it's a man Oliver envisages. Someone bored in his job, perhaps, suddenly brought to life by the case. Someone physically capable and alert. Not someone who eats drive-in McDonald's and tells long stories of his escapades at the bar in his local pub. This man is someone who gets fired up by the old-fashioned battle between what is right and what is wrong.

The hypothetical detective is going to have a short and utilitarian name. Gary or John or Bob. He's going to be mid-forties — not so young that he is fast and careless, not so old that he is slow and uninspired. John Bancroft, he decides. It's a name plucked out of nowhere, but the minute it comes to him Oliver begins to flesh out the armature.

Bancroft is thoughtful — sometimes too intense. He has a quick intelligence and a dogged approach, and quite often he will stay awake all night trying to figure his way through a conundrum. He will know what to do when he finds the Anchor-Ferrers. Oliver can see him arriving here — when? Ten days hence? He comes into the room and hesitates. He doesn't yet know about the evidence on the camera system — that will come later. For now what he sees is Oliver's dead body. He doesn't come to it immediately. He takes his time, using his mind to project what has happened here. What the clues are.

Oliver gives the room careful consideration, tries to see it through Bancroft's eyes. After a long time pondering, he notices Lucia has a pot of pens sitting on the windowsill which the men have overlooked, probably because they are mostly soft felt-tips which could do no harm to anyone. Oliver shuffles himself around and finds he can reach these by stretching only a small way. It makes the wound on his chest smart and pull, but he's able to grab the mug and sit back down without too much pain.

He crouches over the mug, going through the pens one by one, testing them on the back of his hand. Most are old and dried out, but he manages to get two working. There is a small gap between the skirting board and the floorboards into which he finds he can slot the two pens — so a good place to hide them. The remaining pens he puts into the mug, which he returns to its place.

He rolls up his sleeve and makes a mark on his arm. The pen is blue and the mark could almost pass as a vein or a bruise. Then he writes his name, Oliver Anchor-Ferrers, along the inside of his arm and this time there's no mistaking the letters for veins. He pictures someone finding his dead body — he pictures them reading the words on his arm. Stunned by the drama of this image, tears prick his eyes.

He has to push them away with his palm and concentrate to get his thoughts in order.

Beat the next beat, Pig heart. And the next . . .

Lucia's rug, bright red and splashed in a geometric design of silver, is under his right foot. He looks at it for a long time, then he carefully lifts the corner of the rug and runs his fingers across it. He touches the dry felt-tip to his lip and tests it on the back of the rug with a single stroke. The line is fine and clear. He flips the rug over and studies the top — none of the ink comes through. Since history began, man has been finding new and ingenious methods of communicating. It is something lasers can do and it is, Oliver suspects, one of the strongest drives the human race possesses.

He begins painstakingly unpicking a section of the rug's hem — a run of about five centimetres. Then, using the pen, he makes another mark. He folds the hem down, settles the rug on the floor and considers the way it lies on the boards. Not obvious; no one would think to examine it further unless they were searching the room forensically. The way the police might.

DI John Bancroft. If he was conducting a murder enquiry.

20 May I am Oliver George Anchor-Ferrers and I am of sound mind. I love my wife and my children. In the event of my death: two Caucasian men posing as police officers entered this house yesterday morning. No car visible.

    1) 'DI Honey' (command?) 6', 170 lb, age 30–40, pale skin, receding hairline, fair curly hair. Accent British? Public school?

    2) 'DS Molina' 5'10", 160 lb, 25–35 years, dark thick glasses (disguise?) Red hair

(dyed?) Cut short almost certainly military. Distinctive body shape — long arms, wide shoulders. No gloves, fingerprints poss on bedstead (this room), banisters, kitchen on many surfaces.

Please contact the security company which installed my alarm, as they have a code for a hard-drive which will contain further evidence. I will not go into details here as I do not want to risk this being discovered by the men. The security company has the code to unlock the evidence.

I believe that these men have been trained in security. I believe that they are nothing to do with Minnet Kable, that that was a well-rehearsed ruse to alarm us. I believe they are being paid to be here by someone in my industry.

My Wolf missile system has been sold globally, to companies with bases in the UK, US, and Africa. One of these is responsible. I don't yet know which one.

He reads it through, wondering what else to add. Then, unexpectedly he recalls a sentence that is dear to him. Something he read years ago as a student and which could seem childlike and simplistic, yet to him is more profound than anything he can express. It is a quote by Martin Luther King.

Darkness cannot drive out darkness, only light can do that.

He writes it down carefully. Stops and reads it through. Then he adds in a rush:

God forgive me for everything, I think I have killed us all.

THE ROSE ROOM

Lucia sits up and rubs her head, a little groggy. On the other side of the door there are noises. Noises she can't quite decipher. A dragging and the sound of something fraying. For a moment she thinks she can hear Mum crying, pleading. Then the place is quiet again. A strange sound comes: the creaking of wood. But it's not floorboards, it's something else. She stares at the chink of light under the door, trying to make sense of it.

The noise goes on for about ten minutes — then abruptly the light in the hallway is switched off. A few moments pass before she hears footsteps. The door to her room swings open. The hallway is dark behind him, but she can tell in the soft light coming from the window behind her that it's 'Honey' standing there.

He snaps on the light and comes into the room. A few paces behind him comes Molina. They both wear stony expressions.

'What?' she says, looking from face to face.

'What is it?'

Honey holds out his hand to her. He's smiling at her. A broad, glittering smile, as if he's standing on a beach at sunset advertising a holiday resort. 'Care to dance?' he murmurs.

She doesn't answer.

'Oh, come on.' He flicks his hands at her impatiently. 'Don't be a cunt. Get up. Get off the floor. You look pathetic down there. And come with me. Or else you're going to have to learn all about the mandibular lift. You don't want to know about that.'

She glances at Molina, hoping for help, some reassurance. But there's none. He just stands there, his arms folded, blankness in his eyes. This makes her panic even more.

Honey crosses swiftly to the radiator where she is shackled. She swivels round and raises her hand to fend him off, but he's quicker and stronger than she expects and she's no match for him. Before she knows what's happening he has uncuffed her and in a move that shocks Lucia with how expert and unforced his control is, he steps behind her and cups his hands under the hinge of her jaw. Her hands fly to his, but before she can struggle a band of pain shoots through her, so liquid and pure it makes her want to vomit. Her hands flail, turning like windmills in the air, and there's nothing she can do to resist. Effortlessly he lifts her to her feet.

She stops struggling and concentrates on

not falling to the floor. Sets her feet as firm as they can be. Tries to calm her breathing.

'OK.' Honey gives her a shake. 'Now we're clear who's in control. OK?'

'OK,' she murmurs.

'Louder.' He gives her another shake. 'Say it louder.'

'OK, OK — I said OK.'

'Good. Now move.'

He puts his knee in the back of her leg and pushes her out of the room on to the landing. Behind them Molina switches off the light and the hall is in such darkness that, although she knows this landing well, she hesitates, afraid to step forward for fear of bumping into something. She is urged on by Honey and finds herself being forced into a chair. A torch comes on — the beam dances across the floor. The wood of the chair is cool against her bare arms as the men quickly and skilfully fasten her there.

'What's happening? What are you doing?'

Neither man answers. She bites her lip and lets them finish what they are doing. Then, without a word, they leave her. They head down the staircase, training the torch on their feet to guide their way.

Silence.

She sits and concentrates on breathing, soothing herself. Nothing will go wrong — she will not be hurt. The curtains are drawn and she can't see a thing, but she knows she is on the right-hand side of the galleried landing. When they first moved here Mum and Dad had the panels that had been tacked on to the gallery in the fifties stripped away to reveal the original turned and fluted rails. It meant that anyone sitting up on the gallery could look down and see what was happening in the hallway below. Usually it was her and Kiran, who, as nine- and ten-year-olds, would stand shyly in their pyjamas, twisting their bare feet around the railings, staring down in wonder at the grown-up world going on below. During one of those cocktail parties Mum glanced up and saw both of them peering down. She shook her head sharply at them and they slunk back into the shadows.

Now the vague shapes of the railings emerge out of the gloom. There is a camera mounted in the ceiling above the top of the stairs, completely invisible to the uninitiated. It has infrared capability and will be able to see her at this angle. The chair is in the ideal place. That and the camera in Kiran's room suit her vision of the way this will unfold perfectly.

There is noise from the kitchen downstairs, plates and cups clanking as if food is being prepared. The light from under the door seeps a small way into the entrance hall; she can see from here the edge of the tattered old rug. She breathes slowly, conscious of every sound and atom of air around her. She can smell polish where Ginny has been cleaning.

Now she can smell the coffee aroma wafting up from the kitchen. She can hear things too — the men talking, but something else. That odd creak of wood she heard earlier — except now it's not as sharp, it's slow and lazy. And breathing. A controlled, raspy, in-and-out breath.

Gradually, gradually, her senses coalesce and make sense of what else is in the hallway with her. The men, she sees, have exceeded her wildest expectations in terms of shock and intimidation, because, about fifteen feet away something is hanging level with the gallery, directly above the entrance hall where the cocktail parties used to happen. It is large and heavy enough to make the beam creak gently.

This is where the breathing is coming from.

CLUES

Oliver hears the sounds out on the landing. Shakily he strains towards the door, tugging at the handcuff. He would tear his own leg off if he could — would do anything to know what was happening.

'Please!' he calls helplessly. *'Please? No!'*

His voice is pitiful and small and the words choke him. He stops and sinks back to his haunches, trembling all over. He takes deep, gulping breaths to calm himself. His ribs ache. *Keep beating,* he reminds pig-heart. *Keep beating.*

The landing becomes quiet again and at last, when at last his pulse has subsided and he has stopped sweating, he snatches up the pen. He flicks the cap off and continues writing on the rug, more urgently now: *9 a.m.,* he scrawls. *I believe, from what I can hear, that either my daughter or my wife has just been attacked. I don't know the outcome. The house is silent.*

He swallows hard, glancing up at the door,

then feverishly back at the words, using all his willpower to focus on what is important — what he can do. Details. If he is going to die, John Bancroft, his imaginary detective, will want details. Oliver has written everything he can think of, combing his mind for clues: the words the men use, the slang, their clothes, what they cooked, whether they showered last night. He has monitored their actions and their accents. Even tried to smell them to see if he could pick up distinctive whiffs — cooking, as a clue to what they eat, or a scent of suntan lotion to reveal that they have come from somewhere overseas.

Earlier he thought the one who calls himself Molina seemed familiar. Now he's not sure. And if he is familiar, does that mean Oliver's met him in the course of his work? If so where? He can't think. 'Molina' — the name sounds Spanish, though his accent is British. The one who calls himself Honey seems almost twice the height.

The taller one — Honey — is the boss. The names Honey/Molina — not nec. arbitrary. Some subconscious bearing on their real ID? Choosing false names = employing some level of reason. Names start with same letter as real IDs? Names of first pets? School? Street they grew up in? Meaning in a different language: Molina = Mill/Moulin, Honey = Miel/Honig/Miele.

Honey's teeth — slight brown/white striations — does this mean he grew up in an area with high fluoride concentration? Accent English/query antipodean? Or has spent time with Americans/Australians. Not sure yet if partic vernacular/verb combinations/argot.

Molina — glasses — geek look. A disguise, or glasses are necessary — not sure.

He pauses. Throws a glance at the door. All is silent.

Well-researched attack — knew our arrival time and understand well our connection to Minnet Kable. Use of handcuffs — appear to be US manufacture. Implementation inconsistent. Alternates between wrist and ankle. I am secured to the radiator, and so is my daughter.

He pauses, then, his spirits sinking even lower, writes: *Was tied . . . before the noises I have just heard.*

He isn't sure John Bancroft will know what to pull out of this information. Even he isn't sure what any of it means. These men are either more subtle, or far more irrational, than anything he's ever known.

Sudden footsteps on the stairs. Not one of the men, but both. He hurriedly flicks down the carpet and smooths it flat. He licks his finger, hurriedly rubs the writing off his arm and pulls his sleeve down. Then he presses the pen back into the slot under the skirting board and lolls back against the bed. The door opens and the men are there. They click on the light. They are dressed in clean clothes. More proof they've come prepared for the long haul.

'You can have anything you want. Anything. I don't care what it is, I'll do it.'

Honey crouches next to Oliver so he can peer up into his face. 'You know something, Oliver? I love this part. Just love it. I can do it a million times and never get tired.'

'What's happened to my wife? My daughter?'

Honey doesn't answer.

'This is pretence,' Oliver says. 'A veneer. Drop it — get it over with. And then you and I, we're on the same level and we can negotiate. You get what you need from the situation and I get what I need. Whatever it is, we can come to an arrangement. Make this short and sweet for all of us. Reach our objectives — together.'

Still Honey is silent.

'Who are you working for? You're English. Is it a British company? Please, I *beg* of you.'

Honey laughs. 'You're not unusual, Mr Anchor-Ferrers. Nearly everyone begs. In the end.'

'Are you telling me this is the end? For me?'

'No, no no. No no no. Not the end. This is the beginning.'

'Please, no. Please, don't put my wife through anything else. Please, I'll do anything, anything at all — anything you want, I'll do.'

'Yes,' Honey says. 'You will do everything we want. Stand up.'

Oliver hesitates. He is completely powerless — failed by his old man's body. He struggles to his feet, struggling to keep his balance with one ankle still chained. The blood in his body draws itself to the ground and there is pain in his chest. Twenty-four hours ago this would have terrified him. Now it hardly registers. He allows Honey to unsnap the cuff and when Molina gets behind him and pushes him towards the door he doesn't resist.

They lead him on to the landing. The house is pitch-dark. The big tapestry curtains are drawn, but that isn't enough to create this blackness, and Oliver thinks the men must have taped the windows somehow. The way everyone learned to in the Second World War. There is a faint smell of cigarette smoke and antiseptic.

He is pushed into a chair where he is fastened, using, he thinks, zip-ties, though it is far too dark to see for sure. He makes fervid mental notes of the details in case he has a chance to add more to his essay on the rug. Yes — they are using zip-ties. It could be

231

relevant.

'Where's my wife and my daughter?'

The men lock his ankles together. They place something over his head. It is rough against his ears and he thinks it is a box of some sort, closed on four sides with the front and bottom open. He can smell fresh wood, or MDF, can feel it scraping his skin. There comes the unmistakable sound of tape being ripped from a roll and then the box is secured over the top and down to his shoulders so he cannot move his head to left or right. A pause, then a torch is shone into his eyes. He flinches, making the chair jump back a fraction, and feels strong arms securing it in place. He can smell something astringent — like a household cleaner on someone's hands. In his head he goes back to the notes he's made on the rug:

Honey — relevance of? Childhood pet — a dog, a Labrador maybe, Golden retriever? Molina? Molina? Somewhere he visited as a child?

Again comes the torch. He tries to turn away but cannot, so he breathes, deeply, from the diaphragm, trying to keep his pulse steady. Someone — he can't see which man — places fingers over his eyelids. For a split second it flashes on Oliver that whichever man it is will sink his nails in and gouge out his eyes.

Instead he gently opens the lids. The torch

232

isn't shining at his eyes any more, but it up-
lights Honey's face ghoulishly as he peers at
Oliver. A caricature of fascination, he carefully places tape on the upturned lids and
secures them by the lashes to Oliver's brows.
The air stings his exposed eyeballs.

Then, without a word, the men step away.
They go down the stairs and move quickly
across the hall floor. Then the light goes out.
The kitchen door opens and closes.

An unearthly silence falls on the hall. Oliver waits — tensed — ready for something
else. It takes some time for him to realize
that they aren't going to come back. The
muscles around his eyes twitch violently with
the need to close.

He cannot move. He's on the left side of
the galleried landing. He can see shadows,
recognize shapes, and begins to realize there
is something at eye-level across the banisters
that doesn't belong. Something that is bigger
and longer than the chandelier that hangs
there.

LITTON

The area around Litton, viewed on a map, is mostly long wooded tracts, only interrupted from time to time by the blue slash of a reservoir, or the occasional collection of red roofs where a hamlet nestles. Caffery spends a long time drawing out lines radiating from the place the Walking Man found Bear. It's a technique he's seen used by the specialist police search advisors at work, and it's taught him a lot of the questions to ask. The vet says the dog is in good health apart from the injury and the bizarre stomach contents. Caffery's guessing she hasn't been missing for a long time — certainly only a day or two. But how far could a small dog walk in a day or two? And which direction would it go? How long is a piece of string — where do you start in guessing the unguessable?

In the end it's the flip of a coin. He decides to go south of the place Bear turned up, starting in a village at the end of furrowed farmland, because somehow those ploughed fields look like an easier stretch of land for a small dog to have negotiated than the surrounding forests. He drives slowly, trying to get a feel for the area, Bear bolt upright on the back seat, alert, her ears cocked, watching the scenery flash past.

It's a typical Mendip village, tiny and picturesque like a water-colour greeting card with wisteria-loaded buildings and an old pub, its sign creaking lazily in the slight breeze. Hansel and Gretel chimneys sit on the cottage roofs. But the place has an empty, hushed feeling, and as he parks up he senses it's not the right place — that he's off-piste. Sure enough, when he opens the car door Bear shows no sign she recognizes it, just slips mildly out on to the hot pavement and stands, looking around, waiting for him to tell her what to do next.

Ordinarily Caffery trusts his instinct, but he's got no better ideas than this as a starting point, and thinks that if he at least begins to walk he might eventually lock into something important.

Thus he embarks on one of the longest, most fruitless of mornings, trudging from house to house, holding his card in one hand, the dog on the lead in the other, putting cards through the letter boxes of empty houses and stopping to listen to the rambling stories of the elderly, of the desperate for company. The complaints and the pleas, because he's in authority and must be able to do something to help them in their plight with the electricity board. Or the noisy neighbour. You need the perseverance of an ox and the hide of a rhino to do this job.

By lunchtime he's tired. They've worked their way through the village and have entered a wooded area where the houses are further apart, an assortment of two-bedroom cottages with creeper-loaded eaves and gnarled apple trees dotted around, interspersed with huge stone-built mansions with garages and long driveways.

He comes to a modern building with a spanking new Range Rover parked in the driveway. It's an ugly house, painted yellow, and is occupied by a brunette in her mid-forties. She offers him a cold drink, inviting him in. His feet hurt, and he's thirsty. What's more she's wearing tight postbox-red jeans and a white vest top that shows a lot of flesh.

'I've got beer,' she prompts.

After some consideration he declines, accepts a glass of water, a drink for Bear, then heads on his way.

'Should have asked for a laxative for you,' he tells Bear as they come to the driveway of a house. There's a FOR SALE sign in the trees. It has a piece of ivy growing across one corner so it's been here some time. 'We'll make this the last one, eh?'

Together they go up the overgrown driveway, the rain in the potholes soaking their feet, the huge shrubs on either side of the drive crushed underfoot, the patterns of tyres stamped into the leaves. They pass a stables on their left — unused — a stone summerhouse, similarly unused with moss growing in its roof tiles. To their right is a fence and beyond it trees. From time to time Caffery gets glimpses of pale hummocks and he realizes it's a BMX course in there — an unofficial obstacle course, all the hummocks covered in sacking to afford the bike tyres grip.

The house begins to reveal itself above the trees. A Georgian villa, with a side-gabled roof, cracked with age. Caffery and Bear get to the house and Caffery rings the bell. When the door isn't answered immediately he leans out of the gabled porch to see if there's anyone in the garden. No one. He rings again. This time he leans in to the door and puts his ear up to it, checking the bell is working. He hears it clearly, but no one answers.

He turns from the doorway and steps back on to the drive. There are two cars parked in the front — a Land Rover and a smart Lexus in cherry pink. Someone must be home. He goes around the side of the house, the little dog following silently.

He pauses, holding his hand up. Bear stops instantly. There's a fading wooden conservatory at the side of the house with people inside. The windowpanes are steamed with condensation from the many pot plants that are dotted around, some yellowed and dying. But although the glass is semi-opaque he can clearly make out a figure in uniform — a woman, a nurse — and another, someone in a wheelchair. Male or female, he can't tell for sure, but he can see the person is naked from the waist down. He can make out bulky shins. Red-spiked skin. Varicose veins.

The nurse is speaking. He can't make out what she's saying, but he can get the emotion behind it. Irritation. Sarcasm. She's quite short and stocky — Asian, possibly Filipina, he can't say for sure — and her face is etched in a furious scowl. As she talks she works, wrapping something in a bin liner, tying it tight. It's only when she snaps open a bag and begins pulling things out, wipes and towels and a pair of incontinence pants, that he understands the scene. She is changing the woman — he's decided it's a woman just from the length of the grey-blond hair — who has soiled herself.

The nurse stands at the woman's side and bends, so that the woman's upper torso is lying across her back, her arms dangling like cobwebs. By half straightening her legs the nurse is able to lift the woman up from the wheelchair just enough to slip the pants under her. She bends her knees again, lowering the woman, then pushes her roughly back into the chair, fastens the tapes at either side. The woman seems barely aware of any of this. Her head lolls.

The nurse pulls the woman's nightie down over her knees, goes to the table and picks up a dressing gown from the back of one of the chairs. She is about to return when something outside the conservatory catches her attention. She stays where she is, the dressing gown in her hand, staring out. It's not Caffery she's looking at, he hasn't moved or drawn attention to himself, she is looking beyond him — as far as the woods at the foot of the garden.

She is looking at the fence and the treeline where the BMX track is. Caffery turns to follow the direction of her eyes. He sees the faint smudge of the hummocks in there — like sleeping beasts — but nothing moves. There's no noise.

In the conservatory the nurse has snapped out of her trance. She drapes the dressing gown around the woman's shoulders. She crosses to the windows and one by one lets down roller blinds until the conservatory is completely closed off from the garden.

'Are you all right there?'

Caffery turns, caught off guard. Standing a few feet down the path is a very tall, well-built man in his late seventies, leaning on a walking stick. Dressed in a Barbour jacket and baggy brown corduroy trousers tucked into his wellingtons, he has rough grey hair in a mad halo, a huge, almost comical bushy moustache, like an Edwardian villain. His cheeks are tinged pink with anger.

'Have you found what you're looking for? Wandering around as if you own the place?'

Caffery walks carefully and respectfully down the path to meet him.

'I'm sorry, Mr . . . ?'

'Doesn't matter what my name is. What's yours?'

'My name is Jack Caffery.'

'And what are you? Looking to lift a few more lawn mowers? Is that what's in your head?'

Caffery feels in his pocket for his card. He holds it out. 'Sorry — I tried the bell.'

The man sees the warrant card and his demeanour changes. His head, which has been poking out on his neck aggressively, like a turtle, retreats. The folds of skin gather around it.

'Yes. Well, I wasn't to know.' He licks his lips. 'So? Police? What's happened?'

'I'm doing a house-to-house enquiry. Is this your place?'

'Yes — but you can't come in.'

Caffery pauses, the badge half in his pocket. 'I'm sorry?'

'I said you can't come in. The place is a mess — our cleaner hasn't turned up — and anyway . . .' He rubs his nose. Clearly uncomfortable.

'And anyway?' Caffery coaxes.

The man shakes his head. There are broken veins in his nose and his eyes are so slack you can see the inside rims. 'Just — just you can't go inside. It's not a good time for us. For me and my wife.'

Caffery returns the badge to his pocket. 'I'll respect that. I know what it's like not to be expecting visitors, Mr . . . ?'

'Colonel.' The man reaches in his pocket and pulls out a business card. Holds it out to Caffery, who takes it and reads.

'Colonel Frink. I've got one question. That dog.' He nods at Bear, who is snuffling in a flowerbed. If Caffery is very lucky, she's thinking about a bowel movement. 'Do you recognize it?'

'Do I recognize it? No. I'm not in the habit of befriending strays. Why would I know that dog?'

'She's called "Bear".'

'So?'

'She doesn't belong to one of the neighbours? I mean . . .' Caffery indicates the view: the numerous valleys visible from this vantage point, the occasional reddish-brown blur of roofs above the trees. 'The houses round here are spread out — but I guess you meet some of the neighbours.'

'Hardly. In our position we don't have

241

much time to socialize — what would be the point?'

Caffery raises an eyebrow. 'The point?'

'My wife is ill. MS. We're army people and we're only temporary here while we wait to sell the place. We've got no desire to stay in this area, absolutely none.' His eyes stray to the fence where the BMX track is. 'Yes,' he says gruffly. 'The sooner we can get out, the better.'

'You don't like the area?'

'No, we don't. When I retired, we stayed in Germany. We've only come back here because of her health. To be nearer the family.'

'Come back?'

'This was our house. Children grew up here — the grand-children . . .' He trails off at the word 'grandchildren' as if it's tainted with an unpleasant memory. Then he turns and gives the house a look of immense sadness, as if it represents all the misery and woe in the world. The walls are covered in ivy, the trellises all falling away listlessly, pulling pieces of masonry with them. 'Damned management company didn't look after it. It'll sell — to some developer, I suppose. And then we can get the hell out.'

'Don't like the countryside then?'

The man reddens more. 'Mr Caffery —'

'Yes — I'm sorry. Nosy of me. So you definitely don't recognize this dog?'

'As I said before — no.'

'What about Mrs Frink? Would she know?'

'Please,' the colonel says. 'Don't insult us. It's been months since my wife knew anything. Can't speak, can't hear. Bloody mess we're in, if you want the truth.'

'I'm sorry.'

The colonel waves his comment away. 'Now, have we come to an end?'

Caffery considers asking, What's behind that fence on the BMX course that bothers your nurse so much? But he doesn't. Instead he holds his hand out to shake. 'It was a pleasure making your acquaintance.'

'Thank you.' The colonel shakes his hand. 'Thank you and goodbye. You can find your own way out, I take it.'

He turns, using his stick, and makes his awkward, limping way back to the house. His shoulders are hunched, his head lowered, as if it's a fight to hold it up under the force of gravity.

Bear watches him go, her head on one side. Caffery says nothing. Doesn't move for a while, because he's thinking that it's always the same when he meets older people, all he sees is their fragility. All he can picture in his head is his mother — and wonder where she is, what she is doing. Whether she's alive. And if she is, whether she has ever got over losing Ewan and being left with the other child. Jack. The one that, given the choice, she'd have preferred to lose.

'Come on,' he tells Bear, when the sound of the slamming door has echoed out across the lawn. 'Let's go have a look in those trees.'

Handcuffs

Ian is in the kitchen next to the cooker. His hands are behind his back — cuffed. He is standing up on tiptoe and trying to slot them down over the hob igniter, which is the exact shape and size of the cuff key. He contorts and twists his body in the effort. It's a trick he's seen Honig doing. Now he's realizing that Honig has made it look a lot easier than it actually is.

Theo Honig is on his camp bed, idly toying with a giant mug of frothy latte. He has decorated the top of the latte with cocoa powder in the shape of a pair of breasts. He uses a spoon to scoop the froth off the right breast. Puts it in his mouth and closes his eyes, savouring the taste. He whistles to himself breezily — that old song from the film where Dustin Hoffman bangs Mrs Robinson.

Ian twists sideways and then, like magic, the cuffs snap open. He shakes his hands, massages his wrists, stares at the handcuff.

Not that difficult after all. He feels good. He does it again. This time it takes less than three minutes. Ian is the master of electronic devices and networks, computer viruses and manipulating imagery, not sleight of hand or weapons or the things that are Honig's forte. He's impressed even himself with this escape.

Just as he is about to try it again, Honig shakes his head. 'No no — not like that.' He stands and crosses the room, his hand out. 'Give them to me.'

Ian hesitates. The two men are in the security division of a company named Gauntlet Systems. Not a British company, but a global company, with headquarters in New York. Ian has been with the company five years, whereas Honig has eight years under his belt and that, in theory, makes him the superior. Ian would like to argue but he doesn't. He passes the cuffs.

Honig begins assembling them so he can prove just how easy it is. Ian goes to his unmade bed where his bag sits. He begins unpacking the video equipment Gauntlet Systems has given them for this job. By the time he looks up, Honig's handcuffs have come open with a snap. He's holding them up to Ian. 'Ta-da!' he says, straight-faced. 'The Man from Beyond.'

'Very good.' Ian flicks off the lens cap and begins checking the focus. As the technical guy, Ian has to be the one who records everything, because a record is what the boss, Pietr Havilland, wants and is paying for. Ian studiously inspects the camera controls. Fiddles with light balances and colour settings. He does a few practice shots then checks the viewfinder. 'Are we ready?'

Honig yawns and glances at his watch. 'No rush. Keep them waiting. That's where the imagination comes in.'

'Imagination?'

'I believe that's the word I used. The reason we are getting paid so generously is to mess with their heads. Whack-'em-and-run merchants don't get paid shit — not enough for you to haul your arse out of bed. What we're getting is serious money. And why? Because we are expected to be *creative.* That is the whole *point* of *us.*'

He re-attaches the handcuffs and gets on his tiptoes again — unlocks the cuffs for the second time.

'You know who had real imagination?' He slings down the cuffs, wanders over to the table and picks up his cup. 'That Minnet Kable character. I mean, those killings? Un-fucking-believable.'

Ian practises his camera moves — starting with a close-up of the fruit bowl on the table, then a swift pan across to the window, pulling focus as he does. This is just grandstanding from Honig. He pretends to know all about what happened to those teenagers; in

247

truth he knows only what Pietr Havilland has told them.

'What he did with those intestines?' Honig goes on. 'I mean — is that extreme or is it not? And waiting in a cave like that — then, when they come past, bam! — he's on them.'

'You don't know he waited.'

'Yes I do.'

'How?'

'For fuck's sake — what is this? The Spanish Inquisition? It's what happened. Anchor-Ferrers told Havilland when he sold him the Wolf. That's where he got the inspiration for it. Are you going to be like this the whole time we're here?'

Ian hesitates. 'I'm sorry. I'm just nervous.'

That seems to calm Honig a bit. He spoons a bit more latte into his mouth. Eyes Ian carefully — as if he's not sure about him at all. He drains the cup. Puts it on the draining board.

'We've screwed up losing the dog and we cannot afford to cock up again. You're being too soft on the girl — I noticed when we were upstairs just now, you made eye contact with her.'

'The girl? Lucia?'

'Lucia?' Honig shakes his head. '*Lucia?* You see? That's just what I mean. You use her name.'

'I'm just being professional.'

'Professional? If you're a true professional

you'll forget what your lousy little dick is telling you. You're on a short leash after what happened in New York.'

Ian has a rush of anger at the mention of New York. He isn't as experienced as Honig in the field. This is their first time paired together and it hasn't got off to a good start. Ian was chosen for the job because he is a technical whizz and because he spent time in this part of Somerset as a youngster, so knows the land. This made him perfect as the advance party to come and set the scene. But on the final day, when Pietr Havilland briefed them in Gauntlet Systems' New York office, the boss threw a new scenario into the job.

He told them he wanted to use the Wolf murders to further screw with Oliver's head.

Ian was furious. He thought the idea unnecessary and dangerous. There were other ways to scare the family, and he told Havilland as much. He recalls the expression on Havilland's face. He recalls Honig standing at the window with the New York skyline behind him, his face white with shock. Because no one argues with Pietr Havilland.

Soon enough Ian came to his senses. He saw he was in no position to argue. He knew how lucky he was to get the job, and how careful he was going to have to be to toe the line. He swallowed his indignation, apologized for his outburst. Agreed to follow orders. It wasn't his finest hour and it seems

Honig hasn't forgiven the incident.

'So.' Honig wanders back to the oven and refits the handcuffs. 'You'll treat that girl upstairs the same as you treat any target. Understood?'

'Understood.'

'Good.' He nods at the camera. 'Is that thing locked'n'loaded?'

'Uh huh.'

'Get me then.'

With Ian recording, Honig throws the handcuffs off. Holds them up to the camera, grinning. 'Long live the company, long live the Wolf.' He gives the lens a victory fist. 'And *vive le sadisme*!'

THE DONKEY PITCH

Caffery and Bear climb a fence from Colonel Frink's driveway, into the BMX course, and wander around. The place is deserted, but it's been used recently — there are Lucozade Sport bottles and a pile of cigarette ends. The bicycle tyre marks in the earth are fresh. Caffery and Bear traipse through long tracts of mud, past pockets of standing water, a great pile of cut logs seeping red wood sap into the ground. They come to a halt where the path ends at the foot of a steep escarpment.

Maybe this was an old quarry, perhaps it's just natural rock formations that make the drops so steep. Caffery folds his arms, tilts his head back and surveys the cliff. Lots of vegetation protrudes from the cliff-face: hardy, woody shrubs like buddleia, some sycamore saplings. The crown is thick with trees in their first flush of summer, like a filigree against the sky. He drops his gaze back to ground level; obviously this is a place people gather because the earth is churned up, there are discarded drinks cans and an aerosol paint can. A grubby, forgotten bandana in finishing flag black-and-white chequers hangs limply in the lower branches of a birch tree.

Bear glances at Caffery then takes a few tentative steps forward. In the rock face is a crevice, which she pokes her nose into. Her tail wags, her back legs move — not anxious or excited — just curious. Caffery comes and puts his hand on the rock face above her, braces himself and bends to peer over her head.

A little daylight reaches inside. The space is not manmade and it's not big — just enough room for juveniles to crawl into. Which is exactly what seems to be happening here. He's seen places like this before in the woods; even recently he was trailing an absconder from the mental health system who was lying low in a place not dissimilar to this. There's a filthy old sleeping bag and a half-full bottle of Coke on the floor. If someone wanted to they could probably sleep in there, or hide for a few hours, but nothing more. It's not big enough for someone to make a home from. He knows about these things from watching the Walking Man — picking up tips on how to live rough.

He pushes himself back from the cave, wipes off his hands and looks around. Whatever it is about the place that worries the colonel or the nurse, it's not choosing to reveal itself to Caffery.

SUDOKU

Oliver is in agony. The dry air on his eyes is unbearable. The only comfort he can get is by rolling them up into the sockets, trying to catch some precious moisture. The effort makes him dizzy so he tries to keep still, willing an existential calm to come and take over from the physical reality. Minutes pass and nothing happens. There is a sound of someone in the hallway breathing, but no movement from downstairs, nothing. This absence of sensory input is part of the game, he thinks.

'Dad?'

He jerks his head up. Tries to turn in that direction, but the box digs into his collar bone. He is obliged to stay facing the hallway and swivel just his sore eyes. 'Lucia?'

'Dad. I'm scared. What's happening?'

Before he can answer there is a small scuffling noise below. He closes his mouth and focuses on the noise, almost able to feel the musculature in his ears at work, rotating like an animal's. There is movement on the stairs, and on the mezzanine landing, directly below the darkened shape hanging in mid-air.

A breathless pause. Then from below Honey says in a dry voice, 'Lights, please, Mr Molina.'

The lights go on. Oliver jolts back in his chair.

About three yards away Matilda hangs upside down at eye-level to the gallery, suspended from her feet by a rope which loops over one of the cross beams in the ceiling. She twists slowly on the rope, as if there is a slight breeze in here. Like a grotesque chrysalis, her arms have been bound across her chest with gaffer tape. Her mouth has been taped too. Her hair hangs down from her scalp, which is bright red from the rush of blood. Her trouser hems have slithered all the way down her legs and are bunched up around her thighs — revealing a long expanse of flesh. The battered lime-green pumps are still on her feet, their soles still embedded with soil and grass from yesterday in the garden.

Oliver frantically searches for clues she's still alive. Her face, what he can see of it, is bloated and so red it's almost purple. At first he thinks she's been punched, then realizes it's not that — it's because she's been suspended upside down for so long that the blood has gathered there.

He doesn't think he can see her breathing.

He wills her to show some sign of life, but there's nothing.

Just below and behind her is the mezzanine floor where Honey sits on the ottoman with his back to the hall, apparently completely immersed in making notes. There is a cup of coffee placed next to him and he is wearing one of Oliver's sweaters. From the light switch in the corner Molina casually meanders back, yawning. He sits on a chair next to the ottoman and gets comfortable, his arms folded, his legs crossed. Neither man has looked at Matilda above them.

A whimper comes up inside Oliver. A howl. He swallows it down. He sees, across the fifteen feet of space on the opposite side of the gallery, Lucia, tied to a chair. She hasn't had her eyes taped, but she is bound. She too is dressed in what she was wearing yesterday — the neck of her T-shirt slightly pulled off one shoulder to show the whiteness of her neck. She is staring at her mother, a numbed, locked expression on her face. She pretends toughness, Lucia, but she is still his little girl, and if there is one thing he wishes it's that she'd stayed in London yesterday morning.

Now Honey yawns. He puts down the book — it's not a notebook but a Sudoku puzzle book — and recaps the pen. He glances up at Matilda.

'Behaving herself, isn't she, Mr Molina?'

'She seems quiet.'

'She does, doesn't she?'

He stretches his arms in the air, moves around as if he's trying to get rid of a crick in his neck. 'You all right up there, sweetheart?'

The bundle of colour and texture that Oliver knows is Matilda doesn't react. Anything, just the smallest twitch, would give him hope. Perhaps she's alive and is simply unconscious — unresponsive. Or maybe she's immobile because she's decided it's pointless to argue.

'Supposed to be good for your looks,' Honey says. 'A little hang upside down does wonders for the complexion.'

He grabs her by the shoulders and makes a great show of twirling her, spinning her sickeningly. He stands back and opens his hands theatrically, giving Molina a sunshine smile. A Las Vegas magician proving to the audience that there is no chance of there being any tricks or fakes in his equipment.

Matilda's eyes flutter and Oliver's pig-heart jumps. She's alive. She struggles briefly, the tired, almost sleepy movements of a butterfly beginning its fight from the cocoon.

Honey looks up at Lucia and Oliver on the gallery. He gives them a smile, and raises a friendly hand as if they've all just waved at him and he wants to acknowledge their friendliness.

'Mr Molina — please.' He gestures at Matilda, suggesting he's suddenly been overcome with the tastelessness of the situation and can't bear to look at her any longer. 'Please deal with that.'

Molina fiddles with the end of the rope that is tied to the banisters. It comes free with a great creaking noise, and Matilda falls through the air. For a moment it seems she will land on her head, but she comes to a bouncing halt a yard above the floor. Molina lowers her the rest of the way, putting his foot under her head so it folds under and her shoulders meet the floor first. He takes her weight and allows the rest of her body to crumple on the mezzanine.

'Yes?' Honey sniffs, still not looking. 'Yes?'

'Alive still,' Molina replies. He gets a grip on her pullover and lifts her top half, then drags her backwards. He hauls her on to the ottoman in a sitting position. She sways limply, her torso slumping forward, and he stands behind her, holding her back against his leg to keep her upright. Honey turns his head disdainfully, then, when he sees she is seated, he comes carefully to her and bends, looking into her face.

'Sure she's alive?'

'Sure.'

Slowly, curiously, Honey peels away the gaffer tape from her face. The sensation startles Matilda into consciousness. Her eyes flicker and her head jerks back. She takes a convulsive breath. But she doesn't straighten up. Just hangs forward at the waist, swaying gently. A line of saliva lowers itself from her mouth to her lap.

Honey slowly unwinds the gaffer tape holding her arms across her chest. Her clothes are creased and covered in glue from the tape. Satisfied she has stopped swaying and can sit upright unsupported, Mr Molina reaches behind the ottoman and pulls out a video camera. He switches it on and spends a moment or two playing with the focus, his eyes on the screen, then practising a panning motion from where Oliver sits, down to Matilda.

'Mrs Robinson?' Honey crouches in front of her, his back to the gallery. He puts a finger under her chin and lifts it, almost tenderly. 'Hey?' he murmurs. 'Hey?'

Matilda doesn't answer. She is still swaying, still off balance.

'Come on, Mrs Robinson — come on.' He glances up at Molina, who has the camera trained on him. 'She looks a bit worse for wear. I hope she wasn't up there too long.'

'I don't know,' Molina mumbles, but he doesn't come to help. He keeps filming.

Honey straightens and takes her hands from her lap. He pulls her to her feet. She stands unsteadily, the weight down on one hip. She tries to lift her head, gingerly, as if every movement hurts.

'Up here.' Honey pats the ottoman. 'Just jump up here for me.'

When she doesn't respond he bends and grips her left leg at the knee. He lifts it so the foot is resting on the ottoman. Then, putting his shoulder into her back, he pushes her until she clumsily steps on to the ottoman. He gets up there with her and stands next to her with his hands on her shoulders to steady her and stop her falling.

'Hey,' he says to Molina, who has moved round and is filming them from below. 'You know what I'm going to ask?'

Molina hesitates. He lowers the camera and gives Honey a long look. 'What?'

'Hot or not? Remember that game we used to play — is she hot or is she not? It's how Facebook started — did you know that?'

'Yes, I did know that.'

'So?' he says, leadingly. 'So?'

'So what?'

'Mrs Anchor-Ferrers. Is she hot? Is she not?'

Molina takes a deep breath. If he is momentarily unsure he doesn't show it. He lowers the camera and looks up at Matilda. He puts a finger under his chin, like he's admiring a piece of art in a gallery. Scans her up and down slowly.

'She's a good-looking woman.'

'Good-looking as in, you'd do her? Or good-looking as in, you'd admire her? If she was, say, your new girlfriend's mother?'

'I'd admire her.'

'But you wouldn't do her?'

'I dunno. Would you?'

There's a flash on Honey's face, but it disappears.

'I dunno,' he says. He rubs his temples as if he's giving this serious consideration. 'It depends on the circumstances. There's the desperation factor to take into account. You know what I mean — when you're so desperate you'd do a bottle. I'm as guilty of that as the next man. I tell you, I've done it with some things would make my mother faint. Not sure I'd need desperation factor, though, in Mrs Anchor-Ferrers' case.'

He lets go of Matilda. Pauses for a moment to check she isn't going to topple over, and then he steps nimbly down from the ottoman. He puts a hand on Molina's shoulder. 'You're unsure and that's understandable. So let's do something. Let's push the situation a little.'

He smiles up at Matilda. Her head is hanging, her hair straggling around her face.

'Mrs Robinson. Undo your blouse please.'

The air in the hall tightens a fraction. It's as if everyone has just hitched in a shocked breath.

Slowly Matilda raises her eyes to Honey.

'I'm sorry?' she mumbles.

'I think you heard me. Undo your blouse.'

JEWELLERY

Back at his cottage Caffery stops the car, gets out and opens the back door. Bear sits on the back seat looking up at him, her mouth open slightly, head on one side, as if she's trying to gauge his expression.

'Tell you what,' he says, with a nod at the garden. 'I'll let you off lightly. Acres and acres of space, and if you go and do something now I'll spare you the castor oil. How's that?'

As if she knows exactly what he's saying, the little dog trots away from him. She sniffs around a bit then pauses and squats under the lilac tree.

'Call me unimaginative,' he says as he watches. 'But I never pictured myself being so happy to see a dog doing that.'

When she's finished he gets a trowel and a colander and collects what she's done. In the utility room he rinses away the faeces and mucus — no blood, so no more vet bills — and carefully inspects what's left. A gold chain and a wedding ring. He dries them on kitchen towel and takes them into the kitchen, setting them down on the kitchen table.

If this is the Walking Man's idea of a joke, then it's past being funny. Perhaps the note really is from someone in trouble. Caffery thinks he should tell someone. The cops? He *is* the cops. An ally? The woman he knows, the one he half suspects he's in love with. He could trust her with something like this, something he wanted kept under the radar. And the unit she runs is just removed enough from his unit for the news not to get back to his superintendent if she pursued it.

He discounts it. He can't say why, but he doesn't want her involved in this. Anyway, he thinks, if this note is a cry for help then whoever it is has got more chance of being helped with him investigating. If he swallowed his pride and took this note to the superintendent he could picture the lacklustre response it would get. A hoax, that would be the verdict, because ninety-nine times out of a hundred it is.

He picks up the chain and moves it through his fingers. It's unremarkable — a woman's neck chain, designed to have something suspended from it. He's not sure, but he doesn't think it's solid gold — he thinks it's plated, and he can't find any identifying marks on it. The ring however — he picks it up and examines it carefully — the ring looks solid. Now he's into his forties, his vision

263

seems to be getting worse by the day; he finds his glasses in a kitchen drawer, puts them on and studies the ring carefully, turning it over and over between thumb and forefinger.

It's clearly a wedding ring: plain yellow gold with no decorative markings on the outside. On the inside however is a clear inscription.

To Matilda, it says. *From 'Jimmy' on our wedding day.*

Next to the writing is the hallmark and a further symbol. Caffery has to carry the ring to the window and squint painfully to make it out. It seems to be a winged figure, standing next to an eye, or the sun, he can't quite tell.

He stands there for a long time, trying to make sense of it, but he can't.

It doesn't matter. He knows what to do about jewellery — he sat through a morning's course on it in the Metropolitan Police and can still recall the basics of how to identify countries and places of origin. The hallmark has several different stamps. One shows the type of metal — he thinks this one with a set of scales with '750' written inside means it's eighteen-carat gold. The next is the assay office, the place the gold was tested. This one shows a leopard — he can't recall which city that means, but it's either Birmingham, London, Edinburgh or Sheffield. The last one shows the year of the marking — in this case a curlicue G but he can't decode that either because he thinks it varies depending on the assay city. It would be easy enough to find out. He looks back at the first mark in the row. It has the letters 'BCD' stamped in a square. This symbol is the 'sponsor's mark' — in other words it identifies the maker of the ring.

He places the ring on the table, stands back and folds his arms. He's resentful of the ring. It could have had the good grace to be a non-starter. Then he could have gone back to the Walking Man and said, There's nothing. No clues, no chance. Speak to Derek Yates for me anyway.

But it would be a lie. Because of those marks. There's a way to trace it back to the owner.

MRS ROBINSON

Absolute silence in the hallway. No one seems to breathe. Only Honey is relaxed. He stands looking expectantly up at Matilda, puzzled that she hasn't done anything yet.

'Well?' he says. 'Well?'

Bewildered, she raises her head. Oliver sees her face properly for the first time. She is so swollen — the veins in her face are red and prominent, outlined like a road map. She catches Oliver's eye and her expression conveys all the despair and humiliation the universe can contain.

'I'm sorry,' he whispers, though he's sure she can't hear. 'I'm so sorry.'

In a daze she lowers her eyes to Honey, who still has his head on one side, waiting for her to comply.

'You heard me, Mrs Robinson. You heard what I said, and although you don't quite believe what I said, you did understand it. I want you to undo your shirt. Just a bit. Come on.' He leans forward, whispering up at her with a smile, as if he's her lover. 'Undo it. You know you want to. It's all I want you to do — just open the buttons a little.'

'Is that all?' she says distantly.

'That's all. Cross my heart, hope to die.'

Slowly, trancelike, Matilda begins to undo the blouse with trembling fingers. Honey watches for a few moments, then he turns away, as if she doesn't much interest him and now he wants something else to amuse him. He wanders to the back of the ottoman and picks up the Sudoku book, sits down, leafing through the pages to the puzzle he was working on. He pulls a biro from his top pocket, uncaps it using his teeth, and scribbles a number into one of the squares. As Matilda finishes unbuttoning her blouse he is totally immersed in the puzzle, his face a mask of concentration.

The muscles at the top of Oliver's cheeks ache from where his eyes have tried to close over and over again. A few tears of despair sluice across his stinging eyeballs.

Honey scribbles down a couple of numbers, scratching his head with the base of the pen. Eventually, seemingly bored with the puzzle, he closes the book and puts it on the ground and puts the pen in his top pocket. He gives a long bored sigh. Then he glances up at Oliver, and, making a huge play of pretending he hasn't noticed him until now, gives a theatrical start backwards. Then, as if shocked to see Matilda standing there with her blouse half undone, he does the same to her. He rocks slightly back on the ottoman to get a better angle from which to appraise her. Makes a vaudeville expression of shock to the gallery, putting one hand to the side of his face and fanning himself with the other, as if the place has suddenly got too hot.

Oliver lets out a long, slow breath. He wants to die. He wants to die this moment and not live any more of this.

'I've said, whatever it is you want you can have it.'

'Shut up, Oliver. Just shut up.' Honey touches his waist at the point of his trousers button. 'Mrs Robinson? Could you just loosen those a little bit there?'

'What?'

'Just a little.'

'But you promised . . .'

He blows a long snort out of his nose and slams a hand on his forehead. 'You're right — I said just the blouse, didn't I?' He shakes his head. 'You know, I disgust myself sometimes. I'm really shite at keeping promises, aren't I, Mr Molina?'

'You're not great.' Molina raises his eye from the viewfinder. 'It's not your strong point, it has to be said.'

'Yeah — I'm crap. Sorry about that. Now take the fucking trousers off.'

Oliver glances to the opposite side of the

gallery and sees Lucia staring rigidly at her mother. Her face is contained, unreadable. On the mezzanine Matilda puts her hands to her waist and unzips the trousers. She bends and folds them down to her feet. Under them she is wearing tights with a pair of plain white knickers.

'Take those off too.'

'Take off what?'

'The tights.'

There is a long pause. Then Matilda lowers her face and begins to cry.

'Just fucking do it,' Honey says boredly. 'Just get on with it.'

Eventually she does as she is told. She rolls the tights off her feet, almost losing her balance as she bends to pull them off each foot. When they are gathered in a ball she drops them next to the trousers. Tears drip from her face on to the floor.

'And now your bra.'

This time Matilda doesn't pause. She's given up. She unhooks the bra and lets it fall to the floor. Her breasts — large and familiar to Oliver — loosen down into their natural place. On the landing the piece of tape holding one of Oliver's eyes open suddenly gives way. His right eye falls closed and tears lubricate its sore surface.

Honey steps forward and studies Matilda's breasts, his head on one side, his tongue between his teeth. Her hands twitch, wanting to cover herself, but he gives them a sharp look, and they instantly stop moving and subside. He seems to like that, the way he can make things happen just by using his eyes.

Now she is still he puts his face very close to her stomach. Her belly button, folded like an oyster in a shell. Tongue between his teeth, he sticks a finger into it. Jiggles it around.

Then he looks up, smiling like a child. 'I like doing that.' He does it again, his tongue wiggling between his teeth in time with his finger. 'I love it, love it.' He lets his finger trace down Matilda's stomach. He tugs at her knicker elastic and peers inside, frowning. 'I can smell you from here.'

'Don't talk to me like that.'

'I'll talk to you exactly the way I want. Now take these off.'

'No.'

'Yes.'

'You said I didn't have to.'

He rolls his eyes up to her. He looks like a caricature of a supplicant in a religious painting. 'Matilda,' he says evenly. 'I've changed my mind.'

He lets the elastic snap into place and takes a step back, arms folded. She hooks her fingers into the top of her knickers, rolls them down over her pelvis, her knees, and keeps rolling until they drop on the floor at her feet. She stands up straight, her shoulders back, proud in her nakedness, her eyes fixed on a point on the chandelier.

'Mr Molina? I suppose it's obvious you're not interested in Mrs Anchor-Ferrers here. I mean — you've got your young bit of trim lined up over there.' Honey jerks his chin in Lucia's direction. 'Admit it, Molina — you have got it in your head, haven't you?'

Molina doesn't answer. He continues filming.

'And I suppose that begs the question about what you do when you find your fancies turning to thoughts of love — I mean, can you be trusted? Are you a courteous lover, or are you a bit rough? A bit inconsiderate? I hope you're not the sort of freak that Kable was . . .' He pauses. Then continues, in a curious voice. 'Mrs Anchor-Ferrers? Mrs Robinson? How much were you told about the way Hugo and Sophie died? Do you know as much as your husband does?'

'You've told us you're nothing to do with Minnet Kable,' Lucia says angrily. 'Just stop talking about him.'

Honey raises an eyebrow at her. 'Good morning, trim. Are you upset because Hugo was your boyfriend?'

'Shut up about it.'

'I don't think I will. If it's all the same to you.'

Lucia closes her eyes and swallows once, twice, her throat working.

Honey pulls the biro from his breast pocket and taps it thoughtfully against his temple. He begins to pace the mezzanine. He has the air of a college professor in a lecture, thinking carefully through the information he's imparting.

'Let's examine the evidence that Kable actually got off sexually in killing those two poor unfortunate friends of yours, Lucia. I mean, you know that when they were found they'd been placed together, as if they were . . . what's the nice way of putting it? In flag — What's it again?' He snaps his fingers repeatedly, trying to bring the word back. 'In flagrante delicto. I've got that right, haven't I? But the thing with the guts.' Honey makes a circling motion at his own stomach. 'All that nastiness. What was all that about? I mean, I've calculated it and at a guess two people, it makes nearly sixty feet of intestines. It must have weighed — oh, I don't know, with food in it three or four stone in total. That's not easy work, you know. He must have had a motive for that. And what other motive is strong enough to do that than a sexual motive? So I did some research — and what I discovered is that some people are unnaturally attached to the sight and smell and feel of viscera. They love the slime and the blood. Do you think that was what our Mr Kable was into?'

He stops next to Matilda. He uncaps the

pen and holds the point against her stomach, then raises his eyes mildly to Oliver.

'The other thing I read, anecdotally of course, is that for some of these sex freaks where the wound is made is *really* important. For some of them that's the most important thing — can you believe that? It has to be in the right place. Even to a centimetre. Imagine that! A centimetre one way or another and all the fun is ruined.'

He tucks his bottom lip under his top lip and peers at Matilda's stomach.

'Was it an accident, where the girl got pierced, do you think? Or do you think Kable was clear? If so, I wonder *exactly* where he liked the hole. I'm going to guess it's somewhere around here.' He lets the pen trail over Matilda's abdomen. 'Because of what he pulled out of those kids. But where exactly, I wonder?' He uses the pen to pensively lift the soft skin on her stomach. 'I mean, it's difficult to tell with you, with all this flesh. The girl was just a teenager — she'd have been firm in this area, easier to get at.'

He pauses then and holds a finger up to the ceiling to illustrate he's just realized something. For a moment he is absolutely motionless, then he turns very, very slowly back to Matilda and quite deliberately and slowly, he draws a cross just under her navel.

'Don't ask me why,' he says lightly, recapping the pen. 'But let's just say I had to choose something so disgusting to do, then *that* would be the place I'd go for.'

HATTON GARDEN

The sponsor's mark on the ring turns out to be 'Beale, Cohen and Dartford' and the city denoted by the leopard is London. Of course, Caffery thinks, it would be London. The biggest city, the biggest haystack.

London Calling. The opening chords of the old Clash song lodge on a loop in his head. He bangs out the rhythm on the steering wheel and casts edgy glances at the other drivers in the lines of traffic around him. All being drawn into the beating living heart. London calls. It's a magnet, a black hole into which everything will ultimately sink and drown.

He's a Londoner, he knows every inch of the city, but that doesn't mean a visit there isn't time-consuming, expensive and complex. On this hunt he's not bolstered by the luxury of police expenses, and although he's got money in the bank — for years he's had nothing much to spend it on — he still itches with resentment at the petrol receipts, the congestion charge, the NCP ticket.

Hatton Garden has always, to Caffery's eyes, seemed curiously placed. Cheek by jowl with Fleet Street and its giant newspaper offices, which when he was growing up hadn't yet made their switch to the Eastern docks; he still can't imagine how the two places have come to live so close together. The press buildings have gone, but the jewellers are still here — the long hill of Hatton Garden rising up from Holborn to Clerkenwell, overshadowed by the white Ziggurat building, and flanked on both sides by row after row of bullion and diamond dealers. Some are mere holes in the wall, with sliding shutters to speak into, or concrete staircases in the backs of anonymous buildings. Others have shining gilded shop fronts, displays glistening. It's like a Harry Potter movie set.

He finds the jeweller's in a side road halfway up the hill. It isn't big, but the owners have installed a high-security entry system, a two-door airlock bristling with cameras where you have to wait to be allowed to enter or exit. Caffery waits patiently, one hand in his jacket pocket, fiddling with the ring and the chain he's jammed in there. The interior of the shop is dark, but after a moment or two a figure appears. He goes around the darkened shop switching on lights and one by one the display cabinets come to life.

'Sorry.' Caffery holds up his warrant card

276

as the man comes to open the internal door. 'I'm not a customer. You can save the leccy.'

The man lets him in then goes around dutifully flicking all the switches to off. He's about Caffery's age and very small. Like a man in miniature, he wears a respectable suit and his hair cut very short and initially Caffery finds him hard to place. At first glance he'd have said Levantine — something about the angularity of his skull — but the complexion is pale, the hair is fair, and his accent is pure East London. Possibly something Jewish somewhere, but he's as mixed and varied in his blood as London is.

'Michael Beale.' He shakes Caffery's hand, his eyes flitting to the police badge. He registers it but he's not flustered by it. In a place like this it's probably commonplace. 'Welcome. Come in. Do you want to sit somewhere private? In the back perhaps? If we sit out here in the front we're going to be disturbed, I can guarantee it.'

'The back then.' Caffery puts his card away. 'Go ahead.'

They go into the office. It's just a cubbyhole, but it's been decorated like a country bed and breakfast, with family pet portraits in cheap frames on the woodchip paper. A stained net curtain hangs in front of the grimed window. Caffery can't see what lies beyond but he can guess. Fire escapes, wheelie bins and pigeons. It's funny, he's been in the countryside for two years but the city is still imprinted on him like an acid plate.

'What can I do for you?' Michael flicks the switch on the kettle and begins rinsing out the dirty mugs that clutter the sink. 'Is it the robbery again?'

'No. I'm from out of town.'

He pulls the chain out of his pocket and puts it on the table. Michael stops what he's doing. Mug still in his hand, he bends over and peers at the chain.

'Plated. No hallmark. If you're after an identification then you'll be lost, I'm afraid.'

'And what about this?'

Again Michael bends his head and peers at the ring. This time he doesn't dismiss it instantly. He wrinkles his nose so his glasses inch up a bit. He turns his head from side to side, his brow furrowed.

'I've got photos too.'

Caffery's been to the Scientific Support department at HQ. He's not on duty but they don't know that. He's asked them to photograph the ring and has convinced them to backdate the request so it's in his duty time. There are two 8 × 10 photos which he holds out to Michael.

'Yes. It's one of ours. Nineteen eighty-one. Thirty-three years ago. When my father was running the company.'

'Your father? Is he alive?'

Michael shakes his head. 'He went in 1997. BSE, if you can believe it. Ten thousand to one chance of getting it, that's what they told us. Dad told us that if it's a ten thousand to one, somebody has to be the one. To make it fair on the other nine thousand nine hundred and ninety-nine.'

'He'd have made this ring?'

'He'd be the only person who could have made it — we're a small operation.'

Caffery glances up at a dust-covered filing cabinet in the corner. On top of it is a stack of plain blue folders bulging with paper. 'You keep records. Can we find out who it was commissioned by?'

Michael follows Caffery's eyes to the cabinet, but he shakes his head. 'No — they only go back as far as the nineties. And besides, mostly what you see there is appraisal stuff, for insurance companies.' He turns the ring from side to side, squinting at it. 'The gold was assayed here in London — and that makes it a pretty common breed — but . . .'

He stands. He put his mug on the draining board and goes into the shop front. He returns a few moments later holding a jeweller's loupe. He takes up the ring and examines it carefully.

'What is it?'

Michael is silent, turning the ring side to side, his face a mask of concentration.

'I know this ring. I know it. This symbol. I

just . . .' He screws up his face, groping for the memory. Caffery sits quite still, waiting. After a long silence, Michael rocks back in his chair, a triumphant smile on his face. 'Yes, bloody hell, what're the chances? I *do* remember. I was here when it was made.' He digs his finger on the table. 'Right here — in this chair. I remember because Dad was grumbling he had to have special punches commissioned for these two symbols. We didn't use lasers in those days. I must have been — what? Nine? Ten?'

'Who was it made for?'

'The space-junk guy.'

'The space-junk guy?'

'Yes — he was the coolest guy I'd ever met. Something went wrong with the punches, I can't remember, but the guy had to hang around while Dad finished the ring, and I ended up sitting in here with him while he waited. We talked — you know, me trying to be grown-up, rattling on.'

'About?'

'Spacecraft. That's the reason I remember him. He was telling me stories that opened my eyes up like I'll never forget. About how there was this huge asteroid belt developing round the world, made up of bits of old satellites, discarded parts of spacecraft. He said it'd get to the point where you couldn't send a rocket into space without it hitting something. That every time there was a collision it'd put more junk into orbit. I thought it was the most amazing thing I'd ever heard. Brilliant. Absolutely brilliant. I've still got an obsession with space to this day.'

'And his surname?'

'Jimmy?' Michael shrugs. 'Well, I don't remember that. All I remember is the space stuff. Afterwards I just referred to him as the space-junk man. We talked about him a lot — I mean, I talked about him. I became a dreamer. I got a subscription to *Omni* after that, became a Trekkie, etc. I think I bored my parents to death, if you want the truth. I never saw him again though.'

'You can't remember anything else to identify him? His job? Where he came from?'

'I suppose I thought he might be something in NASA. Back then we were still buzzing about the space race, if you recall; it wasn't that long since all that had happened. In my head I must have had some dream he was an astronaut or something.' He shakes his head. 'I was a kid — what can I say?'

'What did he look like?'

'White, tall — I think, but everyone looks tall when you're ten. Especially when you're a short-arse into the bargain, like me.'

'Did he mention where he lived?'

Michael bites his lip, staring into mid-air, concentrating hard. 'This was years ago, mind? I'd forgotten about it all until now.' He shakes his head. 'No. I'm sorry. Nothing.'

Caffery picks up the loupe. 'May I?'

'Go ahead.'

He examines the ring through the glass. It's astonishing the clarity the loupe gives the marks. It's high time he got his eyes retested, he decides.

'The symbols? Mean anything to you? This triangle with the star burst?'

'Masonic, I guess. Not that I know anything about the Masons. I mean — no disrespect — but it's more of a cop thing, isn't it, the Lodge?'

'Depends on the cop.' Caffery sits back and looks again at the photograph. 'What about this — the winged figure. Does that mean anything to you?'

'No. It's nothing to do with the jewellery business. I've never seen it before.'

'You don't remember him saying what it was about?'

'I'm sorry. I'm really sorry. I mean — you know. Years and years ago and all that.'

Caffery gets to his feet. 'Don't be sorry. That you remembered anything at all is a result. You'd be surprised — a lot of people can't remember anything from their childhood. It's just a blur.'

'Well, that's probably because they've reason to forget. I've got nothing to forget. I had a good childhood. I miss it.'

'Then you're luckier than most. Much luckier.'

SUNSET

Evening seems to fall over The Turrets faster than usual. The shadows lengthen rapidly, and almost ahead of time a dark stain creeps up at the edges of the sky. Ian has been down to the bottom of the drive to collect the company car the men left down there earlier, and now he is back at the house, next to the telephone junction box. He is smoking a cigar and watching the few clouds on the horizon. He is thirty-three years of age and he reckons he's seen sunsets in more different countries than most men his age. He's seen the Northern Lights, and he's seen the skies in Africa. He hasn't stayed still very long.

He stubs out the cigar by pinching the end of it. Lets the ash fall to the ground and pockets the stub for later. He doesn't throw things like that away, it goes against his training. Ian was in the Foreign Legion for five years and in the Legion you are taught to live like animals, to waste nothing. It's a hard life — and full of desperadoes. Full of life's chancers. Anyone with little enough to lose that he can walk through a door in Marseilles, five skiddies and a toothbrush in his bag, and know his life has changed entirely. It was like being in some crazy film — *The Matrix* — bam!: everything changes when you swallow that red pill. But it was perfect training for the job he's in now.

When he left the Legion the trend among his peers was to go into security. One firm in particular caught Ian's eye: Gauntlet Systems. They were using a weapon called the Wolf Missile, and the rumour went that it was named after the killings here in the Mendips all those years ago. No one who lived in this area at the time of the Wolf murders could fail to be affected by it, and Ian was no exception. Curiosity drove him into the company, though he never foresaw it leading back here, to Litton.

Ian is cold. He's been out here at the telephone junction box for almost half an hour and he's only in his T-shirt. He collects his tools together and goes back inside.

The kitchen lights are on. Honig is in Oliver Anchor-Ferrers' comfortable leather recliner, his legs stuck out a long way, his pose restful. He's wearing a wine-red polo-neck and jeans, but his feet are bare. In front of him the television flickers — a comedy programme — the canned laughter floating through the room. A plate with a piece of

Mrs Anchor-Ferrers' cake rests on the chair arm. Honig is eating slowly, his eyes locked on the screen.

Ian clears his throat to get Honig's attention. 'Got the car back, but I can't get the phone reconnected.'

Honig seems to stop chewing for a moment, but it's just a pause, then he continues eating, not taking his eyes off the television or giving any indication he's heard. The on-screen audience laughs and he joins in. A lazy, huffing laugh, that makes his cheeks puff out. Ian waits until the noise on the screen dies down, and a little incidental music plays, then he tries again.

'Just thought you should know, I disabled it, but I can't reenable it now. There's something wrong with it.'

Once again Honig puts back his head and laughs at something on the television.

Ian waits. 'So,' he says, louder this time. 'I'm here to report that I can't get the phone reconnected.'

At last Honig turns his eyes to Ian. They're pale and calm. And completely uninterested.

'I thought you were the technical guy — you've had enough time to study the place.'

It was dawn yesterday morning when Ian disconnected the phone, and he was in a hurry. There were so many other things to organize before the Anchor-Ferrers arrived. Gauntlet were worried that there was a hole in their intelligence about the house's alarm system, something that didn't quite add up, as if Oliver Anchor-Ferrers had added something extra to the system that hadn't come out in the research. Ian isn't too worried about that; he's quietly confident there's nothing else to look for. Nevertheless, setting up a signal to disable the alarm when the phone wires were cut tested his technical knowledge to the hilt. 'I'll look at it again tomorrow.'

'Tomorrow's not good enough. We need to send the videos.'

'We don't need ISDN — we can do it from the cell phone. There's reception at the bottom of the driveway.'

'A file that big?'

'Yes. We can sex it up a bit, make it a piece of art.'

'Let's do it.' Honig kills the television, pushes himself out of the chair, shoves his feet, sockless, into a pair of boots and pulls on his jacket. He hooks the keys up from the table and turns for the side door, but stops for a moment. He turns to look back at the kitchen, and gives a long sniff.

'What is it?'

Honig shakes his head. 'Can you smell something?'

Ian sniffs. 'What can you smell?'

'It's probably those fucking innards. Three days — no wonder they stink. In the morning we're taking them out of the scullery and into the forest. Get rid of them.'

THE RAILWAY CUTTING

It's a strange thing, but there have been moments today when Caffery has imagined someone speaking to him. A man's voice — an older man. It's impossible to distinguish words, but the voice seems to be pleading. Caffery dismisses it as tiredness. That and the endless drone of London traffic.

When he leaves the jeweller's he calls Johnny Patel and, instead of turning west, he heads across London Bridge and down towards the part of town North Londoners like to pretend doesn't exist. South London, the badlands. Specifically Lewisham, the borough that has the highest violent crime rate in the UK. It is his home turf, but somehow today he feels like a visitor here. In the countryside, a year can pass on the clock and on the London clock it's just a second — a flickering mosaic of light and colour in which lives change beyond recognition. Always regenerating, always new. It used to be normality to him, now it's like a fast edited animation. His head struggles to keep up with the visual input.

He passes the graffiti-strewn estates and the dank railway bridges, the parks and the high streets. The takeaways, the Chinese fish-and-chip shops, the Indian pizza parlours. And when he stops, puts on the handbrake and turns to stare at his surroundings, his heart pounds as if he's doing something he could get stopped for, questioned.

He is in the road he grew up and lived in for nearly forty years.

He gets out of the car and walks back a hundred yards to a place where cars used to cross a small bridge which straddles a railway cutting. As a child he was always told by his parents that the cuttings were built in the nineteenth century by Gurkhas using pick-axes and shovels. He still doesn't know if that's true, but what he can see is that they're not designed for modern traffic because he finds the bridge has been closed. There's a notice saying it's structurally unsound.

He stands on the bridge and peers down along the railway cutting. The lights on the gantry above are red, sending an eerie glow out over the tracks. Caffery's old house is on the right, set a hundred feet from the embankment. There's a tree in the back garden, hanging over the fence. It's been pollarded since Caffery left here, but it draws him nevertheless. That's where their tree house used to be. Thirty-five years ago there was a tree house.

Caffery measures the gap with his eyes — as he has over and over again — from the back of his old home to the back of Penderecki's garden.

Penderecki's house has a fresh coat of paint, there's been a glass extension added. There are blinds at the windows — blue, with big pink dots. In the old paedophile's garden a children's climbing frame with tyre swings stands in the middle of the lawn. There's a fading plastic Wendy house on his left. Penderecki would love that irony — that children are living here. If spirits do exist then he'd be happily flitting from one bedroom to the other, watching the children in the bathtub. Caffery wonders if the family who live here now know about the house's past. There's a piece of rusting barbed wire at the end of the garden; it must be the same wire that's been here for years, because it sags in the place Caffery has always climbed over it.

He routinely broke into Penderecki's house in the three decades after Ewan's disappearance, when he was still living here. He's torn the place apart — been through it a hundred times. He's thought of everything. He's pulled up floorboards and searched in chimneys and through the attic. He's been round the tiny garden like a bloodhound, pulling up stones and pushing a reinforcing rod into the earth every few centimetres. Nothing.

Derek Yates *has* to know what happened that day. He just has to.

THE PEPPERMINT ROOM

Matilda hears the back door slamming. She watches the arc of headlights cross the ceiling, and listens as a car reverses out of the old outbuilding behind the house. She is manacled by the ankle, though she hardly needs to be. There's no fight left. Her body is transparent, just a shell — no substance and no desire for anything.

Honey made her undress. He humiliated her. But in the end that was all. The assault she'd expected didn't happen. Instead he told her to get dressed and brought her back to the room. 'You look so much better, Mrs Robinson. I don't mean you look better dressed — that would be disrespectful. I mean your face — you look almost normal.'

She pressed the back of her hand into her eyes, made it appear as if she was pushing the hair from her face. She was not going to cry. She would not cry.

'Thank you,' she said, when he finished manacling her to the radiator. 'Thank you.'

Honey — or whatever his real name is — might be a father, she decides. He might have children, because he knows how to twist the screw. He knows how to work everything. He hasn't raped her, he's done something worse, because however much he's humiliated her it is nothing, absolutely nothing compared to the fear he's instilled in her that the next time — whenever the next time is: tonight or tomorrow — it will be Lucia.

That fear sits in Matilda's throat like a stone, not moving, not getting any smaller. That's the cleverness of the men, they know exactly how to hurt a parent.

GEORGE CLOONEY

It takes Caffery almost an hour to drive the two miles through London traffic from Lewisham to Catford, and when he arrives shops are closing, people are making their way home. Johnny Patel's first-floor office window is the only one with a light on; the row of shops below have grilles on the windows. An accumulated black grease of urine and dirt seems to coat every doorway.

'You haven't changed a bit.' Patel stands in the scruffy doorway to his office, cigarette ends and chewing gum under his feet, and scrutinizes Caffery. 'I'd hoped for a bit of a paunch at least, but it seems that's too much to ask. Ungrateful effing bastard. I should slam the door in your face.'

'Always a pleasure, Johnny. Always a pleasure.'

'What have you done to yourself? Here, let me get a good look.' He turns Jack so he can examine him in better light, squinting at his face. 'Is it Botox? If it is, it's a bloody good job they've done. Fillers? You know what — I couldn't tell, I really couldn't.' He stretches his neck out, pointing at his face, inviting Caffery to scrutinize his skin. 'What do you think? George Clooney or is it a fail? More Shane Warne? You can tell me the truth. Come on.' He nudges Caffery. Leans closer. 'I'll give you a hint — I'm hoping for the Clooney answer.'

'It's Clooney. Definitely Clooney.'

'You don't even know who Shane Warne is, do you?'

'Johnny, you haven't changed a bit.'

Patel laughs. He stands back and lets Caffery into the dingy hallway. Years ago this scuffed industrial carpet with the fag burns, the staircase with the ochre line of hand grease on the wall from years of human traffic, wouldn't have been noteworthy. Caffery would have just walked straight past it. But his eyes have got used to the clean green of the countryside; his vision is stripped clear and he sees the scruffiness in detail.

Patel leads Caffery up the flight of stairs. The office is a single room with a partitioned glass area at the far end, rows of dormant computers placed at regular intervals along one side. On each available piece of wall is a whiteboard with names scribbled on it. He is struck by how much it resembles the incident room of a working police station. This is Patel's own business and if Caffery had to guess at the staff demographic it would be: 50 per cent totty and 50 per cent overweight ex-cops all sitting at the work stations, their eyes glued to the screens. Once a cop, always a cop, he supposes.

Patel takes him to a glass cubicle where a desk light is on. He's got three thirty-inch monitors on his vast desk and each has lines of names scrolling down the screen.

'You're not going to like it.' Patel swings a chair round for Caffery to sit. 'While you've been sitting in traffic I've been name-crunching.'

'And . . . ?'

He sighs. 'It's a needle in a haystack. As a population we're not in love with the idea of marriage any more, but back then we were crazy about it. Matilda and James, they weren't common names in the eighties, but I've put in a parameter of two years — starting from the beginning of 1981 — and you're still talking thirty to forty thousand weddings.'

'Forty thousand? Jesus.'

'Yes. And so far about thirty-five between a James and Matilda. That's just in inner London boroughs — assuming they *were* married in London. I mean, I know you got terrier genes in your DNA, Jack, but even you won't be able to bottom out that many.'

'Shit.' Caffery folds his arms and drops his head back, staring up at the ceiling. Patel's right. Even if there was an entire police unit devoted to the task it would take weeks to track down every last name on the list.

He reaches into his rucksack and pulls out the photos of the ring. He puts them on the table. Patel looks down at them. Shakes his head and looks up. 'I dunno. Nothing's jumping out at me.'

'What about the winged figure? Mercury presumably.'

'Mercury the messenger — didn't one of the phone companies use him as a logo or something? And the triangle . . . Masonic?'

'Presumably.'

'Were you ever Lodge?'

'Christ no. You?'

Patel points to his face. ' 'Scuse me, Jack, with the length of our friendship have you still not noticed? I hate to break this to you without warning, but Jack, *I'm not white*. I don't know, the Lodge might have changed now, but back in the day there was no way. No way at all. I never even got the invite.' He pulls his iPhone out and starts scrolling down his contacts. 'However . . . it just so happens I am the networking king, and I know someone who studies heraldry and guilds. Want me to give them a call?'

'Of course.'

Patel finds the number. He dials it. Caffery hears a woman's voice answer.

'Hey, it's me.' The woman says something

297

and Patel's smile fades. 'Yeah, well, I can explain that . . . Hang on.' He puts a hand over the phone. 'I'll take this outside,' he mutters. 'Won't be a second.'

He leaves the room and the last thing Caffery hears him say is, 'I'm at the office, I promise you that's where I am.'

The door slams and Caffery is left in the office alone. He stares at the computer screen. He wonders if it would be like this if he'd stayed in London. Working in a scummy office over Catford High Street. Married, seeing women on the side. In the street below someone is shouting, a dog is barking. He can see a man in a filthy parka, his hair tied back in a ponytail, standing in the door of an off-licence, yelling abuse into the interior.

When Patel comes back Caffery hasn't moved. Caffery watches his old friend, one eyebrow raised.

'What?' Patel says. 'What's that look for?'

'Nice to see you're still the person I once knew.'

'What're you talking about?'

'You're wearing a wedding ring, though I'm sure it's not the same marriage that I helped you destroy. Was that the new Mrs Patel you were speaking to?'

'You know what, Jack — they say a suspicious mind is always a guilty mind. How do you know the person I just spoke to is anything more than a friend?'

'OK, that's a challenge. Tell me — what's her name?'

Patel shakes his head. Rubs his forehead. 'Nina. Why?'

'Nah — you haven't changed.' Caffery gives a small smile. 'You haven't changed. I can tell by the way you said her name. NEEENA.'

'Amen, Father Caffery, thank you for the sermon.'

Caffery says nothing. Secretly he prefers it this way — nothing changing. The bad guys still the bad guys, the chancers still getting away with it. Patel still a skanky old man with the morals of a dingo. It makes him feel he's less of an animal — more human. And not set apart from the world by the fact he can't get a relationship to work.

'She's going to look into it for you.'

'Thank you. I'll pay you for your time.'

'OK, I was going to get to that. I know I owe you big time, but eventually reality is going to come back and bite me in the arse. I've got a tally, OK. I've got this giant favours scoreboard, like at Wembley. And you will thank me for keeping you clearly informed when you're about to go past your credit limit. Won't you?'

'So how much credit have I got?'

Patel thinks about it. 'Twelve hours. That's nearly five hundred quid's worth.'

'Generous.'

'And the other thing is, you'll have to be a

bit nicer about Nina. She might turn out to be the love of my life. Then how will you feel, eh?'

THINK LIKE ME

Oliver doesn't remember the last time he cried and now there's no stopping it. His eyes, still sore from the time they were taped open, seem to have turned into geysers. They just flow and flow and flow.

The men didn't rape Matilda. They let her climb down and get dressed. It doesn't matter of course, because, as with the movie Honey told them not to worry about, the threat is now so firmly planted in Oliver's mind it will never go away. Over and over again he pictures Honey holding the pen against Matilda's white stomach. Pictures the two men smiling up at Lucia. This is worse than the pain of the operation. He sits propped like a spent puppet against the wall, arms flopped helplessly at his sides, his mouth open, tears running down his face. A helpless shuffling old man, incapable of standing straight, let alone protecting what is precious to him.

After a long long time, and only when darkness has fallen outside, he begins to calm himself. There has been hardly any sound from the rest of the house. The men have left the house — he heard a car starting outside. They haven't come back yet.

A presence comes to him. It is a man, dark and lean. He is dressed in a modest suit, off the peg, nothing flashy, and he keeps his hands in his pockets. He comes into the room, moving slowly, deliberately, taking everything in.

John Bancroft. It goes against Oliver's scientific scepticism, but he firmly believes he's witnessing Bancroft entering the room at some point in the future when it is over. When they are all dead.

Bancroft stops now and peers down at something. Oliver's own corpse. Bancroft takes note of it, but he doesn't overreact. Doesn't panic. He is too professional — he's seen this before. Instead he is looking round the room for something, some intangible element which will illuminate the incomprehensible. He stands near the window and closes his eyes briefly, as if trying to tune out everything except the message. Unconsciously, Oliver raises a wavering hand to this spectre, wanting to touch him on the forehead. To get the message to him.

'Think like me,' he whispers. 'Think like me.'

John Bancroft doesn't move.

'Come on, think like me — look at the rug.'

Bancroft's eyes open then, in surprise. Slowly he turns to Oliver. He comes and crouches next to him. Looks at the rug.

Convinced he's in the presence of something spiritual, Oliver flips over the rug, scrabbles the pen out from its hiding place, and begins to write, feverishly:

The fact these men persist in using my connection with Minnet Kable to play psychological games on us only confirms to me that they are working for one of the companies I sold the Wolf system to. I have written a book about my life, it is possible one of the companies I've written about may be threatened by this.

However I sold the system to so many corporations worldwide that I can't list them all here. It would be a jumble of names and histories.

Bancroft puts his finger on the rug and frowns slightly. He has nowhere to start.

Furiously Oliver tries to think of more clues. If he had the name of the company he could fight back. Or, in the event of his death, John Bancroft could. His only chance to find that out is now, right now, while the men are here, giving subtle hints to their identity. But they're giving nothing away. That will be a vital part of their remit, never to reveal who they are working for.

He feels Bancroft's attention wavering. 'Don't go,' he pleads. 'Please don't go.'

But Bancroft is tired of waiting. He half straightens, his eyes raised to the window, as if his name has been called, and then he begins to dim. Like a candle his image flickers and dies.

All that is left is the empty bedroom.

PIETR HAVILLAND

The Chrysler 300C, with its new-smelling upholstery and its radiator grille like the mouth on a baleen whale, is a kind of joke. A pantomime gangster car — it's got no real cachet to it, yet people are so easily convinced, and the 300C looks way out of place in the quiet English countryside. It signals power or danger to the casual onlooker. Not that anyone wanders across these vast parklands of the Anchor-Ferrers, but better safe than sorry, so the men don't put on the headlights as they go slowly down the driveway, out of the gates, and into the lay-by opposite, where the phone signal can be picked up.

Honig feels faintly self-conscious sitting there while in the passenger seat Ian the Geek fiddles with his iPad and his smartphone. Honig's still got serious reservations about Ian the Geek. He's sold himself to Pietr as a shoot-to-kill on-the-balls technical shiznit — and OK, he's had his uses. To give him his due, it was Ian the Geek who learned about the autobiography Oliver is writing. He did that by passing spyware on to Oliver's phone disguised as a Bluetoothed airport advert in a business lounge in Munich. All Oliver will have noticed is the occasional flash of the Bluetooth icon on his phone; when the phone was synced, the virus jumped to his laptop and began installing a custom-built spyware with a keystroke recorder that fed all the information on Oliver's computer to Havilland. This is how Havilland learned that Oliver's autobiography contains information about Gauntlet Systems which could harm the company.

But otherwise Ian the Geek is patchy. Very patchy. And unpredictable. He notched up a fail on getting a landline back into The Turrets, and because Oliver Anchor-Ferrers changed contracts on the alarm installation there's a grey area about the security system that Ian the Geek still hasn't adequately explained. And all that stuff in New York with Havilland? Ian the Geek arguing about bringing Minnet Kable into the operation, as if he was on some moral crusade or something? The hyper-inappropriateness of defying the boss is stunning to Honig. And even more stunning is the fact the bastard seems to have got away with it. Evidently knowing shit about spybots gives you carte blanche to argue with the boss because, while Havilland didn't junk using the Minnet Kable story, he didn't drop-kick Ian the Geek off the job either. Instead he let him go ahead with it, regardless of his outlandish temerity. It's obvious Havilland's completely blinded by Ian the Geek's sleight of hand in the techy department, his nerdy glasses and smart-phones and computers.

Honig watches Ian the Geek closely as he works. Grudgingly, he has to admit, the video he's edited together, encrypted, zipped and mailed *is* pretty good. It shows Matilda naked. It shows her husband watching. Everything Havilland wants is right there in Oliver's face. Confusion, desperation, fear. Havilland is currently in Mozambique — which has the advantage of being in roughly the same time zone as the UK. He is now sitting in his hotel room watching the video. Pietr Havilland hates Oliver Anchor-Ferrers more than anyone on the planet and seeing him helpless like this is exactly what he wants.

When anything threatens his company, Gauntlet Systems, Pietr Havilland doesn't believe in softly softly catchee monkey. He believes in shoot hard, ask questions later — kill them all, let God decide. Like a viper, he paralyses the prey. Or rather, he sends his soldiers to paralyse. And for this he pays very, *very* well. On this job Honig has negotiated a unique pay structure: 25 per cent of their 'bonus' up front, then incremental payments

— each time video evidence of the family's suffering reaches Havilland, another 5 per cent of the payment is sent, which leaves five episodes of torture and humiliation still to come. When their final objective is achieved they will receive a lump sum of 30 per cent — leaving a total of 15 per cent to collect when they get their first-class flights back to New York.

The job is easy to achieve and the financial terms are extremely good. It's a golden-goose job and has been awarded to Honig because of his loyalty and status in the company. It irritates him that Ian the Geek, by default, is being paid in exactly the same way. The anorak. Every day he should be getting down and licking Honig's shoes clean, just to show his gratitude.

He sighs and stares out of the window at the woods that run along the side of the lane. Impenetrable purple and grey shadows.

Honig's a brilliant performer, but that's his only skill. He's not the badass he pretends, not at all. And although he is good at acting, lately he's been getting tired of it. The way he and Ian the Geek were talking to each other yesterday: *Yes, Mr Honey, OK, Mr Molina* — no first names, as if they were in a Tarantino movie and were about to put on loud music and cut someone's ear off — he wishes he believed in it. He wishes he was a proper villain, a hard bastard, someone who could have done every bit of that Sudoku puzzle while Mrs Anchor-Ferrers was hanging from the ceiling.

He's not. The Sudoku book got filled in with nonsense. Honig was concentrating on his act. The act which is making him tired, cold and slightly disgusted with himself.

Honig is British, but at the moment he lives in a modest house on the outskirts of Silver Spring, Maryland, USA. What no one in the company would guess is that his life is changing. He has a brand-new wife, a beautiful half-Puerto Rican girl from New Jersey who works in a beautician's in the local shopping mall. The beauty clinic is called Strawberries and Cream and she is obliged to wear a pale pink tunic and slacks to work. She hates the uniform, thinks it's cheesy. Honig loves it. Her black hair against the pale pink is the happiest, prettiest sight he can imagine.

He would go to the ends of the world for her — do anything just for five minutes of watching her wake and shower and dress, tie her hair back and lean into the mirror to examine her make-up. Usually she kisses him, then puts on her lipstick carefully, outlining the lips before filling in the rest with expert ease. Sometimes, just to wind her up, he grabs her on the way out of the house and kisses her again before she can get out of the door. Then she yells and play-slaps him and complains that she's got to do her lipstick all over again and does he know how much good lipstick costs these days?

Bubblegum Mania. That's the name of her lipstick. He knows because he's got a stick of it in his pocket to remind him of her. He pushes his hand in there and rubs his fingers along the casing. He misses his house, his home. He doesn't like this part of England. It is damp and the valleys mean you can never see very far. He wonders exactly how far away from here the bodies of those teenagers were found. He thinks about those deer intestines, stinking the place up, covered in flies. He doesn't know why they're bothering him so much — it's as if they've left a brief, transient stain in his mind.

Weird bastard, Kable, to have done what he did. Weird-looking too. Long face and strange teeth. What would he be doing at this very moment? He must still be inside — no way he could have been released yet. Is he rocking back and forward on his bed, watching monkeys climbing the walls of his cell? Alien radio beams and TV news presenters whispering secret messages? Or maybe he's actually much more sane than anyone thinks. Maybe he'd be honoured to know someone has mimicked his crime.

Ian the Geek's iPad pings.

'Bingo,' he says, holding it out to show Honig the screen. Four thousand dollars for the video of Matilda has just hit his bank account. That means Havilland approves. It feels good.

'See?' Ian the Geek says. 'Told you we didn't need the landline.'

'There's still no signal up at the house. Which isn't perfect.'

'Why? We can always come down here to stay in contact.'

'Yeah,' Honig says, wryly. 'I mean what's the worst that can happen if we haven't got a phone up there? A couple of tossers posing as cops walk in and tie us up?' He turns the engine on. 'Come on. It's time we ate something.'

THE EYE OF PROVIDENCE

Back in his home in the Mendips, Caffery sleeps well for the first time since Tracey Lamb died. When he wakes his head is clear. He sees where he is going and it feels good and right. His old determination and drive are back.

Cross-matching weddings registered in 1981 in the London boroughs is going to take days. Even if Johnny Patel finds a James and Matilda, they won't necessarily be the right ones. And if he finds the right ones, what are the chances they are still together? The way divorce rates have climbed sky-high, surnames will have changed, people will have moved, dispersed, left the country, died. It's an almost impossible challenge. The Freemasonry lead sounds more promising. He makes coffee and calls Patel, finding him in a good mood. Things must have gone well with Nina last night.

'Just so you know, she's not only beautiful but a very nice person too. With the morals of an angel and the brains of an Einstein. She spent a long time last night looking into this.'

'Generous with her time too, by all accounts.'

'Ahem — remember the deal, Jack?'

'I remember. Go on.'

'OK. So, according to her, all the Masonic lodges have got different symbols. Like the agriculture lodge has an ear of corn, for example. There's pretty much every symbol you can imagine.'

'What about the one on the ring?'

'Mercury? She thinks it's something to do with an engineers' guild down in Farnborough. But the Mercury in their symbol is pictured differently — their Mercury isn't on top of a globe like this one is. She's adamant about that. Now, Jack, have a proper butcher's at the circle in the triangle? The one with rays coming out of it. That's the bit she's not sure about. She says it looks like the Eye of Providence.'

Caffery studies the photographs splayed out on his kitchen table. 'Is that what it's called? I thought it was the all-seeing eye — it's Masonic, isn't it?'

'They do use it — but it's not exclusive to the Masons. Nina says it's one of those images that has been picked up and used all over the world down the ages. Probably came from Egypt originally. It's on the American

313

dollar bill, at the top of a pyramid, which is why the conspiracy theorists say the American government is a Masonic clique — a load of BS, of course. Though when you look around and see the number of US government agencies who've used it as a symbol, you start wondering. Just because you're paranoid doesn't mean they aren't after you, right? But . . . there's a problem.'

'Oh joy.'

'Open your emails.'

Caffery sighs. He pushes his coffee cup out of the way and drags his iPad over. There's a message from Patel with an attachment, which he opens.

It shows a Masonic 'lodge certificate'. Some of the names have been blocked out to preserve anonymity, but it's not identities Patel wants Caffery to see — it's the symbols at the head of the paper. A set square and a pair of compasses arranged in a diamond shape, next to them an eye.

'See what I'm seeing?'

'The same radiating lines, but it's just the eye on its own.' Caffery traces his finger across the screen. From the corner of the room, Bear watches him steadily. 'It's not a triangle. And the eye on the ring is rounder.' He compares the two; the shape of the eye in the triangle on the ring is a circle, whereas the Masonic eye is almond. And though he thought he'd once seen a triangle on a

314

Masonic lodge, it must actually have been this — the set square and compasses diamond.

'Not Masonic then?'

'I'm sorry, Jack. It's a dead end.'

He shakes his head, deflated. His good mood has gone. Maybe he should just open the malt whisky that sits on the counter and get stuck in drinking now, at nine a.m. The road, which a few minutes ago seemed a little more navigable, has suddenly stretched out again — into infinity.

PAPER TIGERS

Morning at The Turrets. Theo Honig lies on his bed, his hand behind his head, and stares at the ceiling. Ian the Geek is snoring on the other camp bed, oblivious — he'd sleep through an earthquake — but something keeps waking Honig, and he can't put his finger on what. In the night three times he woke and went to the windows to check they were closed, but even when he'd checked and checked again he still slept uneasily, his dreams flitting across mashed faces, long scrawls of intestinal matter decorating trees.

He hates this damp rambling old pile of a mansion with its draughts and echoey halls and dark oak panelling. It is supposed to be early summer, but at night the place is freezing. And it smells too. All night long he's been conscious of that smell. He stares at the ceiling; it is damp and peeling in places and seems a million miles away. It must be at least ten feet tall. His ceiling at home is one of those low, functional things, covered in a freckled render so common in American houses. It is painted a pale yellow.

He misses it like crazy. And his wife.

He throws back the covers and pads across the kitchen, feels around in his jacket for the lipstick. He takes it out and winds it so the frosty tip comes up. He smells it, closing his eyes, remembering her soft black hair, the fragrant waxy slide of her lips against his. His wife doesn't know where he is at the moment — she knows he is in England, but she believes he is at a high-level meeting. She knows he works in the arms industry, but he's allowed her to think he works in design. He hasn't the courage to tell her the truth.

As fakes go, Theo Honig thinks he beats the pants off every paper tiger that ever walked the earth.

Oliver Anchor-Ferrers isn't going to die. Nor is Matilda. Nor is the girl, Lucia. None of them are. The whole job is an exercise in fear — in headfucks. Headfucks are Pietr Havilland's speciality. He knows how to inspire terror to achieve his goals. Often that takes time, and in this case it is scheduled to take six days. By the end of which none of the Anchor-Ferrers family will be permanently hurt. At least, not physically. But they will be traumatized beyond belief. As a result Oliver will have withdrawn the book he is working on, and it will never occur to him *ever* to write about the arms industry again.

317

He will feel sick every time he even thinks about it.

Moreover he will never know that Gauntlet Systems was behind the whole thing. That is Havilland's most important caveat: that Oliver Anchor-Ferrers never, *ever* learns the identity of his tormentors. If Oliver finds out Havilland is behind this, he will be in a position to involve the authorities and exact revenge. If he doesn't know then he has no starting point. The family will be too terrified to speak of it again — they will carry it to their graves. The only evidence that any of this happened will be the video clips of the family crying and begging — and those will remain encrypted on Havilland's hard-drive, for him to retrieve and enjoy at his leisure whenever he chooses.

This will be Honig's last job. He's already decided it — the very last. With the money he gets for this he's going to go legit. He'll enrol at one of those big universities in DC. Perhaps he'll go into design. Do the job his wife thinks he is doing. Anything is possible.

He sniffs the lipstick again. His wife's face comes to him. Then, frowning he lowers the silver tube and sniffs the air. His daydream evaporates. He recaps the lipstick and turns, scanning the kitchen.

That is what kept waking him overnight — the smell. It's not just a faint odour any more. The place fairly *stinks*.

318

THE COLONEL

The wedding ring doesn't belong to a Mason, but the marks on it must mean *something*. Caffery spends time googling various symbols, but if there is a link between an obsession with space junk, the image of Mercury and the odd eye in a triangle, it eludes him. He finds references to something called the Kessler syndrome back in the eighties, when NASA put money into mapping the junk that was already in space, but that's long ago. There's a US research programme under the auspices of the Defense Advance Research Projects Agency that might, possibly, be involved in monitoring space junk — its logo, he notices, incorporates the great American Seal and the Eye of Providence. But it's unlikely they'll be able to tell him who owns this damn dog. He's hit a dead end. If he wants the Walking Man to speak, he's going to have to start from square one again.

'Come on,' he tells Bear, who is sitting on the floor watching him. 'We're going back where we started.'

It feels stale and it feels old, but at least the Walking Man can't say he isn't thorough. Caffery and Bear return to the hamlet they set off from yesterday. They knock on the same doors they did yesterday — the names of the houses blurring together: Rose Cottage, Hollyhock Bank, Daisy Dene. On and on, an endless repetition of yesterday. The only difference is that today he has a picture of the ring and two names.

'James and Matilda — they'll be probably in their fifties or sixties. He's got something to do with space. Possibly an engineer? A scientist?'

But his hopes this new information might jog someone's memory are soon in the gutter. Nothing about the ring or the names means anything to anyone around here.

'I know a James,' says the woman in the yellow house. She's wearing pink jeans today — and a striped blue shirt. She doesn't ask him in this time. 'But his wife's name is Maureen. They're in West Bromwich.'

If Caffery's spirits are low then Bear's are even lower. Her head droops further with every door they knock on. Caffery buys a sandwich in the Co-op in the high street and shares it with her, sitting on the stone steps with their backs to the memorial, their heads warm in the sun, the names of the village's war dead behind them. Bear takes tiny morsels from Caffery's fingers with great delicacy.

'You're a well-mannered girl,' he tells her. 'Does that mean you come from a nice family? One of the big houses round here? Or is that my class prejudice at work?'

The sun moves high above the church tower. He's getting tired. That sensation is back — that odd, out-of-body feeling he had in London, of someone trying to get into his thoughts. Someone talking to him urgently: *Listen, listen.* He shakes his head, scrunches up the sandwich wrapper and drops it in the bin. Looks up at the hill rising above the village, to where the gables of Colonel Frink's house can be seen above the trees.

'What do you think, Bear? Do you think the colonel would like a visit?'

Bear looks back at him, her head on one side.

'I agree — he'll be chuffed to all buggery.'

They walk up the driveway in the midday sun, criss-crossed by the gaunt shadows of crows flying back and forward between the lime trees. On their right are the ghostly humped shapes of the BMX track. Caffery can't help thinking they look like ancient burial mounds. As if they should have grave markers mounted above them. He recalls the look on the nurse's face as she turned to look at the BMX track.

As he and Bear reach the front door he fumbles out his warrant card. The colonel is the type to insist on seeing ID — even though he knows exactly who Caffery is, he'll stick to protocol. Even if only to humiliate Caffery. That is always the way with men who've once held rank; they expect the world to go on in exactly the same way, people to bow and scrape, even when the army's just a dim and distant memory.

Caffery knocks this time, not trusting the bell. The door is opened almost immediately by the colonel, who wears a patched and threadbare sweater in olive green over a checked shirt. His glasses are perched on the end of his nose. He's got a glass of whisky in one hand and seems unsteady on his legs without his walking stick.

'What now?'

'Colonel Frink? Detective Inspector Caffery.'

'Yes, I remember you. I do have the faint remnants of a memory span, you know. I can go back further than five minutes ago. Remarkable but true.'

'Can I come in?'

'I don't think so.'

Caffery glances over the colonel's shoulder. Inside the house has the look of a fading chateau, a high-ceilinged hallway with a curved stone staircase leading upwards. Dusty oil portraits hang at intervals along the water-stained wallpaper, and further towards the back of the house a glass-eyed deer's head stares at him from the wall. Evidently the cleaner still hasn't been; the place looks as if a tornado has come through and there's a melancholy, damp smell emanating from inside. In the lighted kitchen at the end of the corridor, Caffery can make out the back of the colonel's wife's head. Hunched in her wheelchair, a thick mop of hair above a pink waffle blanket.

'Fair enough. Just wanted to ask you another question.' He returns the card to his pocket. 'About this dog again.'

'What about it? Has it changed appearance?' The colonel lurches out of the doorway, slopping whisky on the mat. He glowers at the dog. 'Am I going to recognize it better today than I could yesterday? Is that it?'

'I've got some names.' He tugs the laminated print out of the plastic envelope. 'Matilda and James. Possibly known as Tillie and Jim, Tilda and Jimmy?'

'Never heard of them. Is that all?'

Caffery holds out the photograph. 'This is the inside of a wedding ring. Does it suggest anything to you?'

The colonel peers at it blearily, swaying slightly as if there was a wind pushing him off balance. 'I told you, I don't know anyone by the name of James. We haven't been here for years, and like I said, we don't socialize. Now, for pity's sake will you please stop pestering us?'

He starts to close the door, but Caffery, with the old salesman technique, slides a foot in to prevent him. 'Please, Colonel Frink. Please, I've got one last question. The land at the bottom of your garden — where the kids ride their bikes.'

'What about it?'

'Is there something special about it?'

Frink's face grows even darker. 'Is that meant to be a joke?'

'No. I don't know —'

'A detective? And you don't know about that piece of ground?'

'Seriously, I don't. This isn't a game. I'm a long way off my patch. If I've said something inappropriate, then I apologize, but —'

'Inappropriate,' the colonel says dully. 'Utterly inappropriate.'

'Then I'm sorry.'

'Accepted. Now are you going to leave us alone?'

Reluctantly, Caffery returns the photos to the wallet. Fishes his car keys out. This is getting sour. 'I'm sorry — a waste of your time.'

He walks back down the path, Bear tripping along behind him. He's almost across the weed-cracked courtyard when the colonel calls him from behind.

'You walked all this way.'

Caffery stops in his tracks. He waits a moment, then turns. 'I beg your pardon?'

'I said you came all this way for a second time.' The colonel looks something monstrous, filling the doorway. 'Asked the same questions twice.'

'What's your point?'

'Persistence. It's something I like. You could count a hundred men in your regiment and you'd only find one who had true persistence. It's a rarity. Like gold dust.'

'And?'

'You might want to think about speaking to someone in the Royal Signals.'

'Beg pardon?'

'Royal Signals.'

Caffery comes back to the doorway and pulls the photo out. Studies it. 'What? What makes you say that?'

'Mercury — on a globe. It's the cap badge for the Royal Corps of Signals.'

'Mercury on a globe is a symbol for a lot of companies.'

'But that's a particular one. Ever heard of Giambologna?'

Caffery has. It's something his time with the artist girlfriend gave him. It's not usual cop knowledge.

'I have. Italian — medieval, sculptor.'

The colonel raises an eyebrow. 'And they say our tax pennies are wasted. Extraordinary.' He leans unsteadily over the photo, pointing a reddened finger, swollen at the joints. 'Look at it. See the way he's standing — the way he's holding the staff? That's based on a bronze by Giambologna. I know because I did some time in army intelligence. Did a lot of liaising with the various corps.'

'Seems a bit of a leap to me.'

'That's because you don't know. The name Giambologna — can you see your average squaddie being able to pronounce it? Of course not. They shortened it to something the great unwashed could handle.'

'Yes?'

'Yes.' The colonel holds Caffery's eyes. 'They shortened it to Jimmy. Show a signaller that picture of Mercury — the first word out of his mouth would be "Jimmy".'

LEGACY

The sun beats through the skull curtains, making the floor a blood red. Ollie sits hunched over the rug, funnelling all his concentration into what he writes.

It is my opinion that we are going to die in the next 48–72 hours. Probably we will be tortured first.

He touches the pen to his tongue and continues in the painfully cramped script:

I hereby bequeath my entire estate . . .

He pauses. A few years ago, this would have been clear-cut, straightforward. Kiran had done so well for himself, riding the white horses of the nineties and noughties, back in the day when 'investment banker' was still a job title to aspire to. It seemed certain that he would never have a financial worry in his life — unlike Lucia. In the aftermath of Hugo's murder and everything that led up to it, she stumbled and stuttered through life, pursuing one thing after another, but never finishing anything. She's earned next to nothing in her various dead-end design jobs. It had therefore been decided that the lion's share of the estate would pass to Lucia. But what with the upheavals in the banking system, Kiran's star isn't shining so brightly of late. When they got the news from Hong Kong — a second baby on the way, another grandchild to provide for — Matilda urged Oliver to reconsider. They've made an appointment with their solicitors, set for next month, to change the will so the children get equal shares. The solicitor already knows what the terms of the new will are to be, and Oliver's scientific brain struggles to decide if this fact should be addressed in this note. In the end it is the military man, not the scientist in him, that comes to the fore and he makes a decision:

. . . to my wife, Matilda Emma Anchor-Ferrers. In the event that she doesn't survive me, I wish it to be divided equally between my two children, Lucia and Kiran. In the event either child does not survive me I wish the entire estate to go to my surviving child.

Kiran, he thinks, it's going to be Kiran. Because every family member currently in the house is going to die.

Today they tortured my wife, using me and my daughter as witnesses.

I am going to witness further attacks on my wife, and almost inevitably on my daughter too.

There is nothing I can do to stop it happening.

I want to

He breaks off. Stares at the letters, his eyes watering. He was about to write *I want to die,* but he has already written that several times in other places.

John Bancroft will have got the message by now.

DORSET

Recently DS Paluzzi, who has always dressed like a sex bomb anyway, has got even more extreme. Her sweaters are tighter, her skirts and her pink Capri pants more figure-hugging. Her heels have got higher too. This reinforces for Caffery's that since her divorce she's developed an interest in him. It's little things, like the way he sometimes catches her watching him across the office. A stray comment here and there about the tie he's wearing, or did she see him when she was out at a Bristol bar last Saturday night? She could have sworn it was him. Did he have a good time?

It's not the first time this has happened to Caffery at work. He likes Paluzzi, respects her, but he's not above using the situation to his advantage. While he's driving down to the Royal Signals regimental base in Blandford, Dorset, he pairs his phone to the Bluetooth speaker and calls her, asking her to do some digging on what happened at the BMX course behind the colonel's house. Paluzzi tells him the mood in the office has been like a war council, but that the superintendent has gone from red alert to amber, and it probably won't be long before he starts begging Jack to come back to work. Offering him incentives. Then she promises to send him the information as soon as she can get it.

Yup, he thinks as he finishes the call. He was right about her.

He puts in a call to Johnny Patel, who answers sleepily, as if this is two o'clock on a Sunday morning and not a weekday afternoon.

'Hey, Jack. How're the rednecks, my old china?'

'Have I got you at a bad time?'

'No no no — I'm just doing a little, uh, *research*.'

'With Nina the classicist?'

'Like I said — a suspicious mind . . .'

'How's my project coming along?'

'Not good. The clock's ticked out on your credit, Jack, I've got to charge you from now on. I'm sorry, but Nina really needs a Samsung tablet for the course she's on. And there's a pair of Kurt Geigers too. You can't guess what a pair of Kurt Geigers buys between the sheets.' He coughs. 'Not that Nina cares about these things, you understand. Like I said, lovely girl, morals of a nun.'

'It's fine — it's fine. Just start me a tab.

Now, here's the twist. We may have got the wrong names.'

'*We?* Who's the "we", kemosabe?'

'What?'

'Nothing. Lone Ranger joke.'

Caffery sighs. He's tiring of Patel's relentless perkiness. 'It might not be James and Matilda. It might be something else and Matilda.'

'Ohhhkay, so that takes us back a few steps.'

'I know it. And the groom might have a military title in the marriage certificate. The mercury symbol is the badge of the Royal Corps of Signals. And those quotation marks around the "Jimmy" — well, it turns out that's a nickname for the signallers. I'm on the way to regimental HQ now.'

'On your way? What're you going to do there? If everyone in the regiment is nicknamed Jimmy, how the hell are they going to help?'

Caffery surveys the countryside that zips past the car. Hot and still in the late afternoon sun. It's the sort of place the Americans and the Japanese would fly thousands of miles to gawp at: honeysuckle-covered cottages and quaint pubs and churches. To him, in his current frame of mind, there couldn't be a greyer, more desolate sight.

'Well, Johnny,' he says eventually. 'You got any better ideas?'

THE SMELL

All day long the smell hangs around the kitchen, refusing to budge. In between ferrying food up and down the stairs, and trying to get the phone line working, the men try to work out how the hell it's creeping into the house from the scullery where the bucket of intestines still sits.

'Because that's all it can be,' says Honig.

'Right,' says Ian the Geek. 'Unless the dog crept back into the house and died on us.'

But they comb the house, the cupboards and the rooms, and find nothing. They search for vents in the scullery and shove newspaper up into the chimney that the dog fell down, but it makes no difference. What neither of them is in the mood to do, Honig thinks that afternoon, standing in the doorway of the scullery, coffee cup in hand, is move the fucking bucket. Hardly surprising, considering. As the day has gone on the flies have been swarming around the entrails. The noise they're making is like the sound of an electricity pylon on a damp day. They move like a single black entity, undulating as if the offal itself is moving.

The smell is nauseating. He's smelled death and decay before, but this smell has got an extra sweet edge to it. He goes back into the kitchen and chucks away the coffee. He washes the cup then goes around the kitchen, opening drawers, sniffing inside the fridge for the hundredth time. He goes to the coal cellar door and stands there, shining a torch down the wooden steps. Ian the Geek is shuffling about below, checking there are no vents that could carry the smell from the scullery into the cellar, then up through the floorboards. And failing that, no dead dog corpses down there among the coal.

'Hey!' Honig puts a hand on the doorpost and leans into the cellar. 'Geek? You there?'

There's a muffled noise of coal falling somewhere under the kitchen floor. The sound of Ian the Geek swearing. A moment or two later he appears at the bottom of the steps, shining his own torch up at Honig. His face is covered in coal dust.

'Well?' hisses Honig. 'What's there?'

Ian the Geek shakes his head. 'Coal.' He clicks off the torch, wipes his forehead, and climbs wearily up the steps. He is completely covered in coal dust. He goes to the fireplace and starts batting at the dust, trying to get it off his clothes.

Honig watches him in silence. He's deeply uneasy. That same unease he's had since last night. There's something about the smell he can't put his finger on. Why hasn't something — some rat or badger or other — crept in through the open scullery door and eaten the insides of that deer? Suddenly, out of nowhere, he wants to know exactly where Ian the Geek found the dead animal.

'Right,' he says, tipping away the remains of his coffee. 'You're going to move those disgusting things out of the scullery. And then we're going to get in the car.'

'We're going somewhere?'

'Yeah. You're going to show me where you found that damned animal.'

HUGO AND SOPHIE

By five p.m. Caffery finds himself in a pub. It's one of those gastropubs that looks like it's been set up ten years ago and left to run itself into the ground. It must once have had high aspirations, but now it's scruffy — wooden floors with black streams running down the centre where people have walked. The kickboard below the bar, where the punters would rest their feet, is splintered in places, and once smart furniture in bold, primary colours has gone tatty and stained. On a wall between the bar and the window is a blackboard on which have been drawn dog footprints, with names chalked under them — all the loved animals who have been regulars over the years, by the looks of it.

Caffery sits next to the unlit fire on one of the lime-green sofas with Bear, who delicately takes crisps from his fingers. Johnny Patel was right — it was a wasted journey, coming to Dorset. The staff at the Royal Corps of Signals want to help but the historic records from the eighties aren't kept here but in Glasgow, of all places. And to find an individual with nothing to go on but the name of a spouse would take months. 'Jimmy', or whatever his real name is, may have left the Signallers Corps before the wedding; he could, conceivably, still be with the unit, but divorced, remarried. The computations are infinite, it's a dead end.

Caffery has come straight from regimental HQ and stopped here, at the first pub he saw. There's a half-empty beer glass in front of him. If he drinks any more he won't be able to drive, but he doesn't know what else to do with himself at this point.

He pulls out his phone and opens his messages, combing through the spam and the work-related mass-circulation emails. There's one from DS Paluzzi. He opens it and his first thought is that she must *really* like him. She can't send direct from the database so she's transcribed all the information she can find about the BMX course into a pdf file and emailed him. 'Must've taken hours,' he tells Bear as he pulls on his glasses and scrolls through the document. 'Hours.'

What he reads is an instant slap in the face. The BMX course is close to the house, but not quite close enough for shouts to be heard. Fifteen years ago there was a double murder there; the victims were the Frinks' grandson Hugo and his girlfriend. No wonder the colonel is so disjointed and numb, why the nurse stares at the place as if it's cursed.

Caffery hasn't heard of Minnet Kable until now, probably because he's only been in the local force for four years. Kable was a convicted sexual predator. He had raped three young girls just outside Yeovil and had done nine years in Ashworth high-security psychiatric hospital, from which he was released in 1991. In the summer of 1999 he attacked and killed the couple on the BMX course, which in those days was known as the Donkey Pitch.

Caffery lets out a long, low whistle as he reads the next part. A lot of this isn't known to the public and it makes difficult reading.

Minnet Kable must have taken with him a holdall containing everything he needed for the night. An ice pick and a Stanley knife. Probably food and drink too — because the whole thing took over twelve hours.

When he ambushed them with an ice pick Hugo was semi-naked, face down on top of Sophie. In this initial attack Sophie sustained a relatively superficial wound caused from the pick exiting Hugo's abdomen and entering hers. She was bleeding but was able to scramble out from under her boyfriend and run into the woods. However from the very first blow Hugo was doomed. The pick had penetrated the muscle of his buttock into the base of his spine and severed a vital nerve that serviced his legs. He became instantly unable to control himself from the waist down.

Kable didn't inflict another wound on Hugo. He had no need. The boy was paralysed and Kable had the leisure of watching him die. It probably took about five hours. That's why the murders became known locally as the Wolf murders, because the method was the way a dog or a wolf would kill its prey. Wounding, then stalking and containing — constantly corralling — until the victim was exhausted and died of blood loss.

Meanwhile Sophie Hurst-Lloyd was hiding in the woods.

Even fifteen years after the event, and with all he's seen and done, Caffery still finds it hard to take in what happened to her.

Kable must have been enormously confident, because he appears to have allowed her to escape. Apart from the small wound to her abdomen, her body at autopsy showed no other injuries from the initial attack. There was every chance she would have survived if she'd escaped. The forensic fingertip-search team found her hiding place on the third day. The pile of leaves she'd burrowed herself into. They found the attempt she'd made to scratch out a message on a tree trunk.

Mum, Dad, I love you. I'm sorry. I want to come home . . .

There was more writing, maybe an attempt to identify Kable as her attacker, but the words had been rendered illegible with deep gouges that matched the profile of Kable's Stanley knife. Bad luck, or some might call it fate, had led her to choose the most difficult place in the wood to escape from. She'd edged herself back into the angle at the foot of a steep cliff where the cliff formed a U shape. Caffery knows exactly where she was trapped: he and Bear have been there. It's the same escarpment where the cave is. Sophie's misfortune was that she didn't see it. If she had, there would have been an outside chance that she could have survived.

In those days teenagers didn't carry mobile phones. Her choices were to escape, which would have meant passing the place where Kable sat watching her boyfriend die, or to wait. Sensibly, she waited. She waited and she waited. While Venus and Mercury and the moon rose, crossed the heavens and dipped to the horizon, she inched herself deeper under the leaves, keeping her breathing light and steady. In all likelihood, she couldn't see Kable and Hugo, but she did have a watch and she must have thought that twelve hours after the wood fell silent was a reasonable time to wait. She must have thought that by the time the first light of dawn filtered through the trees, when there hadn't been any movement except for the occasional passing fox, the occasional bird, she'd be safe to move.

She didn't reckon on the madness and perseverance of Minnet Kable. He was as good at waiting as she was. He came at her the moment she moved. He cornered her and attacked her repeatedly with the Stanley knife. The report says Minnet was ambidextrous — he'd demonstrated that in attacks before — and sure enough the wounds bore this out. The most vicious punctures were made with a right-handed blow, but some were made with the left — so he'd had time and leisure to switch hands. Sophie took forty minutes to die. Like Hugo, she died from blood loss. Maybe it was quicker in her case because she was already cold and weak from a night in the woods.

Incredible, Caffery thinks, the confidence Kable showed. To contain two fit and healthy teenagers in those relatively public woods — without any panic, for that length of time — knowing he could have been discovered at any moment. How one person could have had that self control — that persistence — is beyond Caffery.

When Kable was finished he extracted the intestines of the teenagers through their abdominal wounds. The pathologist was of the opinion that Sophie was still clinging to life at that point, and could have been conscious of what was happening. Kable draped the entrails in the tree branches, forming the shape of a heart. Then he posed the bodies in what the pathologist believed was the same position he'd first found them in when he attacked them with the ice pick: Hugo on top, Sophie's legs wrapped round his waist. An unholy embrace among the wet leaves. With the intestines hanging above them, the crime-scene photos make the couple look like twins in the womb, attached to an umbilical cord.

The final touch was the strangest. After placing the couple face to face, as if they were kissing, Kable either repeatedly stamped on or battered their heads — the report's not conclusive — but whatever method he used it was forceful enough to break their noses and cheekbones. When the police pulled the bodies apart, the report says, the teenagers' faces were not recognizable as human.

Caffery lets out his breath in a long stream. He puts the phone face down on the table and rests his head back against the wall, mulling it all over. He wonders if jealousy was at work. Perhaps Kable was in love with one of the kids — the guy or the girl, who knows? — and what he did to their faces was his way of punishing them for their intimacy. Mash them together. If they were going to kiss, they had to *really* kiss. That would teach them. The mocking heart shape, and a ring Hugo gave to Sophie which has never been found: it all points to jealousy. And yet the detectives and the case workers at the time were never able to establish a personal connection between Kable and the couple.

Bear nuzzles his hand and Caffery opens one eye, squinting down at her. 'You're right. Interesting, but it doesn't get me any nearer to finding out who you are.'

He swivels his eye to the beer glass. He doesn't think he can face going home tonight. What he wants is to find the Walking Man. To make him talk. To throttle something out of him. But when he pictures it he knows he could strangle the guy, stop him breathing, and all he'd get from him would be a beatific smile — a serene certainty that this was exactly what he'd expected to happen. The Walking Man will never beg for mercy, will never tell his secrets, will never strike deals in desperation. He'll only talk when he is ready.

Caffery closes his eyes and drops his head back against the wall, breathing steadily.

THE DEER

Ian removes the bucket from the scullery and places it in the woods. The intestines stink, and as he walks the flies keep pace with him in a cloud like a cartoon smell, like the smell of gravy in the old Bisto kids adverts. Afterwards he has to bin the T-shirt he was wearing and take a shower. Then he joins Honig and together they get into the Chrysler.

Honig's face is red and hard as he drives. He doesn't speak. They go slowly down the driveway, out of the gates, and take a left turn. They keep going, Ian directing, until they come to a small lay-by.

'Here,' Ian says. 'This is where I found it.'

Evening hasn't reached The Turrets yet, but down here in the shadow of the hill the dark is gathering already. There's a faint chill in the air as they lock the car and head off into the trees.

Ian stops where some rusted barbed wire is looped between trees. He waves his hands around vaguely. 'It was in this area. Why?'

'Here?' Honig approaches thoughtfully, looking all around him. There is nothing. He walks in a big circle, kicking the grass, lifting branches. 'You sure it was here?'

'Yes. I mean, I think so.'

'Tell me what happened. I mean, you find a deer — already shot, you said? What did you cut it with to get the innards out?'

'A . . . a knife.'

'A knife? From where?'

'The kitchen. That knife block.'

'You're lying.'

Ian swallows. 'No, I'm not lying — I . . .'

'Exactly which knife? You'd need to be sure — to butcher a deer, you'd need to have the right knife. Can't just use a butter knife, you know.'

'I didn't use a butter knife. I used one from the knife block.'

Honig narrows his eyes suspiciously. 'Did you wash it afterwards? I didn't see anything that had been washed.'

Ian pushes his glasses hard against his face and blinks. He hates being caught out in a lie. It was one of the things his mother used to love doing — catching him out in every lie she could. Even the small, white lies. *How did you sleep last night? Oh OK. No, you're lying, Ian, I know you didn't sleep, I heard you up and moving around at two in the morning, why do you lie to me?*

He lowers his eyes to his feet. Anything rather than look up. It occurs to him that if he does look up there's no predicting what he might see. Maybe not Honig's face — maybe his mother's looking back at him. Accusing: *You liar.* Maybe something worse.

'I am fucking speaking to you, Geek. Because I am standing here and I cannot see any evidence at all that there was a deer here. No signs of you dragging it to the car. So you're lying to me.'

Ian grinds his teeth. He's got to hold steady. Forty thousand dollars says he's got to hold it together. That and much more — his honour, his pride. So much. 'OK,' he blurts, still not looking at Honig. 'It's true. There wasn't any deer. Just its insides. Here — on the barbed wire.'

'Its *insides*? You found its innards — here on the wire?'

Ian rubs his nose. He still hasn't lifted his eyes. 'Yes. I'd spoken to the housekeeper and I was walking back. I came up through the woods and I just found them. They were there next to the driveway and I assumed — I don't know, I assumed they came from an animal that had been killed or hit by a car or something. Or shot, because someone had been shooting up here — I could hear them. But by the time I got here they must have field-dressed it — got rid of the intestines and carried the carcass. Or . . .' At last he raises his eyes. Honig is staring at him, his face white in the purple half light. 'Or that's what I assumed.'

'Assumed. ASSSS-umed? You fucking dickhead. You're telling me you found the insides of an animal — but no animal?'

'Yes. And I remembered what we heard from Havilland about Kable and I thought . . . what?' He breaks off. Honig is shaking his head in disbelief. 'What? It's not *that* weird.'

'You know what? I think it *is* weird. Just *slightly* fucking weird. In fact totally un-fucking-believable.'

'Why're you so upset?'

'Well, let's start with the fact you lied. Not once — twice.'

'Yes, but not about anything *important*. Jesus, I had a lot to think about — the housekeeper, the phone, the alarm . . .'

He trails off. Honig has turned and is walking away, shaking his head.

'Come on,' he shouts. 'Keep up. We've got calls to make.'

BREANNE

'Do you want some water?'

Caffery opens his eyes. A woman stands opposite him, an array of dirty glasses clasped between her fingers. She must be in her mid-forties, yet she's dressed like a biker chick of twenty in black leather jeans and a tight black vest. Her long hair is dyed aubergine and tied in two plaits that hang to her waist. But the thing which really sets her apart is the scar on her neck, face and cheek. From just under her nose, stretching down her neck on to her chest. She must have had several skin transplants because the bottom half of her face is a different texture to the top half: it is raised but smooth, white and unblemished, while the top half is tanned, with a spattering of freckles across the nose. It's as if someone has cut her in half across the centre of her face and stitched on a different lower half.

'It's OK, you can blink now. I'm used to it.'

'I'm sorry.' He shakes his head. 'I was staring. Rude.'

'Human nature. Makes you normal, not rude. You stare when you're not sure what you're seeing — it's like you're checking to make sure I'm not a threat. That's what pigeonholing is all about too — people do that to keep themselves safe. I've had it all explained to me by the psychiatrist. And trust me — you're as normal as they come.'

'Am I?'

She pauses for a minute, scrutinizing him. Then, at length, she gives a small, ironic smile. Puckered and painful though her face is, there's something weirdly sexy about that smile.

'Staring at me — that's normal,' she says, at length. 'But the rest? Who knows? I couldn't comment. Now,' she nods at Bear, 'does your dog want some water or not? We like to look after the pets in here — that's what makes us the pub we are. That sort of friendliness.'

'Thank you.' Caffery sits up a little straighter and rubs his eyes, feeling suddenly as if he's actually been asleep. 'That would be kind.'

The woman takes the glasses to the bar and returns with a bowl of water, putting it down for Bear. She bends and scratches her head.

'Boy? Girl?'

'Girl.'

'She's part Border, isn't she?'

'I don't know, for sure.'

349

'I think she is. I used to have a Border. She'd sit on the back of my bike. She liked the wind in her hair, had a little bandana — see?' She points to the wall where a framed photo of a shining bike hangs. A dog is perched on the back, its tongue hanging out. 'And that's my before photo.'

The photo next to it shows a young woman in a Harley T-shirt, standing in front of an American diner, a broad grin on her face. Heavy dark hair hangs in wide curls across her shoulders. Her teeth are white, her mouth wide, her eyes clear. She was pretty. Very pretty.

'What's your name, old girl? Eh?' The woman has dropped to a crouch and taken the dog behind its ears, putting its face close to her. 'What's your name, you pretty girl? You so good-looking.' She peers up at Caffery, waiting for him to answer, to tell her the dog's name. He drags his attention away from the photograph.

'Bear.'

'Bear? She doesn't look like a bear — well, maybe a bear cub. Why Bear?'

'I don't know.'

She frowns. 'You don't know a lot about your own dog.'

'It's not mine.'

'You've stolen it? You're a dog rustler. You're right — you're not as normal as you seem.'

'What happened?'

'To my face?'

'Yes. Your face.'

'Acid.'

'Oh,' he says, not knowing what to say.

'Exactly.' She smiles. 'Oh.'

Caffery is surprised to find he's comfortable about studying her. As if there's something in her that almost invites it. As if this peeling away of skin has forced her to make herself naked to the world, and that now she's as happy in this skin as she could be in any.

'How did it happen?'

'If I told you I was blown up in a mine disposal operation in Afghanistan, would that make you more or less impressed by me?'

'It matters to you if I'm impressed?'

'You're a good-looking man — you probably know it. I'm a human being. Not entirely recognizable as one, I grant you, but I am human. Of course I want to impress you.'

Caffery turns his glass around and around on the table. It leaves a wet circular stain and he keeps his eyes on it, because he thinks if he looks up and meets her eyes she'll see the images that are there.

'So,' she says. 'Are you impressed?'

'It would depend. Was it a bomb in Afghanistan?'

She gives a small, dismissive laugh. She straightens, hooks a bar stool under her and sits opposite him, arms folded. She has very

351

long slim legs and very small breasts. The skin on the lower parts of her arms and hands is smooth and lightly bronzed.

'No. I wish it was. I wish I could say it was a bomb or a helicopter accident, trying to save other troops, because half the clientele in here have got some story or other like that, being this close to the barracks. But no. I was born here.' She waves her hand around the pub. 'It's my dad's place — that's him who served you. Manic depressive, or bipolar, or something. We just can't work it out. He's as sweet as you like to everyone around him, but he can't seem to get himself happy. Clever man, too — educated as a physicist, but he couldn't find a job in his field. Hence this place.'

'And you? Army?'

'No, no no. Too much of a layabout, and lots to look after here, with Mum and Dad not coping. No, I was twenty, working here, dating all the boys from the camp — the Signals — you can imagine.' She nods out of the window. 'A natural progression, living so close, to be dating all the grunts. Looking back I think I had my pick, but I chose the bad boy. He was always trying to impress me, always trying to show off — and I loved it. One night he smuggled me into the camp. Could have been court martialled for it, but he did it anyway because I wanted to see — I wanted to know what went on over the fence.

He was in charge of the transport for one of the regiments so he showed me around a bit, showed me the trucks and the maintenance places and —' She breaks off, taking a moment to replay it all in her memory. Then shakes her head. 'Anyway, there'd been a problem with the air-conditioning unit. The batteries they use in the trucks, they're supposed to be kept ventilated because they produce gas and it's flammable — actually, it's explosive. We had . . . you know, we'd stopped what we were up to, then he lit a cigarette and bam! I was right next to a battery and got it in the face. He was completely fine. He's a major now. I saw him on the news in Afghanistan about a month ago.'

She tips her head on one side. Searches Caffery's face for a reaction. He keeps his expression level. It's something he's learned to do over the years: put up a blank wall to stop people peering in. She stares and she smiles, but she can't get past it. So she stands and picks up his glass.

'Another drink?'

He should say no. It will mean he won't be able to drive until at least ten o'clock. He'll have to sit here drinking nothing but coffee for three hours.

'Yes,' he says. 'I'd like that.'

When she brings the glass back and puts it down, he picks it up and drinks half of it at once. He sets it on the table and both he and the woman and the dog look at it in silence for a moment. Something has shifted in the atmosphere. He knows and she knows it. He picks up the glass and finishes the rest in one go, setting it on the table and wiping his mouth with the back of his hand.

'My name's Jack,' he says.

'Mine's Breanne.'

'It's nice to meet you, Breanne,' he says. 'How far down does that scar go?'

THE LAST JOB

Honig stands three metres away from the house, holding up a torch — shining it into the woods. Behind him Ian the Geek is working on the telephone box, using a headtorch to see what he is doing. He keeps swearing and muttering under his breath — so Honig is assuming all is not going well.

He puts his hand in his pocket and closes it around Bubblegum Mania. He wishes he could call her. He is so on edge he can hardly keep still. Animal intestines tangled in a barbed wire fence? Placed so close to the Donkey Pitch where Minnet Kable killed the teenagers? Weird and weirder. Like someone in the area is orchestrating an enormous mindfuck.

When they were at the bottom of the drive and had mobile signal, he did some phoning around, left messages in several places trying to get some intel on Minnet Kable. It sounds nuts, based on animal guts in barbed wire, but suddenly he wants reassurance that the guy is still in the slammer. No one had anything to tell him, though they've all promised to do some digging and get back to him. Then he had Ian the Geek spend half an hour searching the web for anything — any news about Kable being released. They found nothing. But then again, Honig wonders, would the authorities send information like that to the press?

Minnet Kable can't be out. *Can't* be. And even if he were, this would be the last place he'd come back to. Surely? All the same, Honig is utterly rattled by the remains of that animal. It feels as if the air around the house and the surrounding woods is tightening like a fist with each passing hour.

'Anything?' He has his back to Ian the Geek and he keeps his eyes on the furthest boundary, where the semicircle of the torchlight meets the darkness. He is also, out of the corner of his eye, monitoring the back door, which is standing open, the light spilling out. Usually he is level-headed and rational, so he can't explain why he's suddenly as nervous as hell. 'Anything at all?'

'Nothing.'

Honig bites his lip hard to stop himself from swearing. His anger with Ian the Geek is under very shaky control at the moment. Not only does he find it incredible that the guy didn't find anything odd about discovering those intestines, it also seems he can't do

the only thing he's supposed to be good at —
getting the fucking phone working. They need
that phone. Really need it.

He peers into the woods, ferreting around
among his thoughts and sensations for some
logic. He turns the torch beam to the scullery door. Studies it. Now he's thinking about
it, he has the strangest sensation that there's
something he's missed which will make sense
of everything. It's *something* that happened
the first day . . . something someone did, or
said . . .

The thought leaps and skitters away. He
screws up his eyes, rubs his temples wearily,
tries to get it back. But it's gone. Completely
gone. He turns. Ian the Geek is standing next
to the junction box, a pained smile on his
face.

'I'm sorry.' He wipes his face with his
sleeve. Shrugs and waves the pliers at the box.
'I'm shit and I know it. Just can't make it
happen.'

Honig shakes his head. It's cemented his
decision that this is his last job. He's definitely
leaving Gauntlet after this. He's going back
home to Bubblegum Mania.

They go into the house and pull out the
camp beds. Ian the Geek falls asleep quickly,
but Honig is restless and cannot get comfortable. He's a city boy and the noises of the
wildlife outside are alien to him. The night-
song of birds, the bark of foxes. At four a.m.

something large, possibly a pheasant, gets killed — judging by the squawk and shriek. He knows it's just the sounds of nature, but they leave him as stripped-down scared as anything he's ever heard in his life. He keeps Bubblegum Mania on his pillow where he can uncap it and inhale the smell, just to calm him. What has put it into his head that Kable is out of prison, he just doesn't know, but all night he is pursued by the image of a man in the milky dawn, decorating trees with the intestines of two teenagers.

Eventually he gives up the battle, and when first light comes, he pushes back the covers and gets up. He puts on the kettle and drinks two cups of strong coffee. Ian the Geek is still asleep. Snoring. *Plus ça change,* Honig thinks.

He washes his cup, draws back the curtains and looks out. It is dawn and the pink light is filtering through the trees to the east of the house. He puts on his boots, finds a torch, and unlocks the door. He couldn't care less if Ian the Geek, the bovine, gets woken, but he is such a sound sleeper that even the noise of three bolts being pulled back doesn't stop the snoring.

The world is white with dew. Honig knows he's supposed to be a hard-bitten bastard, but even *he* sees something magical about it — sees where that 'rosy-fingered' quote comes from. He wishes his new wife could be here to see it. He'd take a photo of it, if he wasn't superstitious about mixing work and pleasure. In his jacket pocket Bubblegum Mania bounces lightly against his thigh as he walks.

He goes quickly down the path, conscious of the trees still and silent in the mist. Wet dew gathers on his trousers from the lavender in the borders. He has no idea what's leading him out here or what he expects to find — all he has is an instinct that whatever is out of kilter has something to do with the intestines. With moving them to the woods.

He stops outside the scullery door and, still not sure what he's searching for, kicks around in the bright grass, shining the torch at his feet and along the path Ian the Geek used to take the bucket into the trees. He tries not to think about the images that have been woven through his dreams. Stomachs ripped open. Kable waiting in a cave. Waiting. Sometimes he wishes he hasn't read all the paperwork the company supplied about the case.

He pauses, staring down at his feet. Something is there. He picks it up and shines the light on it, examining it very closely. Immediately he is chilled. It's as if the last breaths of those doomed teenagers is floating up the hillside. Condensing cold on his face.

'Fuck,' he mutters. 'Fuck.' He puts the object in his pocket and heads quickly back towards the house.

INTERNATIONAL ART THIEVES

'The woman who is getting that from you every day is lucky.' It is morning and Breanne lies on her back, one arm behind her head, the other resting on the sheet, a cigarette smouldering between her fingers. 'Getting fucked like that on a daily basis.'

Caffery lies next to her on his front, his head turned sideways, resting on his arms. He watches her out of one eye. The scars, it turns out, go down her chest and stop just above her nipples. The acid ate through the T-shirt she was wearing that night, but the bra underneath protected her breasts. There's another small band of puckered skin above her navel where the acid splashed. The place on her face where the skin graft meets the original skin is raised. She's encouraged him to touch it — has taken his hand and placed his finger there. Later he ran his tongue along the groove, his eyes closed, tasting the different textures.

There is only one woman he'd like to be

doing this with on a daily basis and it isn't Breanne, sexy though she is. It's the police sergeant who runs the search unit, the one he's shared so many secrets with over the years. Again he wonders why he hasn't made a move in that direction. He half suspects it's to do with Jacqui Kitson's closure and happiness. All the psychologists say: if you're not healed yourself you can't hope to have a relationship with another human being, and on some level he's sure he's avoiding her until he discovers what happened to Ewan.

Breanne blows smoke in a long line towards the ceiling. 'You're still angry.'

He blinks. Lifts his head up. 'What did you say?'

'I can spot an anger fuck a mile away — and that's what this has been.' She licks her finger and puts it on his shoulder. Makes the hiss of scorched flesh between her teeth. 'You're burning up with it. Who is it? A woman?'

When Caffery doesn't answer she rolls on to her side and drapes her hand over the edge of the bed, groping around on the floor for something. The light from the half-drawn curtains catches the fine invisible hairs on her skin and turns them gold. Caffery doesn't move, he follows her movements with his eyes.

'So . . .' She's found whatever she was looking for and rolls back. It's the black police-issue wallet that contains his warrant card. Propping herself up on one arm, she gives a slow smile and lets the wallet fall open. 'Something we forgot to talk about last night?'

'I had other things on my mind.'

'Nice try. But some things are basic etiquette to mention. You know — before. Not after. It should go with the condom discussion. Is this the real reason you're such a long way from home? I didn't believe you when you said you were just having a drive because it was a nice day.'

'I'm not a good actor then.'

'The worst I've ever seen. And I watch a lot of movies.'

'I was in the camp. I'm trying to trace someone who was in the Signals. Years ago.'

Her eyes gleam wickedly. 'Who are you looking for? An international art thief? Go on, tell me. A murderer? A terrorist?'

'All three. And none of the above.'

'That's a riddle and I don't get it.'

'I mean I don't know who I'm looking for.'

He explains to her about the ring. The image of Mercury and the names Matilda and Jimmy. Breanne lights another cigarette and listens carefully.

When he's finished she sits up and swings her legs off the bed. Goes to the wardrobe and pulls out a white shirt which she puts on, braless.

'Are we going somewhere?'

'Yes. We're going to speak to my father.'

'That's great — though I think it's early to be discussing the wedding.'

She stops buttoning the blouse and gives him a patient, unamused look. 'He's been running this pub for thirty-nine years and he's got a memory like an encyclopaedia. You should have gone to him in the first place, not to the regiment.'

ALCOHOL

Honig sits at the table, his elbows on it, and watches Ian the Geek wake up. The Geek turns and pulls up the covers and tries to go back into his dreams, but each time he does Honig coughs a little louder, until eventually Ian the Geek gives up. 'What's the matter? What's going on?'

'I think it's time you woke up.'

'Wha . . . ?' he begins, but seeing Honig's face his expression changes to one of alarm. 'What?' He sits up nervously. 'What is it?'

Honig doesn't answer. He beckons him with one finger. Ian the Geek hesitates, then gets up from the camp bed and pads over to the table. Honig points at what sits on the table in front of him. Ian the Geek peers at it, frowning.

'What is it?'

'A filling.'

'A filling?'

'Er, yes. That's what I said. Do you know where it came from?'

Ian the Geek shakes his head, bewildered. He rubs his eyes and sits down at the table opposite. 'I don't know. I just don't know.'

'I found it. In the grass. You chucked it there.'

'What?'

'Let me take you back. A piece of "shot". In the intestines?'

Light begins to dawn in Ian the Geek's expression. He picks up the filling and examines it.

'It's not lead shot,' he admits. His face is red. 'It's definitely a filling. How did it get to be in the intestines?'

Honig puts both fists down on the table and tightens his teeth, resisting the urge to drop his head into his hands. He concentrates very hard on not speaking because he knows if he does it will just be a stream of invective. He pushes the chair back and goes to the sink, where he rummages in the cupboard until he finds two pairs of rubber gloves. He pulls the knife from the block — the serrated one that Oliver told him to use three days ago, back when Honig was Detective Honey and they were playing games that Minnet Kable was out of jail and terrorizing the house. The irony of the situation isn't lost on him.

The two men go outside, with Honig stopping to lock the back door carefully. He gives the trees and the gardens a quick scan, then leads Ian the Geek into the dewy morning. They walk down through the gardens, into the woods and stand, hands over their mouths, looking at the mess Ian the Geek tipped out of the bucket. It stinks, but because of the cold at least it's not covered in flies the way it was yesterday. There are just a couple of bluebottles, picking their way sluggishly through the entrails.

Honig holds out the knife and the pair of gloves. Ian the Geek stares at them.

'What?'

'Your job.'

'What?'

Honig nods at the entrails. 'Let's have a look at the "deer's" last meal, shall we? Shall we look at all the grass and leaves it's eaten?'

Ian the Geek swallows. His face is pale in the thin morning light. There's a pause, then he takes the gloves. He pulls them on and squats next to the mess, his face averted from the smell. He doesn't need the knife, the intestines are so rotten the white fascia splits apart at a touch.

Honig watches without speaking, holding his nose, breathing loudly through his mouth. A white mass of maggots plops out. Ian the Geek turns his head away, but continues to unfold the intestines, letting other matter sluice out.

'OK,' Honig says tightly, straightening his back to stop himself feeling weak. 'I think that's what we needed to see.'

Ian the Geek stares up at him, his pupils like pinpricks. It's as if he can't bring himself to look at what his hands are doing, like they're separate entities. 'What? What can you see?'

'I'm not an expert — and it's degraded. But I think I recognize tomato seeds. And that is definitely sweetcorn.'

'I don't get it.'

'No — because you're a dick. The dog didn't come back for these because there's alcohol in them. That's what the smell is — that's why nothing, not a badger, not a fox will touch this mess.'

'Alcohol?' Ian the Geek echoes tremulously. '*Alcohol?* Sweetcorn?'

'Yes, and a filling — swallowed.'

Ian the Geek makes a noise in his throat. He straightens quickly and shakes his hands of the mess and walks quickly to the edge of the trees. He is pulling off the gloves and gulping in air when Honig comes up behind him and gives him a swift clout around the back of the head.

Ian the Geek buckles. *'Shit!'* he yells, his hands coming up to his ears. *'What the fuck did you do that for?'*

In reply Honig grabs him by the back of his fleece and pushes him in the direction of the house. 'Because you are an idiot,' he hisses as they walk. 'A fucking wanker.'

But it's not anger making him shout, and he knows it. It's fear.

TOBACCO

Caffery has given up real cigarettes and he should be repulsed by the smell of tobacco, or angry with Breanne, or tempted to start again himself, but he's none of these. Instead he finds it sexy and brave that she smokes so unapologetically — as if she doesn't give a toss what all the public health announcements say, isn't scared of the scaremongering shots of tumours and cancer cadavers emblazoned across the front of every tobacco pouch.

He keeps his eyes on her, seated at the Formica table in the pub kitchen, sipping tea and tapping ash into the ashtray. She narrowly misses being an archetypal pub landlady by virtue of her intelligence. Her thoughtfulness. In fact the whole family are weirdly placed. They'd look more at home as teachers in a house on the grounds of a nice prep school in the home counties. Her mother seems slightly vague but very educated — no make-up, a floral dress with a shapeless cardigan. Her father — the manic depressive — doesn't seem manic and doesn't seem depressed. Like his daughter, he's whip thin and speaks with an educated voice, and if he seems anything at all it's tired. In fact there's an air of restrained exhaustion about the whole place, from the over-scrubbed floor tiles that have been worn through in places with constant cleaning, to the ancient gas cooker which is old enough to have an eye-level grill.

But in all this weariness, what shines through is how close the family are — how much the parents love Breanne. Caffery wonders what they think about her bringing a man in here, first thing in the morning. She hasn't even brushed her hair, and his own crumpled appearance, his unshaved face, must tell them a multitude of things. But they make no mention of it.

'It's definitely a signaller's ring,' Mr Drew says, squinting at the photograph. 'Unmistakable. But 1981? I can remember a lot of things — a lot of faces, but I don't remember the name Matilda.'

Caffery stares down at the photos. What an idiotic fool's errand he's on, trying to find a single oyster in an ocean. The more the alcohol wears off, the worse it feels.

'Is that all you've got to go on?'

'I know what he looked like. He was white. Tall. Blond or sandy hair.'

370

'Sounds like you-know-who.' Mr Drew raises his eyebrows at Breanne. 'Doesn't it?'

She shakes her head. 'He means my ex,' she explains to Caffery. 'The one who was with me that night. But his wife's name is Carmen. Anyway, he didn't join the regiment until the late eighties. And, Dad, a hundred guys are tall and blond.'

'Was he English?'

'Yes,' Caffery says. 'He had some obsession with space junk.'

'Space junk?'

'Asteroids, exploded fragments from space ships.'

Breanne's father, who has held the photo out for Caffery to take, pauses where he stands, suddenly motionless.

'Asteroids?'

'Yes, or at least, I think so. Or do I mean meteorites?'

Mr Drew makes a noise in his throat. He turns and raises his eyebrows at his wife, as if to say *Well, who would have thought?*

But she's not with him. She shrugs, opens her hands. 'What? Don't look at me like that. I don't know what you're thinking.'

He shakes his head, incredulous. 'You honestly don't remember?'

'No, I don't.'

'You must remember. He used to come in with a bunch of the officers. He'd sit apart from them — over there, at the bar and I was

371

the only one he talked to, we used to talk about cosmic rays and neutrinos and nerd stuff. He'd drink wine. I remember that because in those days no one drank wine in pubs. And yes. It would have been the eighties. Early eighties. Breanne?' He appeals to his daughter. 'You remember the space guy? Don't you? The light guy? He'd spent some time in America, I think. He was obsessed with the things littering space.'

'Dad — I was a kid. And anyway, you know me.' She clunks the side of her head with a finger. 'Memory of a goldfish. Nice castle. Oooh, look at that — what a lovely castle . . . Oh, nice castle!'

'I don't get you two — how can you not remember?'

'Because we're not elephants or computers.'

Mr Drew lets his breath out in a long sigh. He goes into the office that opens out on to the kitchen and begins searching for something, opening drawers, sifting through the piles of junk. He pulls down some box files and sorts through the paperwork and oddments in there until he finds what he's after.

'I knew it!' He turns and gives the other three a victorious smile. 'I just knew it.'

When he comes back into the kitchen he's holding a tattered beer mat. Caffery and the two women both lean over to study it. It is an old Tanglefoot beer mat, something Caffery hasn't seen in years, but the design on it has been obliterated by a biro sketch. The drawing, which has been initialled, shows the Earth, with the continents and oceans depicted carefully. A halo of specks orbits the Earth, from which emanates a series of light rays.

'Yes. Fascinating chap. He used to sit at the bar and sometimes all he'd do was stare at the patterns the sunlight made on the floor. He loved everything to do with light — was always talking about how it changed everything, how powerful it was.'

'A name?'

'No, sorry. Not a clue. Just remember his face.'

Caffery frowns at the picture. The three initials are illegible — nothing more than a scribble. That could be an O or a Q or a C. The second one could be an N or A, and the last one anything — a G, an E, an F or even an X.

He looks up at Mr Drew. 'Do you remember what he was doing for the Signals?'

'No. But I'd be willing to bet it was something to do with space, with the stars.'

'You don't know if he was in the Masons, do you?'

'Haven't got a clue. All I remember is how much he loved light. I remember envying him that love — wherever you were in the world, there would always be light to look at.'

'You sure you don't remember a name?'

Mr Drew scratches his temple, shakes his head. 'No, I'd be lying if I said I knew. He was tall, that's all I can remember. And he came back — I'm sure he did. In fact, I think that was when he drew this. It was years later, after Breanne had her accident. I remember thinking I should say something about it, so that if she came downstairs he wouldn't stare at her.'

'What was he like when he came back?'

'He had a woman with him and kids — can't remember how many. But I assumed it was his wife and family.'

'Matilda? The wife?'

'I didn't ask her name. She was in the beer garden with the children. I exchanged a few words with him. He said . . .' Mr Drew trails off, his eyes drifting up to the left as he chases the memory. There is a long silence, then he snatches up the beer mat, flips it over. 'There — that's it!'

'What?'

He puts the mat between his thumb and forefinger and displays it proudly, moving it so all three people can see it plainly. The words *Columbus Systems, Oxford* followed by a phone number have been painstakingly written out in the same biro.

'What's that?'

'We got talking. He said he left the army when he got married — he was working for a private company. I was in one of those

374

periods where I thought I might be able to get out of the pub, do more the sort of job I was trained for, and this is the company he suggested. I never followed it up though.'

'Columbus Systems?'

'I'm sure he told me they were a navigations company.' He smiles at Caffery. 'Maybe they still exist.'

A Change of Plan

In the kitchen Ian the Geek stands at the sink feverishly washing his hands, pouring great streams of washing-up liquid over his ape-like arms, lathering the red hair on them as if his life depends on it. Honig shoots him contemptuous looks as he paces the kitchen. He is agitated beyond belief. Every now and then he stops to look out of the window at the long driveway.

Ian the Geek is a dick, he thinks bitterly. *Human* remains — the stupid cunt picked up human remains. There's a corpse somewhere out there and whoever created the corpse has chosen to do with his or her intestines exactly what Minnet Kable did fifteen years ago.

'It's him,' he says. 'Minnet fucking Kable.'

Ian the Geek shakes his head vehemently. 'He can't be. It's impossible. Too much — too much of a coincidence. We're trained not to trust coincidences.'

'Yeah, and I'm starting to think our training is shit. Life is made up of coincidences, mate. That's how come there's a name for it: *co-in-ci-dence.* They don't make up words for things that don't happen.' He stops at the window and peers out at the grey mist and the trees. You can't even see the bottom of the driveway. The Turrets could be the giant's castle in *Jack and the Beanstalk,* they're so cut off from the rest of the world, poking their heads up above the clouds like this.

'How far away was it?'

'How far away was what?'

'The cave.' Honig turns and stares at Ian the Geek. 'The place he killed those kids. You do know this area, don't you? That is why you were hired.'

Ian the Geek nods weakly. His mouth is trembling. 'It was at the end of the valley. About a mile in that direction.'

Honig checks his watch. It is half past eight. Offices in London will be opening soon. Havilland placed a lot of conditions on this job, but ultimately there is one chief objective — to get Oliver's book spiked. The payment schedule is weighted accordingly: the bulk of the money — 30 per cent — is payable on Oliver instructing his literary agent to pull the manuscript of *Luciente, A Life in the Light.* If they cut the job short and get out now they'll lose out on the extra bonuses for the videos of the family's suffering that Havilland enjoys so much. But sometimes you have to take what you can and get out alive. Already his heart is halfway back to Maryland and the shopping mall.

'Can I ask you something?'

Honig glances up. Ian the Geek has stopped washing. He is standing with his hands in the sink, soap suds up his arms. 'You've never killed anyone. Have you?'

Honig stares at him and Ian the Geek stares back. His eyes are like saucers, beads of perspiration on his forehead. Ian the Geek sees the answer in Honig's eyes and shakes his head dejectedly. 'Jesus. I'd hoped you'd at least hurt someone. So, all that mouthing off you do is just acting . . . ?'

Honig snatches up a tea-towel and throws it at him. 'Come on,' he says. 'Get dried up. We've got two hours to get our act together.'

'Why? What's happening?'

'We're changing the rules to suit the situation. We're going to cut the operation short. It's time we got out of here.'

Heart Attack

At nine, when Oliver is expecting a tray to come in with cereal, coffee and his medication on it, instead the two men come into the room together. No tray. In spite of himself, he begins to tremble uncontrollably. This is it. Now he will be taken out into the hallway and hanging there will be his daughter. He keeps his gaze lowered. He is beyond humility.

But instead of dragging him out and taping his eyes open, the men sit down. When they don't speak he dares to raise his eyes to them. They are both leaning forward, elbows on their knees, watching him. Their expressions alarm him more than if they'd hauled him outside, because something is different. The tall one, Honey, seems fidgety, a light sheen of sweat on him. They look like they're here to announce a death.

'What? What is it?'

There's a long silence where his pulse hammers in his temples. It's Honey who eventually speaks. 'You had a mild heart attack, didn't you? About a year ago.'

'Yes.' His jaw is trembling. 'So?'

'You owe your life to that heart attack. Without it you'd never have known there was something wrong, you'd never have known you needed an operation, and you'd have been on a one-way ticket to the biggie. It was your body's way of warning you, giving you a chance. Now you're being given another warning, another chance.' He waves his hand, indicating himself and the ape-like Molina: 'My associate and I are like that heart attack: a gentle warning. We're here to teach you how to have a quiet life. That's all. By the end of this you will be the quintessential expert on silence.'

'Silence?'

'Your book.'

Oliver lets out his breath. 'Yes,' he says. 'The book. I thought so. How did you know? It's been a secret. Just me and my agent.'

'Ah yes, your agent: Messrs Bright and Fullman. Now in receipt of your book and trying to find a publisher for it. A phone call to tell them you've changed your mind — that's all we're asking.'

Oliver looks at Honig's pale eyes. 'So there's something in the book that someone doesn't want published? Who?'

Honey shakes his head. 'You're never going to know.'

Oliver looks from his face to Molina's then back again. Once more he wonders what's different — what's making them nervous. Have the authorities been tipped off? Perhaps the doctor has been trying to call to check on him and has raised the alarm. Or Ginny, the cleaner. Or Kiran?

'I don't know,' he says. 'You said before that you don't keep promises.'

'Consider this: you call your agent, have the manuscript spiked . . . then I lapse into my bad habit, break my promise and dispose of you and the ladies. Your bodies turn up floating in the docks. I expect Messrs Bright and Fullman will get wind of that, don't you? And when they do, they're going to mention it to the law. And then all the names in that manuscript of yours will find themselves under a fairly powerful microscope. If, on the other hand, you tell your agent that you're pulling the book for personal reasons and life goes on as normal . . .' He shrugs. 'Maybe it's just me, but I don't see anyone's alarm bells ringing in that scenario.'

'So I call my agent, pull the book. You leave. What's to stop me retracting that when you're gone?'

He raises his eyebrows. 'Even you're not that stupid. After what you've gone through? As for our employer . . . well, you've had a taste of his persuasion. He might not be quite as subtle next time round.'

Honey's right, it doesn't matter if the authorities *are* out there, it doesn't matter if the police are on their way. People in the arms industry are the most tenacious, the most single-minded on the planet. These two men are dispensable; even if this operation were to end with their arrest, there would be someone else equally nasty, equally determined, lining up to take their place. Oliver's best hope is to identify them. And soon. Time is running out.

'If I found out who your employer was, it would change everything. I could come after you. If I did it through the right channels, I could finish the company.'

Honig inclines his head in gracious assent. 'Indeed you could. And as I said earlier, that is never going to happen. You will never know who we work for.'

Oliver puts a finger to his temple. His head is aching. 'If I pull the book, you'll let us go?'

'That's generally how a warning works.'

'My family, me — we'll never hear from you again?'

Honig inclines his head — like a waiter in a top hotel where nothing is too much trouble, nothing unachievable for the right clientele. 'Of course. But tick tock tick tock.' He holds up his wrist to show Oliver his watch. 'We haven't got for ever, you know.'

Oliver closes his mouth in a straight line. There's no choice. He glances at the guitar clock on the purple wall.

'My agent's office opens at nine thirty,' he says. 'Is the phone working yet?'

THE POLICE

It's getting hot outside and Honig can feel
the sweat sticking to his shirt. This is craziness. Complete craziness. Even getting to the
bottom of the driveway to make the phone
call is turning into a thing of stress. Ironic
how he and Ian the Geek are suddenly in the
same situation they dramatized on the first
day to scare the family.

He scans the gardens, checking everything
is as he remembers it. When he's sure nothing's changed he goes to the side door and,
not taking his eyes off his surroundings,
reaches in and takes the key from the inside.
He's already been around the house and
checked every other door is locked — this is
the last one. He slams it shut and locks it.
Checks it. Rattles the door. It is sound.

In the front porch Oliver is standing with
Ian the Geek. He's got the face of a prisoner
on his first day of freedom. He turns and
looks up at the windows, as if trying to see
his wife or daughter up there. Then he takes

a deep, deep breath. For a moment Honig wonders if he's having another heart attack, his face is so blue. But the old man gives a weary sigh. 'Come on,' he says. 'Let's get it over and done with.'

The car is waiting — just a few short steps from the door. Honig would defy anyone to ambush them now. Even someone as nuts as Minnet Kable. Nevertheless he keeps his eye on the treeline as he leads Anchor-Ferrers to the car. He opens the car door, puts his hand on the old guy's head to make sure it clears the door trim as he ducks into the back seat. Just like the cops do to stop themselves being sued.

He slams the door and goes round the rear of the car. He opens the boot and checks what Ian the Geek has put in there. He's transferred the intestines from the bucket into three plastic measuring jugs, taped clingfilm over them, and placed them in the boot. The intestines are small — small enough to fit into three jugs. That probably means it's a woman, which fits in with his image of what Kable would do. But who? And why and where and when? The field with the barbed wire is, weirdly and completely coincidentally, opposite the yellow house where the woman in the red jeans lives. The woman he and Ian the Geek picked out of a hat when they were deciding on the charade to scare the Anchor-Ferrers — mostly because she was kind of a

show-stopper in her car and her tight red
jeans. As far as they were aware at the time,
she was fine. Wouldn't it really be the bol-
locks if it turned out that, not only is Kable
out there but, just like in the pastiche Havill-
land cooked up, the person he hit on was, in
fact, the woman in the yellow house? What a
total headfuck that would be. It would make
him start believing in UFOs and the collapse
of WTC Building 7 and all the other wack
conspiracy theories.

The jugs are jammed up against the wheel
arches so they won't fall over. At least Ian the
Geek is using his head, Honig notes; he's surrounded the jugs with towels. If they do fall
over, there won't be any spillage. At that moment Ian the Geek appears from the back
door, carrying all the smartphones and
headphones and recording equipment they
need. He crosses the short distance from the
door to the car and stands next to Honig.
They both look at the jugs in the boot.

'Have you got something to clean yourself
up afterwards?'

'Tissues,' Ian the Geek says. 'In my pocket.'

'And fingerprints?'

'I've got those gloves you gave me
yesterday.'

'Good. Make sure you bring everything
back with you.'

'That's the one thing I did learn in the
Legion: always cover your tracks.'

At last, Honig thinks, the Geek is thinking like a professional. He hasn't been asked, he's suggested the wisest thing to do is take the entrails back to the barbed wire where he found them. As soon as Oliver makes the call they can take most of the money and disappear. Leave the cops to deal with whatever psycho is out in these woods.

Bubblegum Mania, he thinks. Jesus, Bubblegum Mania. I'm coming home.

He slams the boot and the two men climb into the car where Oliver is waiting. Ian the Geek fastens his belt in the passenger seat and Honig uses the central-locking button to secure all the doors. No one in the car says a word about this — about why they need the doors locked just for a drive down the hill.

'The car smells.' Honig has driven only a hundred yards or so, very slowly for fear the jugs in the boot will capsize, when Oliver Anchor-Ferrers sits up straight on the back seat. He turns his head, craning his face to find the source of his irritation. 'It smells like hell in here. Smells like death. And drink. It smells like drink.'

'It's the rubbish,' Honig says, keeping his hands resting lightly on the wheel. 'We've got to empty the bin bags. All that dog food that got thrown around. It's all in the boot.'

Oliver doesn't immediately accept this answer, Honig can tell just from monitoring his face in the rear-view mirror. The old guy stays canted forward in his seat, his head at an angle, his eyes moving back and forward, as if he's trying to work out what's going on. In the back window behind him The Turrets dwindles to a fairy castle on a Disneyland postcard.

The Chrysler goes smoothly through the electronic gates. It's such a predatory car, Honig feels he should put sunglasses on just to drive it. He wishes again he could stop and take a snap of his situation, a photo of him in the car, in his moment of danger, just so he has something to take home to Silver Spring. Next to him Ian the Geek is checking for messages on his phone. All night they've been discussing how Havilland could have let them go on with their charade if Minnet Kable was actually out of prison. They're expecting some news by now.

'Nothing,' the Geek mouths. 'Zilch.'

'What?'

Ian the Geek frowns, shakes his head looking at the screen. 'No emails either.'

Fuck, fuck, *fuck,* Honig thinks. *Fucking* Havilland can't be bothered to get info this important to them? So they're stuck out here in the boonies with some serial killer planning God knows what, and their own shagging company isn't backing them up?

He's still raging about this when they get to the place he and Ian the Geek stopped yesterday. He parks up and Ian the Geek gets out, goes to the boot. While he's fumbling around back there Honig unbuckles his belt and turns to look over the seatback at Oliver.

'Hey, look at me. Keep your eyes on me. You don't need to know what's going on back there. OK?'

Oliver nods. His eyes flicker but he doesn't try to look back. It's clear he's not happy about this; he's a man who has long been in control of his life, and learning that he can't control everything must be the hardest lesson. Behind him, Ian the Geek is removing the jugs from the boot. He takes one at a time, leaves the first a short distance inside the trees then comes back for the next — getting them out of Oliver's view before he transfers them further into the woods to the barbed wire. When he's done, he throws Honig a short salute through the rear window and disappears into the woods.

Honig sighs and turns to stare out of the windscreen at the tarmac, all the cowparsley hanging over the lane in the sun. It's nine twenty-five. The literary agent's offices open in five minutes. He toys with the filling in his pocket. Turning it over and over. When they're all out of here he's going to post the damned thing to the cops with an anonymous note. Somewhere out in those woods there is a body. Christ only knows what state it's in. Again he wonders how Havilland can be so lax as not to send a message. Incredible.

He begins to assemble the recording equipment, trying to remember what Ian the Geek told him about where to put the USB line. He gets the mic attached and is about to test-run it when a car approaches from the north, coming slowly down the winding lane. Honig lowers the phone and watches. It's a marked car, driven by two uniformed cops.

He is instinctive. He drops the recording equipment in his lap and at the same time reaches a hand back and grabs Oliver around the ankle in a pincer-like grip. 'Don't even think about moving,' he says between gritted teeth. 'If my colleague and I fail, there'll be someone else behind us. We will keep coming until you do what we want. Get it?'

The cop car slows fractionally as they pass. There's a second or two where the man in the passenger seat turns his head to monitor the occupants of the Chrysler. Then the car continues on its way until it disappears in the distance.

Honig lets out his breath. He releases Oliver's leg and continues hastily assembling the equipment. The cops aren't looking for them, but something about their attitude tells Honig they're not just passing through. They're casing the area. Maybe they already know there's a fucking psycho on the loose. Could it be the rest of the disembowelled body has been found?

The net is tightening. There isn't much longer.

CALLING LONDON

'I don't know why you didn't leave this place.'

It is nine thirty-five. Oliver has tried calling his literary agent in London but the phones haven't yet been switched through to the office and are still being picked up by the answering service. So now he is sitting in the back seat, waiting to call again. Honey is in the driver's seat, facing forward, his shiny monk's pate pressed back into his headrest. Oliver can see his eyes reflected in the rear-view mirror. And a faint line of sweat on his brow. You can't act sweat, thinks Oliver. The guy is absolutely terrified. Perhaps the tables are turning.

'Someone like you — you could have got away from all of it, could have escaped. Why keep coming back to the place it all happened? If it was me, I'd have sold up and got myself to the furthest part of the planet.'

It takes Oliver a moment to understand what he means. 'Are you talking about Kable?'

'Doesn't it bother you? Thinking about what he got up to in these woods?'

Oliver leans forward and massages the place on his ankle where Honey dug in his fingers. A police car has just passed. A *genuine* police car, which is likely to have something to do with the men's anxiety. The car hasn't turned up towards the house, but that doesn't mean something out there isn't on the move. Oliver isn't sure whether to feel relieved or more scared. If the police are involved, how desperate will the two men get?

'I said — doesn't it bother you?'

Oliver looks up. Honey is staring at him in the mirror. His eyes are small and intense.

'I don't think about it because it's hardly likely to happen again. Not here, anyway. Lightning doesn't strike twice, whatever you tried to trick us into thinking.'

Honey gives a shiver at that comment. He puts a finger into his collar and loosens it to get some air in there. He leans forward and casts a wary glance out of the window, as if to check they are on their own.

'Gives me the fucking creeps,' he says, staring into the trees. 'Thought of what he did to those kids. Choosing them — then waiting for them in a cave like that . . . then *bam!* Next second they're both dead. It's some kind of sickness, isn't it?'

He waits for an answer from Oliver, but gets none. Honey sighs and checks his watch.

He shifts in the seat, pulls his phone from his pocket and dials the agent again. It connects and begins to ring as he holds it over his head for Oliver to take. Oliver looks at it in silence for a moment. His head is whirring. Connecting dots. He takes the phone. Holds it to his ear.

'Good morning. Bright and Fullman. How can I help you?'

'Oliver Anchor-Ferrers here. I need to leave a message. Have you got a pen?'

'Yes, go ahead, Oliver.'

'Gauntlet Systems. That's G-A-U-N—'

He doesn't get any further. Honey swivels in the seat and grabs the phone from his hand, killing the call instantly.

'What the fuck are you talking about?' He throws the phone down and leans over the back seat, pushing his face at Oliver. *'What was that shit about?'*

'You're from Gauntlet.'

'Bullshit, bullshit, bullshit, you are living a fantasy.'

'I'm not. You are from Gauntlet. Pietr Havilland sent you.'

Honey launches his entire body through the gap and pins Oliver by the throat.

'Fucking shut it,' he hisses, shaking him hard. 'Just fucking shut your mouth.'

Oliver's head clunks against the seat-belt mooring, he claws pitifully at Honey's hands — feeling the tug and ache of the scar on his chest. Dimly he can hear Honey's feet scrabbling and banging against the handbrake, trying to get purchase. 'You have *no* fucking idea what you're up against. None.'

Knock knock knock . . .

Oliver is pressed too far up against the door to see where the noise is coming from, but it's enough to make Honey freeze. There's a long pause where he is so motionless that Oliver has time to see close up the pale eyelashes, the large pores in the side of his nose, the fine red veins in his eyes. Honey's breath comes in and out with a punch of stale coffee and fear.

Then abruptly Honey releases him. He heaves himself back into the driver's seat, muttering under his breath, straightening his shirt. Oliver pushes himself upright with difficulty. It is Molina at the window, knocking on the glass. He is holding a pair of Matilda's pink and yellow rubber gloves and there is an expression of astonished puzzlement on his face to see the two men in the car in this tussle.

'Jesus.' Irritably Honey reaches over and unlocks the door. He pushes it open so quickly that Molina jumps back just in time to avoid being hit.

'What the hell . . .' he begins, but Honey is already gunning the engine.

'Just get the fuck in. There are cops all over the place.'

Molina leaps into the seat, the door still swinging open as Honey slams the car into gear and swerves into the centre of the road. Both passengers are thrown to one side with the force of his fury. The car turns in the direction of The Turrets, Oliver sees, his face pressed painfully against the glass by the motion. It seems they are going home.

Beat the next beat, he tells his pig-heart. *It's not over yet.*

THE ROSE ROOM

A car screeches to a halt on the gravel at the front of the house and in the little box room Lucia props herself up from where she has been lying. She lifts her face to the window and listens carefully. There is the sound of car doors slamming, an angry, half-whispered conversation, the bang of the front door. Shuffling sounds that tell her Dad has been brought back to her bedroom at the other end of the landing.

Lucia stays absolutely still, trying to decode what's going on. The men clatter back down the stairs and she can hear the muffled noise of their conversation coming from the kitchen. She can't hear words but she can pick up on their anxiety.

After a while she moves herself to a sitting position and rubs her ankle where it's tethered to the radiator. Her troll boots sit about a foot away, placed neatly together. Last night 'Molina' brought back the boot she left on the stairs during the struggle on the first day.

She thanked him. She considered maybe smiling, even reaching a hand out to him in gratitude, but the door behind him was open and she didn't want a gesture like that making its way on to the video recordings. Especially now things are starting to happen.

Lucia is almost 100 per cent certain Honig's plan is falling apart, it's unstitching by the second. She's been watching him like a hawk, tracking his movements, and she knows he's a fake, that his bravado is a masquerade. He's probably never even been in a pub brawl, let alone been an international assassin the way he wants the family to believe. It was watching him doing that puzzle when Mum was hanging upside down that gave him away. From where she was sitting she could see he was filling in the squares on the Sudoku puzzle with nonsense. He might know some of the rules — like the best way to torture a parent is to torture the child, which is a truism so old even Shakespeare used it — but the truth about Honig is that while he acts cool he's actually a baby inside. And now he's out of control.

Sure enough, when, five minutes later, the door opens and Honig is standing there with a sandwich and a plastic bottle of water, she can see it written in his face. He's anxious. Really anxious.

'Breakfast,' he says curtly. When she doesn't

immediately take the food he pushes it at her. 'Eat.'

'What's the matter?' She looks past his hands and up into his face curiously. 'What's happening?'

'Just take the food.'

She lets a smile curl her mouth slowly. 'I know. I know what's happening. I know more than you could ever guess.'

'Shut up and take the food.'

'I know you're here because of Dad's work. And I know you're not the person you pretend to be.'

'Take the fucking food.'

He throws the water bottle and the sandwich at her. They land on her thighs and roll on to the floor. As Honig leaves the room she is still smiling.

'I'm so sorry,' she murmurs to his retreating back. 'So sorry it's all going wrong for you.'

As Caffery pulls up outside Columbus Systems' headquarters — forty acres of landscaped grass, fountains and glittering windows on the outskirts of Slough — his phone is ringing. Blocked number. The way most calls from police officers come in, so he puts on the handbrake, switches off the engine and answers it.

It's Paluzzi. 'Did you get the pdf?'

It takes Caffery a moment to remember. The attacks on the Donkey Pitch. Minnet Kable. 'I did. Thank you for that.'

'There was no particular reason you were asking about that place, was there? No other reason?'

'No,' he says slowly. 'Like I said — just curiosity. Why?'

'I don't know. I just wanted to pass something by you. We've got a missing person popped up in Litton, just down the road. It's not connected with your *curiosity*, is it?'

'I'm sure it's not.' Caffery flips a jot pad

out of his glove compartment and takes a pen from his pocket. He crunches the phone between his chin and his shoulder. 'Give me the outline anyway.'

'Lady by the name of Ginny Van Der Bolt. She's forty, white, works as a cleaner, divorced, children have left home, but the daughter's called the local station because Mum hasn't picked up the phone in a couple of days. It's a bit of an odd one. Apparently she's been known to do this before, has a habit of taking off without saying anything — especially if there's been a bit of family discord — so we're not exactly tying ourselves in knots over it. They've been in the house; handbag and car are missing, but passport's there.'

'Suicide?'

'Nothing to suggest that. No sightings of the car. No one here in the office is interested — she's not a vulnerable person — but I was just trawling through the database this morning and this popped out at me because she lives so close to where Kable killed those teenagers. Rose Cottage in Litton — not a million miles away from the crime scene.'

'You said she's divorced?'

'Yes. Her ex is in Wincanton. He hasn't heard from her, but he says he wouldn't expect to.'

'Has Ginny got a dog?'

'A dog? Um — don't think so. Hang on.'

She hums and haws at the other end of the line as she reads through the report. 'No — doesn't say anything about dogs. Says here: daughter questioned, no dependants, no pets.'

Caffery glances in the rear-view mirror and sees Bear watching him seriously from the front seat. 'You sure?'

'I'm sure.'

'OK,' he says. 'Do me a favour, will you? Call the local station and double-check that. If she's a dog owner, let me know, yeah?'

'I'll call you in ten.'

'No — I'm going into a meeting. Just send me a text.'

'It's OK, I can wait until you're out of your meeting.'

'Just the text, OK? And only if this woman is a dog owner. Right?'

There's a slight hesitation. Then Paluzzi says, her voice downcast, 'Fine. I hope you have a nice day. The superintendent is still on an amber, looking likely for a green later this week if you hold out.'

They finish the call and Caffery sits for a moment, looking distantly out of the window at the sun on Columbus's HQ. He's sure he went to a Rose Cottage during his tour of the Litton area, but he can't picture it for the moment. There were so many cottages, and they all seemed to have roses growing round the porches. That area is teeming with people. And any one of them could be Bear's owner.

'Ginny?' He tips back his head and looks at Bear's reflection. 'Know anyone called Ginny?' Bear wags her tail. Opens her mouth. She thinks Caffery's asking her if she wants a walk. He smiles wearily. 'Later. I swear, later.'

He drops his hands on the steering wheel and forces himself to look sideways at the sparkling football stadium of a headquarters. Columbus Systems. So bloody big it's got its own signposted exit on the dual carriageway and its own sports centre. This is just the hub — the company has almost ten thousand employees worldwide. Like every search he's done since he agreed to find Bear's owner, before he even starts he knows he's on to a loser.

'Still,' he tells Bear as he swings out of the car, 'nothing ventured, nothing gained. You stay here and keep the seats warm.'

GAUNTLET SYSTEMS

In the bedroom Oliver gingerly touches the places on his neck where he is bruised. Honey has hands like pincers. Like iron rods. He is trained in the way that most of the men in Gauntlet's security division are trained. They're predominantly ex-military — many of them pulled from the ranks of the Foreign Legion, which might have polished up its image recently, but to Oliver's thinking is still a sinkpot for all the world's desperados. The ones who come out of the Legion have less regard for humanity than they did when they went in.

But they are not invincible. As Oliver has proved.

It is afternoon now. He has been here for hours and no one has been up to see him. Downstairs the men have been arguing in angry whispers. They are thrown into disarray by Oliver's phone call and are trying to work out how to get themselves out of this trap. Because Oliver might be tied up right now, but he has gained the upper hand by identifying them.

All it took was one sentence from Honey when he referred to Minnet Kable *waiting for them in a cave like that*. And Oliver knew.

He has always been open with his clients about the inspiration for his torpedo system — arms manufacturers are not the sort of people to get squeamish over the murder of two teenagers, they've seen much, much worse. In fact, they seem to relish hearing the genesis of his system, a personally profound experience of the couple being wounded by one blow translated into the professional inspiration behind the Wolf. What he's never mentioned was exactly how Minnet Kable approached the teenage couple that night. No one knows for sure what happened, and there has never been any suggestion Kable hid in the cave waiting for Hugo and Sophie. There's no evidence he even knew of the cave's existence, and the idea he waited there to ambush them is a detail Oliver invented once. And once only.

The night he sold the Wolf torpedo to Pietr Havilland.

He remembers sitting in L'Escargot in Soho, Havilland shaking out his starched linen napkin, tucking it in, saying, *So, Mr Anchor-Ferrers, people are saying great things about the Wolf . . .*

Havilland was a notoriously difficult sell. Oliver knew Gauntlet had poured millions into a remotely operated underwater housing, a type of garage where a projectile could wait patiently for its prey to pass. The Wolf had to work in concert with Gauntlet's established system, so Oliver embellished his account of the murders to fit what Havilland wanted to hear. He painted a picture of Minnet Kable targeting the teenage couple in a local bar, stalking them until he discovered they often went to the Donkey Pitch together. Locked into their appearance, their sound, their smell, just like the Wolf, he had crouched in the cave until their individual signature passed by. The same way, Oliver explained to Havilland, he pictured the Wolf torpedo leaping from Gauntlet's underwater housing.

Only Gauntlet Systems has ever had this fabricated version of the murders. No other company. Ergo Honey and Molina are from Gauntlet. Oliver recognizes Molina not because he's an actor or a politician, but from seeing him somewhere in the corridors of Gauntlet's New York HQ.

The literary agency will think nothing of the earlier phone call; they will simply assume he was cut off. If they try to call him back it will take time for anyone to realize things are amiss at The Turrets. But the name 'Gauntlet' has been delivered and the men downstairs now have a huge dilemma on their

406

hands. Not to mention the fact that for some unaccountable reason police are circling the area. Perhaps someone other than the agency has already raised the alarm.

In the kitchen the men's voices are growing louder, more irate. Oliver knows there's still an outside chance that they are angry and desperate enough to kill the family and make a run for it, but to do so would spell the end of their careers — and worse. They will be hunted down by Gauntlet and the police. The secret cameras have recorded almost everything that's happened in the house, and Oliver has faith that John Bancroft, his detective, will pick up the baton now the name 'Gauntlet' has been delivered. Bancroft will make sure justice is done.

He turns over the carpet, licks the tip of the pen to coax out the remaining ink, and begins to write.

Pietr Havilland, of Gauntlet Systems is behind this. I worked with Gauntlet for six months during its period of greatest expansion. Its net worth increased exponentially for a full two years, resulting in global domination in its field. Havilland is rightly terrified of what I have written in my autobiography because he has been covering the immoral acts of his company for several years.

There have been accidents during the development of Gauntlet's underwater weapons programme. In particular, a trial run off the coast of Africa which ended in disaster and loss of life.

Oliver is running out of room. He unpicks more of the rug hem and shifts position so he can write the date of that particular accident: *May 2007.* He adds *Ncala Harbour, Mozambique.* As he writes 'Mozambique', almost like a comment on the place, from downstairs comes the unmistakable noise of the buzzer on the electronic gates. He freezes, the pen held where it is, leaking a loud blue spot into the fabric. Slowly, slowly, he raises his head to the window. Once again the buzzer sounds. A small smile creeps on to his face.

Out there, more than half a mile away, someone is at the gates, wanting to be admitted. It doesn't sound as if they're going to take no for an answer.

CHERYL

There's a line from a song, Caffery can't remember the title or the band, but as he's walking through Columbus Systems' offices, listening to the squeak of his feet on the polished marble floors, the song keeps going through his head. Something about waking up bleeding and drunk in a strange bed — about lunatic women driving you to despair. He thinks about Breanne. Was it him that pushed the button, or was it Breanne? And, if it was her, does that means *she's* the crazy? Are women really nuts or is that just men's neat little abdication of responsibility?

But then he looks at the woman from Columbus's human resources department, and quickly decides that sometimes, yes, women really are as mad as fish.

She's about thirty-five, with white-blond hair clipped very close to her head, long hooped earrings and no make-up, save a slash of red on her lips. She's wearing a nose stud, a droopy floral dress and a boyfriend cardigan, her hands pushed into the pockets.

'I know — I'm not your average human resources chick, am I?'

He looks her up and down. 'Usually it's power suits and nude tights. Hair up, you know — heels.'

'Sexy secretary? Not me though — because Daddy owns the company. I'd be unemployable anywhere else.' She waves a hand around the office. 'Everyone hates me, but I don't care.'

'Are you joking?'

'Only partly. My father does own the company. But I could probably get a job somewhere else if I would toe the line with the clothes. And I don't think the staff hate me — at least, they've never said it to my face.' She gives a low laugh, and bends towards him, her hand next to her mouth. 'But,' she mutters, 'if you hated the boss's daughter, would you be retarded enough to say it to her face? I don't think so. Oh, and before you go and say anything that's going to totally piss me off, I'm gay. I'm a lesbian and I'm extremely politically correct — so you'd better use the right language around me because I get offended very easily and when I get offended Daddy gets offended and everyone's unhappy.'

'I'd never have guessed. You *look* so straight.'

'You're on thin ice.'

'I know it. I'll get to the point. You read my email?'

'Several times. But that doesn't mean I've got you an answer.'

'OK.' He folds his arms. Waits for a moment or two, trying to get the measure of this person. 'But you've got a system, and even if you're only here through nepotism I'm guessing you at least know how the computer works. So will you help me?'

'Take your hand and guide you?'

'Well, I would never put it like that — not with the PC axe dangling. So let's say euphemistically. Yes, euphemistically, I'd like you to take my hand.'

'I love that — cops using long words. It's especially great when they use them in the right context.'

Caffery notices a sign hanging above her desk that reads *One cries because one is sad. I cry because others are stupid and that makes me sad.* There has to be an easier way, he thinks. There really has to be.

'Are we getting anywhere here, Cheryl? Are you going to help me?'

'Have you got a warrant? That's what I'm supposed to say. It's what they all say in the police dramas. And then you're supposed to pull something clever out of the hat — like that you know I've been faking work records, or that the Department of Work and Pensions would LOVE to hear about how five of my

411

mates are employed as consultants when, spookily enough, they have absolutely no experience in the communications field and don't even live in the country.'

Caffery shakes his head, mystified. 'I don't get you — I just don't get you. It's a straight question. Are you going to help me or not?'

'Yes. But only if you tell me about Malcolm Bliss.'

He stares at her. Malcolm Bliss was a freak and a necrophiliac he brought to justice ten years ago in London. 'Do what?'

'As soon as I got your email I checked out who you are. You worked on the Birdman case, didn't you?'

'What about it?'

'There's this girl, you see. She's Ukrainian, new to the company, and I'm dying to impress her. She's so clever — so, so clever, brain the size of a city, and just — Oh, you know, looks to die for. But she's weird too.' Cheryl smiles coyly, showing her perfect white teeth. 'She's an ambulance chaser. Spends all her time looking at car crashes and autopsy photos on the web. A real-crime fan. She eats stuff like this.'

'What's this got to do with me?'

'Malcolm Bliss — she's absolutely obsessed with what he did. She's digging around, trying to find out all the gory details, but she's totally convinced the investigators didn't tell the whole story of what he did to those women. I thought you could, y'know, add some spice?'

In 2000 Malcolm Bliss had mutilated and had sexual intercourse with the corpses of several women. Until now Caffery hasn't completely realized how much the story is in the public domain. He's not sure whether to be shaken by it or not. Especially by the fact this woman seems to be in the grip of a lascivious fascination about it.

'What Bliss did is nobody's business. If there's anything held back from the public it's because the victims' families deserve to be protected.'

'Ahhh,' she says with a smile. 'But you *do* know. You know the details — the ones my girlfriend wants to know. You know everything about it — the way the bodies were, what he did to them.'

Caffery turns his head to one side and scrutinizes her carefully. He's met ghouls before — the ones who want to know all the details. Generally they are women, something he's always found strange, but they're never as forthright and blunt as Cheryl.

'OK.' At length he sits on the edge of the desk and folds his arms. 'But this didn't come from me.'

'I never met you.'

'What do you want to know?'

'Did he have intercourse with them?'

'Yes. We think so.'

413

'And the bodies — were they mutilated?'

'Yes.'

'How?'

'Bliss carved a Celtic cross into their chests. He cut off their heads and there's evidence to suggest he may have consumed them.'

Cheryl sucks in a breath and blood flows rapidly into her face. He can't tell if it's shock or excitement.

'And that's all I can tell you. Enough?'

She nods. He sees her swallow. 'Yes, that's enough.'

'So you'll help me?'

She nods again, as if still absorbing what he's said. 'Yes, I'll help. But I'm warning you — there's no magic button. No database I can just hit search on.'

'You're not computerized?'

'Yes, we're . . .' She swallows. Pushes her hair off her forehead and gathers herself. 'Of course we're computerized, but only going back ten years. Before that it's all paper-based and honestly, you go into the archives and it's like the final scene in *Raiders of the Lost Ark* — you know, where they put the Ark away in that warehouse and —'

'I know. But he might still be working for you. In which case he'd be computerized by now.'

'Uh huh,' she says in the sort of sarcastic, exasperated tone that makes him sure the next word out of her mouth is going to be 'duh'. 'Ye-essss — I'm on to that, surprisingly. I've started a search. On that computer over there — see? I'm going through biogs looking for spouses named Matilda. There is one, but they got married this year and she's twenty-five and he's twenty-six and they live in Buenos Aires, so that doesn't fit your spec. I've gone through all the CVs we've got online, looking for any that came out of the army. But it's a waste of time; we only keep electronic copies of CVs for people who've joined in the last ten years. From what you're saying, he'd have joined us in the late eighties?'

'Yes, from the army. Signals. He knows about radio communication.'

She smiles. 'Never fear. There is a second way.' She goes to a filing cabinet and picks up a wire tray loaded with paper. She brings it back and sets it on the desk with a loud whoomph. Dust flies off it. The paperwork is old and crumpled.

Caffery's heart sinks. 'Intimidating.'

'In the eighties we had a military division. If this "unnamed man" of yours came across from the army he'd have had some military skill set, or if he was techie but more comfortable working on a military application — which a lot of them are in the army; you know, they're working with their own kind — then he'd have probably gone into that division. But we got rid of it in the nineties and

415

lost a lot of staff back then. Dad got fed up with how it was lagging behind the civilian division. That's the way with military stuff, you have to jump through so many hoops to prove stuff is bomb-proof before it goes. It always runs over time.'

'Why do companies bother?'

'The long time is a two-way street: stuff for the MoD always runs over, because once it runs over it brings in more money. The tax-man picks up the bill, bless his heart — how much do we love him!'

'So what happened to the military division?'

'Every piece of paper in that pile is a company where staff who were let go in the nineties could have funnelled their way through to.'

Caffery picks up the first few sheets and leafs through them. Some are letters, some invoices — each has a different letterhead. He puts them back on the pile, dismayed. There must be two to three hundred sheets of paper here. Days — weeks of work.

'I know.' Cheryl opens her mouth and gives him a diamond-bright shopping TV smile. 'But I've got good news too.'

'I can almost see the light glinting off you.'

'I know — blinding, isn't it? Damn, it's tough being this wonderful!'

She swirls around, like she's in some crazy advert for the perfect wife, and walks across the office, sashaying her backside, one hand held up at her shoulder — the index finger beckoning him coyly.

He follows her to a bookcase where an old-fashioned CD player sits, its lights on.

'What?'

'Your good news.'

'What am I looking at?'

She flips open the lid of the CD, switches on an anglepoise and twists it round so it shines full on the underside of the lid.

'Ta-da.'

He feels in his pocket for his glasses, puts them on and peers at it, carefully. There is a small sticker there. It's a triangular symbol: black on yellow, a sunburst in the centre of the triangle. The symbol from the ring.

He closes the lid and opens it, as if he's going to find an explanation for what the sticker means.

'It's a laser hazard symbol,' says Cheryl. 'I recognized it the moment I saw the photos of the ring. We deal in microwave technology, uplink and telecommunications; our speciality is free space optics, which has a huge reliance on lasers. You walk through our factory floor and you see this symbol everywhere — it's pasted on pretty much every work station in the place. If I hadn't recognized it, I should have been shot.'

Caffery shakes his head and pockets his glasses. Not the Masons but something far less arcane, far less mystical and something so close to hand. It's probably stickered under the lid of his CD player at home.

'So he's probably a laser specialist,' Cheryl continues. 'And that narrows down the places he could have moved on to. Which is the good news.'

'The bad news?'

'Ah yes.' She holds up a varnished finger-nail. 'The bad news.' She goes back to the filing cabinet, where there is a second tray, also bulging. She brings it back to the desk and puts it down.

He looks at it, then raises an eyebrow at her, wondering if this is a joke. 'I thought you said you'd narrowed it down.'

'This *is* narrowed down.'

'But there are . . .'

'I know. Hundreds. It's a crazy industry.'

Caffery shakes his head and runs a hand through his hair.

'I'm sorry, Mr Caffery. I wish I could have been more help. You're welcome to borrow these, if you want. I'd like them back.'

Caffery sighs. 'Yeah, thank you,' he mumbles. Then in an attempt at manners he forces an uncomfortable smile. 'Thank you. To get all this together — it must have taken . . . I don't know . . .'

'Four hours. From the moment you emailed me.'

'You were always going to talk to me?'

'Oh yes. Of course.'

'All that stuff about the girlfriend? The one who's such a pervert she wanted to hear the gory details?'

'I made it up. I'm not even gay — I'm a plain old hettie.'

'Seriously?'

'Seriously. Quite fancy you, if you want the truth.'

'And Daddy?'

'Made that up too. My dad's been dead six years. I worked to get this job.'

Caffery sighs. Shakes his head and looks down at the folder in his hands, not quite knowing what to say. 'Well,' he says after a while. 'That's OK — because I made up all the stuff about Malcolm Bliss too. I mean he was nuts — a real pervert — but he didn't eat anyone's head. Or carve crosses in their chests.'

Cheryl nods. 'I know,' she smiles. 'I know he didn't — I know you were making it up.'

'How come?'

'Because you're just like me. Even if you don't know it, you're walking a tightrope. And there's a huge part of you wishing someone would just push you off the edge.'

HOG ROAST

The police car doesn't have its blues-and-twos flashing, but it does have its headlights and interior lights on and the radio cackling full blast. Both front doors are open like wings and the two cops stand with their arms resting on the doors, watching the Chrysler wind its way down the driveway.

Honig gets out. He's dressed in a dinner jacket, the bow tie half undone. This is Oliver's. They've only found one in the house, so Ian the Geek has covered his shirt with a camel coat which they've discovered in a wardrobe. He keeps it buttoned, just revealing the white collar, and he's taken off his distinctive glasses.

They stop the Chrysler ten foot from the electronic gates so they don't drive over the pressure sensor and cause the gates to open automatically. Honig gets out and walks to the gates, bending down to open them manually.

'Sorry.' When the gates have opened he approaches the police car — and stands with his hand resting on the newel post. 'The guy who's coming to fix them has been "definitely coming" for two days now. So here's us having to come down to the gate every time someone turns up.'

'Looks like you were on your way out anyway,' says the smaller of the two cops — a guy in his twenties who is already losing hair at his temples. He nods at Honig's dress shirt. 'Somewhere nice?'

Honig looks down at his clothes. Shakes his head and makes a face as if it's all a big embarrassment. 'I know. Has to be done though — Mum and Dad need someone to, you know, keep up appearances. The local hunt are having a charity barbecue in Blagdon. I can picture it now — actually, I don't want to picture, but I'll do it anyway. Still, it's a hog roast. Every cloud and all that.'

'Hog roast?' The bigger cop grimaces. 'Don't — it's torture.'

'He's on a diet,' says the one with the receding hair. 'Six kilos by midsummer. Don't think he'll make it.'

'Too many donuts?' Ian the Geek tries to make the comment sound witty and convivial, but it fails miserably. The atmosphere lowers a fraction. There's a pause. The larger one eyes Ian the Geek carefully. Then, taking his time, he gives a slow laugh.

'Actually, I can't stand donuts. In fact my

421

weight is a matter of genes and I could eat half of what you eat and, do you know what? I'd still be fat. But that's the problem with stereotypes, Mr . . . ?'

'Raven,' Honig interjects quickly, before Ian the Geek can dig himself any deeper. 'He's my friend Julian Raven and I'm Kiran Anchor-Ferrers.' He holds out his hand to shake. 'This is my parents' place.'

The officer pauses. He's still giving Ian the Geek a sideways glance as he leans forward and shakes Honig's hand. Then he steps back. Adjusts his radio and pulls back his shoulders a little. 'They here, are they — your parents?'

'No, you've missed them. They're in Scotland. Or rather, my mother's in Scotland, my father . . .' Honig looks at his watch and waves a hand vaguely in the air. 'Well, he's somewhere over the Lake District if SleazyJet are flying on time — we're just back from dropping him at Bristol Airport.'

'I think I saw you,' says the smaller one. 'Earlier. Over there — in that lay-by?'

'Possibly.' Honig reaches in his pocket for his phone. 'I'll give him a call, if you want? Is it them you want to speak to?'

'No no, it's just a routine enquiry. I'm sure you can help us, Mr Anchor-Ferrers.' He inclines his head to Honig, then Ian the Geek. 'And your friend, Mr Raven.'

Honig takes the smile off his face abruptly.

'OK, OK. If you want to make a joke, do — be my guest.'

'I'm sorry?'

'You've clearly got a problem with me having a' — he makes inverted commas with his fingers — 'friend.'

The cops exchange glances. The bigger one sighs. 'I'm sorry if we gave that impression. It wasn't our intention, everyone has a right, to his or her sexuality.'

'That doesn't sound genuine. In fact it sounds like you've got that from one of those courses they send you on.'

'I'm sorry if I've upset you.'

Honig shakes his head. 'No. I'm sorry. It's just that Julian and I? We've seen it all — been through a lot. We don't want any trouble, but we have got used to having to defend our choices.'

'We're not here for trouble.'

'Well, if you are, Julian and I will deal with it in a civilized way. Although a legal process is never an easy choice, sometimes it's the only choice. I'm blessed in that I've got the money to carry it all the way through to the end. Let's say that every time lawyers have been involved, no matter how much it's cost, I've made a point for every brother, every sister out there. We get called bolshie, but frankly, if we don't do it, who will?'

The smaller officer reaches into the car. He pulls out a pocket book. His attitude has changed completely. He's gone from swaggering to formal. 'Mr Anchor-Ferrers, Mr Raven, let's bring this whole thing on to a calmer footing. Is that OK?'

Honig and Ian the Geek exchange looks. Ian the Geek shakes his head and puts his hands into his armpits as if he's trying to subdue them, stop them hitting someone. He raises his chin and stares at the stars.

Honig turns his scrutiny to the cop's notebook. 'That looks worrying. Is everything OK? You must be here for a reason other than to harass us.'

'Yes,' says the taller one. 'And whether everything is "OK" or not rather depends on your perspective.'

'That's not the most promising comment I've ever heard. Sounds ominous.'

'Someone local is missing.' The cop takes a couple of paces towards the house and stands, squinting up at it, as if he's an estate agent sizing it up for the market. 'It's a house-to-house enquiry — just to pick up if anyone's seen anything strange. Just to build a picture.'

'A missing person.' Honig manages to get the words out and make them sound innocent. In his head, though, he's seeing the intestines again. The shiny, ruddy line they made in the branches. The three measuring jugs in the boot of the car. 'And under what circumstances is this person missing?'

'Oh, nothing, it's probably nothing at all.

It's not someone who is known for their reliability. Spends a lot of time in the Cart and Horses, according to the landlord — you know what I'm saying. But we have to check to make sure nothing untoward has happened.'

'Not someone known for their reliability? Who might that be?'

'Ginny Van Der Bolt. *Van . . . Der . . . Bolt.* She lives down in the village.'

Honig swallows. Although he doesn't let it show, he has a moment where he wants to put his hand back on the gate, just to steady himself. Not the woman in the yellow house. Closer to home than that.

'Mr Anchor-Ferrers? Are you . . . ?'

'I'm fine. Of course.' He recovers himself. 'Perfectly fine. It's just — Ginny — she cleans for my parents. So I know her.'

'When was the last time you saw her?'

'I'm not sure. I mean, I really don't have many dealings with her. My mother generally does.'

'But she comes up here once a week?'

'Yes. I think it's twice when we're all here, once if we're not, just to check everything's OK.'

'Your mother — has she mentioned anything about Ginny recently? Anything on her mind?'

Honig shakes his head slowly. 'No. I mean, not that I can recall. Is something . . . I mean, you haven't found anything? No . . . *evidence* of her?'

'She didn't have any problems at home? No upsets with boyfriends? Her ex?'

'Not that I can recall.'

'Would your mother know more? Have you got her number?'

The taller cop pulls out a business card and a pen and holds them out. Honig leans against a tree and carefully writes out a number the company uses — one that will always be answered by an anonymous sounding answer service. He hands it back, saying, 'I know she said she was going to be out of signal for a while. You know what it's like up in Scotland.' He looks from one face to the other, licking his lips, not sure who to direct the question to. In the end he turns to the diet cop. 'You do know about what happened here, don't you? In this area.'

The cop looks up at him. 'I'm sorry?'

'The teenagers — back in the nineties?'

There's a pause, then recognition dawns. 'Minnet Kable? Yeah, we know. Everyone round here knows about that.'

'And . . .' Honig says searchingly. 'And I suppose it's nothing to do with him?'

'No.' The cop flips another card out of his pocket and hands it to Honig. 'Nothing to do with him — unless it's his ghost.'

'I beg your pardon?'

'He died about a week ago. Never got let

426

out of Rampton. If your mother calls, get her to give me a ring, would you? Don't worry her — it would just be nice to have a quick chat.'

Honig stares at him blankly. The cop shakes the card at him and Honig snaps out of it, takes the card hurriedly. 'Of course,' he says. 'Of course I will.'

'Enjoy the hog roast.'

'We'll try to.'

The police get into the car and fasten their seat belts. The big one starts the engine and the car reverses in a crunch of gravel. It spins into a three-point turn then heads back down the road in the direction of Compton Martin. Neither Honig nor Ian the Geek speak until the car has completely disappeared and the sound has dwindled into silence. Now it's just the faint click click click of crickets in the field, and the soft shush of a breeze going through the corn.

Honig turns to look at Ian the Geek. The Geek is staring back at him, eyes like open spaces.

'Don't look at me like that,' Honig says. 'I haven't got a fucking clue either.'

THE CELLAR

This is so fucked up it isn't true. So fucked up. Just like Lucia said, it's all going wrong. Honig paces back and forth in the kitchen. He and Ian the Geek have made a show of setting off for the hog roast, in case the cops have bothered to stop and check, but now they are back at the house. For hours they've been trying to make sense of it and decide what to do. But they're getting nowhere.

The Chrysler, which neither of them cares about hiding any more, is parked directly next to the front door. They've left the interior light on. Every instinct is telling Honig to dump everything and run. But Pietr Havilland will find them. They could go on threatening Oliver, but even if he retracted what he's told his agent, he'll be able to come after Gauntlet Systems at a later date. Time is running out. Something beyond all this is at work — something that's outside all Honig's understanding. He cannot for the life of him figure out what is happening.

He takes deep breaths and for the hundredth time talks himself through the list of realities, hoping to comb some sense out of it all.

1. There is no phone line up here.

2. The only phone signal is at the bottom of the lane where the cops are cruising around like sharks.

3. The Anchor-Ferrers' cleaner is missing.

4. It was *someone's* guts he and Ian the Geek took into the forest in three jugs this morning. They were human. The sweetcorn — the filling — the alcohol. (*Someone not known for their reliability. Someone who spends a lot of time in the Coach and Horses, you get what I mean?*)

5. Minnet Kable is dead.

This last detail is the biggest mind-melt of all. He has double-checked that Kable is indeed dead. He is. No mistake about this. There are messages on the phone that Ian the Geek overlooked — he checked the emails, but the text messages from Gauntlet and various others he hadn't bothered to read. Ten days ago Minnet Kable died from complications of lung cancer in the medical wing of Rampton high-security facility. Honig's fury with Ian the Geek pales into insignificance against his complete and utter bewilderment. What the *fuck* is happening here? And how long can he wait until his

429

nerves unzip completely?

The shadows outside have been long and sharp, but now they are getting muddy as ditchwater and twilight is sliding into darkness. He hadn't intended spending another night in this place but he still can't make up his mind, which way to leap. He has changed out of the dinner jacket into his own clothes, but Ian the Geek is still dressed for the 'hog roast' — Oliver's bow tie hanging loose around the collar of his white shirt. His face is red and congested because he's started drinking — a bottle of wine he found in the rack by the window. A cigar sits in an ashtray on the mantelpiece. The tobacco and alcohol go against all the rules, but the situation has got to both of them.

The moment they came back from the encounter with the cops both men went and checked every door, every window. They gave Oliver his medication and checked on Matilda and Lucia, who are still perfectly healthy and alert — as healthy as you can be after three days in shackles. There is absolutely nothing, no evidence to suggest that anyone has been at the house. Yet something feels wrong.

Honig wafts the air with his hand, half hoping the smoke from Ian's cigar will mask the smell that still permeates every centimetre of the kitchen.

'Are you sure you washed out those jugs?'

he says. 'It still fucking stinks in here.'

Ian the Geek nods. Pours another glass of wine. Honig glares at him. The guy is really irritating him. He's got almost as much of the money as Honig has been paid, and has done half the work. He's fucked up from start to finish. From gathering up those innards, to not being able to get the landline working, to not checking the texts from Havilland about Kable's death. There is every chance that when he arrived four days ago he didn't search the place efficiently.

Bad-temperedly he snatches Ian the Geek's cigar and throws it into the sink. Ignoring the other man's indignation he picks up the torch, goes to the cellar door, unlocks it and opens it a small way. It makes a slight groan. The smell from down there is foul. Truly disgusting. Honig licks his lips and looks down at his feet in his clean shoes — they're going to get trashed. Then he realizes he's standing where he cleaned up the blood stains two days ago from where Ian the Geek carried the intestines through the house. Something niggles at him; somewhere in the back of his head in a place he keeps all the things he doesn't want to address head-on, it nudges at him briefly.

Minnet Kable is dead.

Deer don't eat sweetcorn or swallow fillings.

He tries the electric switch — in case it's

suddenly started working again, but it doesn't. He goes down a few steps and waits for a moment to see if his eyes will get used to the light. From here the darkened stairwell falls away into the gloom — he can see nothing. He puts his hand on the banister and ducks his head down, squinting. There is light coming through the floorboards in the kitchen which casts a dim segmented light on to what lies below; you can tell the cellar extends a long way. Ian the Geek has missed something. *Something* bad is down here because the smell is overpowering. The floorboards aren't caulked, there is light shining in dusty slices from the kitchen above. A smell from down here would just rise through the gaps into the kitchen.

He gets the torch from the table, powers it up, and shines it down into the darkness. The cellar stretches way off under the house, past the kitchen and onwards into the gloom. To his left are ranged wine racks stacked with dusty bottles. To his right is a pile of firewood and a litter of boxes containing the usual family stuff — Christmas decorations, old bicycle pumps. Further on is the avalanche of coal that Ian the Geek must have precipitated, but it's only halfway into the cellar and it's clear he can't have covered the entire floor space of the cellar in the time he was down here. The place goes on further — much further.

Honig continues down the remaining steps

and stops next to the boxes of tinsel. He aims the torch at the ceiling and runs it along the beams. He estimates he must be standing under the kitchen table. He can see the darkness where the large rug sits, and, over near the hearth, the smaller rug where the camp beds are. He shines the torch along the rough stone walls, covered in cobwebs and soot — and sees that along the entire back of the cellar rough-hewn logs are stacked, ready for the fire. Pile after pile after pile of them. He's fairly sure Ian the Geek didn't check any of those.

The floor is made of cast concrete and his feet don't make a sound as he crosses to the wall. He walks like a cat, stepping slowly into each new space, and stops, waiting for something to reveal itself. There's a grille in the ceiling at the far end which must come out under the big bay in the front room. Other things are down here — old milk crates, a tent in a red-and-blue cover, a rotting cardboard box full of plastic laundry-conditioner bottles. Piled against one of the brick columns he sees clothing.

He squats and begins to go through it. A woman's clothes, crackling with old dried blood. Bra, knickers, tights in a big jumble. There's a pair of jeans and from them he fishes out a wallet. He flicks it open and what he sees makes him close his eyes.

Ginny Van Der Bolt. The housekeeper.

433

Honig has to count to twenty before he finds the strength to stand. 'Hey!' He reaches up and uses the butt of the torch to knock on the underside of the ceiling. 'Get your tukas down here,' he calls to Ian the Geek. 'Now.'

He goes to the furthest corner and stops next to the heaps of cut wood. This is where the smell is coming from. He bends slightly and rests his hand on the wood, feeling it rough and dusty under his fingers. No movement from upstairs.

'Geek,' he bellows. 'Down here now.'

The torch beam makes the wood seem to swim in and out of the gloom. He moves a log from the top of the pile and casts it to one side. And another, and another. The fifth log is leaning against something soft.

Honig stands quite still for a long time, his heart thumping in his chest. Something large and spreading is under the wood and now he looks down at his feet he can see what's oozing out. He lifts one foot — feels the tacky adhesion there. Upending one of the other logs he finds a hand. It is swollen and black, the nails raised from their beds. There's a ring on one finger — a woman's ring. As he pulls away more logs the body confirms itself as female. Naked. The head is turned away from him, in the direction of the wall, bent at an almost impossible angle as if she is looking at her knees. He's grateful he doesn't have to look at her face. The arm he can see has been sliced by something sharp — she'll have bled from that. The edges of the wound are peeled open and shrivelled like orange skin. He pulls away another piece of wood and sees the gaping wound in the belly.

Honig's chest heaves. He can't tell if it's nausea or because he wants to sob. Kable is dead, Kable is dead, Kable is dead, he repeats to himself. Kable is dead.

EIGHTS WEEK

Matilda lies on the floor, manacled by her ankle to the radiator. Her eyes are closed, she is somewhere between sleep and delirium. All day she has been trying to summon up a better picture of Oliver. Something clean and beautiful and untouched by age and reality.

At last her eyes flicker and a small smile comes to her face — because she can see him. He's young again and he's dressed in a nice suit with a college tie all covered in red pelicans. He's standing in a sunny quad, holding a pair of binoculars. It's eights week at Oxford and he's taken her back to the college reunion. The binoculars are so he can be the first on the top of the boathouse to see his old college team come round the bend in the Isis.

He holds a hand out to her. 'Come on, Matilda my love,' he says. 'Let's go for a walk next to the river.'

She reaches a hand out to him, but as she does tears come into her eyes. 'Oh, Oliver,' she murmurs. 'What are they going to do to us? What are they going to do to Lucia?'

'I don't know,' he admits. 'I don't know.' The light in the daydream fractures in sharp geometric strands around Oliver's face. A rush of blood to the head and Matilda wakes, her thoughts suddenly crystal clear. Her eyes come open abruptly. She sees above her the ceiling, the flaking paint on the ornate cornicing, the ceiling rose and all Kiran's airplanes hanging there. She pushes herself to a sitting position, careful not to put more strain on her ankle, and blinks around her. It's about placing herself into the physical world again, because it is in the physical world that she now has to operate.

Her face becomes fixed, her eyes locked on the peeling paintwork of the skirting board. Something . . . something . . . something — she gropes after the idea — she's missed *something* about this room. She scans the room, her heart beating harder. The years of maintaining a house like this . . . years of keeping on top of the havoc wreaked by two young children intent on destroying everything about the house. The broken furniture, warped doors, torn curtains and dog hair. Missing hamsters, smashed cups and jam on the skirting boards.

Skirting boards. Her eyes turn slowly to the base of the wall. She lowers herself on to her hands, as if she's going to do a press-up, and stares at the gap between the board and the floor. The silvery wire she noticed the first afternoon she was shackled here. She hasn't given it a thought in all this time.

It's like a wave crashing over her. A memory that should have come to her days ago. Why didn't she think?

Her daughter-in-law, Emma. Poor embarrassed Emma. Standing shame-faced in the utility room. 'Matilda, I'm sorry, I think that's my fault.' A plumber's van leaving, and in the sink a collection of debris that had been clogging the washing-machine pump. Fluff and a single wire from an underwired bra. *It's the culprit ninety per cent of the time,* the plumber had said. Who'd have thought: the humble underwired bra, the saboteur extraordinaire of washing machines. But what comes back to Matilda now is Emma's next comment, peering concernedly into the machine. 'I've lost both wires, I hope the other one isn't still in there.'

It happened at about the time Emma and Kiran were first married. The missing bra wire never did turn up.

Matilda blinks. She's looking at it, she's sure of it. Today she is cuffed by her right ankle, which changes the range of her reach. Lying flat on her stomach and stretching hard she finds her hand reaches the skirting board easily.

She raises her chin, licks her lips and

438

focuses on the wire.

This is not over yet. Not yet.

IAN THE GEEK

Honig comes up the steps slowly, his head throbbing. Still Ian the Geek hasn't answered or appeared. When he gets to the top of the stairs he sees why. Ian the Geek is fast asleep in Oliver's recliner. The place Honig usually sits. His head is lying back at an angle, perfectly relaxed, his chest rises and falls slowly.

Honig's hands are smeared with matter, he is holding the wallet of a dead woman, and Ian the Geek has slept through the entire thing, as if it's Christmas Day at his family home and he's just polished off a bottle of port.

He takes long, calming breaths. In his head things are sliding together. But they aren't coming to rest at the places he expects. He looks down again at where the blood drops were on the floor. They're not here now, but he can recall how they looked. He's got a perfect snapshot of them in his head.

He draws an imaginary line from the cellar

door to the sink. He realizes that he'd pictured Ian the Geek bringing the intestines in from the front door, passing the cellar door where they began to shed blood. Now he wonders why he assumed that, and then he wonders why it was necessary to have brought them through the house at all, when Ian the Geek could have simply taken them round the outside to the trees. And thirdly, with a rush he realizes that intestines which have been tangled in barbed wire for any length of time wouldn't still be leaking blood. They'd only be leaking if they had just been taken from the body.

He looks back down the stairs, his pulse racing. Ginny Van Der Bolt in the basement? Ian the Geek's version of events was that he spoke to her then came straight back up here, finding the innards on his way. Which is of course a lie. Like everything else. Like not being able to fix the landline and 'finding' the entrails in a clearing. Like the way he 'checked' all the messages on the mobile phone in the car this morning. How many messages about Kable's death did he surreptitiously delete while Honig was driving . . . ?

The car keys are on the worktop. Honig notes them, then looks back at Ian the Geek, who is still sleeping peacefully, a half smile on his face, his arms folded across his chest. Honig estimates the time it will take to get to

441

the keys and get into the hallway — out to the front door. Tongue between his teeth, he bends and silently lowers the torch to the floor. He is halfway across the kitchen when Ian the Geek's eyes snap open.

He smiles pleasantly when he sees Honig, but doesn't try to sit up.

'Pleased to meet you,' he says with the same slack-mouthed nonchalance that Jagger used in 'Sympathy For The Devil'. 'Have you worked out who I am yet?'

HEADACHES

Storms move across Somerset again. Claps of thunder shake the windows of the little cottage in Priddy, making the books on the shelf shudder. The computer on the desk sends a dim glow across the bedroom to where Caffery sits, on the edge of the bed, his head in his hands. There is paperwork scattered around him, and he is pressing his fingers hard into his scalp — fighting the headache that has been nibbling at him all evening.

This investigation, this insane challenge to find Bear's owner, is turning to mud in his hands. He's cross-checked the first ten companies Cheryl — the head-messing HR girl — has given him. She's right, they all have some involvement with lasers, and some connection with Columbus which was, just as Cheryl said, restructured in the nineties, the military division sold off. Since the nineties Columbus's various offshoots and fledgling companies have divided and re-divided into a morass of different corporations. It's mind-

443

boggling.

He lowers his hands and glances across at Bear, who is fast asleep on the end of the bed. Her ears are moving as if she's dreaming of a long run. Rabbits and a ball being thrown.

OK, he thinks, hooking the phone out of his back pocket, and scrolling until he finds Johnny Patel's number. One last chance. One last-ditch effort.

Patel answers after seven rings, just as it seems the call will divert to the answering service. He sounds out of breath. 'Hi, hi, Jack. Hang on —' Caffery hears the shuffling noise of him covering the phone and whispering to someone. Hears something creak. Then Johnny. 'Hi, Jack, sorry. How's it going?'

'I take it I didn't wake you?'

'No, mate. No sleep on my planet.'

'Hard work, Johnny. I pity you. You're not at the office, I guess that'd be too much to ask.'

'I am, as it happens. Take it while you can, take it while you can. What can I do you for?'

Caffery sighs. 'I don't know. I'm in a dead-end street, shit creek, Johnny. Sort of last-chance saloon stuff. I've had a tiny bit more info come through.'

'Oh joy.'

'Yeah — about fifty companies, with, say — oh, I don't know — average four hundred employees apiece, past and present. It's all hard copy, but I can scan it and zip it over to you. If you compare the names of the employees with your wedding registration records, you might get a name pop out at you.'

'Yeah,' says Patel. 'No problem. Hold on a minute, I'll just press my "compare-all-married-names-with-all-names-in-the-scanned-files" button. It's right here, it's got a giant pink light on it, just begging to be pressed. There we go — done it. Should have your answers this time next year.'

'OK, OK. I know it's not that simple. Stick with me, though — there has to be a way through this. You've got a stack of names you've already pulled out, so it shouldn't be all that hard to take the names and cross-match them?'

'You're right, but Jack, old man, it could take ages. I mean day after day after day. Weeks. I haven't got OCR — at least not one that actually does what it says on the tin. I might end up having to key the names in manually.'

'But it could be done — in theory? Even if it takes time?'

'Uh, yes. In theory. But it is time to look hard at what we're trying to do. The sheer needle-in-a-haystack element to this. Are you sure this is worth it?'

Caffery is silent for a moment. Since yesterday morning he's slept just four hours. He feels no closer to his goal than he was four days ago.

'Just do it,' he says.

He finishes the call and rubs his eyes. He stays like this on the edge of the bed for almost five minutes, fighting the rising depression in him. It's not working — he can kid himself that between them he and Johnny are going to dive into this mess and come up holding the magic shining clue, but that's not going to happen. In a week's time he'll find himself with an invoice from Johnny amounting to thousands and nothing to show for it. It's like being told in the coldest possible terms that you're going to be drowned. And saying in reply, *OK, bring it on.*

He shakes his head and raises his chin, wondering how to shed this mood. He'd like to speak to the woman he knows, the one with the specialist search unit. She would have an opinion. She would bounce him back to enthusiasm in the blink of an eye. He stares moodily at the phone, picturing what she would say. She'd tell him to stand up and fight. She'd tell him to stop being so defeatist. And he'd probably end up angry with her and it would all go to shit. Instead of making a phone call he finds two paracetamol in the bedstand drawer, fills a glass with the whisky and swallows them with a slug. He refills his glass and leans back on the pillows, eyes closed, the tumbler resting on his chest.

He's got to deal with this. He can't just let the mystery disappear into the ether. He can't let the sickness, the headaches and the dreams, back into his life. Some people can do that thing with boxes — they can strap any unwanted thought down in a box and never open it. Caffery's never been able to do that. Never.

The last cogent thought he has is that this is all the Walking Man's fault. The fucking Walking Man who could answer his question in a second if he just had a mind to. Put all of this to bed and release him. Caffery thinks it. Forces himself to think it again, so it's ingrained and he doesn't forget it. And in the process of the second thinking he falls into a deep sleep, poleaxed at last by alcohol and exhaustion.

THE KILLING OF
GINNY VAN DER BOLT

Ginny Van Der Bolt died four days ago. It was sunny — a fresh breeze — nothing to complicate things for Ian, and as he climbed the giant stone steps of The Turrets he wasn't anticipating anything. It was only when he saw the front door standing slightly ajar he realized it wasn't going to be straightforward.

He pushed the door open and came silently into the hallway to hear a radio playing in the kitchen, to smell polish and bleach, to see a basket of fresh-cut flowers in the hallway. To glimpse, across the threadbare kilim and flagstones, Ginny Van Der Bolt in the downstairs shower room — on her knees, back to him, scrubbing the toilet. Wearing jeans and a T-shirt, blond hair in a ponytail, round backside sticking up in the air.

She heard the door latch. She raised her head. A strand of hair dangled across her forehead, and there were clogged specks of mascara around her shocked open eyes. Hurriedly she pulled off her rubber gloves and fumbled in her pocket for her phone. Maybe she recognized him from years ago when he lived in the area, maybe it was just the uncertainty of an intruder, but she was terrified.

'Don't come near me.' She jabbed a number into her phone. 'Whoever you are, respect what it's like to be a woman on her own.'

He took another step towards her and that was enough. She began to scream. She scrambled out of the cloakroom and bolted into the kitchen. He followed her through and found her at the back door, battling to negotiate the locks and keep her phone in her hand. In that second he knew what he had to do.

The Wolf is still inside him. All these years later. He may have been around the world since then, but his killing instinct hasn't left him.

When he joined Gauntlet he didn't know he'd be back here, recreating all this. He's been pulled back here by circumstances and a little help. When Pietr Havilland ordered him to use the murders of Hugo and Sophie to scare the family Ian balked at first. Then he saw arguing was only drawing more attention to himself, and now he's accepted it the irony is delicious. That Havilland should unwittingly be hiring Ian to re-stage his own killings? It is his private joke, one of life's quirky twists. The death of Ginny Van Der

Bolt, that too tumbled on to him from nowhere. Thrown in by fate. He had to make of it what he could. Let instinct take over.

Now he's here. Beginning the end.

Honig stands in front of him. His face is flushed and hot. He pulls off his filthy sweat-shirt, throws it on the floor and sits at the table, his filth-covered hands limp and forgotten at his sides. He stares and stares and stares.

'What,' Ian says, 'are you staring at?'

'You.'

'What about *me*?'

'You,' he says woodenly. 'You grew up here. That's why Havilland chose you for this.'

Ian nods. 'Correct.'

'And Minnet Kable? He was . . . ?'

Ian takes a long sip of his wine. He places the glass down very carefully — in exactly the place it was sitting before, the same slight circular stain in the wood of the table. Then he wipes his hands carefully on his napkin.

'I haven't been very lucky in my life in general, but with Minnet Kable I was . . .' He opens his hands. 'What can I say? What were the odds? If you read the reports you'd be amazed how slack the investigation was. Two teenagers? In a lovers' lane? There was more stray DNA in those woods than there would be on the floor of a brothel. The cops were floundering. Kable was . . . a miracle. A serial confessor, yes, but a miracle for me.'

Honig shakes his head very very slowly. 'A serial confessor?'

Ian nods. For fifteen years he has hidden behind this unexpected magical occurrence. That someone would walk into a police station and confess to a crime he didn't commit, that's not unheard of, but that the authorities would believe him? That it could get to court and result in a conviction? Miracle is the only word for it. Kable was going down anyway for a string of other offences and wanted to get into the mental health system rather than the penal system, so he claimed the murders of Hugo and Sophie as his own. They were clearly committed by a maniac, after all. Ian chooses to think of Kable's conviction as a sign from the Almighty, the universe, and every spirit guide known to man, that he is protected by the divine. He is above the law.

'I know, I know. Amazing but true.' He gives an embarrassed smile and clears his throat. 'I'm sorry — you're right. It was wrong of me not to have told you sooner.'

Honig has complete and utter disbelief in his eyes. Ian can't help but marvel at the man's pain — his pure *agony* to be in the presence of such evil. As if Ian is toxic, while Honig is on the other side of the glass, in the land of the brave and the good. Clean and white and incorruptible. With his 'Noo Joisy' wife and her strawberries-and-cream tunic.

Bubblegum Mania in his pocket like a sacred string of rosary beads. He's got some neck, Honig, with this presumption that his right to shock is unique — after all the things he said about sadism, cruelty, torture. He still believes he's different. Still imagines he's the only one who has to work to gain the love of his woman. Not so. Not so.

'This can't be happening.' Honig turns his hands over and over, examining the matter clinging to them as if he's only just noticed. The electric light overhead reflects dully off the bald top of his head. He pulls from his pocket a plastic pouch of antiseptic wipes, peels away the protective tab and tugs out a handful. Begins to wipe his palms.

Ian extends a finger, reaches over and prods him on the top of his scalp.

Honig jerks his head up, his eyes wild.

'What? *What?*'

'Stop doing that. Stop it.' Ian opens his palm. 'Give me the wipe. Stop doing that and concentrate on what's happening.'

Honig's eyes flick from side to side. He's assessing his options. But he passes Ian the wipe and slumps down, his hands limp on the table — as if he's disowning them.

'Please don't overreact,' Ian says.

'But *why*? Why the hell are you here? How did you . . . you know. All this?'

'The money's nice. A bonus — a great bonus, but my real prize is . . .' He jerks his head towards the ceiling. 'Up there. The Anchor-Ferrers. They're what I really want.'

Honig's mouth droops as that sinks in. Ian wants to laugh out loud. This man, this *fake,* who is such a show off, such a dick and a bragger — it's completely sailed past him that the whole thing, the information about Oliver's proposed book being passed to Gauntlet, it's *all* been set up. Ian's jockeying into position, everything, every day, every hour, every *second,* has danced around his need to get in here and torture the Anchor-Ferrers.

'What the hell did they do?' Honig asks. His voice is shaky and low. 'What did they do to you?'

Ian laughs. He rolls his head back. Moves it around on his neck until it clicks. Lets his gaze go up to the ceiling. 'Or, more important, why don't you ask what the hell I'm going to do to them?'

SCISSORS IN THE PEPPERMINT ROOM

Matilda is back in herself. There is no longer a hole where her head should be and the gap where her heart was is now packed fat with determination. She has spent the last ten minutes pulling apart the stitching of one of her canvas gardening shoes. Now she holds the tongue of the shoe in her fingertips and strains to edge it under the skirting board where the bra wire is lodged. She misses the first time, so she shifts her position to give herself a better angle. Takes a deep breath and gives another try, reaching further this time. There's a fractional sound of metal catching on wood, then the wire pings out from its place.

She snatches it up and stares at it in her hand. Unbelievable and wonderful. She gets back on her knees and twists herself, rotating her ankle in the cuff so she is facing the section of board Ollie nailed up all those years ago. This time her fat, dull fingers don't matter. She has the wire, which slides into the gap with such ease it's almost laughable. Within seconds she's got purchase and then, just like that, the board pops off in her hand, jerking her backwards.

She lies there for a few moments, her breath whistling in her chest, staring at the cobwebby treasure trove behind the board. She can't quite believe it's been so easy — and that there is so much in here. Thank God Oliver was angry that day. He didn't move a thing, oblivious to the squeals and pleas of the children, he just sealed everything in. Like relics in a museum, it's all here. Pencils and pens, a protractor and . . . she can hardly believe it . . . the plastic red handles of *scissors*. There are scissors too.

She reaches through the cobwebs, pulls out the scissors and studies them feverishly. They are rusty and small, but still better than she could have hoped. She could maybe remove the rust with the bra wire if she's clever enough. For the first time in four days, she allows herself to feel optimism.

She is prepared to die — quite prepared — but perhaps now there is a chance she can take at least one of the men with her.

BUBBLEGUM MANIA

Ian the Geek's drunkenness is heavy and medieval in its nature. It is gone midnight but he insists Honig sits at the table and they talk 'like civilized people'. Honig finds it hard to speak. He is still struggling to take it all in, his heart hasn't stopped pounding. But he sits, and tries to engage in conversation, while his brain processes the new information.

Opposite him sits a monster. A man who can happily make decorations with another human being's insides. Honig still hasn't decided why, though over and over he's asked: *What's the vendetta about? Why this anger?* Each time the expressionless answer has been, *Because I hate them. Don't ask again.*

So Honig has to fill in the spaces himself. He imagines Ian the Geek joined the Legion knowing it was a safe place he could hide in case Minnet Kable changed his story. Did he anticipate Gauntlet would have a conflict with Anchor-Ferrers? Or was that a happy accident? The discovery of Oliver's autobiography via the phone virus? Was that really picked up on routine surveillance? Or was it all too convenient? It is possible Ian the Geek himself flagged up its existence to Gauntlet.

In this new light it makes sense that Ian the Geek squirmed so violently that day in the New York office. Resurrecting the Wolf killings hadn't been part of his plan; it must have seemed very dangerous to him to go along with that masquerade. But he adapted, incorporated the orders into the job. If he's adaptable enough to do that without much more than a twenty-second argument with Havilland, then he's very capable indeed. Very capable.

'So.' Ian the Geek opens another bottle of wine and pours another glass. 'It'll be morning soon. What are our plans?'

Honig doesn't answer. He doesn't know what to say.

'OK, I'll tell you. Between you and me, I think we're running out of time.' Ian the Geek lowers his chin and moves his eyes meaningfully towards the driveway where they had the conversation with the cops. 'I think we're in the final straight, old man. Now, your job is to tell Havilland whatever you want to save your hide. I will never see him again anyway — he will never find me. I am invisible.' He puts down his napkin. Leans back in the chair, his ape-like hands folded over his stomach. 'That's my position. How about you?'

Honig gives a small acknowledging nod. His face is on fire. He thinks of his wife at home. It's early evening in the USA and she will be eating ice cream in the Baskin Robbins next to the beauty parlour. Her favourite flavour is 'America's Birthday Cake'. Ian the Geek could track her down. He's the sort who would. There's an old Japanese saying: 'The bamboo survives because it bends, it stands not rigid where it will break, but flexes.' By being the bamboo Honig will continue to live. He will return to Virginia and sit in that mall with his wife and they will eat America's Birthday Cake ice cream. He is going to pretend indifference to Ian the Geek's behaviour. When he's got away from here he will throw himself at the mercy of Havilland. He will be honest. He will tell him the truth from start to finish. He will return Havilland's money. He would rather be poor than be part of this any longer.

'Ian . . .' He clears his throat. 'It seems to me we can't win. Anchor-Ferrers has given away our identity — we're screwed. We won't get the money, we won't get peace. That makes us both on the run.' He scrapes back the chair. 'So it's time for me to go now. Leave you to it.'

'Uh.' Ian the Geek stops him by simply raising his wine glass. He shakes his head. 'No.

That won't work. I need the car, so you can't have that. And it's a four-hour walk to the nearest train station.'

'Four hours is fine — I'm happy to walk four hours. I'll get my stuff and be gone.'

'I'm sorry, but I don't want you to walk so far. It's bad for your feet. You will wait for me. We drive out of here.' He puts both palms together, fingers extended in an arrow shape — pointing to the driveway. 'OK? You will wait until I've finished. We drive out of here together.'

'Finished?'

'Yes. Finished what I came here for. Do what I've wanted to do for years.'

Honig sinks weakly back into the chair.

The bamboo bends, so it doesn't break. Bends so it doesn't break. His heart races. America's Birthday Cake. Bubblegum Mania . . .

Eventually, painfully, he speaks: 'OK. I'll wait. But I don't want to know any of the details.'

'And I know you'll understand if I ask you to wait somewhere secure.'

'When will it happen?'

Ian the Geek looks at his watch, his lips move noiselessly, his right hand is moving through the air like a clock hand, suggesting he's trying to work out how long each act will take. 'I'm going to sleep now so I'm fresh. I'll start in about four hours' time. And it'll take me two hours — possibly three. You might want to take a book in case you get bored.'

LIGHT RAYS

The clouds cling to the Mendip Hills like sluggish wraiths. Periodically a crack of lightning illuminates the landscape, throwing all the trees and hillsides into startling sudden relief — an X-ray landscape, no place to hide.

Caffery lies face down on the bed, still dressed, only his shirt unbuttoned. He's asleep, but one leg dangles near the floor. Habit from years of being on call in a London murder squad. Always ready for the phone message that would tip him out of bed, out on to the cold, beer-smelling streets of Lewisham. Out to the scene of the most recent killing. In those days it wasn't the illegal guns coming in with the Caribbean gangs that claimed the most victims; in those days the most common weapon was a pub stool or a beer glass. Those are a faraway land, those days. Tinged in pink and gold, with the faint smell of cigarettes and petrol leaving oily rainbow stains at the edges.

On the bed now he twitches slightly, half raising a hand as if to rub his face. He's dreaming. In his dream, orange rays crisscross the sky. The lights are coming from people when they speak — their words translated into long orange beams which radiate through the air and bounce off anything they encounter. *Think like me, think like me,* they whisper. *Think . . .* The rays finger the heavens, find the surfaces of distant planets. They bounce back to the Earth. Lasers. In the dream he wants to follow them — to find their source. To find the light man.

The perspective of the dream changes abruptly. Now he's suspended above the globe, witnessing the continents jutting out into the thrashing sea. Seeing clearly the sum of all the human chatter, like a mist rising up from the surface of the planet. He sees a light and knows, instinctively, he has no choice but to follow it. He's hurtling towards it — fast, too fast. It begins to blind him and his hands come up to shield his eyes from the light. He can make out details: a figure standing at the source of the light. A man, sunburned and lean as leather, dark tangled hair. He's standing next to a fire, his face is turned upwards, watching Jack coming out of the sky at him. He looks neither surprised, nor alarmed. His face breaks into a knowing smile.

Caffery is nearly on him, his hands out to

throttle him, when he wakes, jerking upright on the bed, breathing hard.

It takes almost a minute for his heart to stop banging. For reality to come back down to him and for him to realize there's nothing in this room to defend himself from, that whatever's produced the adrenalin rush isn't an external physical entity but something he's conjured from dreamland. The computer is still on, Bear is blinking sleepily at him from the end of the bed, and out of the window the sky is already showing the first signs of dawn.

He takes a long, deep breath. Presses his hands into his sides and drops his legs off the side of the bed, bent over, his head lowered. Staring at his feet — still in his shoes.

It takes him a long time to get his breathing steady. Then he looks up.

'Come on,' he tells Bear. 'Let's go find the old bastard.'

THE CHRYSLER

Honig can't believe this. Ian the Geek has gone casually to the camp bed, dropped on to it, and fallen asleep. Fully dressed, he is snoring loudly. His complacency, his blind arrogance, is incredible.

For a long time, sitting at the table, his hands resting in front of him, Honig watches Ian. If he is capable of what he did to those teenagers on the Donkey Pitch all those years ago, then what does that mean for the Anchor-Ferrers? Honig's guess is that he will make the living members of the family watch the first two killings; somehow he thinks it will be Matilda who is killed first. Then Lucia. He can't imagine what Ian the Geek has planned for her, but he's sure Oliver will be forced to watch it all before he dies. Oliver is Ian the Geek's ultimate target, and he has no brakes or sense of the taboo. He'll probably make the family do things to each other before they die. After all, he will have the time and the leisure.

Honig bends down silently. He unlaces his shoes, prises them off and pushes them under the table. He waits a moment or two, but Ian the Geek continues to snore so Honig stands and crosses the room, his back straight. He finds his bag with his passport and wallet. He closes his hand over the Chrysler keys that lie on the kitchen table. Turns to see if he's been heard.

Ian the Geek sleeps on.

Moving as quietly as a cat, Honig pads to the hallway, hesitates, then walks silently to the front door, lifts the latch as silently as he can. He opens the door a crack. It makes a low creaking groan which seems to echo up the stairs and around the huge panelled hall.

Honig takes a long, shaky breath through his nose. Holds it. There is a pause in Ian the Geek's snoring, but it is momentary — he settles back to his steady rhythm. Honig breathes out. It's incredible how fast his heart is beating.

He's not going to risk opening the door further, so he slides himself through the gap he has already made. He goes to the Chrysler and unlocks it — not by using the remote but the key in the door lock. Mercifully it's not the type of alarm system that bleeps to acknowledge being switched off — instead the indicators flash on and off silently, the light bathing the walls of The Turrets orange.

He reaches inside and switches off the

interior light. Tongue between his teeth, he turns and looks back at the house. Silent.

Ian the Geek is still asleep.

THE PEPPERMINT ROOM

Matilda is in her usual place on the floor between the fireplace and the window. She is exhausted — her neck aches and her hands are almost bleeding. Miraculously she has managed to sharpen the scissors a little, but neither they nor the bra wire will release the handcuffs. Tears of frustration pour down her face. She wants Oliver. She wants him so badly it's like a taste in her mouth or a pain in her belly.

The front door opens. A sly but distinctive creak. She jerks her head up and stares in the direction of the hall. She hasn't seen the men since lunchtime, though she's been able to hear them coming and going from Oliver's room, opening and closing doors. Twice today they have left the house in a car, but each time they've come back. They've been talking and cooking downstairs all evening. They stopped talking a while ago; she thought they must have fallen asleep, but now it seems not.

Silence. The faint clicking vacuum of anticipation — as if the house is holding its breath, only the tiniest crack and creak of the muscles between its ribs giving the game away. She strains her ears, willing out a string of concentration that winds through the crack under the door and slides down the stairs into the hall.

For a long time nothing. Then the tiniest tap of a footfall on the front doorstep. A long pause. And then, quietly, distinctly, comes the crunch of gravel and the sound of a car door opening.

Matilda lets her breath out. She gets on to her knees.

Something is happening. It's all beginning to happen.

BUG SCREENS

Honig is neither valiant, nor brave. He is self-serving and, like most people, he will usually take the easy route out of any situation. He has never been more aware of that than he is now, standing next to the opened driver's door of the Chrysler. Silently he reaches across the seat and releases the handbrake. He turns the key, but doesn't engage the engine. Hands on the steering wheel, he braces his shoulder against the front door rim and puts his weight against it.

There's a long moment where the car doesn't move, but at last, slowly, slowly it begins to inch forward. His eyes dart between the car and the curtained windows of the kitchen where Ian the Geek sleeps. The sound on the gravel is minimal — a faint popping noise — getting more frequent as the car builds up speed.

When the Chrysler has enough momentum he leaps into the driver's seat. The steering and the brakes are heavy without the engine, but he wrestles the car along the drive, hauling it round one hairpin bend, then another, until he is hidden from the house. He lets the car trundle into the space next to the Anchor-Ferrers' Land Rover — a small bay off the driveway surrounded by bushes. He brakes hard. Drags on the handbrake.

He gets out of the car and stands in his socks looking back at the house. None of the windows on the bottom two floors is visible from this hiding place. All he can see are the windows in the turrets. The sky in the east is getting paler. Dawn is on its way already. A sudden picture comes to him of his own modest house in Silver Spring. Weatherboarding and bug screens on the windows — a fading and peeling swing set on the coarse front grass where the wild onions come up each spring. It's a relic of a forgotten ex-tenant, but Honig's wife insists on keeping it. *Just because,* she says sweetly, *just because one day . . . maybe if we're lucky . . .*

Sometimes in the spring evenings if he is at home they sit on the swings and drink Sol beers with wedges of lime pressed inside the mouth of the bottle.

Honig is no hero, but he knows this much. Even if Havilland lets him off the hook, he will not be able to go home and look his wife in the eye if he hasn't at least tried to do something good and valiant in his life. He

470

can't leave the Anchor-Ferrers family alone with Ian the Geek.

His hand closes around Bubblegum Mania in his pocket. He looks up at the windows. There's a key in his pocket too. One which will unlock handcuffs. Mrs Anchor-Ferrers and Lucia can walk on their own. They can run. Oliver Anchor-Ferrers? Well, if he has to, Honig will carry the old guy out of the house on his back.

SUNRISE

During the day the Walking Man is invisible — he is the same colour as the land, going, head lowered, in a straight line across the grey unploughed field. At sunrise and sunset, like the prey of a crepuscular predator, he is easier to find.

Caffery is a natural-born hunter. Relentless.

He drives for two hours — and it's not far from dawn when he finds him. He is on the gravelly perimeter of a kale field, next to the hedge, cooking breakfast over his campfire. Caffery pulls the car up to the farm gate and gets out.

The Walking Man is prepared for Jack's visit. It's not for him to hide, or behave in a cowardly fashion. He will face Caffery the way he faced him in the dream, no hint of panic or defensiveness. Just a slight smile on his face.

As is always the case, he doesn't acknowledge Caffery's arrival, just continues pottering, using a stick broken from the hedgerow to lift the sausages and check they're cooking.

Bear is uneasy. She knows something is going to happen. When Caffery clambers over the stile into the field she doesn't follow but stays on the other side, hesitant. He glances back — sees her, notes her behaviour, and ignores it. He's not going to be turned back now. Leaving her there, he heads straight across the field, not sticking to the footpath but mowing a trampled line across the crop in the shortest possible route.

He gets closer and closer. The crop crunches under his feet as he nears, the sweat gathers around his neck. The Walking Man, sensing trouble, puts the pan down and slowly straightens. But he doesn't turn to look at Caffery.

Caffery isn't a gym freak, he drinks and he's an ex-smoker, but he knows his body, he's muscular and he trusts his strength in most situations. He's an instinctive fighter — tooth and nail. He springs at the Walking Man, launching his whole weight on to his shoulders, one arm in a stranglehold around his neck, his knees coming up to get a purchase around his back.

He expects the Walking Man to go down like a tree, but he doesn't. He resists, his wiry frame shaking with the effort. A small grunting noise comes from his throat as he takes one or two compensatory steps to keep his balance, but he refuses to go down. There's a long silent struggle. Two men who look like one. A freakish, writhing beast silhouetted against the sky.

Caffery tears at the man's hair, rains punches on the side of his head and neck. 'You've made me,' he hisses into his ear. 'You've made me do this.'

Eventually, without warning, the Walking Man sits. He simply folds his legs in half and goes down where he stands. Caffery is unprepared and is jolted into a half somersault, coming to land a metre away on his back.

He doesn't bother to get up. He drops his hands over his eyes and lies there on the ground, breathing hard. He knows the truth: he knows that the only person who's lost anything is him — Caffery. He's lost his temper and his dignity. The Walking Man meanwhile has kept complete control of the situation.

Eventually Caffery takes his hands from his eyes. He rolls his head sideways to look at the Walking Man. He too is lying on his back, his hands at his sides. He hasn't moved or spoken. Caffery props himself up on an elbow, wondering if he hasn't actually killed the bastard.

But the Walking Man's not dead, he's alive — very much alive. His eyes are open, watching the clouds cross the sky. He is smiling serenely.

'You know what, Jack?' He drops his head to the side to look at him. 'A great man once said that the definition of insanity is doing the same thing over and over, expecting the results to be different.'

'You fucker,' Caffery hisses. 'You old fucker.'

THE COB

Oliver is drifting, dreaming that he's with Matilda. They are standing on the Cob at Lyme Regis and it's the day he asks her to marry him. It's the most romantic place he can think of — this is just before the French Lieutenant is an international sensation and it's not crowded with tourists. It's a place he loves to walk in the winter, the wind streaming around his face, the light so pellucid he has to squint.

It is his birthday, the thirteenth of December. A wind is whipping the waves into a milky froth and when he pushes the ring on her finger her skin is wet with brine and the ring slides on smoothly — it doesn't crinkle or buckle. Afterwards they go to a pub and sit in front of the fire. Matilda turns her hand over and over to look at the sparkle of the ring. The sea water on her face and hair dries slowly into a fine white frosting.

That white comes back to him in the dream. Except now it's scales, not a frost.

Matilda smiles. The smile cracks some of the scales off. They fall with the noise of glass. Under them the skin is red and raw.

'You have met Molina before,' she says slowly. 'But not at Gauntlet. You met him once before. Many many years ago. You didn't like him then.' She touches Oliver's face with a hand that's like gossamer. 'Deep inside I think you've always known the truth.'

He wakes, his heart thumping. The room is silent, the beginnings of a pink dawn coming through the window. Matilda's face slips away like shattered light. He lies still, suddenly shocked as if one of the cold Lyme Regis waves has crashed over him. What Matilda has told him in the dream has peeled back something in his memory. Under it is a truth, nastier than any truth he's ever guessed at before. So horrible that at first he refuses to even consider it.

Eventually, with an effort, he pulls himself to a sitting position and, blinking, fumbles the pen out from under the skirting board. He begins to write.

Something I have until now only suspected in some shuttered corner of my mind . . . something which is impossible for any man to face head on. I don't know why it's taken me so long to admit it, because I must have always harboured this suspicion on some deep, deep level.

477

Kable, wherever he is, is an innocent man.

Oliver pauses. He puts back his head and tries to picture John Bancroft in the room. He sees him standing in the middle of the rug, just in front of the mirror. He sees him looking all around, taking in the scene. 'Look at me,' Oliver whispers. 'Look. Please look. Please look at what I am writing.'

Slowly John Bancroft turns. He comes and crouches next to Oliver. The old man's hands are shaking as he shows him the rug. 'Read it, please, read it.'

Bancroft reads. And when he has finished Oliver writes more.

Incredible, yet possible, even in this day and age. I believe he was wrongly convicted. He didn't protest his innocence at the trial, perhaps that is why he was convicted so easily. Without his confession there wasn't much evidence — hardly any DNA at the scene to connect him to the killings. I may be wrong in my suspicions, but you — whoever you are (John?) — I think you will read this and use it as a piece in the puzzle. I cannot believe what I am going to write next. And yet it is what I believe to be the truth.

THE PEPPERMINT ROOM

Matilda sits upright against the radiator. Her hair is wild, her eyes wide. Her ankle is torn and bleeding from the scissors, but her frantic attempts to remove the cuff have come to nothing.

There's a creak in the hallway. Someone is out there. It's one of the men coming up the stairs. He's trying to do it silently.

She quickly assesses the distance from the door to where she lies. Then, trying to make as little noise as possible, she rearranges herself, shuffling her bottom across the floor and twisting so her manacled foot is pointing towards the door and her torso is nearer the fireplace. She lifts her right knee and tucks her foot behind her left leg, which remains out straight, locked to the radiator. Then she rolls her upper body to the right, into the wall. The scissors are open, the blades ready, concealed under her body.

Another creak on the stairs. Nervous sweat runs down Matilda's sleeves and soaks her blouse. She hopes it's Molina, the smaller one, and not big, tall, balding Honey. She doesn't think she'll be able to fight Honey — there's too much of him. The door opens. Her heart is like an animal scrambling to escape. She breathes through the fear, low and deep.

The light comes on. She wills her eyelids not to flutter and give her away. Then a footstep next to the bed, soft, as if he's tiptoe-ing. She keeps her ribs rising and falling steadily, imitating sleep. It's Honey, she's sure of it. He's the only one nasty enough to creep up on her. He is behind her, one foot up and to the left of her face. She dares to open one eye and through the curtain of hair sees a shoe, and recognizes it.

Good shoes. Yes, it's Honey.

'Mrs Anchor-Ferrers,' he whispers. 'Keep still, don't say anything.'

She feels his hand on her shoulder, tugging to turn her to face him. She tenses. There is a beat, a moment where it could all change — then it's over. She unrolls, uses the mo-mentum to bring the scissors down. She has time to register the look of surprise on his face, his finger up to his mouth as if to say *Shhhhhhhhh,* before the thin pointed tip of scissor blade lands in the side of his foot, just above the top of his smart shoes. It goes in. She feels and hears the small pop of his skin under his sock.

He crumples in surprise, dropping to his knees in pain. She pulls out the scissors and stabs again. This time she gets the blade into his neck, just next to his collar.

'What . . . ?' he stammers. *'Wha— ?'*

Blood wells up from under the scissor blade. It races along her fingers, makes a silky crimson glove round her hand. She pulls the scissors out. Something clatters on the ground and Honey gropes shakily at her, trying to stop her. She scrambles her leg around clumsily so she is kneeling in front of him. He makes no attempt to move away from her, but sways slightly on his knees like a tree in the wind, his hand clasped over his neck. Blood is pulsing through his fingers — bright, almost fluorescent red like spilled ink from a child's fountain pen, soaking into his collar.

'Whu . . . Whu . . . ?'

He screws up his face, as if a terrible noise has started in his ears, then crumples forward, his face hitting the radiator with a loud clang. She swings the scissors again — woodenly, her joints stiff and shocked, her vision blurred by tears. She doesn't know why, but she thinks the back of the head is the place to aim for. The point of the scissors goes into the tender V at the top of his neck. He lurches forward but it's the force of her blow and not his own movement. A spurt of yellowish vomit comes out of his mouth and his hand moves numbly around in the air, as if trying

481

to bat a cobweb away from his face.

Then, quite suddenly, he's still.

She sits back on her heels, breathing hard. Along the line of opened scalp she can see the bloodied insides of his skull. So quick. So quick and so easy.

The scissors fall from her hand and she begins to shake. How has it come to this? How has this happened?

BACK TO THE START

Anger can clear a person's thoughts like a blast of air. Caffery is winded and the clumsy somersault he executed over the Walking Man has left his back sore from where he landed on a stone, but he's not drunk any more. He's coming into a hyper-alert phase and a renewed determination has opened up in his head.

He stands next to the car, his hand in the small of his back where it aches from the fight. He stares up over the hills that surround this place, at the new sun making pink patchworks of the clouds. Something familiar happens — excitement is in his veins. He's thought for a long time he'd lost that capability. But no, it's back. Ferocious. He is going to make this work. He is not going to be beaten. It just needs one last push.

Bear is waiting for him at the car, her tail wagging cautiously, as if waiting to see his mood now he's returned. Caffery eyes her, thinking back from the beginning, putting everything he knows into order. A little dog injured and unclaimed. Found only a mile away from the place Hugo Frink and Sophie Hurst-Lloyd were murdered. A woman from the same area missing.

A triangle appears in his head. At one apex is Bear — abandoned with a cryptic note on her. At the second is Ginny. Missing. There's a third point that connects these two — it's something connected with Minnet Kable and the way Hugo and Sophie died, but Caffery can't quite make that apex swim out of the murk into clarity.

Kable knew the Donkey Pitch — he'd been seen there in the past — but the only example of his DNA at the scene was found fifty yards away, while there was none found on the victims. It's the third point on Caffery's triangle, but it's fuzzy and vague. Something's not right about it.

Bear begins to bark excitedly. Caffery shakes his head, amazed at her insight. If it didn't sound completely crazy he'd say she knows what he's thinking. She knows they aren't giving up yet.

A Man of Principle

Fifteen feet beneath Kiran's bedroom, on his camp bed Ian opens one eye and smiles at the ceiling. He's been listening to Honig creeping around the house — moving the car away, going up the stairs. Bless Honig — for he is a man of principle. And if Ian's ears don't deceive him Honig has gone the way of many men of principle. He has tried to save the family and now he is dead. For his ideals. What a waste.

Of course he was always going to die one way or another. Maybe not quite *this* way — but Ian can work with the circumstances of his dead body in the room overhead. He is going to frame Honig for the terrible fate that will visit Oliver Anchor-Ferrers before morning. When Pietr Havilland hears Ian's version of events in the house he'll be so shocked, so infuriated about what Ian and the family suffered at Honig's hands, that he'll overlook the fact that the one caveat of the job — Gauntlet's identity being protected — has been breached.

Ian yawns and gets up. He reaches under the dining chair and slowly pulls out Honig's sweatshirt from where he dropped it. It has traces of Ginny Van Der Bolt's DNA all over it. Ever since they arrived here Ian has been weaving an intricate fabric of veiled hints at Honig's untrustworthiness. Three days ago he warned Pietr Havilland that Honig's behaviour was 'erratic'. While Ian was disposing of the insides of Ms Ginny Van Der Bolt, the one who played Kiss FM too loudly, he took the opportunity to email Havilland the video of Honig in the kitchen, holding his fist up to the camera — baring his teeth.

Vive le sadisme.

Ian attached the message: *Sir — I am uncomfortable in this man's company. I feel his connection with this family may be deeper than he has revealed. More to follow . . .*

Now he puts the sweatshirt in a holdall and adds the wet wipe and the video saved on a memory stick. Things are stacking up nicely. When this is all over Honig will be revealed as the person who really killed Sophie and Hugo all those years ago. That he has returned to continue his spree, choosing the family as his next victims. When his corpse is examined they will find traces of Ginny Van Der Bolt on his trousers and under his nails. In his pocket will be Sophie's engagement ring. Missing since 1999.

Ian gets changed into something more comfortable. He needs to be able to *move* for the next part.

It is getting light outside as he goes slowly up the stairs, holding the banister. He intends to start with Matilda.

From the bedroom doorway he surveys the scene. She has killed Honig in a spectacular fashion. There is blood everywhere and he is lying on the floor face down, his ear hanging off on a flap of skin. There's something bloody and yellow next to him which might be an eyeball or a lump of fat — it's impossible to tell. Matilda is next to the body, backed up against the fireplace, her teeth chattering with shock and fear. In her hands are clenched a pair of scissors which she points fiercely at Ian. He is able to disarm her very quickly with a kick. For all her ferocity she isn't strong. And she's in her sixties — no match for him.

'Shut up now,' he tells her quietly. 'Don't move.'

He pulls Honig's ear on its flap of skin back so he can see the bloody skull — checks he's dead. Then he throws the duvet from the bed over him. All the time Matilda cries silently. Ian passes her a towel to clean herself with, but otherwise he ignores her.

When he's finished with Honig's body he crosses the landing and goes quietly to the door of the rose room. Opens it a crack and peeps in. Lucia is staring up at him from where she sits, on the floor. She looks a mess with her hair all over the place, in her black jeans and T-shirt and her bruised eye. But she's still hotter than hell. Sexy sexy sexy. A slutty punk goddess among all the chintzy roses: snowy skin and melted mascara.

He doesn't step into the room, but waits for her to speak. Her lips are dry, he notices. She licks them, he watches the action carefully, watches her tongue. She finds her voice. 'What's happened? I heard some . . . things.'

'Don't you know?'

She doesn't cry. Her eyes flicker past him, to the opened bedroom door where the body lies. 'I think I can guess.'

'Don't guess — come and see. Much better to see for yourself, don't you think?'

'I suppose.' She talks like a marionette, her jaw moving up and down woodenly, like it's hinged. She knows, of course, what's happened, but she still doesn't quite believe it. 'I guess.'

He steps in and undoes the cuffs. He's careful not to touch her, though he can feel her eyes on him and knows she's wondering when it's going to happen. 'Put your shoes on,' he says, passing her the pair of troll-patterned Doc Martens. 'You need to be able to walk.'

She hesitates, but eventually pulls the boots

on. Laces them with intricate care. When she is finished he offers her his hand. There is a long pause, then she takes the hand and lets him pull her to her feet. She stops for a moment to smooth her clothing down, as if preparing herself for a public ordeal. She shakes her head, swallows hard and faces the door.

'OK,' she says. 'Let's do it.'

He takes her arm and leads her across the landing. He's left the light on in the room where Matilda is, and as they go he uses his foot to push the door open wider. It swings back with a long creak. Honig is in there, face down on the floor, his torn head just visible above the fluffy green-and-white striped duvet — which has wicked out a dark semicircle of blood from his neck. Matilda is still on the floor, clutching the towel — crying and crying, her mouth open like a bewildered child in a war zone.

'Jesus.' Lucia balks. She stands quite still and stares into the room. 'Oh Christ.'

'Lucia.' Matilda stretches out a hand. *'Lucia.'*

But Ian shakes her. 'Don't answer. We're not going in there. Come on.'

She resists his attempt to move her on. She puts sinew and steel into her legs so she is jammed in place.

'Come on,' he says, giving her another nudge. 'Come on.'

'Lucia!'

'Oh God.' She shakes her head and puts her hands to her face. 'God.'

'I don't know why you're doing this. You know what's going to happen.'

There's a small pause. She is very still. Then eventually she drops her hands and nods. She lets him lead her away from the peppermint room, one jerky step after the other, like a horse being led towards something it fears. They stop at the door to the amethyst room. It is closed.

Lucia's breathing is heavy; he can feel her small, hot ribcage rising and falling under the T-shirt.

'Push the door open. Give it a push.'

She does and the door swings open. Ian stands behind her, holding her arm, and allows her to survey the scene. The purple room is filled with sunlight — it comes through the half-drawn skull curtains and throws red patches on the floor. Two huge purple ostrich feathers flitter lightly in the draught from the door. Lucia's idols gaze placidly out from the purple walls: Marilyn Manson and Dita Von Teese. Patty Hearst. Something in their faces suggests they are studiously avoiding looking at the other person in the room.

Oliver Anchor-Ferrers. Seated on the floor below the window, his right foot handcuffed to the radiator.

'OK,' Ian says lightly. 'Let's get started, shall we?'

ROSE COTTAGE

He drives fast, throwing the car around the bends in the country lanes. So fast that Bear has to lie down on the back seat to avoid being thrown on to the floor. The first time he went to the Frinks' house the colonel mentioned the cleaner hadn't turned up for work. Ginny Van Der Bolt, according to Paluzzi, is a cleaner. Caffery isn't sure why these two facts haven't registered earlier with him, but now that they have, things are ticking away in his head.

He goes impatiently through the early morning traffic. Past the forests and old mills and tythe barns. The sun is up and at the country bus stops one or two people are waiting to head off to work — already a couple of mothers with children in tow, heading out to breakfast clubs and then work. When he gets to Rose Cottage, Ginny Van Der Bolt's, he recognizes it. He's knocked here before and dismissed it. Today he puts his face up to the window of the front room, his hand curved over his eyes to block out the reflecting sunlight, and tries to see the hallway. Then he stands in the back garden with Bear, his arms crossed, wondering what to do. Break in through the kitchen window? Phone Paluzzi and open the whole thing up?

'What do you reckon?' he asks Bear. 'Do you know the person who lives here?'

Bear's ears prick up slightly. She puts her head on one side, trying to understand what he's saying.

He shakes his head. There's nothing more he can do. He's got to start again, comb through everything he's seen and find what he's missed.

'Come on,' he says. 'Let's go see the colonel.'

MATILDA

This is the beginning of the end. Matilda is sure of it. It was that glimpse of Lucia that did it — standing in the doorway — pale-faced, her clothes all crumpled the way they used to get when she was a teenager and would fall asleep fully dressed — an expression on her face that Matilda will never be fully able to describe. It was only a few seconds, then Molina forced Lucia away across the landing. Yet the encounter has signalled quite clearly to Matilda that the end must be coming.

Something deep comes over her; an old, primordial sense of herself as a human being facing a death that may not be far away. It brings with it a heavy solemnity that feels as big as the universe. She stops crying and allows herself to rest. Honig's drying blood tautens and dries her skin. The scissors have been placed high on the bed, she can see them glinting from the corner of her eye. Well beyond her reach — not even worth trying.

But there *will* be something . . . Something. She takes deep breaths and squares her shoulders to face the door.

Sure enough Molina reappears a few moments later and this time he's wearing latex gloves. He begins undoing her handcuffs. He hasn't said an angry word about Honig's murder. If anything, he's been too calm, almost nonchalant — conveying the sense that though he finds this turn of events a trifle unexpected, it is far from insurmountable for him.

Those gloves though . . .

'What's going to happen now?' she murmurs, turning her face up to his. It's almost intimate, this — this physical closeness. 'What's happening? What are you going to do to us?'

Molina doesn't answer. A shutter has fallen behind his eyes. He might not just be a criminal, she thinks, he might be insane too. As insane as Minnet Kable — guided by voices even. Or he might just be desperate.

He grips her by the elbow and lifts her to her feet. She sags slightly, letting him take the weight, thinking that if he believes her to be submissive he might relax his vigilance and give her the chance to hit out at him. He guides her towards the door. She goes, each step heavy and leaden as if she's a Frankenstein's monster in flat metal boots. Her eyes fall on the scissors — they drift from her line of sight and she feels their loss the way she'd feel a parting lover's.

He pushes her towards Lucia's room — the amethyst room. Matilda watches the door panelling getting bigger as they get close. She thinks she knows what she's going to see on the other side. Oliver and Lucia.

Molina opens the door and with it the room reveals itself to her — worse, because its familiarity reminds her of how they've been invaded. Lit from the tall windows with their deep window seats, it looks like something in a museum. The floating skull curtains move slightly from the breeze in the open windows; all of Lucia's posters are still there, not moved. All her black jewellery on the skull-and-crossbones stand on the windowsill — still there. But the room isn't the same.

On the floor under the window sits Oliver. He is wearing the same clothes he was wearing three days ago and he hasn't shaved. There's a grey stubble on his hollow cheeks. His shirt is dirty. He raises his eyes to hers and gives her a brave smile, but she isn't fooled. This is defeat.

'Matilda,' he says. 'Matilda.'

Lucia is a yard or so away at the foot of the bed — not restrained. Her face is white, her black hair is mussed all over the place and she's clearly lost weight in the last few days because her bones are like shadows under the skin. But there's poise and delicacy about

496

the way she's sitting. Her feet in the multico-
loured boots she so loves are pointed, and
the purple bed throw that she bought from a
London company in the King's Road and
brought down here when she decorated this
room, is uncreased and immaculate. If this
was any other circumstance you'd think that
Lucia was in a high-gloss spread for a life-
style magazine. She stares and stares at
Matilda as if her mother is a ghost.

'Sweetheart,' Matilda says, tears coming
into her eyes. 'Sweetheart — I love you. We
both do.'

Lucia swallows hard. There's a pulse in her
long white neck beating frantically, but her
face is expressionless. She has always been
good at hiding her feelings — it's one of Lucia's talents. 'Mum. You're covered in blood.
It's everywhere.'

Matilda looks down at herself. Lucia is right
— the blood is everywhere. Even though
she's rubbed herself with the towel, it has
soaked her clothes so they stick to her. Her
thin arms are plastered in it. She starts to say
something but from behind Molina pushes
her down into the empty chair. He uses the
cuffs to manacle her right foot to one of the
legs. With a jerk he pulls her right arm
backwards. She has to thrust her body forward at an awkward angle to stop her shoulder dislocating. He binds her hand to the bottom of the chair back with something thin

and plastic — a zip-tie, she thinks.

He backs away and now, in spite of the painful position, she can assess the room. Oliver to her left, Lucia in front and, beyond the bed, Molina, his back to her, locking the door. Lucia isn't tied in any way — she is simply sitting there. Matilda doesn't know why Molina hasn't restrained her — but he's underestimated her if he thinks she isn't going to move. Kiran is the most successful of the two children, but Lucia is the cleverest — she can be a wildcat. Now as she watches Molina sullenly from behind her mussed-up hair, her dark, intelligent eyes are taking in everything he is doing.

Lucia's strength and will are like a smell in the air. She is planning something, and Matilda thinks Molina is going to regret not tying her.

He turns to face the room. He pulls from his pocket a Stanley knife. Oliver takes a sharp breath and straightens, tries to get to his feet. Molina doesn't seem to notice. He frowns at the Stanley knife, turns it over and over in his hands, examining it as if he's never seen it before and is curious to know how it works, what it does.

He goes to the window and looks out, surveying the trees as if he's remembering something. The Stanley knife dangles at his side. Next to Matilda, Oliver takes another shaky breath, but he doesn't speak and when she twists her neck around she sees he is weeping quietly. On the bed Lucia hasn't moved an inch. Her fists are clenched in the satin bed throw.

'Please,' Matilda blurts out. 'Please, for your sake — stop and think.'

He turns from the window. 'Beg pardon?'

'Stop — and think. Do you understand what you're doing? I mean *really* understand?'

'Do I *really* understand?' he mimics. *'Really really really?* What do you think? Do I look as if I *really really* understand?'

She swallows and puts her head back.

'I'll tell you what I think. I actually think you *don't* understand. I think you have no idea. Someone must love you. I am sure there is someone. A parent? A sister, a brother, or a son? A wife, a girlfriend?'

'What?' he whispers, as if he cannot believe she has the temerity to speak. *'What did you just say?'*

'You heard me. Do you have someone who loves you?'

Molina's mouth opens. He blinks once. Twice. He doesn't know how to answer. She's got him. Somehow she's got him.

'You have, I can see it in your face. And you love them back. Before you do . . . whatever it is you're going to do . . .' Her voice is shaking, but she goes on. 'Please stop and imagine what the person who loves you will think. The person you love? What will she think?'

He stares at her. The colour in his face is high. She thinks, though she can't be sure, that there's a tiny tear glistening in the corner of his eye.

He shakes his head as if he can't think about it. He turns to the window, squinting as if the sun is too strong. 'There is someone.'

'And she loves you?'

'I think she does. I believe she does. I wouldn't be doing any of this if it wasn't for her — I've done everything for her.'

'Then ask yourself — what will she think? What will she think of this? Of what you're doing?'

There is a long, long moment where Molina is completely still — absolutely motionless, not taking his eyes from her face. The silence seems to stretch around the room. Into every corner, into every ear, into every brain. Matilda can hear her own heart thudding. And in its echo she is sure she can feel the heartbeats of her daughter and her husband.

Then Molina turns away from the window. He comes and kneels next to Matilda. He is so close to her she can smell him; she can smell cooking spices and tobacco and wine and aftershave and suntan lotion. She can see the thick line of lashes where they grow out from the fleshy upper lid. She can see the red hair and freckles on the backs of his hands.

He is a human being. He is a little like Kiran in some ways — the same age. The same height.

She speaks softly. 'Yes. I can see, I can see you don't want to do any of this. I can see how difficult this is for you.'

He nods silently. Anguished.

'This is dreadful for you,' she whispers. 'Just terrible, my dear.'

'It is,' he says hoarsely. 'It is.'

He holds his hand out to her — the way Kiran would hold out his hand as a child — wanting her to walk with him down the garden path. Or come to the ice-cream van. She grasps Molina's hand and squeezes it. 'There there. There there. Don't you worry, dear. It's going to be OK.'

He nods again. He gives her a watery smile. Reaches up and quickly, gently, draws the Stanley knife down the inside of her arm.

Before she can understand what's happening he gets to his feet.

'That's it,' he says. 'That's all — it's all over, all over.'

Her mouth falls open in disbelief at the blood which seems to leap up in a long line down her arm. Oliver begins to howl. Molina takes Matilda's hand and bends it inwards at the elbow, presses it to her stomach as if he's a caring doctor, or nurse. 'There you go.' He pats her hand reassuringly. Leans his head in to hers and kisses her on the temple. 'It won't be long now. It won't take very long.'

MRS FRINK'S MEMORY BOX

The gables of Colonel Frink's house are still and silent in the early light. Caffery looks at them thoughtfully, picturing Mrs Frink in the wheelchair. The nurse. The fear and the sadness that sit over this place like a blanket. He looks at the treeline, the BMX track where the Frinks' grandson was murdered. Then he lets his eyes trail slowly back up the hill to the house, measuring the distance. The woods are silent, only the occasional early butterfly flitting to and fro. Wild garlic grows in waxy carpets between the tree trunks, the sunlight makes a hopscotch of shapes coming through the branches overhead. Incredible, what happened in there, so close to the house.

In the Frinks' driveway two cars are parked, but the house seems unusually quiet. Instinctively Caffery slows his pace, tries to tamp the noise of his feet on the gravel.

He gets to the front door and has lifted the knocker when he notices Bear has stopped and is staring at something out of sight around the side of the house. He lowers the knocker, careful not to make a noise. Goes silently to join Bear.

About ten yards away, on the rickety piece of veranda above the overgrown knot garden, is the colonel's disabled wife. Her wheelchair has been placed so her back is to the house. She is hunched over so far her nose is nearly touching the blanket. Her hair falls down like curtains, covering her face. Her pink swollen hands sit helplessly on the waffle blanket. There is no one else to be seen.

'Mrs Frink?' Caffery approaches cautiously. 'Hello?'

Slowly, very slowly, the woman's head turns to him. Her face is puffy, the skin stretched. But her eyes are bright. They flicker across his face.

'Are you OK?'

He touches her hand. It is freezing. The blanket is thin — too thin to be any protection. He looks up at the house — there's no one to be seen. He jams off the wheelchair brake with his foot and begins to push her inside, jolting across the flagstones.

As they near the door she whimpers. Her hands rise weakly. When he stops to push open the back door she puts her chin up and speaks one word, clearly. 'No.'

Caffery hesitates. 'Mrs Frink?'

'That's my name.' Her voice is hoarse and cracked but it's clear and educated and quite adamant. 'And please — I don't want you to take me inside.'

'I thought you couldn't speak.'

'I'm sure you did.' She licks her lips. It seems to be an effort to hold her head up. 'That's what he wants you to think, but I can.'

'The MS?'

'It doesn't stop me speaking. Now, please, don't take me back into the house.'

'You can't stay out here. It's too cold.'

'Then a coat. The hallway.'

Caffery hesitates, caught between wanting to do the right thing and doing what she asks. After a moment, he leaves her where she is and goes into the warm kitchen, where the Aga pumps out heat. The place smells dank and sour, there are dirty tea-towels all over the kitchen, and plates piled in the sink. He crosses to the doorway and is about to enter the hallway when a noise from above stops him. He stands, his hand on the door, and swivels his eyes to the ceiling. The floorboards creak and bounce. Something is banging against the wall in the room overhead.

The nurse's handbag — he's sure it must be hers — crocodile-skin effect with a gold clasp, sits on the floor in the hallway. It looks expensive.

OK. So now he understands. The colonel's getting what he needs from the nurse and the nurse is getting what she needs from him. Angry, Caffery goes to the coat stand and pulls three coats off. Outside, Mrs Frink meets his gaze sadly — as if she's ashamed — and for a long moment neither of them speaks. Then she lets her head droop back to where it was before, almost touching the blanket. He feels her arm. It's as cold as ice.

He sighs. 'You've been out here hours, I'd say. Not minutes.' He puts the coats around the old woman, tucking them in. 'How did you get out here? You didn't wheel yourself, did you?'

'No. They bring me out.'

'And how often does this happen?'

'Most mornings. Not often at night.'

He wheels the chair down the path a small way into the sunshine, until they are out of earshot of the house. Next to a small garden bench he puts the brake on the wheelchair. He sits opposite Mrs Frink and studies her. The veins under her skin are visible. Her eyes are blue. Close up he sees she's not all that elderly — maybe in her mid-seventies. She's not stupid and she's not losing it. Not yet.

'Why won't he let anyone speak to you? Why does he pretend you're losing it?'

She rolls her eyes to him. 'Because of what I would say.'

'About that, you mean?' He jerks his head in the direction of the house. 'About what's going on in there with the nurse?'

'Yes.'

'How long's it been happening?'

'I don't know. I lose track of time. Probably since we lost Hugo. Our son and daughter-in-law still won't talk to us. They blame us, I think, because it happened here. They think we could have stopped it somehow.'

'But that was years ago. Fifteen years at least.'

'Fifteen?' she says tremulously. 'Yes, I suppose it is fifteen now. And I'm glad. I've been so hoping I'll be able to forget it all soon.'

'The nurse hasn't been with you all that time, has she?'

'Yes. She was Hugo's nanny first. And now she's mine.' She gives a half-hearted smile, as if it's a joke she's practised several times. 'Marina.'

'Marina?'

'She's been everywhere with us. Everywhere he was posted, she came too. I don't blame Charles for it. I do still love him.'

'*Love* him?'

'I do. I keep thinking it'll blow over. I haven't been a proper wife to him, not since Hugo went. I lost a grandson that day, and a son, you might say. But my husband — he lost all of those. And a wife too. Men take things like that much worse, don't they?'

She smiles tremulously at Caffery, her eyes searching his face as if she's trying to commit it to memory. As if these days everything she witnesses needs to be scrutinized thoroughly so she can carry it on safely to the place she knows she's going.

'I've got a photograph. Of Hugo. Would you like to see it?'

Caffery hesitates. He's seen Hugo's face — there are family photos of him in the extensive files he read through the other night. There are also photos of him naked, his face bound tightly to Sophie. And autopsy photos of what his face looked like when it was unwrapped. Caffery still can't comprehend the force that was needed to break a person's face like that, and what drove Minnet Kable, who knew neither of the teenagers, to such barbarism.

He realizes Mrs Frink is still smiling expectantly.

'Of course,' he says. 'I'd love to see a photo. Where is it?'

'Under the chair.'

He gets up and looks in the basket under the seat of the chair. There are wipes and handkerchiefs and an empty bottle of glucose drink, and, nestling under everything at the bottom, a large box. A crude painting of a lion on the lid, it looks like something the Frinks may have acquired during an Asian posting — as if it's from India or Nepal. He straightens.

'Is this it?'

'Yes. Thank you, dear.'

She opens it and with shaking hands begins to take out the contents. There are letters and newspaper cuttings. A birth certificate and some baby portraits. She pauses at a photo of a young man. Dressed in straight-legged jeans and a white shirt, his hair worn short and neat. He is standing in front of the gates to a large house, squinting in the sun.

'Hugo?'

She nods. 'On his way to summer camp. That's where he met Sophie. He fell for her — we all did. He had lots of girls after him, but she was the one.'

She begins to say something else, but the memories have overwhelmed her. Caffery notices tears leaking out of the sides of her eyes. He crouches next to her and fumbles out his cloth handkerchief, using it to dab at her eyes.

'I'm sorry, dear. I am sorry. Silly old thing — that's what I am. A silly old thing, crying like this.'

Caffery lets her take his handkerchief. He holds her other hand, rubs it gently to get some circulation going. She's still so cold, in spite of the sunshine. It's as if she'll never warm up.

'Who are you?' Mrs Frink stops wiping her eyes and gives him a watery look. 'Why are you here? Are you from the hospital?'

He shakes his head. He straightens and fumbles around in his pocket for his card.

'I'm police.'

He holds out the card and she takes it cautiously. 'Police?'

'Yes.'

'Why are you here?'

'I'm here to . . .' He pauses. 'It's a courtesy call — to see how you're doing.'

'A courtesy call? After fifteen years?'

'We like to visit the people who've suffered in these circumstances. Even years later when everyone else has forgotten.'

'How lovely.'

'Do you mind if I have a look at the things in the box? I didn't know Hugo. It would be nice to get a feel for him.'

She holds the box out to him with shaking hands. He takes it and sits down on the bench again. Begins to sort through the things.

'He was a good boy. Always a good boy. Very good at sports — he had a place at Durham, you know. He was going to go up that September.'

'A talented boy. No wonder the community felt his loss so deeply.' Caffery speaks the words woodenly, automatically, not really thinking what he is saying because his attention is no longer on Mrs Frink but on what he is looking at. It is a photocopy of a painting, folded and made into a card.

He lifts it from under the other objects and tilts it sideways to catch the sun. It shows a globe, floating in a darkened sky. An amateur painting, with the vague flavour of a religious image, nonetheless it's clear in its depiction. It shows a ring of material, like the rings of

Saturn, circling the globe ethereally. And shooting out from the earth are light rays.

He opens it. Inside are written the words:

Our sincerest condolences on your terrible loss. With much love, warmth and affection. From Lucia and all the Anchor-Ferrers. The Turrets, Litton

Caffery doesn't move for a moment. Then he lowers the card and stares at Mrs Frink.

'What is it?'

'The Anchor-Ferrers?' he says distantly. 'The Anchor-Ferrers.'

PIG-HEART

Matilda is next to Oliver, facing him, her hand tucked up under her chin, her head on the floor, her hair streaming out around her. Her feet are bare, warm and heavy where they rest on his shins. The woman he has loved for forty years, limp on the floor next to him, where she has been placed by the monster who calls himself 'Molina'.

Oliver buries his face in her hair. She smells of the soap they use in the house — the white stuff with the carved face in the top of the cake. Matilda, he thinks, the light shatters in a million pieces when you walk into a room. The laws of physics themselves are helpless in your presence.

Oliver's not going to struggle. There's no more to struggle for. Not now that Matilda is dead. She is soft and limp against him, but there is no hot breath on his face, no heart dancing against his. Just a heavy stillness, the creeping wetness of blood, and cooling skin. Her face in its familiar place, inches from

him, as if they are asleep in bed, sags sideways. Her eyes are still bright. But they see
nothing and they don't blink.

Molina has made them lie together like this,
on the floor. A mockery of a loving couple.
Oliver squeezes his eyes closed. This is
damnation. It is the dark hole at the centre of
the universe. Tears roll out of his eyes and
soak into her hair. He takes Matilda's dead
arm and places it over his ribcage, as if she is
holding him. The cameras haven't covered
what's happened in this room, but John
Bancroft will deduce everything, Oliver has
to have faith in that. There is nothing else he
can do. Nothing nothing nothing.

'I love you,' he murmurs to Matilda. 'I love
you.'

She will go to heaven — or wherever it is
that the good and the thoughtful go. That's
where she is now, whatever heaven she has
spent her life dreaming of, he's sure she'll
have got there. While he — well, he is going
to hell. He can't see any way round that. For
the role his chosen job has played, and for
the warnings he ignored. He will go to the
coldest place in the universe, where particle
storms rage and his heart beats in fear two
hundred times a minute for eternity.

Keep beating, keep beating . . .

'Hey.' Someone shakes him on the shoulder.
'Hey, come on — look at me.'

Slowly, numbly, Oliver opens his eyes. He

513

sees Molina kneeling next to him. He's taken off his black sweatshirt and is wearing only a T-shirt. In his left hand is the Stanley knife. His arms aren't as muscled as Oliver imagined they would be. In fact they are thin and long and freckle-covered. But that inadequacy means nothing — not now.

Lucia is still on the bed. She isn't bound but she isn't trying to fight either. Behind her Patty Hearst stands like a towering statue.

Oliver says, 'Kill me. Kill me. Just kill me now. Put that knife in my head, put it in my chest.'

Molina ignores that. Ruminatively he prods the back of Matilda's head. 'Look now. This is your chance. You can do whatever you want and she won't argue. All the disgusting things you wanted to do that your wife wouldn't let you? Now's your chance. Don't be embarrassed. We've got open minds — me and your daughter.'

'Kill me. Be a man for the first time in your life and kill me.'

'No. I won't.'

Oliver meets Molina's eyes. He runs his tongue around the inside of his mouth. Though part of him has already gone — already moved on from this life — he can't die without telling this man what he has worked out. Matilda hasn't died the way Hugo and Sophie died, but it doesn't change anything. Oliver knows the truth. Just for a moment, for one more moment, what is left of him is going to hold itself together:

'I've met you before,' he says slowly. 'I don't know your real name, but you grew up in Litton. You were a fighter and a thief. Then, fifteen years ago, you came through my front door and stood in my hallway downstairs. The moment I saw you, I knew you were wrong. I knew you were everything that was bad. Maybe on one level I even guessed what you had done and I —'

'Shut up.'

'You're not the person you think you are — you haven't got what it takes.'

Molina's face changes. He tilts his head sideways. 'Cunt,' he says. 'Perfect cunt. You tried to keep me from the only thing I ever gave a shit about.'

'Thank you,' says Oliver. 'You've answered my question. Now kill me.'

Molina breathes in and out. His face is red — he is furious. He gets to his feet and walks around the room once or twice, like a caged animal. He stops in front of Lucia, who sits silently on the bed, knees drawn up, her eyes like reflective black holes, her face raised to him.

'Well?'

'Well what?' she says.

'Get up and help me.'

There's a long pause. Whatever is going on in Lucia's head, Oliver can't tell — but he

515

knows this is the moment his life has been galloping to all these years. Eventually, her expression fixed, she pushes herself off the bed. Molina steps forward and grips her by the elbow. Not roughly. She doesn't struggle — she hasn't put up any sort of a fight yet. She allows him to lead her towards her parents.

He stops her at Matilda's head. Lucia's feet are inches away. Oliver rolls his eyes up and sees them, boots with pastel-coloured faces on them. Black soles that seem as big as buildings from this angle.

'Right,' Molina murmurs to Oliver. 'Now is the time — your decision. You do something to her body or I'll make your daughter do something. Which would you prefer?'

Oliver stares at the feet. Fifteen years ago — a few weeks after the Wolf killings — Lucia came home with this man 'Molina' and tried to introduce him to her father. Oliver recalls coming down the stairs and seeing him standing proudly next to her in the hallway with his hand out. Oliver was a piranha for character judgement and took no prisoners with Lucia's boyfriends. He formed an instant dislike to 'Molina' and didn't bother hiding his feelings. He simply nodded at the young man at his daughter's side, bypassed the offered hand, not bothering to listen to the introductions, and continued into the kitchen.

Oliver never found out his name and Lucia never tried to bring him to the house again. That's why he, 'Molina', hates Oliver and Matilda so much. He blames them for keeping him from Lucia.

He sucks in a breath. It's going to be his last. He locks his throat tight — the time has come. If Molina won't kill him then Oliver is going to have to do it himself. His lungs bloom hard and sore in his chest but he fights them. He fights pig-heart — tells it *Thank you, thank you for the time you've given me. But now I don't want you to keep beating. I want you to stop.*

It shouldn't work — no one should be able to will themselves to death, no one can beat their body's stupid, dull desire to survive. But the new valves the doctor has given him — the valves of a pig — can be overcome. They can't stand up to Oliver Anchor-Ferrers and his determination.

Lucia lifts her right leg. There's a pause then the pastel-coloured boot kicks Matilda in the face. It withdraws and does it again. And again.

The last thought Oliver has is a prayer — a prayer that Matilda has got safely to the place where there is sun and lightness and brilliance.

Somewhere she is safe from Lucia.

OLIVER ANCHOR-FERRERS

Mrs Frink hasn't met the Anchor-Ferrers but she recalls Lucia, the daughter, who dated her grandson Hugo for a while before his death. Mrs Frink doesn't know much about the family, she thinks they still live in the area, and when Caffery quizzes her she decides she remembers the cleaner, Ginny Van Der Bolt, saying she's done some work for the Anchor-Ferrers too. Ginny hasn't turned up for work this week, she says. The Turrets is . . . she has to dig deep to remember where the house is. It's . . . on the other side of the hill — very remote.

'Lucia was a nicely brought up girl,' she tells him. 'A little troubled, I think she never forgave Hugo when he finished with her. I don't know what became of her, where she is now.'

Caffery puts the box back under the chair. He clicks off the wheelchair brakes and begins to push her towards the house. 'I'm going to take you inside now. Whatever your husband's been doing, let's hope he's finished. See that business card?'

Bewildered, she looks down at it in her hand.

'That's my number. If any of this gets too much for you, call me, will you?' They reach the conservatory. He pushes her into the warmth. He can see through the hall into the living room. The nurse is standing with her back to him in the hallway, checking her reflection, refreshing her lipstick. She doesn't hear Caffery. He watches for a moment then goes back into the conservatory. 'In fact,' he tells Mrs Frink. 'Call me anyway. I'd like to know how you're getting on.'

He bends and, not knowing quite why, kisses her head. Then he pulls his keys out of his pocket and begins to trot back down the driveway. Bear, who is sitting patiently on the lawn, jumps up and canters after him. When they reach the car they are both out of breath. They get in and Caffery grabs the file that's on the front seat, hastily shuffling through the paperwork Cheryl gave him, scanning the pages he read last night. His mouth is dry, but when he finds what he's looking for he's so elated his pulse doubles.

It's a company in New York called Gauntlet. He whisked past it last night, but no matter how much his logical brain had told him to ignore it, something about it must have stuck subliminally in the illogical part — because now he is looking at the same name as is on the card in Mrs Frink's memory box.

Oliver Anchor-Ferrers.

It isn't the kind of name he's been expecting. Some part of him must still be expecting it to be James, or Jimmy. It takes him a moment or two to accept 'Oliver'.

He fumbles out his phone. Dials Johnny Patel who, for a change, answers sounding awake and ready to talk.

'Yes, what? Are you calling to tell me the cheque's in the post? Because that goes down on the list of world's unlikeliest promises. Along with *I promise I won't come in your mouth.*'

'Oliver Anchor-Ferrers,' Caffery says. 'He married Matilda in 1982.'

Patel is momentarily dumbstruck. 'What?'

'Oliver Anchor-Ferrers. He's on the list of directors of one of the companies I scanned to you.'

Patel whistles. 'Does this mean I don't get paid?'

Caffery digs his thumbnail into the groove between his teeth. He's got a radio which he can use if he needs to call help. He should make this official. He really should. But no. He's going to go that one step further. Just one step further.

'Johnny, you need to get me some info on him. I've got no 3G out here so you'll have to do it for me — I just want the bare details.

If you have to pull in a favour from the firm, then do it. I just want the broadest outline. Phone numbers, etc.' Caffery reaches into his glove compartment and pulls out the police radio, his quick-cuffs and his CS gas. He puts them all in his pockets and starts the engine. 'Johnny? He's got a place down here. It's called The Turrets. I'm going over there now. If I don't call you and tell you I'm sitting in the pub with my first pint in say . . .' he checks his watch '. . . half an hour, then you know what to do.'

'Getting you loud and clear, mate. And, Jack?'

'What?'

'Don't get yourself into trouble, OK?'

'Are you trying to say you care about me?'

'No. I'm trying to say you haven't paid my bill yet.'

LUCIA

Both her parents are dead. Her father stopped breathing a few minutes ago and hasn't shown a sign of life yet. Nor will he. Her mother has been dead almost twenty minutes. They deserve it. They've had it coming for years. Her hatred for her parents is enormous and intricate. For years she has been the black sheep, never understood by either of them. Dad was even going to change his will in favour of Kiran. Her brother, who has always been in the limelight, always the golden-haired boy with praises heaped on him, while she's languished in the dark corners of the family, the shadow soul, black rings under her eyes and sullen words in her mouth. Meanwhile Kiran has flown with white wings — travelled far and brought grandchildren into the family. The mere fact of reproducing makes you superior and godly, as everyone knows, and more deserving of attention and money.

She feels about her family the way she felt

about Hugo. The day he left her and gave Sophie an engagement ring. Her bitterness is boundless.

'Happy now?'

She looks up. 'Molina', or rather 'Ian', is sitting at her desk, watching her steadily. She's almost forgotten he's in the room. He's taken off his nerd glasses. He looks quite good without them. She's not sure how she feels about him at the moment. He's done as he's been told, mostly. He used her tip-off about Dad's book and alerted Havilland to the book's existence, Gauntlet's security wing took up the baton and Ian just had to ride the wave in to shore.

It's been elaborate, but it's been worth it. Even the initial assault staged with Ian, when she got her bruised face, was delicious and worth the pain. It's all played into her sense of the dramatic, a kind of gothic intricacy she loves, and every tiny twitch of anguish in Mum's face, in Dad's face, has been an ecstasy. Especially their distress when Lucia was 'threatened' by the men.

'Are you, Lucia? After everything? Are you happy now?'

She sits down, crosses her legs. Puts her elbow on her knee and leans forward to hold his eyes. 'Ian,' she says sweetly. 'I'm not sure.'

His smile drops away. The veins in his eyelids are dark blue. 'I'm sorry?'

'You put the whole thing into jeopardy by

bringing Hugo and Sophie into it.'

'I've *told* you, I didn't have a choice and I couldn't warn you. It was a last-minute thing. Havilland's orders.'

'Well, it was stupid — so fucking stupid.'

'Yes, so you keep telling me.'

'And Bear? What went wrong there?'

Ian glowers at her. He reminds her of a sullen little boy.

'Ian?' she says sharply. 'Answer me: what happened to Bear? We agreed you'd put Bear with *me*. And you let Honey — whatever his name is — say some screwed-up stupid things to me. So no — in answer to your question, I'm not really. Not really that happy at all.'

IAN AND LUCIA

The pulse hammers away in Ian's temples. He says nothing, but he is struggling — as he always seems to struggle in issues around Lucia — to keep his temper. She has no idea the power she exerts over him, nor the pain he's been in the last three days at the way she's treated him. Every opportunity she's had, every time he has come alone into the rose room to give her food or take her to the toilet, she's let him know in fierce whispers exactly what she thinks of his idiocy in bringing Hugo and Sophie's murders into the scenario. She won't listen to his excuses: he had to obey orders, that keeping Honig unsuspecting wasn't easy. Instead she goes on and on. And the dog . . . the fucking dog. She's done his head in over that.

'You could have stood up to him,' she insists. 'Told him Bear was going to stay with me. You have no idea what it was like, knowing she could be hurt.'

He studies her. She never ceases to impress

him with her enormous capacity for cruelty. Sitting in a room the way she has for three days, anything to increase the distress her parents went through. Ian isn't keen on his own parents, but even he can't imagine the depth of her hatred. It is so Lucia. *So* like her. She wouldn't have missed this for the world. She was exactly the same at the Donkey Pitch all those years ago. She taught him more about sadism in that one night than either Honig or the Foreign Legion could have taught him in a lifetime.

Ian opens his hand to her. 'We're in trouble — I'm going to get us out of it. Give me the ring.'

She licks her lips. Looks down at his hand. 'What ring?'

'What ring,' he says laughingly. 'You know what fucking ring.'

Lucia has Sophie's engagement ring and Ian intends putting it in Honig's pocket, thus sealing the idea that Honig was the Wolf killer all those years ago. That he's come back and done the same thing to Ginny, to Oliver and Matilda. Ian will need to put the Anchor-Ferrers' DNA on him too — he will have to transfer the blood from what's left of Matilda's face on to Honig's shoes, just in case Gauntlet can't discreetly cover this mess up, and the police have to get involved too.

'Give me the ring.' He's impatient now. 'This is dicking me off.'

She stares at him, her face flushed, incredulous he's being so bold. His heart is racing, but he holds her eyes, determined not to look away. She can make him walk to the ends of the earth — but he will always show her that he is a man.

There is a strange light in her eye as she slowly, slowly raises her hand. He expects her to slap him, or scratch at him. He is ready to stop her if she does. Instead she puts her hand inside her bra. Pulls the ring out and places it in his hand. He shoves it in his pocket.

'Lucia. One thing.'

'What?'

Ian clenches and unclenches his fists. He hates himself for even asking it. He should be stronger, but he can't help that nagging sense that if it hadn't been for the happy circumstances of his position in Gauntlet he might never have seen or heard from her again. After the Wolf killings years and years went by and he didn't hear from her — she claims it was that she couldn't track him down, but he suspects she didn't try that hard. Not until she knew how he could help her.

'Tell me you're not using me. I couldn't take it again.'

In reply she strokes his face. Gazes at him with a look of such adoration he feels ridiculous for his doubts. 'Ian, I missed you all that time. We're back together now. OK?'

The slight warm drag of her small fingers across his stubble is perfumed and soft. He closes his eyes momentarily.

'That's it,' she whispers and when he opens his eyes again she has her head on one side and is smiling curiously into his face. 'That's it — that's my darling. There.' She catches up his hand and pushes it against her flat stomach. She eases it down into the front of her jeans, inside the elastic of her knickers.

His fingers are coarse and dry against the smoothness of her stomach. They catch at her skin. She keeps pushing his hand down until he can feel the hot, wet tangle between her legs. She pivots her hips slightly apart so her thighs open and he can get better access. He slides his fingers into her and instantly he's lost. He takes his hands out of her jeans and pushes her clumsily towards the bed. She tumbles on to it, her hair falling around her eyes, her head going back on the pillow.

She jacks up her hips and unzips her jeans. They are covered in her mother's blood, and they leave long dappled scars on the sheets as she rolls them down. She kicks them aside and pulls off her knickers, then lies back, her arms above her head, smiling at him secretively — her knees open just enough so that he can see what he wants to see.

Her eyes are very black. He knows her from all those years ago, has been to hell and back with her, has been inside her body scores of times — and yet he's never known what's happening in her head.

'Yours too,' she says.

He stands and unzips his trousers, kicks them aside. He pushes down his shorts and lies on top of her. It's the end of all the longing and the fear and the hurt.

THE TURRETS

The Turrets stands high above a tree-filled valley, almost at the crest where the treeline gets blue and hazy. Caffery parks in a secluded lay-by at the bottom of the drive and stands for a moment assessing the place — the long lawns sweeping up to it, the giant cedars of Lebanon casting their austere shadows on the grass. The house is as sombre as the name suggests, made of dark stone with two turrets and a stone tiled roof that seems to absorb the light naturally.

He's been past this place before. He recalls passing the curved stone walls on either side of the entrance on his way into Litton. Ironic.

On the back seat of the car Bear is on high alert. She is staring out of the window in the direction of the house. Caffery opens the door and fixes a lead on her. She jumps out and begins to pull in the direction of the house. He smiles. They've come to the right place.

'Good girl.' He lifts her and puts her back

in the car. Cracks the window and closes the door. 'You're a good girl. You stay here, now, OK? Don't bark, don't move.'

She shuffles agitatedly on the seat, moving her hind legs as if she's thinking of jumping up or barking. But he holds his finger to his lips and she subsides. Watches him forlornly. That's one more thing he knows about this family — the Anchor-Ferrers — without ever having met them. They might not have chipped their dog, but he admires how well they've trained her.

The gates to The Turrets are electric and closed. When he climbs over them he wonders if he's going to break some infrared security beam that will alert the owners. But nothing happens and he drops on to the gravel driveway. He stops for a moment and lets his eyes travel up the hill. Rhododendrons and hydrangea ramble out from the treeline — not in flower yet, but they make him think of coastal regions of the UK — bringing the faintest whiff of adventure and exoticism to this inland valley.

What does he look like to someone inside, he wonders, someone in one of those turrets? Small and insignificant.

Suddenly he is uncertain. He has found where Bear lives, but that's not enough. Now it's not the Walking Man driving him but his own curiosity and moral compass. He needs to know what has happened to Oliver Anchor-

Ferrers and to find out who attached the note to Bear's collar.

He puts his hand inside his jacket to re-assure himself the radio is there, ready. In situations like this he's trained to slide away and call for backup. So what is the right thing? Right? Who defines right and wrong and how far down the list of *what ifs* and *what abouts* do you go? He doesn't know.

In the end the person who wins out is the crazy Jack. The Jack who occasionally gets into dumb street brawls when of course it's the wrong thing and will do no one any good. Maybe that's just the way he's always going to be.

He begins to walk carefully and deliberately up the drive towards the house.

EYES

The morning rays come through the red skulls and lie across the bodies of Oliver and Matilda. On the bed Ian shifts. He drops an arm over Lucia's waist. She doesn't react, just continues breathing steadily, in and out. In and out, her eyes closed.

He studies her sleeping face. She's so relaxed. He's going to have to wake her — they have to get moving — to get out of here. The cops looking for Ginny will only hold off so long before they come back and start asking questions. Ian uses his index finger to lift the lid of Lucia's right eye. She doesn't react so he raises his head and takes the time to study the iris. He can see all the veins and the different layers of protein that go to make up the white of her eye — like albumen. It's so typical of Lucia that she will lie here, not moving, and calmly let him inspect her eye. She's got an innate sense of what is dangerous and what isn't. It's as if she can detect it in the hairs on her skin, like an animal can.

He's her puppet. She orchestrated this entire scenario, carefully planning it so her parents were dealt the most hurt and anxiety. Pietr Havilland isn't the only person who wanted videos of Oliver suffering, Ian made them for Lucia too. She is going to watch them over and over, she will eat them up, will absorb every second of pain. Gorge herself with it.

She's been the orchestrator all along, just as she was the night Hugo died. She dealt the first blow with the ice pick and it was she who hounded the bleeding and weak Sophie through the woods all night — Lucia going calmly, combat gear on just like Patty Hearst in that poster. It was Lucia who decided how the bodies should be arranged at the end. After all, she said, that *was* what they'd come there for in the first place. He remembers her expression as she stamped Hugo and Sophie's faces together. Almost crying in her victory and fury. The way she tightened her teeth, braced her hands against a tree trunk to get leverage — pushing the couples' heads together so hard that nothing was left of them. Every pop of gristle, every snap of bone went through her like a shiver. Every burst vessel that released a new line of blood into the moss.

When she finally finished with the bodies it was nine a.m. The whole thing had taken over fourteen hours. And Lucia wasn't even tired.

It was as if she had just sprung from a good night's sleep.

He is awed by her. Awed and scared and completely in love.

'Hey.' He drops the eyelid and kisses her. 'Time to wake up, sleepy head.'

She smiles lazily. Yawns and rubs her eyes. She seems about to put her arms around his neck and pull him down again when a noise from downstairs makes them both sit bolt upright in bed — staring wide-eyed at each other. The doorbell. Echoing up the staircase.

Ian tips his legs off the bed and pads to the window. Naked. He draws the curtain back a fraction and presses his face to the window-pane. Squints down.

'Who is it?' Lucia is pulling on her clothes.

'I don't know.'

'Well, what do we do? Ignore it?'

He shakes his head. 'The back door's open. Whoever it is can just walk in there.'

'Who do you think it is?' 'The cops?'

'The cops?' she hisses. 'What the fuck're you telling me?'

He turns away from the window. Scrutinizes her. 'You look a mess,' he says bluntly. 'Seriously, you might as well have been in a cat fight. You stay up here.' He pulls on his trousers and shirt and shoves his feet into his shoes. 'Be quiet, don't make a noise — let me deal with it.'

THE TURRETS

The sound of the doorbell dies on the other side of the big front door and then there's just silence. A long silence that reaches out into the garden and finds the flowerbeds and the lawns and the forests beyond. Caffery stands in the porch, arms crossed, staring at the fields, the huge trees. He takes a few steps down the lawn, then stops and turns a full circle. Slowly, slowly, assessing. An ugly white Chrysler is parked further down the drive, the family's Land Rover next to it. He knows it's theirs from Johnny Patel's information package. There's a tennis court — neglected, holes in the guard netting.

Then behind him, from inside the house, a noise. The sound of locks being pulled back. He turns just as the door opens.

'Hello?'

The man who stands there, blinking at the light, is stocky with a big head. He wears a T-shirt and sweatpants and his gingery hair stands in disarray up off his forehead. There is no one in the hallway behind him. Caffery lets his eyes rove all over the scene, trying to tease out anything wrong or out of the ordinary. A stained-glass window presides over everything — there are a few pairs of muddy wellingtons on the stone-flagged floor and a basket piled with potatoes that have gone to seed. Dog leads hanging from a coat rack. But nothing weird. No panic or defensiveness in this man's face either. Only vague bewilderment.

'Have I woken you?' Caffery says, scrutinizing him carefully.

'Yes. Yes you have.' There's a pause while the man rubs his eyes. Draws his hand down his mouth and ruffles his hair. 'But — it's OK. Sorry, you just caught me off guard.'

'Detective Constable Caffery.' He flashes his warrant card and sees the man's face change instantly. It droops, the way people's faces do fall when the police arrive out of the blue. 'What?' he says. 'What is it? Is something wrong?'

'I don't know. You tell me.'

'I'm sorry?'

'I said, you tell me. Is everything in the garden rosy? Everything OK with you?'

The guy's face drops even further. His gaze darts anxiously around the garden as if he thinks Jack might not be alone. 'I don't get it. What's this about? What's happening? Is everyone OK? Emma? I've just spoken to

Emma — she's OK isn't she?'

Caffery crosses his arms. 'Your name? Sir?'

'My name? It's Anchor-Ferrers. Why? What's happening? Are you going to tell me? I'll shut the door if you can't tell me, because this is starting to mess with my head and I —'

Caffery holds up a hand. 'Calm down. Nothing's happened. I just need to ask some questions. Is that OK?'

'Questions?'

'Yes. I've got no one with me. I'm alone. OK?'

The man nods hurriedly, his eyes still flickering nervously round the garden. In the half an hour since he left the Frinks' place Johnny has provided Caffery with a pretty comprehensive snapshot of who the Anchor-Ferrers are and he's coming to know the people he's been looking for this week. Matilda and Oliver. Especially Oliver. Caffery knows that the daughter, Lucia, lives at home, and over in Hong Kong is the son. A banker. His name is . . .

'Kiran.' The man wipes his hand on his T-shirt and, without letting go of the door, extends his hand to Caffery. 'I'm Kiran Anchor-Ferrers.'

Caffery hesitates, eyeing him carefully. He's given Patel's file all his concentration, tried to digest everything there. But there are lapses. He tries now to recall what he learned about Kiran. Hong Kong. Banking. What else . . . ?

He places his hand in Kiran's. The hand is warm. As if he has, indeed, been asleep. Another pause and then they shake.

'Kiran Anchor-Ferrers?'

'That's right.'

'Is this your house?'

Kiran gives a nervous laugh, glancing up at it, as if to say *Chance would be a fine thing.*

'This? Christ, no. It's my parents'. I'm just babysitting — I don't live here. I live in Hong Kong.'

'Your parents?'

'Yes. My parents. What about my parents . . . ?' He trails off. Then, as if he's seen a message in Caffery's expression, his face crumples pathetically. 'Oh no. It's Dad, isn't it? I told him he shouldn't drive after the op. I told him not to go out this morning. I told him over and over and over . . .'

'No.' Caffery keeps his voice level. His attention is peeled white now, trying to absorb everything he can about this situation. On the face of it, this guy is telling the truth and his own brilliant deductions about Bear and her owners are all wrong. Maybe she's somehow been stolen. Maybe the note on the collar really was a prank after all. He doesn't know. 'It's not that. It's the dog. Your dog. Your parents' dog?'

Kiran's mouth widens. 'Bear? Is she OK?

Mum and Dad have been giving themselves nightmares over her. Is that what this is about? Oh please God, please God. Say it is. Bear?'

'Yes. She's been found.'

His face breaks into a smile. 'No! You haven't found her, have you? You really have found her? That is great, great news. You can't imagine how great.' He stands back, his hands opened, a broad, uncontained smile spreading across his face. 'Come in, come in. Mum's going to be delighted when she gets home. You've saved us all!'

EMMA

The house is scruffier and more spartan than
Caffery expected from the amount of wealth
he imagines Oliver Anchor-Ferrers has
amassed. The floors are stone, only softened
by the occasional threadbare runner. The
radiators are old thirties rads — not because
someone's dumped a load of money on the
local reclamation yard, but because these are
the radiators that were installed at the same
time as the place's first central heating
system. The walls are of lumpy plaster. It's
sort of elegant and nice to look at, but sort of
awful too, because it feels so rusty and cold.

Kiran Anchor-Ferrers leads him into the
kitchen, which is not quite as bleak. Though
faintly dilapidated there's an Aga and lots of
gingham-topped jam jars. A panelled door
into a darkened passage stands half open —
a cellar perhaps. There's a smell, something
dank and rotten like death. He tries to picture
eating here, and finds he can't.

Kiran, on the other hand, can eat. He's

woken up now he's reassured Caffery isn't here to report his parents dead and when they've got into the kitchen he stands at the sink stretching and scratching his belly, opening and closing his mouth. Moving stuff in the kitchen around. Filling a kettle and opening cake tins.

'So,' he says, straightening up from a cupboard from which he's pulled two plates. There is more colour in his face. 'Where is Bear? Mum's going to want to know — the moment she comes home she'll need to know.'

'She's at the local shelter. I'll leave you with a form you can fill in — it has all the details of how to get her back. But maybe first you could tell me something.'

'Yes?'

'I'm just a beat copper — I mean, I'm not uniform, but you know, I still get the tail end of cases, I go out with a set of instructions and I never know the head end of what I'm dealing with. For example, I know your dog has been found, but I was never told how she went missing in the first place.'

'How she went missing?'

'Yes. You'll think it's nuts, but that's just the way I go about things. I like to know the beginning of the story. It helps me tie up the end. How did she go missing in the first place?'

Kiran gives him a winning smile. 'Didn't

anyone say how?'

'No. That's what I mean — I just get part of the story. Always want the rest.'

'Sit down.' Kiran nods to two chairs positioned to face the vast stone inglenook. 'No fire, now, but it's always the centrepiece of the house. Everyone just — I don't know — gravitates to it.'

'Thank you.' Caffery sits in one of the chairs. He crosses one leg over the other, folds his arms. A pile of old newspapers sits in the corner of the inglenook, just a foot away. Soot smears the stone and the ashes haven't been cleaned out, but there hasn't been a fire recently. There's a pile of washing up in the sink and a load of dirty laundry on the floor. In the corner two camp beds are propped against the wall.

Kiran says, 'I'm making builder's tea. Nothing fancy here. Is that OK?'

Caffery watches him pour milk into the mugs, stir it. He comes over and hands Caffery a mug. Then sits down and gets himself comfortable.

'Bear. That's what you wanted to know about?'

'Yes.'

'Well, the story isn't that much of a story: she was here one minute — next minute she wasn't. We had the whole family in the house, no one was paying that much attention to the dog. You know what it's like when there are 'grandchildren.'

'Grandchildren?'

'Yes. I've got a daughter. Saffy.'

Caffery knows Kiran has a daughter. 'Saffy. Where is she now?'

'She's with my mum and dad. And my wife. Emma. Who are all safe — I hope.' He laughs nervously. 'But you gave me a fright, turning up like that.'

'I'm sure they're safe. Nothing to suggest they're not. Where are they today?'

'At Horse World. In Dorset. They're due back this afternoon — I'm not sure whether to call Mum and tell her about Bear, or what. Give her a great surprise when she comes in? What do you think?'

'I think that's a good idea.' A fly is buzzing noisily in the window. The place really stinks. 'So tell me, Kiran. What do they get up to at Horse World?'

'Usual kid rubbish. You know, look at horses. Go down slides and stuff.'

'Slides? Is Saffy old enough to be doing that?'

'Old enough? Yes. If not, Emma will sit her on her knee and go down with her.'

'You're not worried about that?'

'Worried? No. Why, would I be? She's a toughy, Saffy. Tough as old boots.'

'I wasn't just thinking about Saffy. I was thinking about Emma too.'

'No,' he says dismissively. 'She'll be fine.

Loves that kind of thing.'

Caffery watches Kiran steadily. Kiran, Kiran, he thinks. I don't know your real name, but you have been so clever. Not clever enough though. Because Emma is pregnant. The real Emma is eight months pregnant and there is no way you'd be so dismissive.

Emma is not on a slide in Horse World in Dorset.

Emma is eight months pregnant and probably still in Hong Kong.

One of the flies from the doorway comes and lands on the rim of Kiran's cup. Both men look down at it. Then Kiran raises his eyes and meets Caffery's.

Caffery smiles.

Ian Molina

Since the introduction of Airwave, the new police communications network, all officers carry a radio — even plain-clothes. Usually they wear it in their shirt pocket under their suit — or in the pocket of their trousers. Caffery's is in his shirt and switched on. To send out a distress signal is a simple matter, he merely passes his hand inside his suit, hits the emergency 'Status Zero' button, and it'll open the mic for ten seconds, alerting anyone in the area that an officer needs urgent assistance and giving police comms his GPS location. It works even in places no phone signal can reach.

But he isn't going to do that. Not yet. He isn't going to let 'Kiran' — or whoever this guy is — know he's on to him. He's going to walk out of that door and reassess everything. Speak to Paluzzi and Patel, decide how to let the constabulary into the situation. He stands and extends his hand.

'It's been nice to meet you.'

The man gets up and shakes Caffery's hand. 'And you. It's great to hear about Bear.' Caffery makes to withdraw his hand but the man holds it firm. 'Really good.'

'Yes. Goodbye then.'

But the man is pressing his thumb hard into Caffery's wrist. Caffery raises his eyes, finds him smiling at him, one eyebrow raised quizzically. 'What about the forms?'

'The forms.'

'For Bear. Have you forgotten them?'

There's a long silence. Caffery sees he's been caught. He holds 'Kiran's' gaze, keeping his eyes steady, while his attention darts around the room, making a rapid mental list of every available weapon. He quickly rehearses his movements — left hand into his shirt to send out a radio burst, his right hand snatching up the fire poker from the grate.

The man keeps the fixed smile on his face. 'Beat copper?' he says. 'Your card says Inspector, not Constable. A plain-clothes inspector going out to tell people their dog's been found? I don't think so.'

Caffery snatches his hand away. He twists towards the fireplace in one move, his hand going into his suit and firing off the radio burst. He can't fumble out his CS gas in time, so he grabs up the fire poker with the other hand and twists back, the poker poised above his head. The whole thing has taken less than three seconds.

'Kiran' is standing in the centre of the room, his hands held out, joined together at the wrist. A universal gesture: I'll come willingly.

'Seriously — I know the game's up. To be honest with you — after what I've done to those people upstairs? I'm glad for it to be over.'

Caffery scans the room, assessing everything he can.

'Honestly,' says Kiran. 'It's been a shit life, and part of me has been wanting this for a long time.' He holds Caffery's eyes steadily. 'I mean it. And when you see the . . . uh, mess I've left upstairs you'll think it too.'

'Is that what the smell is?'

'No — the smell's from the one I did four days ago. She's in the cellar.'

Caffery studies him suspiciously. Looks at the proffered hands.

'What's your real name?'

'Ian Molina.'

'Ian Molina?'

'Yup.'

Caffery doesn't believe it for a moment, but he'll worry about that later. He lowers the poker so it's pointing at the guy's face.

'OK, *Ian Molina.* Walk to the cooker.'

'Molina' waits a beat, then, just as Caffery thinks he's going to bolt, he walks quietly towards the cooker. Caffery follows, the poker still at the ready. He scoops his cuffs from his pocket and holds them out to Molina. 'One on your right hand.'

'Are you going to take me into custody?'

'Put the cuff on the right hand, like I said.'

Molina obliges, a patient look on his face. 'Is that going to be real custody, or is it going to be the sort where I get fucked in the arse then trip down the stairs?'

'Now drop the cuff behind the handle.'

'Or choke on my own vomit? I mean, once it gets out what I've done to the people in this house, I don't think I'm going to be safe anywhere.'

'Just do it. Then close the cuffs.'

Molina gives a long sigh — as if he's struggling to keep his patience with this trivial charade. But he obeys, dropping the cuffs down and snapping them closed so he's chained to the cooker. He stands, his head back, whistling a small tune, his left leg jerking like someone keeping time with an inaudible sound track.

Caffery checks the cuffs are secure — gives them a good rattle. In his inside pocket, out of habit, he carries nitrile gloves. He pulls them out and snaps them on. He stands for a moment, contemplating. Measuring the path from here to the hallway. 'Where are they?'

'Hmm?' Molina says, with mild interest. 'Where are who?'

'The family.'

'The family? They're — oh.' He shrugs.

'They're pretty much everywhere now. Once I got started I found it difficult to restrain myself. You know how it is.'

'Upstairs?'

'Mostly. Yes.'

'The police are going to be here in less than ten minutes.'

'Good,' he says drily. 'I'll look forward to it.'

Caffery waits a beat or two longer, watching Molina. Then he turns and steps into the hallway. Sun is coming through the huge stained-glass window. Now he sees it is the same as the picture on the condolences card sent to Mrs Frink. A globe, long shards of light emanating from it, a family depicted in a field, the father swinging the daughter around — her legs flying out gaily behind her. The son and the mother are seated on a nearby stile, watching and smiling. Light bounces off everything — the trees, the sky, even the human figures emit rays. The mother in particular, Caffery sees. Matilda Anchor-Ferrers. She has the most light coming from her.

He goes to the long staircase and begins to climb. A minstrel's-gallery-style landing is ahead of him, several doors opening from it. What the fuck is in those rooms? He climbs heavily for two or three steps. The next two steps he makes a little lighter. The next two very light. Before he can see the landing he comes to a halt.

Hand on the banister, he waits. Counts to ten, holding his breath. Then very, very gingerly he removes his shoes, turns and, using the edges of the stair treads where the wood is firmer, makes his way back downstairs. He crosses the hall to the rack of dog leads, takes two and goes swiftly and silently back to the kitchen door. It is still open a crack. He positions himself next to the hinges and peers through.

Ian Molina is on tiptoe. He has slid himself to the far end of the cooker and is standing in an awkward position, his tongue between his teeth, concentrating hard, trying to remove the cuffs using, Caffery thinks, the tiny igniter phlange on the hob.

There is a small click. Caffery pulls his CS spray from his shirt pocket and goes into the room swiftly, unravelling one of Bear's leads through the fingers of the other hand. Molina's head comes up in surprise. He has no time to react before he gets a full face of CS. Caffery uses his right hand, the elbow raised to protect his mouth from the spray, and with the left swings the dog lead around Molina's knees. The CS, combined with the blow, brings Molina crashing down like a tree, screaming in pain.

'You fucker, you fucker.' His legs kick wildly. The freed handcuffs swing from his wrist. 'Get your fucking hands off me.'

Caffery squats next to him and grabs his hair. Gives him a shake. 'Hey, stop that. Just relax. Lie on your front.'

Molina rolls painfully on to his side. He is struggling to breathe, coughing and retching. With all his might Caffery grabs him by the feet and pulls him away from the cooker, across the floor, his head bouncing, his T-shirt rucking up to his underarms. He throws him against the radiator, face down, and cuffs his hands to it. You're not supposed to leave a CS victim, but Caffery's beyond caring. He uses a dog lead to tie Molina's feet together.

'You didn't think I was that stupid, did you?'

Molina opens his sore mouth. His lips and eyes are swollen. 'You don't have to do this.'

'Yes, I do.'

'You *don't* — it's too much, *wanker.*'

Caffery's satisfied with the ties. He steps back and, because there's no point in doing things by halves, he leans over and gives Molina a second faceful of CS gas. The guy twists and throws his head back and struggles to drag in a breath. A second dose could kill him. Caffery shrugs at the thought.

'*You* wanker,' he says. 'You're the wanker, I'm the good guy. Try to keep the two clear in your head.'

Think Like Me

An old injury of Caffery's comes back to haunt him as he climbs the stairs. Years ago he had his calf muscles half ripped out of his leg and something about the exertion in the kitchen must have tripped it off again, because the pain shoots through him with every step. That and the ache in his back from landing on a stone in the field. Old git. Losing it. He has to use the banisters to haul himself up the last part.

A few steps from the top he slows. Not because of the pain, but because of the blood on the landing in front of him. It lies in gelatinous ribbons across the floorboards. A rug, another ancient kilim, has been crumpled and kicked as if in a struggle. Ahead of him a door is ajar.

'Hello?'

Silence. He approaches the door and uses his foot to push it. It swings open to reveal a room with high ceilings and green striped curtains at the windows. It should be bright and breezy, but everywhere are long loops of red-brown blood. On the floor, under a green-and-white striped duvet, lies a man. He's dead, Caffery doesn't have to check on that — you don't lose that much blood and live to talk about it. There's a wound at the back of his skull, at the top of his neck. A deep, hair-matted hollow, the inside of his brain visible, congealed and hard where the air has dried it. He's got blond hair and although it's hard to tell, he looks to be in his thirties. His hand, outstretched and motionless, has a good Tag Heuer adorning the wrist, so possibly he is money, or new money, or just a poser. Either way, he doesn't fit into any of the profiles of the family Caffery's memorized.

Bad guy, Caffery thinks. Almost certainly.

He holds on to the door frame for a moment and takes a mental shot of the room with the body. He doesn't take his hands off the frame, but turns just his head to the right and looks along the landing. He freezes in his head everything he can see there: an opened door — beyond it a room with pink, red and white rose-decorated walls. There's a pair of handcuffs next to a radiator — radiators are great places to manacle human beings. But there's no one in the room.

A noise to his left; he turns suspiciously and looks in the opposite direction. There's a door at the very end of the landing — slightly open — and a triangular slice of reddish sunlight comes from within the room and spreads across the floorboards. Everything is completely still.

Oliver Anchor-Ferrers is a clever man. He turned his fascination with science into a glittering career. His brain will have been working on his situation constantly. Caffery presses his own brain into the same pattern — trying to see the hallway through Oliver's eyes. He looks up at the ceiling. The Turrets is remote — if he was Oliver, what would he do to protect his family? Cameras. There must be cameras somewhere. Caffery has had experience with hidden cameras before — he knows how cleverly they can be disappeared in a room.

He lets his eyes rove across the ceiling and within sixty seconds has found it. A tiny reflective eye like a dot of black, lodged in the oak panelling. Everything he is doing is being recorded. Most people would walk straight past and not notice it.

Cautiously he crosses the landing, the floorboards creaking gently under his weight. He nudges open the door, sees what's there, and has to stop. Has to pinch his nose and take long breaths from the diaphragm, forcing his ribs to lift.

He's come to the heart. He is slap-bang into the nub of what he's been circling for the last few days.

The room is painted a deep purple and strange faces stare down at him from the wall. There's a poster of Patty Hearst aiming a gun at someone just out of sight. The window is open and a small breeze lifts the voile curtains. A woman's body lies on the floor, dressed in brown slacks patched with blood. Her hair is thinning and yellowish grey — this must be Matilda. He cannot think what Molina has done but her face is destroyed. Her arm is draped loosely over a second body. A male, old. He lies on his side, embracing her. Caffery is sure this is Oliver Anchor-Ferrers. The man he's been tracking all this time. He doesn't need to know what Oliver looks like to be certain. Yes, there are physical clues, he fits the age bracket — but it's more than that. Something indefinable.

He drops to a crouch and closes his fingers on Oliver's wrist to check his pulse. Oliver is dead. Caffery presses his fingers into the man's hand. 'Shit, I'm sorry, mate. I should have got here sooner.'

'Help.'

A woman's voice. He turns sharply.

'Help me. Here. I'm here.'

He stands. Goes quickly to the bed, and sees on the floor on the other side a woman lying there, her hands bound to the leg of the bed with a pair of tights. She's got very dark, very clear eyes with thick dark lashes. Her black hair is in disarray, she's covered in

556

blood and she's been beaten — her face is swollen and bruised on one side. She is quite naked. White skinned and defenceless. But she is alive. She's silently watching him with big black eyes, as if she's seeing him from the other side of the universe. As if her soul has gone away to a very very distant place and she can only just make him out as a fellow human being.

He checks the family snapshot he's crystallized in his head.

'Lucia,' he says. 'You must be Lucia.'

She nods mutely. Her eyes are watering.

'I'm police.' He fumbles out his card and holds it up to her. 'DI Caffery. Are you hurt?'

'Where is he?' Her mouth is trembling so she can hardly get her words out. 'I heard you downstairs — what's happened to him?'

'He's secure. He won't be going anywhere. Are you hurt?'

She squirms, tugging at the tights which are looped around the bedstead. 'Let me out of these. Help me.'

'Wait. Keep still. You need to tell me — the one downstairs, is he on his own?'

'There are two.'

'Two? One of them is tall — blond?'

'I think he's . . .' She jerks her chin up — in the direction of Kiran's room. 'I think he's . . . my mother was in the room, I don't know what happened . . .'

She begins to shake. He wants to touch her

— to reassure her — but checks himself. He's not a human, he is a cop. A machine that has to account for everything. Evidence and behaviour.

'The other one? Short, redhead?'

'Yes.'

'No one else?'

'Just them.'

He gestures to the bodies on the floor. 'Are these your parents?'

'Yes. We've been kept for four days.' She twists, trying to get out of the bindings.

'Wait, wait. Keep still. Tell me — what's happened to you? Are you sure you're not injured?'

'No — not injured, just . . .' She breaks off. Tears are standing in her eyes.

'Just what?'

'The one downstairs, he . . . he . . . What he did to me, I can't even begin to . . .'

Caffery lets out all his breath. 'OK, OK, I understand. Now, Lucia, I know this is difficult, but you've got to do one more thing. You've got to listen to me. OK?'

She nods.

'I'm on my own, but there are people coming. I'm not going to come any closer because if you don't need medical attention I don't want to destroy any evidence. I'm going to find something to cover you first.' He hunts around, finds a sheet folded in a cupboard. Places it over her body. 'There — now take it easy. Take it easy.'

'Is it going to be long?' she whimpers. 'Please please *please*. I can't stay here much longer. I can't.'

LUCIA AND THE DETECTIVE

The detective produces a small Swiss army knife, selecting a blade. He opens the scissor tool and begins to snip through the tights. 'I'm not going to undo this knot,' he tells her. 'I'm going to cut it. The scene of crime guys prefer it that way.'

Lucia knows that sometimes the best acting is the silent kind because people will interpret silence to suit their interpretation of the situation, so she doesn't speak while he works. She's good at acting. She's been doing it for years — pretending to the world that she can live in this family. All she has to do is force a little hitch into her breathing to mimic fear.

Inspector Caffery is very near her as he studies the knotted tights she's used to bind herself to the bed. She can smell a faint tang of aftershave and something else — wood smoke maybe. She can see the details of his windcheater jacket and the sinews in his wrists. He is good-looking. Actually — no, not exactly good-looking, his face is too careworn to be a poster boy, as if he's had too many late nights. But he's got this slow, calm confidence about him that's riveting — as if there isn't much in the world could shake him. When he came in the front door earlier she could tell just from listening to the conversation he had with Ian, even without being able to distinguish the words, that this isn't a man used to having to explain himself. He simply walked in as if it was his God-given right.

Lucia believes men like this are secretly confident about one thing: how they perform in bed. She wants to smile, but checks herself.

'Who tied this?' Caffery asks.

'He did. Why?'

'He hasn't done a very good job of it.' He snips through the nylon and immediately she is released she rolls into a foetal curl, shivering, pulling the sheet tight around her. 'God,' she mutters. 'God.'

'It's OK — stay where you are. It won't be much longer.'

'I want a bath.'

'I know, I know. And as soon as my men get here, you can. You've put up with a lot — you just need to be patient a while longer.'

He pulls another glove from his pocket and drops the knot from the tights into it. He puts them in his pocket then he goes to the window and looks down, towards the driveway. She watches him. Her DNA will be on

561

the knot — but some of it will be Ian's too. When Ian went to answer the door she used the tights to swab between her legs, picking up traces of their sex.

She was going to call the police herself — from the first hotel she and Ian got to. The moment she was alone. She'd have said she'd been abducted. Lucia has no intention of staying with Ian — he is right, she's using him. Again. Just like she did on the Donkey Pitch that night. Ian is just an ignorant animal. He's pretended to be a technical genius but he's only taken what she's told him and used it. She told him about the book, and she calmed his fears that there was something hidden in the alarm system. The idiot didn't question her and it never occurred to him to adequately check the house for spy cameras.

The cameras will tell the police the story the way she's planned it: with Ian as the predator.

'What?' Caffery says suddenly. 'What did you say?'

She blinks at him. He's turned from the window and is frowning.

'Nothing. I didn't speak.'

He scrutinizes her, as if searching for signs she's lying. Then he turns and slowly scans the room. He wears the expression of someone listening to a distant sound — straining to interpret music or a voice from a long way away. After a long silence, he turns to her again.

'Have you been held here all this time? In this room?'

'I was in the other room for four days. He brought me in here this morning — the man, Ian — the one who let you in.'

'You know his name?'

'I overheard the other one calling him that.'

'Where was your father kept?'

'In here, I think. I don't know exactly . . . Why?'

Caffery doesn't answer. He turns abruptly and stares at the radiator. He goes to it, crouches and runs his hand under the radiator pipes. There are scuff marks on the skirting board. There's a series of grooves on the copper feed pipe where Dad was manacled. DI Caffery stays crouched there, his fingers on the pipe.

Something about a foot away catches his attention. It is something dark — just visible under the skirting. It's one of Lucia's pens, which appears to have fallen there from the desk. She can't imagine why he is paying this pen so much heed. But he is intent on it and picks at it until it rolls out on the floor in front of him. He studies it for a while. Then he puts his elbows on his knees and appears to be concentrating — his eyes darting around the room, taking in everything.

After almost a minute he moves. He tips on

to his knees, puts his hands on the floor and looks up under the radiator.

'What are you doing?'

He pushes himself back. 'I don't know.' He sits on his heels and looks around again. Another minute passes then he leans over and rolls back the hem of the rug. He looks at it intently, then he pulls from his pocket a pair of reading glasses, which he puts on. She can't see what he's noticed on the rug, but he spends a long time studying it. His face is locked as if he's reading.

'What is it?'

He shakes his head. 'Your dad was a clever man. He's written a diary here.'

'What does he say?'

'He's talking about . . . well, he's talking about Hugo Frink.'

She nods. Bites her lip. 'Yes,' she says waveringly. 'Hugo used to be my boyfriend.'

'I know. Hugo's grandmother told me.'

'What does Dad say about it?'

'He just says that someone was convicted for their killings —'

'Minnet Kable.'

'Minnet Kable, but your father thought it was a mistake.'

'I know.'

'You know?'

She tucks her arms under her and massages the flesh of her right breast, which has been bothering her the last few days. There's a tiny indentation in the skin where Sophie's ring has left its mark. She's worn it inside her bra for years. A hot coal against her skin — a memory she needs to wear like a sword in her side. Hugo gave it to Sophie, as if to say Sophie was a princess who deserved only the best. A ring. A piece of jewellery, which is supposed to be the way men treat the women they care about most. Hugo never treated Lucia like that. Now the ring is in the pocket of Ian's jeans.

'Yes. I know it was a mistake. I know who did it. The man downstairs. Ian.'

GOOD GUYS AND BAD GUYS

An armed response unit was parked in a lay-by, drinking takeaway coffee in their smoked-glass X5 when Caffery's 'Status Zero' radio burst was routed through Communications. They were the nearest and the sergeant self-authorized, immediately flicking on the wailers and the high-intensity strobes hidden in the radiator grille of the X5, sending the vehicle steaming up the winding B roads in the direction of The Turrets.

In the amethyst room Caffery hears the noise. It pricks the edge of his consciousness for less than a second before the sirens are killed and silence comes back. That's protocol. From now on he won't hear anything from them — no sign they're on their way. There will be no warning. Not until the moment they appear — coming from the trees. And then the forests will bristle with men — marksmen, dog handlers and support groups.

Lucia is sitting up now — her pale arms wrapping the sheet around her knees, locking him in her steady black gaze. 'What do you think?' she murmurs. 'Do you think she's all right?'

Caffery can't recall what she's been saying. His mind has been working so hard. So hard. Flitting back and forward between the noises outside — the steady approach of the cops — the long sentences on the underside of the rug — and the girl sitting opposite him.

'I missed that. Say it again.'

'My dog.' She sniffs. Wipes her nose with the back of her hand. 'That's been the worst of it. My little dog, I think she's dead.'

There's a crackle from somewhere outside. Both of them turn to the window.

'Is that them?'

He holds a hand up to silence her. There's a pause, then the unmistakable feedback of a loudhailer. 'Police —' says the voice. 'Come to a window and show yourself.'

Caffery gets up and goes to the window. He throws his warrant card out. It flaps and pirouettes down through the air, landing face up on the gravel.

'DI Caffery. MCIU,' he yells. 'I sent the 'Status Zero' alert.'

There's a brief silence. A distant call of a crow, winging its way over the treetops, echoes through the air, wraps itself around the walls of the old house.

'Is someone in there armed?'

'Negative.'

'Any immediate danger to life and limb?'

'Not that I can see, but you should clear the house regardless.'

'There's a marksman over here watching you. I'm coming to get what you've just thrown down.'

'Sure. I know the routine.'

Caffery leans out of the window, his hands raised palms outward. The shadows — which when Caffery walked up here were long — are shortening now, creeping their way across the lawn and back into the trunks. As if they sense something amiss and want to be somewhere safe. The man who emerges from the side of the building casts almost no darkness on the gravel. Like a vampire or a ghost.

He's wearing a Kevlar vest and ballistic helmet but he doesn't hang around. He bends and snatches up the wallet. Walks back to the trees. There's a long hiatus — the sounds of radio crackle.

'What's happening?' Lucia whispers from behind.

'They're checking my ID.'

There's a burst of static, a crackle of the radio, and then the man shouts, 'Is it safe to come in, Inspector Caffery?'

'It is.'

'How many souls in the house?'

'Including me, six.' He makes it into two syllables, the way they are trained to speak on the radio: 'SIX-UH.'

'Injuries?'

'Three fatalities. One suspect detained in the kitchen — cuffed — unarmed, needs paramedics, he's had a CS blast. And another in the bedroom with me. Under guard.'

'Sorry, sir — is that a suspect or a witness?'

'Suspect. Confirm: I said two suspects. One with me, under guard.'

A creak behind him. He turns. Lucia has appeared less than a foot away in the gloom. She is naked, her hands are raised. He reacts just in time, catching her by the wrists and holding them above her head. She writhes, spitting and kicking out at him with her bare feet.

'I'm the *victim* — I'm the victim. Change what you just said. Change it *now.*'

Caffery digs his fingers into her wrists hard. She's fierce but she's small and he's happy to use excessive force. Whatever it takes. The last words Oliver Anchor-Ferrers wrote are hot and fresh like a burn in his head:

I think you will read this and use it as a piece in the puzzle. I cannot believe what I am going to write next. And yet it is what I believe to be the truth . . .

Oliver knew. In his last hours Oliver had worked out what his own daughter had done.

Minnet Kable was ambidextrous and that is

569

why he was so easily convicted. It was a key piece of evidence the prosecution hung a hat on. But actually Hugo and Sophie were killed by two people working together. How else could they have been confined so effortlessly in that wood? It was two people monitoring them — waiting for the life to seep out of them. It was the man who calls himself 'Molina' and my daughter, Lucia.

Caffery shakes her now. Angry. She drops to the floor still spitting and twisting, but he doesn't release his hold on her. The left-hander was 'Molina' — Oliver has noted on the rug he is left-handed, a tiny observation he's made. But it was the right-handed killer who inflicted the most ferocious blows on Hugo and Sophie. Maybe Sophie's last words, obliterated by the knife, had identified Lucia.

From downstairs comes a splintering shudder. Lucia stops struggling. She snaps her head back and stares at the door. Another noise. The whole house seems to rock.

'It's the entry team,' Caffery says. 'On their way up. Sometimes they're a bit heavy-handed.'

Lucia sees time is limited. She comes out of her fury quickly and lowers her chin, her bright black eyes swivel up, assessing him from the floor. Processing the situation. 'You're insane,' she mutters meanly. 'Who are you? Not a proper cop. You're an evil shit. You won't get away with it.'

'Someone once told me that the stripe of the goat is to look into the eyes of others and see itself staring back.'

'What the fuck're you talking about?'

'You're right. I'm an evil shit — I am a liar and a cheat and not a good human being. I break the law and I have broken people along the way. But all of that, Lucia — it makes me lucky. Because I can look at people like you, I can look in your face and see my reflection. I know when I'm in the presence of evil, Lucia. I do know. It's my gift.'

PART THREE

Amy

In Chew Valley, the sun has already set. Some of the houses are dark save for a few garden lights and the occasional glow of a late night TV. One of the darkened windows is the bedroom of Amy. Five years old.

She lies on her back, holding her teddy, Buttons, in the crook of her arm. Her eyes are open, she's watching the shadows on the ceiling. Mummy tucked her in a long time ago but she can't sleep. There are so many things to worry about: maths lessons and Mrs Redhill telling her off today for running after the whistle went after first play, then Daddy going on and on about how it's important to listen to the teachers.

She's worried too about what's on the other side of the window. When she went downstairs earlier, when she couldn't sleep, Mum and Dad was watching a programme on the telly. When she came in the door they quickly switched the channel, like they always do when there's something adult on the telly.

Some things kids aren't supposed to see and when you get into year 1 and you get to go on the pooters at school then you got to have 'Parental Controls' and that'll stop all the bad things off of the Internet from hurting you.

Except Amy was standing in the doorway for a bit before Mum and Dad noticed and she heard lots of what the man on the telly was talking about. It was all about something horrid what happened to a family. Some nasty men got into their house and hurt them. The man said the word 'murder', which is a horrid word that means someone got a knife and stabbed another person in the tummy. It makes Amy shiver to think about that happening. She hugs Buttons the teddy bear really tight, trying not to cry. She doesn't understand why someone could be nasty enough to want to put a knife into someone else. A whole knife.

God won't let the nasty man who done the murder into heaven. He'll put out his long fork and say, 'No, you bad man, go away.' And that won't be all because the bad man will have gone to prison too, even before he gets to heaven. The police will have put chains on him and put him in a special car and taken him to a place like that spooky place in London with the big black birds and the men in red coats.

She pulls back the covers and slips out of

bed. Still clutching Buttons, she pads to the window and pulls the curtain back. Everything out there is still and silent, without any people walking around. The garden is quiet. Sometimes a fox comes into the garden late at night. Or rabbits, which makes Dad yell because they eat his flowers.

But there's nothing out there now. Just the moon on the grass, and the bird bath with the water all still. She thinks about what a horrible person it must have been to do those nasty things to another person. She hopes they're not near here, trying to creep into her garden like the bunnies do.

From the trees on the other side of the valley comes a line of smoke. Same as when Dad's having a bonfire. It's a straight line going up into the sky, like it's pointing at heaven where God is. She smiles now because she thinks it belongs to the man with the beard, the one who took the puppy. He smelled like smoke.

The reverse Santa Claus man is a good man. He came to the end of Amy's garden yesterday afternoon, when Mum and Dad never knew, and he talked to Amy for ages. He said that men who do nasty things like what happened on the news are the unhappiest men on the face of the earth coz of the way they feel inside. He said they are hurting — the way it hurts when you fall over, except on the inside. Amy thought he meant the way what she feels when Daddy shouts or Mrs Redhill says something nasty about maths.

Reverse Santa Claus said that the puppy ain't not a puppy at all but a grown-up proper dog and he has found her owner. Her owner is a policeman, 'parently, called Jack, and that makes Amy feel better'n'better than anything, because like everyone knows there's no one kinder nor more stronger in the whole wide world than what a policeman is.

Suddenly, looking at the line of smoke, Amy has an idea. She thinks she knows what she's going to say when the boys at school all talk about how they're going to grow up to drive tractors and be in the army and shoot people. She's going to say: 'Well I ain't. I'm going to be a police lady like the one what came into school to talk about traffic and cross the road. I'm going to be a police lady and boss all the nasty men into prison.'

And as soon as Amy thinks the thought a lovely feeling comes over her. Really nice and warm an' cosy like the feeling you get when you walk into someone's house for a birthday party and smell chocolate.

She hugs Buttons closer, kisses his head, and goes back to bed. She pulls the covers up and closes her eyes. She knows she's going to go straight to sleep now — she's not worried any more. Everything, Amy thinks, is going to be fine.

Just fine.

THE TRUTH

The countryside is dark and silent — only the vague ghostly shapes of cows in the fields. Caffery pulls up in the car park at the foot of the path that leads to the 'Reflection Grove', cuts the engine and leans forward in the seat, peering up into the darkness.

It is ten p.m. The debriefing has taken six hours. Six wearying hours of giving statements and going through the formalities of Lucia Anchor-Ferrers' arrest. They've swabbed every inch of him and made him go through elaborate plans of the crime scene so they know where to concentrate their search. He's had to explain the events of the day over and over to a whole line of SIOs, he's faced the wrath of the superintendent, he's transferred money into Patel's online account, he's emailed the council about Mrs Frink's welfare. He's faced down every obstacle so all that remains in front of him is this. The final truth.

His heart thuds in the silence. He doesn't

know what's made him come to this specific place — except maybe instinct and a faith in the Walking Man's sense of irony. Sure enough he can make out the dim red glow of a fire, the spreading fingers of gaunt bramble silhouetted against it. The Walking Man has allowed himself to be found. Which means he knows the game is coming to an end. If he has any truth, any knowledge at all about what happened to Ewan all those years ago, it's going to come out now.

All Caffery's clothes have been taken away by the CSI team and he's wearing the borrowed uniform of a police technician — blue serge shirt and trousers, a navy fleece. He pushes his V-Cig into the fleece pocket, zips it up and climbs out, dread in his belly. Bear jumps out behind him and follows him through the gate. It's been five days since he was here. A part of him wishes he could get straight back to the way he was on that showery morning. A part of him really doesn't want to be here, doesn't want to know.

As he gets nearer, he sees the Walking Man's fire has been made next to the willow pagoda; the orange reflections of flames dance on the underside of the woven roof. A nearby log has been covered in sleeping bags to make a seat. A dead girl's monument. A place to talk about children that have been lost and not found.

He comes into the circle of red light thrown

out by the fire and stops, the heat on his face. He stares at the Walking Man. The Walking Man stares back. Under the dirt on his face he has a cut lip and bruises from when Caffery attacked him last night.

The Walking Man rummages in a rucksack and pulls out a bag full of leftover breakfast.

'Hey,' he tells Bear. 'Come here. Come and eat something.'

The whole time Bear has been with Caffery she's been reticent with other people. Friendly when enticed, but reserved on the whole. Now however she doesn't hesitate. She trots across to the Walking Man and stops at his feet, staring up at him expectantly. He sits and unwraps the bag and feeds her a few scraps.

'She my dog now,' Caffery says.

'You're social services for dogs. She's from a broken home.'

'Yes. I found where she lives. She's never going back there, but I found it.'

'I know. I've seen all the comings and goings.'

'Yes. Of course. You know everything.'

The Walking Man nods. 'I know a lot. Sometimes more than I want to know.'

Caffery sits down on the log. Puts his elbows on his knees. Sensing his mood, Bear leaves the food and comes back to him. She leaps up on to the log next to him and nuzzles his arm. He's so glad she's here. He can't stop his hands trembling. The Walking Man bends and opens the plastic quart-bottle of scrumpy. Pours out two mugs. Caffery takes one of the mugs. Tries to drink and finds he can only manage small sips.

'OK.' He wishes the cider would work fast. 'Tell me.'

The Walking Man sighs. Shakes his head, lets his eyes travel across Caffery's face. 'Jack Caffery,' he says sadly. 'Jack Caffery.'

Everything is in those words — everything. Suddenly Caffery's mouth is watery with adrenalin, the hairs stand up on his arms. Whatever the Walking Man has found out — it's bad. He forces more of the cider into his mouth. More. He's going to need it.

'OK. Tell me.'

'I don't know where his body is — probably never will.'

Caffery is silent for a moment. Then he begins to laugh, low and nasty. 'Funny. Funny funny. I've had enough of you. Now tell me what you've found out.'

'It's the truth — believe it or don't believe it. I said I don't know where your brother's body is. I've said that as plainly as I can, and it's the truth.'

Caffery blinks stupidly. It *is* the truth. He knows it from the Walking Man's expression. 'Then you haven't kept your end of the bargain — you fucking old bastard. I've waded through shit to keep my end of the bargain and you've brought me nothing new and now you —'

The Walking Man holds up his hand to silence him. 'Jack, you can threaten me, beat me, arrest me. But you can't make something out of thin air. I don't know where the body is. It has been buried — disposed of to protect people. Really, you have to believe me, I don't know. But I have spoken for a long time to Derek Yates, and I've discovered something about Ewan's death that you have never suspected.'

Caffery closes his mouth. A cold wave of apprehension goes through him, like nothing he's ever known before.

'The circumstances of your brother's death, Jack, are not the circumstances you think. Ivan Penderecki didn't kill him. Your brother was raped — several times. I'm sorry. But he survived the experience with Ivan Penderecki.'

Caffery is motionless.

'At least, as far as it can be said that still breathing, eating, shitting and sleeping is surviving. He survived for years. He lived on and on, Jack, he reached adulthood. All the time your family was in mourning, he was still living.' The Walking Man drops his head. 'I'm sorry,' he murmurs. 'But it's true.'

Caffery sags with the weight of disbelief. He cannot get his jaw to unlock. Ewan didn't die as a child. *Adulthood.* He reached adult-hood.

'He died ten years ago. Tracey Lamb was inside. She instructed someone to bury his body eight years ago — by then we can only assume it was a skeleton. Mr Yates in Long Lartin doesn't know who she instructed or where they buried him. He only knows how he died.'

The dread is so paralysing his lungs feel like stone. As if every breath takes the crack-ing of molecules and atoms. 'How — how did he die?'

'You produced evidence at a bail hearing — so I am told. Videos you sent to the CPS? To make sure Tracey Lamb wasn't bailed? It stopped her being released. She was your brother's carer — the only person who cared for him — whatever meaning the word "care" carried in her lexicon. When she went into prison, your brother was left by her, incarcer-ated somewhere . . .' He trails off, and for the first time ever Caffery sees sadness in his eyes. Sadness for another person. 'You know what I'm telling you, Jack. He is dead, he starved to death — or died of dehydration, however one dies in those circumstances. But it wasn't Penderecki who killed him. You did, Jack. You did.'

Caffery puts the mug down clumsily and gets to his feet. He walks unsteadily away from the fire until he comes to a tree, and stands there, his hand against the trunk, breathing in and out, in and out. His hand fumbles for the V-Cig in his pocket but can't find it, and anyway he wouldn't be able to smoke it now. He wants to spit. He wants to vomit. He concentrates on his breathing — concentrates on not letting the cider come back up in a sour rush.

Above his head a bird appears quite suddenly, lit orange from the firelight below. An owl, wings spread like lace. It glides silently and purposefully, as if it's aiming for a place far beyond the copse, but as it crests the trees a sudden, ferocious gust of wind assaults it head on. The owl is thrown back on the air. It flaps frantically for a moment, as if it's been hit by a bullet, and sinks briefly before it can recover its balance. Then, determinedly, it straightens, presenting its chest to the wind and beating its wings, pushing against the current. A fighter. Determined. And yet it makes no headway — for the moment it seems caught — destined to hang there constantly, struggling with all its life-force just to stay still.

The sight of the owl makes Caffery cry. Shuddering, he puts his head against the tree trunk and stands there, letting the tears fall out of his eyes on to the ground.

If he had been born a different person, would the world have hurt less than this?

When the wave dies down he turns, his face

a mess, and stares over his shoulder at the fire. The Walking Man is watching him steadily. For once the expression on his face is not antipathy or game-playing. Instead it is sympathy.

'Mr Jack Caffery,' he says slowly. 'This is the truth, but don't be afraid of it. Your life will be different from this day on, but you will survive. You will continue.'

'How do you know?'

'I know because you and I? We are the same person.'

ACKNOWLEDGEMENTS

Thank you to the following people who helped me with the technical details in *Wolf*. Tony Agar, DCI Gareth Bevan (Avon and Somerset Major Crime Investigation Unit), Kirsten Gunn (Sergeant, Royal Corps of Signallers), Anne O'Brien (copy-editor), Dave Welch (MD, Ramora UK) and Hugh White (Home Office Pathologist).

For selflessly lending me her name and allowing herself to be murdered, I thank you Ginny Martin.

Thank you too for the unwavering support of everyone at my publishers, Transworld (too many to mention), and everyone at my agent's office — especially Jane Gregory (agent nonpareil).

As always my greatest debt of gratitude is to my friends and family, especially Bob Randall (who contributed the majority of the research), Lotte G. Quinn, Susan Hollins and Mairi Kerr.